A Deal With The Reaper

MADISON LAWSON

Paperback: 979-8-9989108-0-7
eBook: 979-8-9989108-1-4
Audiobook: 979-8-9989108-2-1

Library of Congress Cataloguing-in-Publication Data available upon request.

First edition 2025

Dirty Deeds Publishing
Saginaw, TX 76179
www.madisonlawson.com

Book and cover design by Qamber Designs.

Content & Trigger Warnings

This book is a *dark romance*, meaning there are several dark themes, explicit language, and scenes that may be upsetting for some readers. That being said, please read responsibly. Your mental health matters.

Below is a non-exhaustive list of content and trigger warnings; however, if you're not worried, I suggest skipping this list, as it does include spoilers! If you have questions about the content warnings, please email me at **madisonlawsonbooks@gmail.com** or through my website, **madisonlawson.com**.

- Murder, serial killer impulses, torture, blood, and violence (I mean, she's a serial killer, so there's a lot of violence)

- Framing people for crimes

- Mentions of gangs

- Substance abuse and addiction, drugging others, and forced rehab

- Mentions of rape (not depicted)

- Mentions of suicide (not depicted)

- Mentions of child abuse (not depicted)

- Abandoning a child (not depicted)

- Mentions of kidnapping (not depicted)

- Death of a child (not depicted)

- Pretty much every bad thing possible happens to a child at some point, but none of it is depicted on page

- Explicit language and sexual content including, but not limited to: CNC/dub con, restraints, choking, breath play, forced orgasm and orgasm control, threesomes, pierced genitals, knife play, getting turned on by murder, semi-public fucking

But don't worry, the dog doesn't die. I'm not a monster.

To everyone who can't decide if she wants to be the psychopath or fuck him.

Why not both?

ONE

June

Whoever said that women prefer clean, impersonal methods of killing clearly never met a woman in their life. At least, not one like me.

The best part of a kill is being close enough to feel each precious puff of air leave their lips and see their pupils expand when they realize they're going to die. I relish the final, weak fluttering of their pulse as their heart works in overdrive to stay alive. There's nothing as satisfying as the irony that the harder their heart beats to stay alive, the more blood it expels from the body through one of the many stab wounds, and the faster they die.

"Please," Jared begs, the sound little more than a gurgle around the blood filling his mouth. "No more."

"Do you remember what you said when Clarissa begged you to stop hurting her?" I ask, dragging the tip of the knife in a circle over his knee, though not applying enough pressure to break skin. He shakes in fear, hands tied behind his back and ankles secured to the legs of the chair bolted to my basement floor.

I've only been with Jared for five hours, and he's already

showing signs of giving up. I'm trying not to be disappointed, because I *knew* he'd be weak, but it's difficult. I'd been looking forward to savoring this for as long as possible. Several years ago, I could last a year before succumbing to the urge to kill. Recently, I rarely make it eight months.

This time, it's been seven.

"Let me refresh your memory." I push in the knife, exhaling with relief when I feel his skin give under the pressure. "You said, 'This is your fault, baby. If you'd just obey me, I wouldn't have to hurt you.'" The knife hits bone, and I let go, letting it protrude from his thigh. Blood slowly seeps from the wound, joining the red-tinged piss and vomit puddling beneath him.

Why these men *insist* on peeing themselves is beyond me. The suffocating, acrid smell is the worst part of my little hobby.

"How do you…" Jared's question breaks off into an involuntary groan of pain.

I lean down to his level, grab his chin, and jerk up, forcing him to meet my gaze. His eyes struggle to focus, and I know I'm losing him. I squeeze harder and reach down with my other hand to grab the handle of the knife, twisting slightly, and he screams, becoming more alert, finally focusing.

"Clarissa escaped you almost five years ago, and yet you're still an infection in her life. Nightmares, trust issues, low self-worth. You even stole her ability to have children. Did you know that?"

He tries to shake his head. "I didn't…"

"Shut up!" I spit the words and let go of his chin, straightening my spine. "I've been following you for *months*. You're still a drunk who takes his own insecurities out on women. I've seen your new girlfriend leaving the ER covered in bruises and bandages and with her arm in a cast."

"Why?"

Always that stupid question. They know why. They shouldn't have to ask.

"Because you're a waste, and you don't deserve the chance to hurt one more person."

"You Issa's girlfriend or something?" he asks, disdain and a bit of strength returning to his voice. He thrives on hatred.

They all do.

I grab the knife and yank it free. His scream is louder than before, and I cut it off by wrapping my hand around his throat.

"No, asshole. I'm her therapist." I thrust the knife into his chest, leaving my hand as close to his skin as possible so the blood coats mine. The life drains from his eyes, and I soak up every second. Only when I'm certain he's dead do I pull the knife free, stand up, and look around the basement.

Thank God for drop sheets, I think as I begin cleaning, erasing all evidence of Jared's presence.

~

Weekly Taco Tuesday with my friends is more enjoyable than it has been of late, now that the need for blood has been satiated.

"What did you guys do this weekend?" Sadie, my best friend, asks, swirling her strawberry margarita. Her black hair is slightly longer than normal, nearly reaching her shoulders, and she's wearing thin-rimmed, pink glasses. Typically, wearing glasses means she either had a long day or a late night. Or both.

"Vanessa surprised me with a trip to Vegas," Rose says. Her hazel eyes brighten when she talks about her girlfriend, and I can't help but smile. She's one of the happiest people I know, and it's always refreshing to spend time with her.

After Rose finishes telling us about her trip, Evelyn gives the same answer she gives every Tuesday night. "Worked late at the office." Sadie and I share an incredulous look, and Rose lightly admonishes Evelyn for never resting. She ignores us, as always. "These kids don't have anyone else to fight for them!" As a child social worker, she takes her job more seriously than anyone I know. Except maybe myself.

"We know, and we're very proud of you," Sadie says. "But you're going to burn out. Then you won't be any use to the kids."

"Whatever. Let's team up against June. She worked all weekend too!"

I hold my hand over my heart. "Et tu, Brute?"

"Is that why you didn't answer your phone at all on Saturday?" Rose asks. "I figured you were skydiving or fighting alligators or something."

Better. I was murdering the abusive ex of one of my clients, then cleaning his blood off my favorite knives. "I wish. I had paperwork to catch up on."

"Could've invited me," Sadie says, pointedly looking from me to Evelyn. "I would've made paperwork fun."

I smile. "Next time."

Sadie launches into a story about one of her brothers, spinning her glass in her hand. A bit of strawberry margarita flies over the rim, landing on the table like a splash of blood. For a heartbeat, memories surface, like the sight of red liquid is a fist around my spine, yanking me back in time to when I was fifteen, lost in the haze of red. That day, a fire, the need to kill, burned in my chest, and it hasn't completely gone out since. Sometimes, it's nothing more than a few lumps of coal that occasionally flicker with lingering heat. Other times, like last week before I snagged Jared, the flames are so tall and hot that I'm shocked no one can see sparks in my eyes.

Only taking a life smothers the fire enough for me to survive its heat. Something about ridding the world of another abusive, selfish, and pathetic man acts like a bucket of water in my chest.

Sadie absentmindedly wipes the spilled margarita away with her napkin, freeing me from the flashback. Mentally shaking my head, I banish the dark thoughts so I can enjoy this normal night with my friends.

Hopefully, I have seven months before I need to worry about the fire burning too hot to ignore again.

~

"There are bruises all up Amber's arms," my client, Jennifer, says, tears streaming down her cheeks. "The police said there's nothing they can do if she doesn't report him because she's an adult. She's twenty-one! That's hardly an adult."

"What did she say when you asked about the bruises?" I ask, leaning forward to pass her the box of tissues. She accepts them, blowing her nose loudly.

"Nothing. She just got mad at me then stormed out of the house. I haven't heard from her since."

"That was four days ago?"

"Yeah. Monday. She sent me a short text yesterday telling me to stop calling."

This isn't the first time Jennifer has spent an entire session talking about Amber, her niece. She became Amber's guardian five years ago when her sister, Amber's mom, passed away in a car accident. First, it was Amber's decision to drop out of community college. Then it was tattoos. Then she was mixed up with the wrong crowd.

"She knows you care about her." Before I can say anything else, she barrels forward, snot dripping from her nose.

"He's hurting her, I know he is."

"Her boyfriend?"

She nods. "I told her to break up with him. He's dangerous!"

"Because he's in a gang, right?" I ask, surreptitiously checking my notes from Jennifer's previous sessions. I put "gang" in parentheses because to someone like Jennifer, any group of guys with tattoos is a gang.

"A biker gang. I forget what they're called. Something awful like Sons of Hell."

"Saints of Purgatory?"

Recognition widens Jennifer's eyes. "Yes! How did you know that?"

"I've seen them around before. Their jackets are memorable." I keep the fact that I make it a point to know as many of the major players in Tucson's criminal world to myself. You never know when you'll need a patsy to take the fall for a messy kill.

"This isn't the first time she's come home hurt," Jennifer says unnecessarily. I have a list of everything she's told me, every possible injury at the hands of that man. "A black eye, bruises, one time she got stitches up her shin. She said it was from a motorcycle wreck. Shouldn't that be enough to get her away from him? What if she never leaves? I've seen the statistics. Fifty percent of murdered women are killed by their partners. What if Amber is next? I'm supposed to protect her!"

"Playing the 'what if' game will only fill your head with false reasons to feel guilt and fear. You're doing everything you can. You're always there for her. She knows she has somewhere safe to go, and that's a precious thing, Jennifer."

"But she's not safe, and now… I don't know what I'll do if something happens to her."

"Try not to go to the worst-case scenario. Take a

breath." I pull in a long breath through my nose and blow it out through my lips, waiting for Jennifer to mirror the action.

The session continues with more tears as we attempt to work through her fears so she can think more logically. I send her home with extra tissues and a reminder that she can call me if she needs anything. Then I have a blessed thirty-minute break before my next client arrives.

I take the time not to relax or eat but to research the Saints of Purgatory. There isn't much about them online, though I do find the obituary of an older member who died last year. It seems most of the Saints are younger now, in their twenties, thirties, and forties. There aren't many recent arrests attached to the club, but I know for a fact that the members have used it as a conduit for criminal activity in the past.

Flipping back in my notes from Jennifer's appointments, I find the name of Amber's boyfriend and quickly discover he's the leader of the Saints of Purgatory.

Three weeks after a kill is too soon.

But as I stare at his name, an ember sparks.

Theo Zervas.

TWO

Theo

"Shut the fuck up, Raph!" I shout across the bar where Raphael is needling Luna about her most recent fuck buddy.

"Yeah, everyone knows you're just jealous of Luna's ability to actually get pussy!" Nico adds.

"Not helpful, Nico," I say, glaring at the boy a few seats away from me. At twenty-two, he's our youngest member and often tries to overcompensate with a filthy mouth.

"Sorry, boss," he says, still grinning.

I click my tongue in exasperation. Behind me, Luna says something about Raphael trying dick instead, then there's a sharp increase in noise when the two move from words to fists. They quickly attract a crowd, and I'd be shocked if the others aren't betting on the outcome of the fight. I look at the plaque of the three cardinal rules we live by hanging on the wall behind the bar, wondering if I should intervene or let them battle it out.

Saints of Purgatory
Family First
Respect
Don't Get Caught

I could tell Raph and Luna they're not obeying rule two, but if *respect* meant *don't fight or bother each other,* then we'd all be kicked out by the end of the week.

"Leave 'em be," James says from my right side before knocking back his whiskey. "They're all getting antsy. We haven't had a job in a while."

"I know."

"And you're still sticking to your decision not to pursue that job Kip brought us? The Phoenix car show?"

"Definitely. It's too risky," I say, slightly disappointed. Eight years ago, I would've been all over it. The risk was part of the rush.

But eight years ago, I wasn't in charge of these idiots. And I still thought I was invincible.

"Whatever you say." After a moment, he adds, "You've been distracted lately. What's going on? Is this about Amber?"

"No."

"That vein in your neck says differently."

"That's from Raph and Nico."

"No, your Raph and Nico veins are in your arms. That vein is your chick-vein."

"I didn't realize I had specific veins for each person in my life."

"You don't, just the ones that piss you off the most."

"Which one is yours?"

"Forehead."

My lips twitch with a hint of a smile, something James is proficient at causing. We may not be related by blood, but he's been my brother for fifteen years. Longer than the rest of the Saints, all of whom I consider family.

"Must be why I have a constant headache," I say.

"You have a headache because you never shut your damn brain off," he argues.

"If I shut off my brain, these idiots will kill each other."

"That's why you have a great vice president to keep them in line."

I raise my brows. "You sure you have time between all your vein cataloging?"

"I'll always make time for you, T." He claps his hand on my back and stands from the bar stool, not wavering despite the four whiskeys he drank in two hours. "Shut your brain off so we can do a job and get these idiots under control. Maybe take a page out of Luna's book and go find a quick fuck. Take a break from Amber. You know one of the boys will be happy to keep an eye on her for a night."

"I can handle her," I say, a bite to the words.

James holds his palms out in surrender. "Sorry. Just consider it. Let me know if you need a wingman." Then he turns and walks away, probably to pull Raph and Luna apart before one of them does lasting damage. With how often they fight, you'd never guess that they're best friends.

I tap the bar, silently requesting another beer from Axel. He slides me one, and I chug half of it in one gulp, my head pulsing with pain and unwelcome thoughts of Amber.

"I fucking hate it when he's right," I mutter. I don't even like her that much. She's just young, hot, and skilled at getting me off. She shouldn't be invading my head like this.

She's becoming a distraction, and not the good kind.

It's time to get rid of her.

~

A month later, I lead the Saints out on a job to steal several cars to sell to Basil. It helps calm everyone, quenching their thirst for action. Two weeks pass without much issue, though Daryus, our sergeant at arms, did briefly get arrested for beating someone up at the Iron Cage. The guy deserved it. If *I'd* seen him slip drugs in anyone's drink, especially Bella's, I would've killed him. Thankfully, Daryus only spent one night in jail. The guy never pressed charges, thanks to our cameras catching him in the act of trying to roofie Bella, and we have friends in the police department.

So, all has been quiet with the Saints. Though a certain blonde bitch has proven more difficult to dump than I expected.

I'm changing my bike's spark plugs, contemplating permanent solutions to erasing her from my life, when Kip, our head road captain, walks in. He crosses his arms and leans against the wall a foot away.

"What do you want, Kip?"

"Luna passed along a meeting request from a possible client, if you're interested."

"Chop job?"

He shakes his head. "Solo kind."

I nod, a hint of excitement in my chest. I enjoy these jobs more than the chop ones that involve the entire club. The solo jobs only ever involve me, James, Luna, and occasionally Kip. They're not secret, but we don't talk about them openly due to their sensitive nature. It's best when as few people as possible know about each one.

"Who is it?" I ask.

"His name is Henry. He's the dad of a friend of one of Luna's thousand siblings," Kip explains. He gives me a rundown of the job, though without many details.

"Should we be worried about his connection to Luna's dad?" I ask. Her father, Judge Hugh Mcintyre, is infamous for his merciless rulings, and he got worse when Luna joined a criminal motorcycle club.

Kip shakes his head. "He seems legit, but I'm having Benny and Zion tail him for a few days just in case."

"Good idea." I'm always happy for business, but our

services are becoming slightly too well-known. These kinds of things are better left hidden in the shadows. Still, I could use a distraction, so I tell Kip to set up a meeting.

~

"Ready to go, T?" James asks, pressing a bag of frozen peas to his jaw, where his opponent got in a decent hit. The underground fights have garnered more attention recently, and the bigger crowds mean more difficult opponents but also heftier paydays. He still demolished yesterday's fight and remains undefeated, though that's only because I've never entered the ring with him. Thankfully, his bruise isn't horrible, or it'd draw too much attention.

"Yeah, let's hit the road."

We're meeting Henry at one of James's favorite cafes uptown, somewhere well-lit and crowded. New clients always want to meet in public places. They feel safer, even though it increases the risk of being overheard.

Henry is automatically identifiable by his constant nervous glances, like he's waiting for a killer clown to jump out at any minute and slice off his ears.

I join him at the table while James waits to order our coffee, then immediately wish we'd switched roles when one of the sexiest women I've ever seen walks in and stands behind him in line. Her ass is sinful in her jeans, and her long blonde hair is begging to be grabbed.

Biting the inside of my cheek, I rip my gaze away from her and look back to Henry.

"As I was saying, it's best that we have another meeting somewhere more private to discuss details before James and I plan how to complete the job."

"Complete the job… You don't mean…" Henry looks around, then pulls a finger across his throat. I barely hold in a groan.

"No, we don't do that." *Usually,* I mentally add. "Each job is different. It depends on the client's needs. You tell us the problem you need efficiently and quietly taken care of, like to get rid of evidence, destroy blackmail materials, or make someone disappear, and it'll get done."

"How do you make someone disappear?" he asks, voice so quiet I almost don't hear him.

"By getting creative. Typically, by manipulating circumstances until they're forced to move away or ensuring they're arrested and sentenced for a crime."

"I think that second option will work for my... problem."

"And what is your problem?"

"Luna didn't tell you?"

"She just told us that your son has gotten mixed up with some bad guys."

James comes to the table to wait until our drinks are called and adds, "Bad guys with endless resources." He's the more reliable researcher between the two of us, so he's the reason we know that Henry's son goes to college with Luna's youngest brothers, the twins, and lives in a similar tax bracket. "It's a group of trust fund kids who get thrills out of pushing limits, both their own and other people's, right?"

Henry nods. "I'll admit that we didn't do the best in raising Cameron to be down-to-earth. We wanted to give him opportunities we never had. But we definitely didn't raise him to treat others like playthings. Or to gamble with his own life so carelessly. He was arrested for drunk driving last month, and that's not the worst thing those boys get up to. Their leader is the son of some real estate mogul, and he has an affinity for convincing the others to risk their lives for his own enjoyment. Cameron and his buddy came home with several bad burns once. They refused to tell me what happened, but there was a story on the news about a resort burning down. It was the off-season, so no one was inside, but the authorities labeled it arson. Cameron's friend's dad owned the resort."

I tap the table, nodding solemnly. Sounds like a classic rich boy tantrum. When silver-spoon kids throw fits, millions of dollars and the lives of poorer people are almost always at stake.

"No one questioned Cameron or his friend?" I ask.

"I suspect the friend's dad smoothed it over," Henry says.

The barista calls James's name just as he's asking a question of his own, so I get up to retrieve the drinks. When I turn, holding a cup in each hand, I notice the sexy blonde sitting at a high bar that serves as a communal table. Her eyes are on a book in front of her, and she's slowly stirring her coffee.

"T," James says, snapping me back to attention. I set his tea latte in front of him and sip my cold brew.

"I'm assuming it's the leader you want handled?" I ask.

Henry looks around again. His paranoia at being overheard is the most conspicuous thing about this meeting. "Yes," he whispers.

"It's extra for well-known and well-connected people. It takes more to make something stick when the target can buy their way out of most corners."

"Whatever, I'll pay it," Henry readily agrees. "I just need to get my boy away from them before he dies."

Though James and I agree to take the job, I can't help but think this won't be the end of it for Henry's son.

Removing one bad influence won't save someone determined to ruin their life.

THREE

June

Once I find Theo, it's easy to keep him in my sights. He doesn't do much beyond hanging out at the bar he owns, the Iron Cage, or the clubhouse two blocks away, working in his garage, riding with the Saints of Purgatory, and visiting the gym with his right hand, James Hartley. Amber is almost always there, dangling on his arm and staring at him like she's waiting for him to snap.

My decision to kill Theo solidifies the second week of following him. I'm sitting in my car, parked in front of the Iron Cage with the seat reclined and windows down. The bar's door swings open, releasing the sound of music with a loud bass, and Theo and Amber pour out. I'm close enough to see their mouths moving, but I can't hear individual words, even when the door clicks shut, muffling the music again. She's crying and reaching for him, swaying like she's drunk. He grips her wrists, yanks her forward so their chests are pressed together, and snarls in her face. Her shoulders pull in as she attempts to make herself smaller.

Her shout of pain is perfectly audible when he shoves

her. She stumbles, throws her arms out, and barely catches herself on the wall.

"Pull yourself together," he yells. Then he rubs his head, turns, and stalks away.

I watch him climb on his bike and ride off, all while Amber cowers against the wall, holding herself with too-thin arms. I'm about to leave when another man, also wearing a Saints of Purgatory jacket, walks out, sees Amber, and shakes his head. At his appearance, she runs over and throws her arms around him, sobbing into his neck. The guy hugs her close, but it doesn't take long for his hands to reach her ass. I stay long enough to watch his piss-poor comforting turn into a sloppy drunken make-out session.

During Jennifer's next appointment, she tells me that Amber and Theo are in a fight, but Amber is too afraid to break up with him. Then, that night, Theo rides to his house, Amber on the back of his bike. When he pulls her off, her legs cinch around his waist, and she tugs off his helmet to kiss him while he carries her inside. I leave, knowing I won't be seeing either one of them again soon.

The next time I see Amber, I wish I hadn't left. Because she has two black eyes and a split lip.

After that, her presence is less consistent, and when I do see her with Theo, she's more subdued, less overtly trying to get his attention. She drinks more, though, if her stumbling is any indicator. She also seems thinner every day, and the dark circles under her eyes never fade.

Nearly a month into tailing Theo, I watch him and the rest of the gang steal four luxury sedans during a convention downtown. They then sell them to a guy named Basil, who lives a life of extravagance that's probably paid for by this agreement he has with a group of outlaw thug bikers. Theo and the Saints bring him nice cars to massacre and sell in pieces to the highest bidder.

For some reason, I'm disappointed. Like I expected more from the leader of the roughest biker gang in Tucson.

I shouldn't have. No man who pushes around his girl is truly impressive. They're always sniveling boys afraid of their own shadows. Everything else is an act.

Theo Zervas is no different.

~

Thanksgiving comes and goes. Sadie returns home to LA for the holiday, and Evelyn, Rose, her sister, Maple, and I spend the day together, all without decent families to celebrate with. By December, the flames inside start to tickle my ribs. It hasn't even been three months, so I double my visits to the kickboxing gym and gun range, two of the most reliable ways of releasing pent-up energy and blowing temporary cold winds through my body.

On Saturday, I don my black, torn jeans, a too-small tank top I stole from Rose, and black combat boots. The tattoo nearly covering my left arm sells the image of a girl who belongs in a biker bar. It's a cemetery with fourteen small tombstones, all but one engulfed in flames. I had the most recent headstone added over five weeks ago.

I arrange my dirty blonde waves in a messy bun that looks effortless but requires nearly half a can of hairspray and apply smokey eyeshadow and fake eyelashes. It's nine-thirty by the time I leave my house and head to the Iron Cage, which is already crowded when I arrive, just as planned. I don't want to stick out any more than I have to. The bouncer, a man so big he could easily crush me between his fingers, gives me a short nod, waving me in.

Not a threat, he's probably thinking.

I'm never a threat.

My ears throb with the onslaught of hard rock spilling from the speakers, and my nose wrinkles at the smell of cigarettes, alcohol, and sweat. The place is filled with Saints and wannabe lookalikes. Ignoring the instincts that tell me to pull free the knife I have strapped to my thigh, I make a beeline for the bar and sit next to a man wearing the Saints of Purgatory cut. He has dark skin and braided black hair, and I subconsciously flip through the files I've started for the core members. I'm confident this is Raphael, the club's tail gunner and close friend of Luna Mcintyre, the club's treasurer and the only girl with a named rank.

At my appearance, Raphael turns, surreptitiously checking the space around me, making sure I'm alone. He then gives me a wide smile, showing off crooked teeth that are oddly endearing.

"What is a stunning young creature like yourself doing in a place like this all alone?"

Could he be more cliche?

"Who says I'm alone?" I respond, though I follow the words with a half-smile.

"Your boyfriend hiding in the shadows?"

"Oh, I don't have a boyfriend." Right after answering, I look away, radiating uncertainty with a hint of insecurity.

"How about I buy you a drink? You really shouldn't hang out alone in a dump like this."

Dump? He practically lives here.

"Uhm…" I say, pulling my bottom lip between my teeth.

"No strings attached, promise!"

I hesitate for a moment, just long enough to keep him hooked, then agree. He instantly turns to the bartender and says to make me whatever I want.

"What's good here?" I ask. *Please don't say beer,* I think. I've never developed a taste for the stuff.

"The IPA on tap is delicious."

Of fucking course it is. "Okay, I'll try that." The bartender pulls the tap to fill a glass, then slides it to me. I thank him and turn back to Raphael. "I'm Maryanne."

"Raphael," he says, offering his hand. I take it, shaking once, then reaching up to tuck a strand of hair behind my ear.

From there, it's easy. I talk with Raphael and choke down the beer. Then I let him pull me into the center of the bar where he grinds against me with the beat of the music. In any other situation, I'd appreciate his sense of rhythm. Now, though, all I can think is, *where the hell is Theo?*

I wasn't planning to talk to him today, but I wanted to get close. This is the first contact I'm making with the people in his world. I would've preferred if he were here so he could at least see me on the sidelines as a random girl, but not a threat. Any sense of familiarity with me, even foggy, will help lower his guard on the final day.

But I spend two hours with Raphael and never see Theo or Amber. There are several Saints among the crowd, and James is obvious when he walks through the bar, thanks to his thick red beard, matching red hair, and towering height, but no other major players show up. Finally, I announce I'm leaving, shut down Raphael's invitations back to his place, and agree to give him my number, which is for the burner I bought with cash. Then I leave, desperate to get home and wash off the night.

Raphael calls the next day but I ignore it, not wanting to be too important in his life or memorable to the rest of the gang. He calls and texts several more times, his last message including a few choice words about me being a tease.

I wait for two weeks before returning to the Iron Cage on a Thursday when I know Raphael won't be there because he'll have his son for a visit. I dance with Luna, a short girl with tattoos climbing up her neck and dark, cropped hair. I have my arms wrapped around her neck, our hips pressed together, when Theo makes his first appearance.

He's standing at the back of the bar, gaze sweeping the whole room. I quickly look away before he catches me staring. The next time I look up, he's gone.

I dance with Luna for longer than I probably should, but she's genuinely fun, and for a blink, there are no thoughts in my mind but the music, the smoke in the air, and the feel of fingers against my exposed skin on my back.

Then she starts to press her lips to my neck, and I take the first opportunity to slip away before I leave a lasting impression.

I manage one more trip to the Iron Cage, and though there is no Amber or Theo, I do hear an interesting conversation from two guys standing off to the side.

"That little bitch needs to go. For good."

"Valor, seriously, dude! You need to keep your mouth shut."

"You can't like her any more than I do."

"I don't, but I trust the boss. He'll take care of her."

Unfortunately, I don't hear anything else, and I pause hunting to attempt enjoying the holidays.

When the fire starts licking my brain, I visit my tattoo artist to add flames to the most recent gravestone on my sleeve. Then, the second weekend of January, Jennifer calls my personal phone.

"Ms. Graves," she says, voice thick with tears.

"Jennifer, is everything okay?"

"No, no. I don't know what to do. I haven't heard from her in three days!"

I swallow a reply that it's normal to go several days

without talking to someone. Especially when you're in a situation like Amber. Instead, I respond, "Tell me what happened."

"She sent me this cryptic text a few days ago saying she was going to be out of touch for a while. But I *know* it's not from her. I can tell. I mean, the texts *look* like she wrote them, but it's *not* her. I swear."

"I believe you, Jennifer. You have a mother's intuition. That means something."

"Not according to the police."

"You talked to the cops?"

"Yes, but they said there's nothing they can do."

"The cops have a lot on their plate," I say. Which is true. We also don't have the best department here in Tucson. Not that I'm complaining. It makes my hobbies way easier to manage. As far as I can tell, the police don't even realize there's a serial killer in the city. And Jared was my eighth kill since moving here after college five years ago. Though their bodies are never found, and I'm not stupid enough to leave behind evidence or a signature.

"Have you checked her apartment?"

"I don't think she's been there for a while. I can't find her. I don't know what to do." Her words end on a sob.

"Breathe, it's okay. Where are you? What happened?" I ask, wanting to know what *exactly* made her call now.

"I'm outside some dive bar in Palo Verde. He's here drinking with his buddies."

"Palo Verde? Why are you there?" My heartbeat ratchets up. The Iron Cage is in Palo Verde.

"I need to find Amber, and I know he knows something, so I've been looking for him. I finally found him, and when I asked about Amber, he just laughed. He *laughed!* Then he told me to stop worrying about her and move on with my life. He did something to my Amber. I know it."

"Jennifer, I need you to get in your car and leave," I say, grabbing my keys and quickly locking up my office. "You're not safe there."

"Amber—"

"She's not there at that bar, is she?" I interrupt.

There's a shaky breath on the other side, followed by fresh sobs and I think the word, "No."

"Then you can leave. Getting yourself hurt won't help Amber. Call the police and tell them what he said, but you need to leave first." I don't want the police involved, but it'd be highly suspicious if I didn't suggest she call them.

"Okay… you should've seen his face, Ms. Graves. He did something to her, and he doesn't care at all. My baby. He just… he laughed."

"I know. Are you back in your car?"

"Yes."

"Good. Now call the police, then go home and get some rest."

There's a long pause before Jennifer whispers, "Okay."

"It's going to be okay, I promise," I lie. Because it's not going to be okay. "*He'll take care of her,*" the biker had said. Amber's injuries have gotten worse, and by the way I've seen Theo handle her, there's no doubt in my mind that he did "take care of her."

Amber is gone. Probably dead.

The only consolation is that Theo will be joining her in the afterlife sooner rather than later.

~

I would've liked a few more weeks watching Theo. Planning and, preferably, making contact. But Jennifer's call incentivizes me to speed up the timeline. Logically, I know if he did something to Amber, then killing him sooner won't help anything. But the flames curled around my ribs don't care about logic. They just want to incinerate something.

Every kill is different. This one just won't have any interaction with my prey until the final day. Which is fine. It just means I'll have to drug Theo. I can't take him down by force, and I don't have time to seduce him back to my place. Plus, he won't trust me enough to walk into my basement like Jared did.

Theo must be alone when I strike, away from any cameras or witnesses. I need space and time to get him into my car and to my basement.

My plan will work. The worst case scenario is a too-quick kill and a left-behind body with no trace of me. Hopefully, it won't come to that.

I struggle through Taco Tuesday with the girls. All three act the same as always, showing no sign of noticing anything is different.

Can they really not feel the heat emanating from my chest? Or see the sparks in my eyes?

My calm goodbyes and gentle hugs in the parking lot bely the bonfire under my skin. Having most of Theo's schedule memorized at this point, I don't hesitate before heading to the small playground on the very edge of Tucson's north border. I never learned why Theo comes here on the second Tuesday of every month, but he does. Or at least, he did in October, November, and December. My plan hinges on him repeating the habit this month.

The last three times, he didn't arrive until after midnight, so I park across the street and double-check everything. I have my midazolam syringes on hand and diazepam syringes in the car in case he needs more later. The back of my car is covered in plastic wrap, there are no weapons within range of where Theo will be in case he wakes up too early, and my mask is waiting on the passenger seat. I don't expect him to get free, but I don't want him to see my face until he's secured in the basement.

My heart nearly jumps in my throat from anticipation when I hear the familiar engine of a motorcycle drawing closer.

Right on time.

Theo parks, climbs off the bike, and hangs his helmet on the handlebars. He walks to the playground with his hands in his pockets.

Sheathing the knife I'd been sharpening, I tuck a syringe up my sleeve, pull on the mask, and jump from my car. I walk on the balls of my feet across the street and pass the motorcycle, which I'll come back to dispose of after he's safely tied in my basement. I think the knowledge that I've destroyed his precious bike will be just as torturous as anything else I'll do.

Roaring flames and a thunderous heartbeat fill my ears. Theo is standing completely still in the middle of the playground, unaware of his approaching doom.

A foot away from him, I pull out the syringe and lift my arm, aiming for the major artery in his neck. Thumb hovering over the plunger, I bring my hand down, needle glinting in the moonlight.

My arm freezes halfway to his neck.

No, it's stopped.

By Theo's hand.

He'd reached up and grabbed my arm faster than I could process.

My lips part in shock, and I fight against his hold.

"Now is really not the time."

It takes a moment for the words to penetrate the roaring in my ears. I belatedly realize Theo said them, and he sounds pissed.

Instinct replacing shock, my left hand reaches for the sheathed knife. Once again, my movement is thrown off course. This time, it's from Theo turning to face me. He briefly lets go of my right hand but knocks the syringe out of my grip before I can attack. Then he spins me around and shoves me so my back is pressed against the pole of the swing set. He moves closer, towering over me and pinning my arms at my side, then positions his feet outside of mine and brackets my legs with his, restricting any possible movement.

Too slowly, I put together what's happening.

Theo took control. He stopped me before I could drug him.

I can try fighting, but he's more trained than most of the men I take down.

I'm fucked.

"Did you really think I would be that easy?" he asks.

I blink at him. His eyes are browner than I realized. I thought they were black, but nope, they're dark brown. Like a mix of ebony and mahogany.

He sneers. Some might call it a smile, but it's much too sinister for that. It's the look of a predator about to devour his prey.

"But nice try, June." Then he rips off my mask.

FOUR

Theo

She stares up at me with crystal-clear blue eyes. There's a danger behind them that anyone could get lost in, and I almost wish to submerge myself in the water of those irises.

Her mouth thins with anger, and her jaw flexes. I expect her to try and knee me in the junk, so I begin moving my leg to stop her. Instead, she throws her head forward with so much force that pain explodes where she connects with my nose. Tasting blood at the back of my throat, I nearly lose my grip on her wrists. But I just grunt and squeeze my legs tighter to keep from stumbling. She struggles under my grip, her hip briefly brushing against my groin.

And *fuck* if my dick doesn't threaten to harden at that momentary contact.

"That was rude," I say, sniffing past the sharp pain in my nose. Blood fills my mouth, and I don't hesitate before spitting. Red saliva lands on her chin, and she gasps in shock. I almost grin at her look of wild indignation.

"Let me go," she demands, thrusting her hips forward. The motion is meant to throw her opponent off balance, but all it does is elicit a groan from me and mix a confusing amount of lust into the situation.

If I'd known she would finally make her move tonight, I would've had a quick fuck beforehand to avoid this exact reaction.

"So you can go for that knife at your side? Or the backup syringe I'm sure you have hidden away?" I shake my head. "I don't think so."

"I don't know what you're talking about."

"Oh?" I cock an eyebrow. "You mean you weren't planning on drugging and killing me tonight?"

A flash of surprise fills her icy eyes.

"This isn't a spontaneous attack. You're much too prepared and controlled for that," I continue, drawing on my weeks of research on her.

I first noticed her following me about two months ago. It was her at the cafe when we met Henry. She never looked our way, but she chose a seat between a very old man who reeked of tobacco and an overweight woman chewing gum louder than should be legal, despite there being two free tables in the cafe at the time. The chair she chose was the only one that put us right in her eye line. Later, she left the cafe after James and I started our bikes and followed us all the way to the clubhouse, though I wouldn't have realized if I hadn't already been watching. She's plainly an experienced stalker. She was never closer than two cars away.

From then on, I always had my eyes peeled. Several times a week, she'd be there, just in the periphery, until her first time in the Iron Cage, when she flirted and danced with Raph. I was in my office the whole time, watching the security cameras. I could tell she wasn't dancing *for* Raph, but she was still moving her body like a professional, swaying her seductive hips as if to lock men into a trance. Raph thought he was going to get lucky, but I saw the way her eyes were constantly scanning, searching for me. Poor guy lamented about being blown off for days.

Then Luna got her attention. For a moment, I wondered if Luna actually would get lucky. But, of course, June was too smart for that.

James is the only person who knows about my shadow, and neither of us has been able to find a connection. June has never met any Saint of Purgatory as far as I can tell. I've definitely never met her. James thought I fucked her at some point, but I would've remembered. Early on, I realized she was the type of woman to unintentionally carve a home in my memory.

On the surface, June Graves is a typical, kind-hearted girl from New Mexico with a slight edge and taste for adventure. She moved to Arizona a few days after her twenty-second birthday. Her mom and stepdad still live in the suburbs of Albuquerque, and her stepsister lives in San Antonio with her son. She's a therapist who occasionally volunteers at the children's hospital. Her best friend, Sadie Oliver, owns a little plant nursery and has a Great Dane and several semi-regular 'boyfriends' coming and going. They both meet two other friends every Tuesday for tacos and margaritas. Evelyn is a social worker addicted to working, and Rose lives with her girlfriend, Vanessa. June is a badass at kickboxing and a regular at Vanessa's hot yoga classes, two things that resulted in *very* long cold showers after I first witnessed them. Her criminal history is made up of a single parking ticket.

Oh, and she apparently stalks dangerous men, like the leader of an outlaw motorcycle club, and attacks them in public parks in the middle of the night.

I knew her intentions weren't pure, but figuring out what they *are* has been excessively difficult. James snuck into her house three weeks ago while I led her on a long ride around the city, and fortunately, though unhelpfully, she didn't have an 'evil plans' journal or a picture of my head on a dart board. But he did find a suspiciously clean basement stocked with rolls of plastic drop, a gun that turned out to be registered, and a toolbox with several odd tools, like a carving knife and a vial of drugs, locked in a giant safe. More importantly, he planted a bug in her house.

Turns out, June talks to herself. Rarely full sentences; more like a few mumbled words fall from her mouth without permission. *"Giant asshole... need a ton of drugs... could seduce him... can't wait till March."*

Our best guess is she wants to kill me. *Why* is the real question.

James thinks she's a hired assassin. I have no idea what to think. She's dedicated, whatever her intentions are. I've rarely seen anyone so focused and committed to something as June is to hunting me down. That really shouldn't be as sexy as it is.

"You think I'm trying to kill you?" she asks, putting on a respectable act of surprised innocence. "I could never do that."

"I don't believe that for a second. You may look helpless, but I have a feeling you'd be able to take down most men twice your size."

In a flash, she drops her mask and hisses, "Bigger." Then, in quick succession, she spits in my face, twists her body to the side, yanks her arm out of my grasp when it loosens in shock, throws her elbow into my neck, drops, and rolls away.

Coughing, I wipe away her spit and turn to grab her. Unfortunately, she's gotten her knife free and slices down, catching my forearm. A gasp of pain rips from my lips, and

I jump back, instinctively covering the cut with my hand. Blood wells against my palm.

"Fuck!" I curse, looking from the wound to June. In addition to her knife, she now has a new syringe out.

I should be worried or angry or *anything* but what I am, which is impressed.

She really can handle herself.

"You know I have a gun, right?" I ask.

"Then shoot me."

My eyebrows raise, but I don't reach for the gun. I can hear James yelling at me in my head, calling me an idiot and telling me to shoot the bitch, but I don't want to.

"Not all of us resort to violence to solve our problems."

She laughs once, though the sound is more like a bark. "You wouldn't know how to live without violence."

"You think you know me after following me for a few weeks?" Again, there's a moment of shock in her eyes, like she's never been discovered before.

Has she done this before? *Why?*

She recovers from her shock quickly. "I know more than you think."

"Aren't therapists supposed to help people, not hurt them? And, you know, not judge a book by its cover?"

"I've seen more than just your cover."

I wink. "Want to see under my covers?"

She grimaces. "In my nightmares."

"Nightmares can be fun if you do them right."

"That makes no sense."

"Then let me show you." I lunge. She learned from her earlier mistake and doesn't underestimate my speed, dodging and swinging out with the knife. I block her arm and prioritize grabbing her other wrist so that pesky syringe doesn't get anywhere near my skin. I'll most likely survive a stab wound, but if she gets those drugs in me, I'm done for. I'm not sure what it is, but my guess is midazolam or diazepam, both of which she owns in excess.

The edge of her knife slides against my side, leaving a trail of stinging pain, but I don't think it's a deep cut, and the effort of trying to stab me puts her on the defensive. A few seconds later, I've swept her legs out from under her and tackled her to the ground, mulch crunching under us. She struggles, but I manage to land on top of her, knees on either side, hips anchoring her to the ground, and feet hooked over her ankles to stop her from kicking or getting leverage. I pull both her arms up, knocking the syringe and knife away, and crush her wrists under one hand. When we stop moving, I have her small form locked beneath me, our faces inches from each other and our hips lined up. I could easily grind down and get a moment of relief from the aching desire that formed during the fight.

I smirk down at her. "Good try again, June. But you're out of your league."

"Fuck you."

"Anytime you want."

A drop of blood falls from the cut on my arm and lands on her forehead. I expect her to flinch, but she doesn't move a muscle.

Curious.

"Tell me, what *exactly* was your plan? Drug me, then what?"

Her lips press together.

"You've been following me for months. Why?"

Nothing.

"Did someone hire you?"

A blink.

"No?" I say. "So, this is all for you? That's even more interesting."

Her resolve not to respond seems to break on its own. "Why?"

"Because that opens a whole realm of intriguing possibilities. This is too planned to be a crime of passion. So, what is it? Revenge? What for?"

"You have so many enemies that you don't know?" she asks. But her voice has a note that suggests I'm not completely correct about her motivation.

"I didn't hurt you personally. There's nothing connecting us."

Her lips return to that thin line. She's either regained control or she's afraid I'm on the right track.

"Are you doing this for someone else?"

There's a barely noticeable movement in her throat from a small swallow.

"You weren't hired, but you are acting on behalf of another. Is this an act of altruism? Man, volunteer work sure has gotten weird."

She turns her head away, breaking the connection between us. Suddenly, I want to force her attention back to me and wrap my hand around her throat to keep it there. But I know if I move, she'll attack.

"Who did I hurt so badly that you decided to kill for them? I've looked into you. I don't know any of your friends or family."

She refuses to meet my eyes.

"June?"

The sound of her name on my lips must piss her off because she jerks her head back and bears her teeth at me, lifting so her face is even closer to mine. "Fuck you!"

"Ask nicely."

She drops back to the ground, letting out a seething breath through her nose. A whiff of something crisp and sweet fills my nose, like juniper and apple pie.

I can't help it. The pinched expression on her face is fucking hot, and my pants are so damn tight. I lower some of my weight, pressing our hips together. I know she feels how hard I am because she sucks in a breath, and her eyes go wide. But she doesn't try to pull away. In fact, I could *swear* her pupils expand. I wonder what I'd find if I were to reach down and dip my hand into her pants.

"I'll fuck you all night if you ask," I say, rolling my hips against her and relishing the little hitch in her breath.

"I will kill you." She tugs her pinned hands and tries to pull her knee up to throw me off balance. Despite the desire I'm pretty sure I see in her eyes, she won't give in to that. If I try to push her further, I'll just get distracted, which she'll use to her advantage.

So, I still my hips and lift slightly to create much-needed distance.

"I know I'm not a good person, but I don't think I've done anything murder-worthy. At least, not in the last several months."

She scoffs.

"You disagree?"

Nothing.

"Tell me, what did I do to earn such a fatal punishment?" I think of all the people I've hurt, stolen from, betrayed, and even killed, wondering if one of the lives I've taken was connected to June somehow.

"The fact that you don't know speaks volumes to who you are."

I frown, more confused than ever.

"Did I fuck your friend or something? Or…" I think through the rest of what I know about her life. Outside of her friends, volunteering, and following me, the only other thing she does is work.

It hits me.

"This is for one of your patients, isn't it?"

The slight widening of her eyes is all the confirmation I need.

"So you're getting revenge for a patient? That's taking your job a bit too far, don't you think?"

Her burning anger is tangible in the heat of her skin.

"How many times have you done this? Killed for a patient?"

She doesn't answer, of course, but her eyes do flick away for a second. I can't help grinning at this sexy, unhinged, violent little murderer I have pinned under me.

"But I'm the bad guy?"

"No one I've ever hurt has been innocent!" she says, finally losing control of the lock on her mouth. "I've never killed someone helpless."

"No, you just drug them before they can fight back."

"They deserved it. All of them."

"I don't doubt that."

"You deserve it!" she yells, pulling at my grip and arching her back to try and break free.

"Probably."

"Let me go!"

"If I do that, you'll try to kill me again. And I can't have that."

"So, what are you going to do? Kill me instead?"

"I should," I say. I really should. This woman isn't as innocent as she appears. I can't go to the cops with a story that a seemingly law-abiding twenty-seven-year-old woman half my size tried to kill me, the notorious leader of a motorcycle club everyone knows is part of the one percent of MCs that engage in criminal activity. The cops would throw me in jail for the sheer ridiculousness of the suggestion. But I can't let her go, because her next attempt might not fail.

She's a threat, no matter what she looks like on the outside.

My job is to eliminate threats, both to myself and the rest of the Saints.

The only real option I have is to kill her.

But I don't want to. She's just so *intriguing*.

"So, kill me. It's not like you have a problem killing women."

"No, I don't," I say, honestly. "I don't discriminate based on gender. If someone needs killing, it doesn't matter what they've got going on between their legs, I'll get the job done."

"You're disgusting."

"I like to think of myself as a feminist," I say. "Equal rights and all that."

"That's fucked up logic."

"What would you have me do? Let you go just because you've got a pussy? Right after you tried to kill me?"

"Either let me go or kill me, because we can't lie here forever."

Fuck she's right, we can't.

"Okay. How about a compromise?"

She freezes, her lips parted. Confusion and disbelief replace the anger in her blue eyes.

"A compromise?"

"Yes, little reaper. A compromise." I smile again at the scowl on her face from the nickname. "You came here because you wanted to kill me, right?"

She slowly nods, as if unsure where I'm going with this. Honestly, so am I.

"Well, are your plans time sensitive?"

"What do you mean?"

"I mean, do you have to kill me tonight, or can it wait?"

Her mouth opens, then closes, like she doesn't know how to answer.

"Your motive for killing me is some misguided sense of justice based on one side of a story you got from a patient. I assume that your weeks of following me have not just been to learn my schedule, but to prove to yourself that I'm the type of man deserving of death."

She bites her bottom lip, and I know I'm right.

"You can't really get to know someone from a hundred yards away. I'm not saying that I'm a good man, because I'm not, but I also might not meet whatever your necessary criteria is before you kill someone."

"You definitely meet the criteria."

"I probably do. But you don't *know* that. Not yet. So, here's the compromise. You have to wait one month, then you can kill me."

It's obvious that's not what she expected. She freezes, blinking at me with shock. "What?"

I nod, realizing how fucking stupid this is but not able to stop myself. "You can kill me in a month, and I swear, I won't stop you."

The gears visibly turn in her head. She frowns, searching for the trick in my words. "Why? What's the catch?"

Clever little reaper.

"The catch is that for that month, you don't get to follow me from a distance. You have to be right by my side."

A wrinkle forms in her forehead as her frown deepens.

James is going to stab me for this when I get home.

"For the next month, June Graves, you're mine. You're a Saint of Purgatory."

FIVE

June

For a moment, it's not Theo's strength holding me down, but shock. Disbelief that what I heard him say is what he actually said.

Become a member of his gang? Absolutely not.

However, he was right that typically part of my process is getting close enough to validate a client's claims. Though I haven't been able to do that with him, I also haven't seen Amber since a glimpse almost two weeks ago when she looked exhausted and broken. She'd tried talking to Theo, but he had shoved her away so hard that she fell, landing hard on her ass. He didn't even check on her. Just stalked off, leaving her to cry by herself. Then she'd disappeared, and Jennifer remains convinced Theo killed her.

"Why would I do that?" I ask, thoughts struggling to stay focused on my task.

"For the reason I just said. After a month, I'll let you kill me without a fight." He pauses and tilts his head, as if considering. "Unless the fight is part of the fun for you." His dark eyes gleam in the moonlight, and I remember how hard he'd felt when our hips rubbed together.

Heat gathers between my legs and rises in my cheeks.

"If I say no?"

"I don't think you're in the position to say no." He looks pointedly up at where his hand grips my wrists, then down to where his knees are pressed against my sides, keeping me pinned.

"What's to stop me from killing you as soon as you let me go?"

"The fact that you don't have any weapons and I do."

My teeth grind together. I wish I could argue, but I'm not stupid. Without weapons or the element of surprise, I don't stand a chance against him.

"What about a few days from now? I could agree, then decide to kill you in a week."

"You could, but that's not in the spirit of the game."

"This isn't a game!"

"You won't be a full member, of course. Not without a bike of your own," he continues, unbothered by my words. "Typically, you'd have already put several hundred miles on the road before becoming a prospect. Then the club would vote on you joining. But seeing as I'm the president, I think we can work around that."

"Lucky me," I mumble. I move my fingers, attempting to find leverage against his hand.

"Other than that, you'll be like any new prospect."

"A psychopath?"

Theo pushes forward, smoothly ignoring me. "You'll need to go through an… initiation. It's customary for our newest members to move into the clubhouse or with a veteran. As you're so determined to kill me, it makes sense for you to live in my house."

I start shaking my head before he finishes speaking. "Fuck no. In what world would I move in with you?"

"In a world where we both walk away from this playground alive."

"I'm not moving in with you! I have a job. I have a life!"

"You can keep taking appointments. And I won't keep you from Taco Tuesdays with your friends."

"I'd like to see you try." I fill my voice with a threat that honestly means nothing right now. If Theo wanted me dead, he could've killed me ten times over.

Fuck, he could've hurt Sadie, Rose, or Evelyn. How could I have missed this? When did he notice me? Has he had one of his gang members following me? I should've fucking noticed. I promised myself years ago to *never* get careless or complacent. That's how you die or go to prison.

Which are my options right now. Or, worse, he could go after my friends. That's the one thing I'll never allow.

"Other than that, you're with us. You come to the Iron Cage and hang out with the crew at the clubhouse. You take riding lessons with either me or Luna. You'll come to church and pitch in with jobs. When we're on the road, you ride with me."

"No."

"You'd rather die than ride on a motorcycle?"

"I'd rather die than join your gang or live with you."

"And James."

"Yeah, because that makes it better," I mutter, sarcastically.

"Are you scared of what'll happen if we're under the same roof every night?" He slowly lowers his body, and anticipation makes my muscles coil. "Think you won't be able to stay out of my bed?"

A laugh rips from my throat even as my skin prickles with heat. And not the I-need-to-feel-a-heart-stop heat that radiates from the flames. "You're delusional."

He cocks an eyebrow. "Am I?" With his free hand not

wrapped around my wrists, he traces my side, thumb brushing briefly under my breast before moving over my navel. I try to wiggle away, but he still has me fully pinned. His fingers hover at the waistband of my pants as he leans down, chest pressing against mine. "If I go further, I bet I'll find you soaking wet."

"I will cut your fucking hand off," I threaten, happy to hear my voice isn't blatantly coated with need. Still, there's a traitorous pulse of desire growing between my legs that's made worse by the intoxicating scent of this man, a mix of exhaust fumes, coffee, and natural musk.

"Are you afraid of wanting me?" he taunts.

No. But I am on fire in a new way, and I'm worried he knows exactly how to coax these sweeter flames.

"Agree to my compromise, and I'll keep my hands to myself."

"No."

His hips push against mine, and I hate how good that feels. "Come on, little reaper. Become a Saint."

"You're insane."

"I also have more resources than you. Did you really think I came here tonight, knowing you're following me, without a fail-safe?"

My brows raise.

"If I don't go home safely, the cops will receive some interesting information on you."

"Bullshit." He doesn't have anything on me. He can't. There's nothing to find.

"Do you really want to call my bluff?"

I want to say yes out of spite, but I haven't lasted this long by making decisions based on pride. Only being overly cautious keeps me off the police radar.

"It's just one month," he adds. "It's the best deal you'll

get. Hell, you may end up enjoying it." As if to prove his point, he nudges at the top of my pants, still not slipping underneath but reminding me of our compromising position. "So, what do you say?"

This is ridiculous. Absolute madness.

But I have to face reality. There's no other way I'm leaving this playground both alive and without the fear that his bluff isn't just a bluff. He might have something on me. Or he might have one of his biker buddies fabricate evidence against me.

It's a risk I can't take.

Teeth practically glued together from hatred, I snarl, "Fine."

He smiles. "You're agreeing?"

"Yes. Now get the fuck off me."

"Are you sure?" his hand raises back to my breasts.

"Get. Off. Now."

"If you insist." He stands, and the loss of his weight makes me feel far too light and cold, despite the continuous fire under my skin.

"Take the night, little reaper. Pack a suitcase. I'll pick you up from your office tomorrow afternoon," Theo says. I think I hear his footsteps as he walks away, but I have no idea how long it takes after the sound of his motorcycle fades away before I finally stand on shaky legs.

I look around, unsurprised to find he took my syringes and knives, including the one strapped to my calf that I hadn't pulled free.

He left. I'm alone.

Until tomorrow.

When he expects me to become a Saint of Purgatory.

SIX

Theo

"You *WHAT*?!" James shouts, face turning nearly as red as his hair.

I shrug, applying antibiotic ointment to the slice on my forearm. I cleaned and bandaged the cut on my side before James walked out of his room, saw the blood, and demanded answers. Hearing the story, everything from the syringe to the fight to the deal we struck, has done nothing to calm him down. In fact, his pacing in the living room only grows more intense, while I pinch the skin on my forearm to inspect the damage.

"Did you forget that this chick is a *murderer* who tried to kill you an hour ago?"

I wave my hand in the air, brushing off his concern. "Who here isn't a murderer?"

"It's not the same and you know it!"

"She's not going to kill me, James." I dig for the largest bandage in our First Aid kit. The slice needs stitches, but I don't want to do it myself, and calling Valor, our resident doctor, would mean dodging several questions I have no desire to answer.

"Except you told her she could!"

"In a *month*. Do you really think she'll still want to kill me in a month?" I apply the bandage, then start wrapping my arm, watching James come to a stop directly in front of me.

"I think she's crazy, and you're not nearly as charming as you think you are."

"If it comes to that, then I'll let you and the boys do what you do best. Protect your own," I say, even as something plucks in my chest at the thought of what they'd do to June to protect me.

"You'd go back on your deal with her?"

"No. I won't try and stop her from killing me. I never said anything about what the rest of you would do."

For the first time since this conversation started, a smile fights through the anger and fear on James's face. It's not permanent, though, and soon he's back to scowling. "What will you tell everyone about our new member?"

"That her name is June, and she has a vicious streak. They'll love her."

"*I mean*," he stresses, "What will you tell them when they learn she can't even ride a bike? Or that she's *moving in with us*? I'm not sure if you know this, but you don't scream boyfriend material. No one is going to believe that, overnight, you have a girl important enough to move in with you and join the Saints, who doesn't even own her own bike."

"I'll buy her a bike."

"You can't just throw money at this problem, T."

"Why do I need to tell them anything?" I ask, throwing my hands up in exasperation. "I'm their leader. I don't have to explain myself to them."

"You're the best damn leader the Saints have seen in decades, and that's not because you do whatever you want without explanation. They trust you. You can't throw that away because some murderer made your dick hard."

I curl my hands into fists and wonder if the vein in my forehead James claims responsibility for is bulging. Part of me wants to end the conversation by decking him. But James is my second for a reason, and I can't throw June at the Saints and expect everyone to make it out with all their limbs.

"We'll tell Luna the truth," I say. "Kip will get a version of it. Not that she wants to kill me, but that we've come to an… agreement that she has to last a month with us if she wants to pay off a debt." James's look is unimpressed, and I forge forward before he can argue. "We'll tell the rest she's my girl, but I want to see how she gets along with the family before we take it any further. All those are versions of the truth."

"She's not your girl."

"She is for the next month."

James shakes his head, a muscle popping in his jaw as he bites back several retorts I'm sure are simmering in his throat. "I don't like it."

"Well, it's already done."

"Theo…"

I stand and step over the coffee table so I'm right in front of him. He might be two years older than me at thirty-three and an inch taller, but I still have a good fifteen pounds on him. "You didn't meet her, James. She might not be a biker, but trust me. She has what it takes to be a Saint."

"Being a killer doesn't make you a Saint."

"She's not just a killer. She's…" I roll my lips together, unable to properly explain this woman to him. He'll just have to meet her. "She's one of us. You'll see."

"I hope you're right, T. Because if she's not, if she tries to kill you again—"

"I know," I interrupt, squeezing his shoulder. "But she's not stupid. She knows she'll be outnumbered here. She'll be armed, I'm sure, but she won't try killing me. At least, not right away."

James's glare is unamused. "You're an idiot."

"Thanks. Now, I need to shower. Tomorrow, we get a new roommate."

I turn, heading to the private bathroom inside my room. Just before I shut the door, I hear James mutter, "We're so fucking dead," and I don't try to stop the smile from forming.

~

I text Luna to come over the next morning, and she waltzes in with a box of donuts, a Red Bull, and two cups of coffee, earning a dramatic kiss on her cheek from James. I sit her down to deliver the news, and she's predictably more excited than wary that I've invited the serial killer targeting me to live with us.

Her first question is, "She's that sexy chick who came to the Iron Cage a couple of times, right?"

James groans from the kitchen.

"Yeah, that's her," I say.

"Fuck yes."

"You realize she wants to kill Theo, right?" James says.

Luna shrugs. "We all want to kill him sometimes."

"Are you sure you two aren't siblings?" James asks, gesturing between us.

"Could be. It's not like my dad is the most committed husband."

"*Anyway,*" I say, reclaiming their attention. "I'm picking her up this afternoon. Don't forget that no one else knows all of this. Kip thinks—"

Luna cuts me off with a waved hand. "Yeah, yeah, I got it. Fake dating and all that. You realize about fifty percent of romance books start with fake dating or enemies to lovers? You're doing both of those with this little charade."

"He's only doing the enemies part," James corrects. "I don't foresee them becoming lovers. Beyond the inevitable hate-fucks they're sure to have."

I have to agree. As hot as June is, she's not girlfriend material, and I'm *definitely* not boyfriend material. I don't want a relationship, anyway. Not when the last one turned out so poorly.

"Please, don't. Just let me go." Amber's pleas fill my mind, and I look down at my hand, expecting to see them stained red. But they're clean, and Amber is gone.

"Does that mean I can go for it?" Luna asks.

"Absolutely not." The response snaps free before I can stop it. At James's narrowed eyes, I add, "Remember, the crew thinks she's my girl. And rule two…"

"Respect your fellow member and don't touch their bike, girl, or cut. Yeah, yeah, I got it," she says. "What about after the month is over? Can I go for it then?"

"I doubt you'll have the chance," James says. "I don't care what Theo promised. The moment she tries to kill him, she's dead."

Luna groans in disappointment, and I fight down the sudden anger at my best friend. More to avoid speaking than because I'm hungry, I grab one of the kolaches from the box on the coffee table and shove half of it in my mouth, letting Luna and James carry the conversation from there.

An hour later, we all ride the short distance to the clubhouse, where I find Kip in the garage. I feed him the half-truth about June, and though he's not ecstatic, he doesn't argue.

I borrow James's Jeep to pick June up since I don't know how much stuff she's packed, and by the time I pull into the lot, parking diagonally across three empty spaces, she's already walking out, keys in hand. Her eyes land on the bright yellow Jeep, and her nose crinkles.

"You were actually serious?" she greets.

"Of course I was. Where's your bag?"

"I didn't pack one. I'm not moving in with you." She turns away, unlocking her little Camry.

It takes three long strides to reach her. I push the front door shut before she can pull it fully open. "That was our deal."

"I changed my mind."

"That's not an option."

She grits her teeth. The small motion captures all my attention, and my hands flex with the desire to grip that jaw between my fingers.

"I'm not moving in with you."

"Fine, then you're moving into the clubhouse."

"With a dozen of your criminal underlings? No."

"Thought so. Lucky for you, I have an extra bedroom. Sheets are brand new, and Luna even brought over some fancy pillows."

"I could kill you in your sleep."

I sigh in frustration. Of course, she's not going to make this easy. "Look, you may be Miss Never-Do-Anything-Wrong on the surface, but don't forget about a certain little packet of your misdeeds ready to anonymously go to the cops."

Her eyebrows pull together. "I think you're lying."

Partly. "You might not leave evidence, but I have a recording of you talking about killing me. Plus, the knives, drugs, and rolls of plastic drop sheets in your soundproof basement would raise a few brows."

Briefly, her eyes widen at the mention of her murder paraphernalia James found a few weeks ago. Then she carefully pulls the surprise back and stitches her expression into one of unconcern. "I've never talked about killing you to anyone."

"No, but you *do* talk to yourself. And you're not very good about sweeping your house for bugs."

This time, she doesn't bother covering her fury. "You didn't."

"I had to know why you were stalking me, didn't I?"

"Talking about doing something is different than doing it. In case you forgot, you're alive."

"And I'll remain so, because if I turn up dead before this month is up, those cops will receive that little recording, which proves premeditation and points all eyes to you. It doesn't matter how good you are; no one is perfect. The reason you've never been caught is because no one has ever suspected you. The moment they do, your luck will change fast."

With every word, her face darkens further, fury swirling in her eyes. "You're a psychopath."

"Nice to meet you, Kettle." When she doesn't react, I let the smile fall and say, "Oh, come on, June. It's just a month. You're brave enough to survive in the big, bad biker's lair for a measly four weeks."

"It has nothing to do with bravery."

"Good, then let's go." I gesture to the Jeep.

She doesn't budge. "I'm not leaving my car here. And I don't have any clothes or anything!"

If I wasn't annoyed, I might've smiled at her acceptance. "Then I'll follow you to your place, and you can pack before we head back. But you'd better hurry. The crew is eager to meet their fearless leader's new girl."

"I'm *not* your girl!"

"I couldn't tell my family that you want to kill me, could I? You wouldn't last an hour."

"So you told them we're dating?" She sounds more appalled at our cover story than about joining the Saints.

"Most of them. No one would believe you're a prospect. You can't even ride."

"You've said that before, but how could you possibly know I can't?"

"Can you?" She presses her lips together in response. "Well then. Ready to go?"

Five minutes of arguing later, I'm following a very angry serial killer to her house. Her closest neighbor isn't far, but the high stone walls provide plenty of privacy. When I start following her inside, she whirls around and says, "You're not coming in."

"Fine, but I'm going through your bag. Don't want you bringing any pesky drugs or weapons."

In response, she stomps to her front door and slams it shut behind her. I lean against the Jeep while I wait. Sooner than expected, June returns, locks the door behind her, and strolls to the Jeep, glaring at me the whole way. I silently hold out my hand, and she thrusts over the large duffle bag, huffing in irritation. With a chuckle, I carry the bag to the back seat and unzip it to examine the contents. Ignoring the lacy underwear and surprisingly large bras takes an incredible amount of self-control. Once finished with my search, making sure to feel the seams for hidden compartments, I turn to face June, who has her arms crossed.

"Arms out," I order.

"What?"

"I need to pat you down."

"Absolutely not."

"You think I'm stupid enough not to check you for weapons or drugs? Arms out, little reaper."

"Stop calling me that." She scowls.

Fuck, she's cute.

"Arms."

She finally obeys, though not without grumbling, and I start the pat down. I'm extra thorough, rubbing every inch of her arm and cupping her breasts. She tries slapping my hands away, but I ignore her, feeling along her bra over her shirt for the tell-tale feel of a weapon tucked away. Next, I pat down her waist and legs, dragging my hand slowly over her crotch. My own groin tightens as I imagine doing this without all the clothes in the way.

"Hurry up, pervert," she bites out.

I move my hands down her legs, making no effort to speed up the process. At her calf, I feel what is unmistakably the handle of a knife. I lift up her pant leg to reveal the hunting dagger strapped to her leg.

"I'm not going to your house without at least one weapon for self-defense," she says in response to my raised eyebrow.

"No one is going to hurt you. Either at my house or the clubhouse." Still squatting, I look up to see her frown. I like this view, especially what's in front of my face.

"Like I'd believe you. It's a biker gang. You're not exactly known for your respectful treatment of women."

I stand, deciding that I need a clear head, and being in that position was doing me no favors. "First of all, it's a Motorcycle Club, not a 'biker gang.'" She opens her mouth, but I barrel forward before she can speak. "Second, don't make assumptions based on a generalized stereotype. Third, even if we lack certain social customs, we do have rules. A code of conduct every member lives by and would never break. One of those rules is that you respect your fellow members and don't touch their property, specifically their bike or their girl. Since they all think you're my girl, no one would dare touch you."

"I'm not your property."

"Why am I not surprised that's the only part you care about? It's just a saying, little reaper. No need to go all murderous."

She crosses her arms, not balking as she stares me down without a hint of fear. "I don't know anyone in your *club*, and your rules mean nothing to me. I'm not giving you my knife."

Part of me, the part most influenced by James, wants to argue. But I like the idea of her walking around with a giant dagger strapped to her leg. It makes me feel better to know she's armed and ready to defend herself, even if I trust all my members.

"Fine," I agree. Then, the corners of my lips climb up. "Look at us, making progress. We came to that compromise so much faster than the last one."

She rolls her eyes and doesn't respond before turning and climbing into the passenger side of the Jeep. Neither of us speaks until I've pulled out of the driveway.

"How will I get to work every day?" she asks.

"I'll take you."

"Really? You'll drive me half an hour every day to my office and pick me up every evening?"

I shrug. "Sure."

"You really have nothing better to do with your life?"

"I like riding, little reaper. You should know that about me by now."

"Why are you calling me that?"

I glance at her and am momentarily stunned at the sight of her piercing blue eyes and dark blonde hair flapping in the wind. "Isn't it obvious?" When she doesn't respond, I say, "Your last name is Graves. And you're a killer. Thus, reaper."

"I get that. But *why?*"

"It's a nickname. You've never had a nickname?"

"Of course, I've had nicknames," she mutters in a not-quite-believable way.

"With a name like Graves, I'd expect several nicknames. Especially considering your hobbies."

"I don't know what hobbies you're talking about."

I smirk, curling my fingers gently around the steering wheel when I turn onto the main road. "You know, your taste for thrills. You're an adrenaline junkie."

"No, I'm not."

"Yeah, you are," I argue. "I've seen your posts online about skydiving and rock climbing and shit. It's nothing to be ashamed of. Most of the Saints are adrenaline junkies. That's a large reason why they started riding in the first place."

"And you?"

I steal another look at her. She's started relaxing, even pulled a leg onto the seat. "What about me?"

"Are you a biker because you're an adrenaline junkie?"

"Among other reasons." I say it with the unspoken order not to ask any more questions. Of course, she doesn't look like she's about to heed the warning, not with that curiosity swimming in those ocean eyes.

"What are the other reasons?"

"I think you'll like riding," I say instead of answering. Her frown shows she didn't miss the evasion. "You'll like the rush."

"I've ridden before. My foster dad would take me to school on a bike."

"You were in foster care?" Though I looked into June's life, I didn't go past her high school years, when she lived with her mom and stepdad.

"For a few years when I was a kid. My mom was in prison." There's more to the story, I can tell, but the flat tone makes it evident she doesn't intend to share.

"I was in foster care, too," I say, surprising myself. Besides James and Luna, I don't talk to anyone about my childhood. But something in my chest yearns to talk to June; to tell her she's not alone with a bad childhood. At least eighty percent of the Saints have some fucked up story. "My mom died when I was twelve, and my dad bailed not long after. Since I was a teenage boy, and a poorly behaved one, no one wanted me. By the time I aged out of the system, I'd been in thirteen different foster homes. Some were okay, but most were as bad as you'd expect."

The rumbling of the Jeep's high profile tires fills the silence, and I expect to see pity on June's face, or judgment that I perfectly fit the stereotype. But when I look at her, all I see is casual acceptance and understanding. Maybe a hint of curiosity.

"You ever consider therapy?"

I laugh, shattering the uncomfortable silence. "They made me see a counselor in high school and at juvie."

"Well, yeah. But I mean as an adult. You should try therapy with a clinical psychologist."

"Ten minutes together, and you're already ready to throw me in a padded room?"

She rolls her eyes. "Don't be so obtuse. You must know therapy is more than that. Everyone could benefit from talking to a professional, whether you have a complicated web of trauma or not. And don't forget that I've been watching you for months. Much longer than ten minutes."

"Do you offer all your victims a pre-murder therapy session?"

"I'm serious."

"I know you are. What about you? Too good for therapy?"

"I do go to therapy."

I glance at her in surprise. "Really?"

"Of course."

"And what does your therapist have to say about your… murderous tendencies?"

She clears her throat. "We all have vices."

"Yes, we do," I say before turning on the radio and ending the conversation.

Twenty minutes later, I'm parking the Jeep at the end of a long line of bikes in the clubhouse's front yard.

"Looks like everyone is here," I say, counting sixteen total bikes. Before jumping out of the Jeep, I look at June. To my surprise, she looks genuinely nervous, biting at a hangnail on her thumb.

Realizing I'm looking at her, she pulls her hand away and fills her expression with fake, but admittedly believable, confidence.

I smile. "Time to officially meet your new family, little reaper."

SEVEN

June

I'd love to retort that these people are not and will never be my family, but I'm worried my voice will come out shaky, and no way in hell will I let this man know how nervous I am. So, I keep my mouth shut as I follow Theo to the front door.

The music blaring from the house is louder with each step, and I can feel the bass pumping into my stomach. The house is huge, bigger than I'd expect for a small biker gang. Before I can think twice, I ask, "How do you pay for this?"

Theo looks at me over his shoulder, pausing so I can catch up. "We're lucky in the finance department," he says. "With all of our different... income revenues, we could afford this place, which also has a two-bedroom apartment over the garage where Luna and Bella live."

"Income revenues?" I ask, thinking about their chop jobs and drug dealing.

He shrugs. "The Cage brings in a good amount, and every member pays minimum dues. Kip and Zion have generously fronted quite a lot. Kip sold several apps he coded in college for insane sums, and Zion has a deep trust fund.

Luna donated a good amount too, until her dad cut her off, and Nico, our youngest member, has his own trust fund and very little impulse control."

I hum in acknowledgment of his answer, then turn my attention to the long line of bikes, trying to label which Saint belongs to each. I'm pretty sure the emerald green Harley is Luna's and the big one with tall handlebars and a low seat is Raphael's, but that's all. I pause at a gorgeous sleek black and brown bike.

"Admiring the rides?"

I whip my head around at the new voice and find myself staring up at James, Theo's best friend and right hand.

And my new roommate.

"It's a Scout Bobber. Benny's. He's been eyeing Valor's Chieftain, though." He's leaning against the side of the house, holding a cigarette in one hand and his phone in the other. Tattoos peek through the top of his black shirt and climb up his neck, disappearing into thick red hair. He's wearing the club's cut, as always, and black boots. There's an uproar of laughter from behind the front door, making my muscles tense.

James blows out smoke and flicks his cigarette to the ground, where he grinds it under the toe of his boot. "Welcome, June. I would say it's nice to meet you, but I'm not going to lie."

"James," Theo says, almost like a warning.

But I appreciate James's unwillingness to pretend. "Likewise."

"You're both alive, so that's a win, I guess."

Part of me really hates that James, and Luna, apparently, know the truth about my situation with Theo. It puts me at risk for anyone, much less three members of an outlaw motorcycle club, to know that I've killed people.

The other part of me is thankful because at least around them, I won't have to pretend to be Theo's loving girlfriend.

"Barely," Theo says. He nods to the front door and asks, "How's the crew?"

"Excited. Confused. Anxious to meet their president's possible new Ol' Lady."

"Excuse me?" I say. "Old lady?"

"It's a term of respect," Theo interjects. "Refers to a member's partner. Not every girlfriend is one, though. An Ol' Lady is more. It's a bond we respect as much as the bond between fellow members." Then he faces James and adds, "June is *just* my girl."

The look they share is oddly somber. James nods. "I know."

Growing uncomfortable, I add, "I'm not even your girl."

"You need to be a better actress than that if you want anyone to buy this bullshit."

"Yeah, we're not off to a great start, little reaper," Theo says. "Try to limit the amount of disgust you show toward me around the others. Now, come on. Let's get this over with." He reaches out and grabs my hand, wrapping his large fingers around mine. I tug at his hold, but he just squeezes and yanks me closer to his side before whispering, "Play along." Then he opens the door and pulls me past James into a surprisingly nice home overflowing with bikers.

We walk into a giant living room with a pillar holding a fireplace in the center. Several couches are spread through the space, and a dining room table sits on the right side of the room, where Nico and another guy are sitting. The inviting smell of roast pork emanates from deeper in the house, where the kitchen must be.

We're only a foot inside when one of the members,

Valor, I think, meets my eyes, beams, and turns around, calling, "They're here!"

Everyone cheers, and my eyes flick around the space, fight or flight response sparking to life. I've seen all these people before, dancing among them at the Iron Cage, but this is the first time they're all looking at me, expecting something.

This is also the first time one of my targets has been at my side, holding my hand. Theo adjusts his grip so his fingers interlock with mine. Without thinking, I lean closer.

Valor turns back to us and throws an arm around my shoulder. He's not a huge guy, but his touch is still an unwanted weight. "It's great to finally meet you!" He steps back, and I hope he doesn't notice my slight flinch. "I'm Valor, the Saints of Purgatory's secretary."

I *almost* say, "I know," but catch the words before they form. "Nice to meet you. I'm June."

"Yeah, I know," Valor says. "I mean, I didn't twenty-four hours ago. Then we get this message last night from our boss," he nods to Theo, "that we're gaining a new hang-around in the form of his girl."

"She's not just a hang-around," Theo says, voice dangerously low.

"Yeah, yeah." Valor waves him off. "To say we're all intrigued is an understatement."

Before I can respond, Luna pushes Valor out of the way and stops in front of Theo. She's wearing a short leather skirt and her branded jacket over a lacy bra. "There he is. Our fearless leader." She kisses his cheek, then turns to me, a sultry smile decorating her face. She's close enough that when she pulls me into a hug, our cheeks press together. "And his personal reaper," she whispers. Amusement lingers in her eyes when she releases me. "I'm genuinely happy to see you again."

I blush at the memory of that last visit to the Iron Cage, when I'd danced far too long with Luna and almost lost myself in the simple pleasure of it.

"Alright, that's enough," Theo says, pushing Luna back.

She holds her hands up, palms out. "Sorry, I get it, she's your girl."

I'm not his girl, I think.

But Theo pulls me further inside, introducing me to his brothers and sisters without letting go of my hand. I know it's just for show, and he might be holding me close because he doesn't trust me, but something about it still keeps the flames momentarily banked in my chest.

Familiar names and faces blend in my mind as he introduces me to the Saints. There's Bella, a tall, lanky girl with dark skin surprisingly free of any tattoos or piercings, who is a bartender at the Iron Cage. Next is Daryus, the Saints' sergeant at arms. He has bulging muscles and sneers at me, already not my biggest fan. Theo guides me away from him, and we have a brief moment alone. He nods toward a trim man with buzzed black hair who's watching us with suspicion from the other side of the house.

"That's Kip."

"I know," I say, inwardly reminding myself of the unique cover story he fed to Kip.

Theo chuckles. "He's my third, our head road captain, and has been a member for years. Almost as long as me. He's probably the smartest guy in our crew, including myself and James."

"Wow, how humble of you to admit that."

"A good leader knows his people well enough to recognize areas in which they're superior." He says it like he's quoting someone else's words.

"Why isn't Kip the leader then?"

"He doesn't have the instincts like me and James. And he has no leadership skills."

Before I can respond, Raphael slides into our path.

"Hey, *Maryanne,*" he says.

"I guess you know my real name now." His bruised pride at being given a fake name is obvious in his frown.

"Right, June. Sorry about the uh…"

"Butt-hurt angry misogynistic text because I didn't call you back?"

Raphael bites his bottom lip with a sheepish half grin. "Yeah."

"No worries."

"Don't be so quick to let him off, babe," Theo says. Somehow, his voice is both light and angry. Like he's joking with me but fighting anger toward Raphael.

"I didn't know she was your girl then, boss," Raphael says, fear lacing his words. So far, all the members have seemed at ease around Theo, but Raphael is providing a glimpse into the potentially lethal side of Theo's leadership. Sure, the Saints respect and love him, but they're afraid of him, too. At least on some level.

"She wasn't yet, technically. But that night was the first time I saw her. Well, the first time she stole my breath, that is."

I tilt my head back to look at Theo, searching for the hint that he's lying. There's none.

"I never really stood a chance, did I?" Raphael asks.

"No," Theo and I say at the same time.

Raphael winces dramatically and holds a hand over his heart. "I can't hold that against you. I mean, he *is* the boss."

"So, my rejection is okay because I rejected you for another guy? What if I just didn't want you?" I ask, bristling. Sparks singe my throat as the fire roars. Suddenly, Raphael looks like a great option to help douse the flames.

But, *no,* he hasn't done anything. Nothing that makes him deserving of death. That's just the heat talking. The need for blood. It's only been four months since Jared, but deciding to kill Theo early was kerosene on the flames. They won't go back down on their own.

"Alright, that's enough," Theo says, nudging Raphael out of the way and pulling me forward. There are more people in the kitchen, and the delicious aroma of cooking meat, but Theo pulls me through a door into a pantry packed with food. He turns me so we're chest to chest.

"You're okay," he whispers.

"I know." The sound of a cracking flame only I can hear nearly makes me flinch.

His brows pull together as he studies me. "What is it? What do you need?"

"I don't know what you're talking about."

"Yes, you do. You're fighting something. You *want* something."

"I'd like some food. And space," I say, eyes flicking down to the lack of distance between our bodies. With every breath, our chests brush against each other. I'm not sure if the burn in my face is from our nearness or the fire.

Theo shakes his head. "Something more. It's been growing all night, I've seen it in your eyes. But just then, when we were talking to Raph, you… left the conversation. You were in your head."

"That's where my thoughts are."

"Come on, little reaper. Talk to me," he whispers, lowering his head an inch.

"Why would I do that?"

His lips part and eyes soften, then he snaps his mouth shut and steps back, putting a foot of space between us that I thought I wanted but now feels like a chasm.

"You're right," he says with a heavy sigh. "Just know this. We all have things eating away at us. Some of us have itches we have to scratch. If you need something, whatever it is, you can tell me. I bet I can get it for you."

The pantry fills with silence, and I grope for some way to respond. Finally, when all I can think about is getting out of this small closet with him, I say, "I need my freedom. So, if you want to give me anything, give me that."

For a moment, I think Theo looks disappointed, but a blink later, he shakes his head and reaches past me to grab the doorknob. "How about we settle for food?"

This time, when I follow him back into the main part of the house, he doesn't hold my hand. For the next two hours, we talk to his family of bikers, eat barbecue, and I struggle through lies about loving Theo and being so excited to move in with him and join the Saints. He occasionally touches me with a short press of his leg against mine or a brush of his knuckles along my hand, but he doesn't interlock our fingers again.

By the time we're driving to his house, I start to wonder whether this next month won't just be difficult but impossible.

And not for the reasons I originally thought.

EIGHT

June

Theo parks in front of his house, which has an enviable amount of space between it and their closest neighbor, grabs my bag from the backseat, and heads to the front door without looking back. Instead of a key, his front door unlocks with a code under the handle, which I learned weeks ago.

Following him inside, my eyes scan the interior, mentally matching it with the floor plans I've already memorized. It's an open plan with the kitchen to the left of the front door, the dining space to the right, and the sunken living room directly in front, two steps lower than the rest of the space. There's an L-shaped sectional and a lone chair in the center, with a TV mounted over the fireplace. Two hallways are on either side of the entryway, one to the main bedroom and bathroom and the other to two bedrooms and a second bathroom. The space is spotless, every surface clean and tidy.

"Your room is down here," Theo says. He kicks the front door shut and walks down the right hallway into the first bedroom. It's small, barely enough space for a full-sized bed and a dresser. He sets my bag on the freshly made bed, where there are embroidered throw pillows.

He points to the middle door in the hallway. "That's the bathroom. Fresh towels are under the sink. Let me know if you need anything else."

I toe off my shoes and sit on the edge of the bed. "I need to be at my office by eight in the morning."

He nods. "Luna will pick you up at seven thirty."

"I thought you were taking me."

"Disappointed?" he asks with a noticeably forced smirk.

"Just stating the obvious. Not even a day in and you're already reneging on your promise to take me to work. It'd be easier if I just had my car."

He shakes his head. "Not happening."

"You worried I'll leave?"

"I know if you want to leave, you won't need a car to do it. But I don't feel like combing every inch of your car for weapons and drugs, so you'll have to deal with one of us taking you to work."

"*One* of you?"

"Don't worry, little reaper. It'll be me as often as possible. I just have something to take care of in the morning. I'll pick you up, though." He winks, and I grind my teeth together.

"I don't care."

"Sure you don't." He gives me one last searching look before walking out, leaving the door open behind him.

I jump up and throw the door shut harder than I intend, feeling like an insolent child. After allowing myself ten minutes to lie flat on the bed and brood, I force myself to unpack, change, brush my teeth, and climb under the covers. Sleep is elusive, and I'm still awake when James gets home two hours later. I listen to him move about the house, take a shower, then shut his bedroom door. After that, I'm in and out of consciousness until six a.m., when I decide to get ready for work. In the kitchen, I find a full pot of coffee and an empty mug in front of it, which warms my chest with something that *isn't* the searing fire.

Theo made enough coffee for me. I know it could all be for James, but there's enough for at least three cups.

It doesn't mean anything, I tell myself as I pour the coffee. Forcing rogue thoughts away, I stroll to Theo's bedroom, planning to search it for any possible information on the man I'm planning to kill in four weeks. Unfortunately, the door is locked. I don't have time to pick it, so I'll have to wait until I'm alone, which may never happen.

It's seven twenty when the rumbling sound of a motorcycle approaches the house. Outside, Luna is straddling her emerald bike, her helmet's face shield pushed back so her green eyes are on display. Unlike last night, every inch of her skin is covered by long leather pants, tall boots, gloves, and a Saints of Purgatory jacket.

"Hey, killer!" I can hear the smile in her voice even over the roar of the engine. She holds out an extra helmet, and I wonder if they got it for me or if they all have extra helmets for possible passengers.

"Don't call me that," I say, taking the helmet and pulling it over my braided hair.

"Why not?"

"Why do you think?"

"It's a fitting nickname," Luna says.

"Exactly."

"You afraid someone will hear me calling you killer and instead of knowing that's a normal nickname for someone as fucking sexy as you they'll immediately think, 'Oh, she must be an actual cold-blooded killer?'"

I scowl. Between "killer" and "little reaper," these bikers are practically labeling me as a murderer.

"Well, are you coming?" Luna asks when I don't move. She's still shouting over the engine, and it's astonishing that bikers don't constantly lose their voices from all the yelling they do.

With a huff, I step closer and throw my leg over the bike behind her. Once sitting, I look around for something to hold that isn't Luna. Finding nothing, I tentatively place my hands on her waist.

"Don't be so shy!" She grabs my hands with her gloved ones and pulls them further, forcing me to lean forward, front pressed against her back. "Hold on tight, and keep your bag between us." She picks her foot up, revs the engine, and the next second we're moving. Luna quickly increases speeds until it feels more like flying.

It's exhilarating. I watch the world move faster than it ever has in a car and stare at the road inches from our feet. One wrong move and I'd be indistinguishable from a flattened possum on the shoulder. Luna would probably fare better thanks to her riding-appropriate clothing. Still, the idea that death is a blink away sucks the gravity from my bones. The wind whips at our clothes and even the flames in my chest. I close my eyes, lifting my head back to enjoy the ride. Unfortunately, it's over much too quickly, and soon we're stopping in front of my office.

"See you later, killer." I start to return her helmet, but she shakes her head. "That's yours. Theo bought it yesterday."

"Really?"

She nods. "It's the best. Over eight hundred dollars. He got you gloves, boots, and a jacket, too. He's picking them up today."

"I have gloves and boots."

Luna shrugs. "Theo is particular about the gear we wear."

I noticed they often look uniform when riding as a unit, but I thought that was mostly due to their jackets.

"Well, thanks," I mutter, holding up the shockingly expensive helmet.

"Thank the boss." She winks. "He didn't want his girl getting hurt on the road."

"Not his girl."

"Sure." The way she says it makes it obvious that she doesn't believe me. She doesn't give me a chance to argue before riding off, leaving me feeling unsteady. It takes a few moments to gather myself before I can walk inside and start preparing for my appointments.

NINE

Theo

After last night, I'm even more anxious for this appointment. There's more to learn about June, and this is as good a place to start as any.

I take James's jeep again since I'll have Benny's dog with me. When I asked to borrow the mutt, he hadn't asked any questions, just told me not to let her off leash or to eat anything suspicious.

"I'll leave the door unlocked so you can drop her off whenever, boss," Benny says, passing me the bright pink leash. The dog, Ellie, is a large Pit mix who is far too excited to see me. I bet that'll change when we get to the vet.

"Thanks again, Benny."

"No problem. Ellie loves going on adventures. Don't you, girl?" He flips his septum piercing up into his nostrils, then squats in front of the dog, letting her lick all over his face. "Have fun with the boss."

Ellie spins in circles then follows me to the Jeep, jumping in and plopping on her butt without needing to be told. Her tongue lolls out the side of her mouth the entire drive, and even though I strapped her leash in, I keep one hand on her until we arrive. It takes twenty minutes after checking in and waiting in a little room before the vet finally walks in.

"Hello, I'm Dr. Fields," she greets. "Who do we have here?" She's a curvy woman in her late thirties with a thick mane of curly red hair pulled back into a wild ponytail and a face covered in freckles.

"This is Ellie," I say, gesturing to the dog.

The doctor squats down, letting Ellie sniff her hands before reaching out to pet her. "You're very sweet, Ellie."

"She's great," I say, trying to sound like I care.

Dr. Fields stands and picks up a clipboard. She scans it, then asks, "So, we're just doing a checkup today?"

I nod. "We recently moved here and wanted to establish a new vet."

"Smart idea," Dr. Fields says, returning to Ellie's level to check her ears.

"Yeah. We're here for my sister," I lie. "She went through a pretty bad breakup recently and needs the support."

The vet talks as she examines Ellie, who seems more than happy to receive all the attention. "Wow, that's good of you. To move for your sister."

"Well, her ex is crazy. I'm worried for her safety."

"Oh, I hope she's okay." I hear a slight tilt to the doctor's voice, as if she's finally clicking into the conversation.

"Me too. I told her not to date him, but of course, no one listens to me. But now she's free, and I think she's going to file a restraining order against him."

"That's very brave." Dr. Fields takes longer than is probably necessary to look at Ellie's teeth, as if trying to distract herself from my words.

"I know. I'm glad she's free of him, and I'm here for her, but I think she needs more help. I mean, this guy really fucked with her, you know? I think she needs to see someone. A professional."

The vet gives a little hum to show she's listening but doesn't say anything. I hesitate, hoping to sound conversational and like her answer to my next question doesn't really matter. "Do you know of any therapists in the area?"

Dr. Fields's hands freeze for a millisecond. Then she seems to shake herself out of the stupor and pats Ellie's head once, whispering, "Good girl." She stands and turns to me, pulling in a breath. "I actually do know of a good therapist. My, uh, friend, who was also in an abusive relationship, sees her and says she's great. Her name is June Graves."

I smile. "Thank you. I'll look her up."

"Now, are we doing any vaccines?"

"Not today." After a few more formalities, Dr. Fields starts to leave and just as she reaches for the door, I ask, "Is your friend doing any better? The one who sees the therapist?"

Dr. Fields looks back at me. "She is."

"So, there's hope for my sister, then?"

"Of course there is."

"Even while that asshole is still free and alive? Is your friend's ex in prison?"

There it is, I think. A glint in the vet's eyes, like she's holding onto a shameful secret. "Actually, her ex disappeared last year. And, honestly, she's doing better than I've seen in a decade."

"Thank you."

Dr. Clarissa Fields dips her head forward and leaves. I pay for the appointment and take Ellie back to Benny's house, my mind on overdrive.

Clarissa Fields doesn't have a friend who sees June. *She* sees June, which I learned while watching June at her office. I set up the appointment with Clarissa last week mostly out of curiosity and a desperation to learn more about June. But after our encounter two days ago, I did some research and learned that Clarissa Fields had an ex who went missing last year. And from the fire in June's eyes last night, her vice is obvious.

I'd bet the entire Saints of Purgatory that Clarissa's ex is dead and that the last thing he saw was my little reaper's grin as she quenched the thirst for blood that must live under her perfect skin.

I don't know if the ex was her most recent victim, but I do know I'm her next one, and I can guess that she chooses her victims based on the confidential information patients give her. I'm not sure who's been talking about me to June, but that doesn't matter now.

What matters is figuring out who her next victim would be if not me. If I can help June move her murderous attention to a new asshole, then maybe she won't try killing me again, and she'll make it out of this month alive.

Thankfully, now that she lives with me, going through her things will be much easier.

~

I tuck my helmet under my arm on my way to the front door. A bell jingles when I pull it open, and a young woman on a couch looks up at my entrance. I nod in greeting and lean against the opposite wall. An older woman, one of the other therapists June shares this building with, opens her door to let in her next patient. Upon noticing me, she lets her eyes trail over my body, taking in the visible tattoos, biker jacket, and helmet with a frown.

"Can I help you?"

"Just here to pick up June," I say, smirking at the surprise that flits over her face.

"And you are?"

"Her boyfriend." The lie isn't necessary, not here, but I want to see her reaction.

It's worth it. The woman steps back and lifts her hand to her chest, not bothering to hide her shock and horror. She opens her mouth, probably to call me on my bullshit or demand more information, but June's door opens before she gets the chance.

"I'll see you in two weeks, Sarah," June is saying to a girl who can't be older than eighteen. The girl nods and wipes tears from her cheeks, avoiding looking at anyone else as she exits the office.

June, on the other hand, looks straight at me and freezes in her doorway, eyebrows pulling together.

I beam. "Hey, babe."

Anger fills June's eyes, but she manages to keep from scowling. "You could've waited outside."

"I wanted to see your office."

"I'm not sure this is *appropriate.*" Her eyes dart from me to the older woman still standing shocked in her doorway to the younger woman waiting uncomfortably.

"Then why don't we head out?" I suggest. "You have your helmet?"

Instead of answering, June turns around and walks back into her office. I follow, kicking her door shut behind me.

June turns, glaring at the shut door. "What are you doing?"

"Waiting for you to get your things."

"Why did you shut the door?"

"Privacy."

"Look," she bites, letting more of that fire shine through her professional facade. "I might have agreed to your inane plan of joining your gang—*club*—but that doesn't mean you can just show up at my office. This is my job."

"I'm aware. I'm here to pick you up, remember?"

"Next time, wait outside."

"Like a dog?"

She lets out a muffled scream of frustration. "Mess with me all you want, but coming in here could make other people uncomfortable! This is supposed to be a *safe* place for my clients."

"What about me simply standing in the waiting room is *unsafe?*"

She gives me a deadpan look, like I asked the world's dumbest question. "It's not like you present an image of respectability."

I raise my eyebrows. "Really? You're going to tell me that some tattoos, long hair, and a leather jacket are so scary that I can't walk into specific buildings? How pearl-clutching grandma of you."

"That's not what I mean, and you know that."

"I don't know that."

"Theo, it's pointless to fake ignorance that your look might be intimidating to some people. Especially to traumatized women already dealing with male-centered trust issues."

"Oh, I get it," I say, feigning a look of dawning realization. "You live by a 'judge a book by its cover' philosophy. Makes sense. Because no one looking at you would possibly think, 'that's a terrifying serial killer who wouldn't blink twice about slitting my throat.'"

"Theo!"

"But one look at me and that's the first thing that comes to their mind, so it *must* be true," I say, smoothly ignoring her shout.

"I'm not doing this with you right now."

"No, let's do this." I stride forward, closing the distance between us as frustration cracks through the wall of amusement. "You don't know anything about me. You think you've figured me out because of some muddled, likely false, second-hand accounts of my actions and a few weeks of following me. The way I choose to dress and live makes me less-than and not worthy of stepping foot in your perfect little world of propriety. It doesn't matter how much blood is on your hands because you look like an average trust fund sorority girl with an altruistic need to listen to people whine about their issues. Hide your tattoos under silk blouses and murders behind innocent Taco Tuesdays all you want, but you can't fool me. I see you, little reaper. *All of you.* So, how about you stop gripping onto your two-dimensional idea of the world and face the fact that you might've been wrong about me?"

She glares up at me, our faces less than a foot apart. The intoxicating scent of fresh juniper and warm apples emanates from her skin, threatening to cloud my mind. Her words are low as she says, "Is this your attempt at guilt tripping me into believing you're the victim here?"

"No. I'll never claim to be a victim. But I won't let you turn me into an evil villain so you feel justified in killing me."

"So, I'm the bad guy?"

Fuck, this woman is maddening. My fingers curl into my palms, and my muscles tense, yearning to either punch something or rip her clothes off.

"Your need for there to be a bad guy at all is why we're in this mess."

She blows an infuriated breath out of her nose like a dragon about to breathe fire.

My voice drops an octave, and desire swirls low in my gut. "The truth is, little reaper, that we're both villains, and the sooner you accept that, the better."

Her lips press tightly together, and, needing distance, I step back, breaking whatever spell had us locked. Seeing her helmet on the floor under her desk, I reach down to grab it and take a moment to suck in a deep breath before turning. I hold it out, and she takes it without a word. The energy sucked from the room, I mutter, "Let's go," and pull open the door, heading outside without looking back.

TEN

June

I expect Theo to drag me to the clubhouse, but he clearly wants to be as far away from me as possible after our fight. He drops me off at the house, tells me to stay put, then leaves, the sound of his roaring bike lingering long after he's gone. Part of me wants to storm from the house to spite him, but exhaustion wins, and I drop onto the couch, turning on NCIS reruns.

I scroll through the group chat with Sadie, Evelyn, and Rose, which is overflowing with unread messages. Guilt bites at the lining of my stomach as I think about all I'm keeping from them, but it's not like I can text my three very normal best friends 'Hey, sorry about your work drama, but at least you're not being blackmailed into living with the guy you tried to murder for the next month.'

I have to tell them *something*, though. They'll eventually learn about Theo. I wouldn't put it past him to show up at Taco Tuesday and dangle our fake relationship in their faces. But my fingers refuse to text anything right now.

Tuesday. I'll tell them on Tuesday. That'll give me a few days to figure out *what* exactly to tell them.

~

My second morning in Theo's house is similar to the first. He's already gone when I exit my room, lured by the aroma of freshly brewed coffee. Though this time, he included a note next to the coffee. The first thing I notice is the way Theo writes his g's. They dip far below the line, the bottom half looped up like a noose.

Then I read it and immediately crumple it into a ball and toss it in the sink disposal.

Luna taking you to work. I'll pick you up. Don't forget about the club meeting tonight.

"We have recycling, you know."

I jump and spin around to see James watching me. He's shirtless, tattoo-covered chest on full display.

"Oh, I was just…"

"Taking your anger at T out on an innocent piece of paper? I can tell." He opens the cupboard above the coffee maker and pulls down two mugs, handing one to me.

"Thanks." I grab it by the rim and take a careful step back.

"There's no need to be so on guard all the time. No one is going to hurt you."

I scoff.

James fills his mug to the top and sets the coffee pot on the counter between us. "T gave his order, and we all follow it, whether we agree or not."

I keep my attention on him as I fill my mug, leaving an inch of space for creamer. "Why?"

"Because he's the president."

"I mean, why did he give the order? Why is he doing this?" No matter how much I think about it or replay Theo's words in my head, I can't come up with an adequate reason.

James studies me for several uncomfortable seconds, then shakes his head and says, "Because you're a predator."

I frown and am about to ask him to explain when the front door swings open and Luna flies in, dropping her helmet on the dining table.

"Killer!" she calls. Eyes moving from me to James, she lowers her voice. "Do you take requests?"

"What?" The Saints must have a silent way of communicating because I constantly feel like I'm missing context that's obvious to them.

"Murder requests?" Luna clarifies. "My brother definitely deserves to be on your hitlist."

"Orion again?" James asks. He leans against the counter, sipping his coffee despite it still being scalding hot.

Luna nods and walks between us to open the fridge. "Yes. He won't leave me the fuck alone." She pulls out a Red Bull then casually hops onto the counter, crossing her legs. "Orion doesn't think a motorcycle club is appropriate for a Mcintyre. He's been trying to make me quit since they found out I joined."

I remember reading that Luna comes from a big, somewhat well-known family, but somehow, I completely forgot. "Your dad is a judge, right?"

She rolls her eyes. "He's hoping for a Supreme Court nomination, and according to Orion, having a daughter in a 'gang' will ruin his chances." She makes air quotes around the word "gang" then cracks open the Red Bull. "You'd think having nine children with three women would be more detrimental, but no, all that matters is that his kids have prestigious careers."

My brain automatically filters through the mental files on Luna. Her dad, Hugh Mcintyre, has nine children, three from his first marriage before his wife died of cancer, four from his current marriage, including Luna, and twins from an affair. Instead of negative press about his affair, he was able to spin it to his favor by welcoming in the twins and publicly apologizing for betraying his wife, who was somehow incredibly understanding and forgiving of her husband's infidelity.

"Orion is a surgeon," I say without thinking. "Third child, second oldest boy, and the last Hugh Mcintyre had with his first wife before she died. Five years older than you."

Luna's mouth falls open, and James frowns, his gaze becoming more intense as he stares at me. A second later, I realize that normal people wouldn't have known all of that because *normal* people don't learn everything about a stranger's friends while planning to murder said stranger.

"You forgot to list his star sign," Luna says sarcastically.

It's Sagittarius, but I don't say that. Instead, I mutter, "Sorry."

"Did you memorize the family tree of every Saint?" James asks.

"No," I answer truthfully. I investigated each of them but only thoroughly researched the officers, those closest to Theo. James was the most difficult to research. All I really learned was that his father, Rocket, was the last leader of the Saints before moving out of the state over four years ago.

Luna grins widely. "Liar. You totally stalked us."

I clear my throat and attempt to move the conversation away from me. "What did Orion do?"

"Same as usual. Called me at the ass-crack of dawn to chew me out for being involved with a bunch of criminals. Apparently, Aurora took a B and E case involving a biker. Not a Saint, just a random biker."

Aurora is the second Mcintyre child, and she's following

in daddy's footsteps by becoming a prosecutor. She has a reputation for being as ruthless as her dad and is, unfortunately, just as good at her job.

"I'm sorry, Lu," James says. "Just ignore him. He'll give up eventually."

"No, he won't. Dad already cut me off. He said if I don't get my act together soon, Dad'll be forced to publicly renounce me as a member of the family."

James gives her a commiserating look. I shift uncomfortably.

"So, how 'bout it, killer? Wanna off my brother?"

I snort. "Kill a guy with a judge father, prosecutor older sister, and lawyer younger brother? I don't think so."

"Bummer." Luna shrugs. Then she rolls her shoulders as if to shake off the thoughts of her family. "Well, you almost ready to go?"

I look down at my body, still wearing pajamas and no shoes. Then I check the time and curse. Abandoning my coffee on the counter, I run back to my room to get ready.

The day passes quickly, and when my last appointment cancels, I don't text Theo. Instead, I use the free hour and a half to call an Uber and return to my house. I make quick work of grabbing another knife, my gun, a burner phone, and the drugs Theo threatened to tell the cops about. I already have the thumb drive with all my research on Theo and the Saints, which I hid in my shoe when Theo picked me up on Wednesday. Smiling, I rush out to the Uber and tell him to take me back to my office. I spend the drive thinking through possible ways to get rid of Theo, but each option ends with the Saints coming after me for revenge. Too many of them know what I was planning to do to their beloved leader, so unless I have a perfect alibi, they'll know if I kill Theo, and I wouldn't survive a day. But even if I never get to finish the job, simply having my supplies and weapons is comforting.

Unfortunately, the euphoria from outsmarting Theo evaporates when he arrives to pick me up, holds out his hand, and says, "Gun and drugs, please."

My jaw drops. "How—"

"Did you really think I didn't plan for you to do something like this? Come on, little reaper. I'm not an idiot."

Fury coaxes the fire. "What did you do? Plant a tracker on me? Put cameras in my house?"

"You can keep the other knife, but not the gun or drugs. I'll give them back at the end of the month."

"No."

Theo smirks. "Want a repeat of Tuesday night? Maybe this fight will end differently and won't leave you so… frustrated."

My face burns. I know we can't fight in the middle of the office, and there's no way in hell I'm letting him that close to me again. So, I retrieve the gun and little bag and drop them in Theo's still outstretched hand. He tucks the gun in the back of his pants and zips open the bag, studying each vial to ensure I didn't take out any drugs or syringes.

"Alright, let's go. We have church to get to."

~

The Saints of Purgatory's Friday "church" meeting feels eerily familiar. Sitting among the group of people who all want their voices heard, I try to locate the origin of this odd sense of familiarity. There are simultaneously a dozen fights brewing between the bikers and, somehow, a strong undercurrent of unity and love.

Then it hits me. The foster family I lived with from ages seven to thirteen, the best years of my life. The family consisted of two biological children, two adopted children, and two to four foster kids at any given time. It was constant chaos in that house. There was never a quiet moment, even in the middle of the night, and my foster parents encouraged input from all the kids, which meant there were a lot of *discussions.* Arguments, however, were banned. I remember always being on edge, prepared for an imminent fight. But whenever it got close, our parents would shut down the conversation, postponing it until everyone calmed down.

That's what this meeting feels like. I wouldn't be surprised if the group walked away with dozens of broken noses and black eyes and an even stronger familial bond between them. It's disorientating.

Theo doesn't look immune to the stress of the meeting either. I have the perfect view of him from my spot in the corner. I see every time his fingers flex in annoyance and how he grows tenser by the minute, the veins in his arms threatening to pop. He sits at the front, James next to him, and only speaks to steer the conversation back on topic or shut someone down.

No one acknowledges me until an hour into the meeting when Daryus says, "Are we just going to ignore the fact that a hang-around is here?"

A dozen heads spin in my direction, as if his question was permission to look. I straighten my spine, carefully not lowering my eyes.

"She's not a hang-around," Theo says.

"Well, she's not a member or prospective," Daryus argues.

"He's right. No one else brings their girl to church," Raphael says. Then he adds in a heavier voice, as if referring to a collectively painful memory, "Not anymore."

"Yeah, I'm not sure she should be here, boss," another guy says.

A few others voice their agreement. I bite down hard, fighting the desire to stab someone.

"That's enough." Theo doesn't yell, but the words are the most threatening he's said so far. Every single person goes silent and alters their posture, either cowering back or straightening like soldiers falling in line. "June is here as my guest, and she will continue to come as long as I want her to. She's to be treated like one of us until I say otherwise. And if I hear one more complaint, I'll start assigning dirty work and stripping patches and privileges. Understood?"

I scan the faces of the bikers. Some, like Daryus, look angry. Others, like James, nod. Luna's wide, cheery smile nearly making me laugh.

"Anything else?"

No one speaks, though several must want to.

"Fine. Then we're finished. I'll see you all tomorrow."

Luna told me their weekly churches are typically several hours long, so Theo ending it after an hour sends a ripple of unease through the group. Those looking at me quickly turn their attention away, like they're afraid of staring too long and pissing off their leader.

Theo stands and crosses the room, meeting my eyes and jerking his head forward in a silent command to follow. My instinct is to stay seated, not to follow the big angry biker while armed only with a knife, but my legs push me up anyway. I find Luna in the crowd, and though she's not smiling anymore, she does give me an encouraging nod. Taking a breath, I head outside, preparing for another fight.

Except when I reach Theo on the front porch, he doesn't look mad. If anything, he looks sad.

I stand a foot behind him, wondering if he expects me to apologize. But I didn't do anything wrong. This was all his idea. I'd gladly stay at the house while he attends these dumb *church* meetings.

Despite that, I'm still shocked when Theo breaks the silence with a soft, "I'm sorry."

"You don't have to cancel the meeting. I can walk back to your house." Or I could go to Sadie's. It's not like he'd know. Though he does have cameras in his house, so he may check on me.

He shakes his head. "James can finish up."

"But—"

"I don't want to go back in, June. Let's just go."

Hearing him call me June is jarring, and my next question, if he ever took one of his previous girlfriends to club meetings, vanishes from my throat. I distinctly remember Jennifer complaining about Amber going to meetings with her "gang-banger boyfriend," fearing that it meant she was being initiated. Except Raphael said no one brings their girls.

Instead of asking, I nod and follow Theo in silence to his bike. We don't speak until we're at the house and I'm heading to my bedroom.

"You can stay out here if you want. I was going to watch a movie."

The last half hour has thrown me so off kilter that I don't automatically say no. The therapeutic analyst side of my brain kicks into gear, replaying recent events and scrutinizing Theo's words.

The club members are suspicious of outsiders, that much is plain. Hang-arounds, people like me who aren't members but spend time with the club, are normal, especially at the clubhouse or Iron Cage when they're just relaxing. But they're more protective of formal events, like meetings. Something specific happened to make them especially distrustful of strangers—girlfriends—hearing club business.

And that distrust not only angered Theo but sucked the fight out of him. I doubt he's just telling me I can watch the movie with him if I want to. He's *asking* me to stay with him, in his own way. He won't let himself appear vulnerable or weak, especially in front of me, a known enemy, but he doesn't want to be alone.

Whatever the experience was that created a distrust of strangers among the Saints must've affected Theo more than the others.

Was it Amber? I can't see how. She was an innocent twenty-one-year-old girl. Maybe what he did to her put them at risk, and instead of getting angry at their leader, the club collectively blamed Amber.

I need to know. Everything Jennifer told me was second-hand information from the perspective of a worried parent. I'm fairly certain how the relationship ended, but I have no idea what got them there. I assumed Theo was just a violent asshole who went too far one day, an unfortunate ending to many abusive relationships.

I'm not so sure about that anymore. And I won't learn the truth by avoiding Theo.

So, I shrug and say, "What are we watching?" I ignore the visible relief in his eyes and how his muscles relax.

"What kind of movies do you like?" He kicks off his shoes and drops onto the couch, snatching up the TV remote. "Let me guess, *Saw* and *John Wick* are your favorites."

I roll my eyes, sitting on the other end of the couch. "First of all, those are great movies. But for your information, my favorite movie is *Across the Universe*."

He gives me an incredulous look. "The hippie one where they're all on drugs? You do realize those people are *pacifists,* right?"

"It's The Beatles. How can you *not* love that movie?"

"Okay, well, we're not watching that."

"Fine. What's your favorite movie, then? *Ghost Rider?*"

"Ha ha, very original."

"Well?"

"I'm not telling you."

My lips tug into a smile. "What is it?"

A barely noticeable red tint spreads across his cheeks.

"Oh, my god. It's some stupid chick flick, isn't it? *Sweet Home Alabama*? *The Notebook*?"

"Isn't it misogynistic to call traditionally female-loved movies 'stupid chick flicks'?"

"You're not going to distract me from this."

"It's *Interstellar*," he says, though I don't need to be a therapist to know he's lying.

"It is not!"

"Drop it, little reaper."

"I'm going to ask James. Or Luna. I'll bet they know."

The blush deepens, and he reaches over to stop me from lifting my phone. "Okay! Fine. It's *Tinkerbell*."

For a moment, I think he's still joking, but the truth is etched in the lines of his forehead and shining on his cheeks. I lean back, staring at him with more confusion than ever before.

"*Tinkerbell*?"

He nods.

"The 2008 animated film?"

"It's a good movie."

"I'll have to trust you on that."

He averts his eyes. "Right. So, what do you want to watch?"

I permit the subject change because I can sense pushing this further would be a bad idea. "The new Marvel movie?"

"No, those are all the same movie. It's boring."

"That's the point. You know what you're getting. Awesome fight scenes and witty jokes."

"What about *Rocketman*? You like musicals."

"I like the *one* musical."

"Alright, no musicals. *Once Upon a Time in Hollywood*?"

"Gross, that's one of those stupid movies the critics rave about but actually has no point. Let's do *National Treasure*. It's a classic."

"Really, little reaper? Are you obsessed with Nicolas Cage or something?"

"He's an enigma, okay?" I shout, throwing my hands out.

"Whatever you say. Let's just scroll Netflix."

So, we do. It takes thirty minutes and several arguments until we agree on a movie.

"I still don't think we should watch a Christmas movie in January," I mumble even as I pull my legs under me and reach into the bowl of popcorn Theo prepared.

"*Die Hard* is not a Christmas movie."

"Is to."

"Just because it's set at a Christmas party does not mean it's a Christmas movie."

"Are we really doing this again?"

"Just as long as you know you're wrong."

"Alright, Tinkerbell."

He glares at me, but there's no real heat in the look. We settle into a comfortable silence of watching the movie with occasional commentary. James gets home halfway through and drops onto the couch between us without a word.

"Jamesy," I venture, pitching my voice up an octave. "Tell Theo that *Die Hard* is, indeed, a Christmas movie."

"Oh, my god! It's not!"

"Sorry, T, but she's right."

"HA!"

"I hate you," Theo mumbles to James, who just shrugs.

I'm still grinning when I turn back to the screen, and by the end of the night, I've nearly forgotten about the awkward club meeting or my earlier fight with Theo.

ELEVEN

Theo

I'm able to shake off the memories faster than I ever have. The anger was fleeting and the grief was only crippling for a few minutes. Even the mention of *Tinkerbell* didn't launch me into an inescapable pit of sorrow. Watching a movie with June, teasing each other like we're not enemies who might kill each other any second, felt so normal, so light and easy, that I could smile and laugh without drowning in guilt.

The night ended so much better than I could've expected.

I shouldn't be surprised when it doesn't last.

"I'm not going to waste a day riding on your motorcycle for no reason," June says, her arms crossed as she stands in her bedroom doorway.

"This was part of our deal."

"Why do you care? You don't have to babysit me. I'm not going to burn your house down while you're gone or run away. I know I can't leave without you turning me in."

I frown. "Because the point of this is for you to get to know me and the club. I won't always make you ride with us, but Saturday rides are important. Everyone goes."

"Everyone? Including '*hang-arounds*'?"

I nearly flinch at the memory of Daryus and Raphael's anger last night. They have valid reasons not to want outsiders at our meetings, but the way they looked at me, the way they looked at June…

I shake my head. "Girlfriends and Ol' Ladies join rides. So do prospects."

"How long are these rides?"

"A few hours. Typically, we ride a couple hundred miles."

"Hours?!" June shouts. "Absolutely not."

"Come with me today, and you can skip next week."

"How about I skip today and go next week?"

"No."

June throws her head back with a groan. Then she turns back into her room and slams the door. I wait a few minutes. Before I can barge in to throw her over my shoulder, the door opens.

My breath catches. She's wearing the riding clothes I got her, the jeans hugging her every curve and her shirt low enough to give a hint of her tits. Despite how covering the outfit is, my dick still twitches at the sight.

"Perfect." I bite my cheek, trying to put a leash on my libido. She's wearing a jacket and jeans, not lingerie, for fuck's sake.

We pull on our helmets and gloves, then head to my Springfield. On the motorcycle, her hands move from the seat to the back of the bike, like she's afraid of touching me, even though she's ridden with me several times already. Rolling my eyes, I reach back, grab her wrists, and yank her forward, forcing her arms around my waist. She lets out a little yelp, and I smirk. The smile grows as her hold tightens with every second.

We meet the crew outside of the clubhouse, and everyone falls into formation, James at my side and Daryus and Kip behind us. Raph, as the tail gunner, picks up the rear on his custom Harley chopper.

As soon as we're rolling, my head clears and my muscles loosen, finally free from all the shit pulling me in different directions. Then June shifts an inch, her fingers curling into my shirt beneath my cut, and the brief freedom is punctuated by thoughts of the little reaper pressed against my back. The feeling of her body molding into mine as we ride is torturous, and I consider rerouting our ride just so I can get rid of her. But then she'll feel like she's won, and she already got too much power last night. So, I suck it up and use all my willpower to ignore how painfully tight my jeans become each time June's fingers flex their hold a few inches above the waistband.

She relaxes when we reach the open road outside city limits. I feel the moment her fear melts into joy, then elation. My little reaper is addicted to thrills. She thrives on the risks of life, like me. Pretty soon, she'll be looking at bikes at three in the morning.

Several hours later, our ride ends at the Iron Cage. We rhythmically pull into the lot, parking our bikes side by side. The absence of the roaring exhaust pipes is louder than the ride itself, and as soon as I swing my leg off the bike, tension begins creeping back into my muscles.

June stumbles as she tries to follow, her legs wobbling. I grab her arms to steady her. "You okay?"

She shakes me off. "I'm fine."

"It's like trying to walk on land after a month at sea!" Luna says, bounding over. "Don't worry, killer, you'll get used to it."

"Doubtful." Without another word to me, June pulls her helmet off and follows Luna into the Iron Cage.

"Looks like Luna might be stealing another one of our girls!" Raph shouts. I turn, aiming a death glare at him. His mouth snaps shut, and he has the decency to look sheepish.

"Chill, dude," James whispers.

"Fuck off." I carefully don't look for June inside, instead heading behind the bar. The bartender, a young woman much tougher than she looks, dips her chin in my direction. I pour a glass of whiskey, down it, and fill another, which I take to the back office. James follows and sits in the chair in front of my desk.

"Did you see Matthew when we were on 80?"

I nod. "He broke formation twice. Something's going on with him."

"Think it's Krissy?" he suggests, referring to Matthew's fiancé, who is, frankly, a bitch.

"I don't care what it is, he needs to get his shit together."

"I'll talk to him."

"Thanks."

"And you?"

"Look, June is—"

"No," James interrupts. "I mean last night. The meeting. I know that wasn't about June. At least, not completely."

"It was about the guys respecting me."

"T, don't pretend with me. The last two women you trusted enough to bring to meetings did a number on you. All the Saints remember that." He pauses, then corrects himself. "Well, all the Saints remember Amber. And those of us who knew you seven years ago never want to see you go through anything like *that* again."

He's worried, I know, but the words still feel like screws in my jaw. James was as affected by Scottie as I was, and even now, almost seven years later, his eyes glisten from the memories.

"That isn't going to happen again."

"The guys don't know that. All they see is you bringing this stranger into the fold, calling her your girlfriend, moving her into your house, and snapping at anyone who looks at her the wrong way. In their heads, either we'll all be burned again, or something will happen and we'll lose one of the best leaders the Saints have ever had."

My eyes fix on the antique model motorcycle on the desk as I let his words settle between us.

"But that's not what I'm talking about," he says. "You were thinking about her last night. Both of them."

"I don't give a shit about Amber—"

"Not Amber."

The following silence is the kind with a heartbeat of its own. It's a silence that fills the space with memories that could be deafening if you let it. We both see it. We both feel it. My body coils, preparing to fight an invisible and intangible threat.

But the real threat has long since passed. Now, the only danger is my own mind finally caving to the memories.

"I can't think about her."

"I know."

"I wasn't thinking about her."

"Okay."

James and I stare at each other for an indiscernible amount of time. He won't force me to talk about her, about *them*, he never would. He'll just read the thoughts in my eyes and sit with me for as long as it takes for the memories to return to their padded boxes in the basement of my mind. If Rocket were here, he'd tell us to nut up and face our feelings. But James's father is several states away, running from the past in his own way.

One day, we won't be able to run anymore. One day, the silence will break, and the memories will destroy me.

Until then, I'll keep the boxes shut however I can.

I sigh, throw back the remaining whiskey, and stand from the desk. James mirrors my movements. "Come on," I say. "Let's go get shitfaced."

TWELVE

June

"Bitch, where the fuck have you been?" Rose demands. Her box braids swing forward, brushing my arms when she pulls me in for a hug.

I pray to whoever is listening that the fire in my chest will stay in control for at least the next two hours. "What do you mean?"

"You disappeared!"

"I did not," I argue, taking the last available seat at our unofficial table. Donovan, our normal Taco Tuesday waiter, brings four margaritas before I'm fully settled.

"You kind of did," Evelyn says. "Even I texted in the group chat more than you last week."

I look at Sadie for help. She sips her strawberry margarita, then says, "I'm with them."

Well, this is happening now, I guess. "Sorry, I… uhm, sort of met someone and did the annoying thing where I got swept up in him for a bit." Which is true, just not in the way they're thinking.

Their reactions are immediate and predictable.

"I'm sorry, *what?*" Sadie yells so loud that several tables give us dirty looks.

"You're just now telling us?" Rose says.

"Who is this guy?" Evelyn asks, distrust lacing the question.

"I'm sorry. I almost told you guys on Saturday but decided to wait so I could see your faces." Lie. I waited because I'm a fucking coward when not carving up sadistic men.

"Then tell us to come over! You know I would've," Sadie says.

My lips roll between my teeth. "Uh, yeah. Well, I've been at his house since Friday." I figured a weekend is more digestible than six days.

"WHAT?!" Sadie and Rose yell. Half the restaurant glares at us, causing my cheeks to blush.

"Time got away from me. I didn't want to go home," I lie.

"Again, I ask, who is this guy?"

This is the part I've been most nervous about. I can't lie without risking exposure. There's no chance the girls won't look him up. Then they'll try to have me committed for shacking up with the leader of an outlaw motorcycle club.

"His name is Theo."

"That's a hot guy name," Sadie says, tucking strands of thick black hair behind her ears. She's recently gotten a haircut, so it's once again styled like a bob.

"Theo who?" Evelyn demands.

"Don't freak out, okay? And no more screaming." I pause, take a breath, then say, "Theo Zervas. He owns a bar in North Tucson."

"Oooh, we love a business owner," Rose says.

"Does this mean we get free alcohol?" Sadie asks.

My laugh at the question instantly dies at the look on

Evelyn's face. Her lips are parted, eyes widened, and her eyebrows cinched together. "Please tell me you're joking."

"What, why?" Rose asks.

I nervously run my finger through the salt on the rim of my glass. "No."

"What the hell, Graves?" Evelyn slaps her hand on the table. "What are you thinking?"

"What're we missing?" Sadie asks. "Is there something wrong with owning a bar?"

"The type of bar this guy owns, yes."

"How do you know what bar he owns?"

"Because I know who Theo Zervas is," Evelyn says.

"It's not like that, I swear," I promise, more truth in that than anything else I've said.

Sadie leans forward so she's nearly in the middle of the table. "Somebody please explain what's so wrong about June finally getting laid? For four days straight?"

I groan. "Theo is also in a club that some people might consider bad news."

"He's the leader of a biker gang full of criminals."

There's a beat of silence following Evelyn's pronouncement. Then Sadie sits back and says, "That's kind of hot."

"Sadie! It is not!"

Relief pulls my lips up, and I'm eternally grateful for Sadie Oliver.

"Who doesn't want a bad boy every once in a while?"

"I don't," Rose says.

"How about bad girl?"

"Oh, yeah, that's hot."

"Guys!" Evelyn hisses. "June is dating the leader of a *GANG,* and all you have to say is 'that's hot'?"

"Club," I say. All four of us blink slightly at the correction I hadn't planned to make.

"What?" Evelyn asks.

"It's a motorcycle *club*, not a gang."

"They're criminals."

"It's still not a gang."

"Who cares?" Evelyn says.

I open my mouth, then close it again because I don't care. I shouldn't care.

"He's not a drug dealer or trafficker or anything like that," I say. I spent months watching Theo, and of that much I'm certain. He occasionally partakes in recreational drug use, but he doesn't sell anything beyond alcohol. Other Saints do, especially Axel and Bella, bartenders at the Iron Cage, but none of the super hard or dangerous drugs. And I've never seen them sell to children.

"Notice how you didn't deny he's a criminal," Evelyn says. "Come on, June. You should know better than most people not to get involved with someone like this."

"She's just having a little fun," Sadie says. "It's not like she's going to marry the guy."

"Definitely not," I say.

"Then why see him at all?"

Because I don't want him to turn me into the cops for being a serial killer. "Because it's fun, like Sadie said."

Evelyn's look is full of disbelief, like she's realizing I'm not the person she thought I was. I feel tiny under the terror of what she'd do if she knew who I truly am. I know what people would think. Hell, I'm a therapist. If one of my clients told me they were having fantasies of murdering people, I'd report it and suggest testing them for antisocial personality disorder, psychopathy, or another mental illness.

Unfortunately, knowing those things does nothing to fix what's wrong in me. Because I know people would say there's something wrong with me, even if I don't think there is. *I* think I'm doing the world, and my clients, a favor.

But what I think doesn't matter. It definitely wouldn't matter to Evelyn.

She'd be disgusted. She would turn me in. I would lose everything.

"Just be careful," she says. "You know how slippery slopes like this are."

"Speaking of slippery, is he a god in bed?" Rose asks.

I choke on my margarita and start coughing. Thankfully, the question is exactly what I need to pull free from the thoughts that threaten to nail me to a wall of anxiety.

"We are not having that conversation," I say.

"Boo, lame," Rose says. Then she turns to Sadie. "You always have good sex stories. Who had the honor of getting you off this weekend?"

Sadie's eyes remain on me, like she's debating asking more questions. For a second, I think she sees fire leaping in my eyes. Then her expression morphs into a smile, and her attention turns to Rose. "Lionel, and let me tell you, he's getting much better."

Relief loosens my muscles, even as they feel like they're melting from the heat of the flames that were fanned by that conversation, not doused. By the time we leave and I'm climbing in an Uber that I convinced Theo to let me take, one thing has become painfully clear.

I'm not going to make it three more weeks.

I need to kill someone. Soon.

~

Thursday morning, I don't have to be in the office until eleven. Unfortunately, instead of using that time to sleep or relax, Theo insisted that we have our first riding lesson. I argued, even suggesting I help around the club or hang out with Luna, who has quickly become my favorite Saint. But he refused, so now I'm standing in the middle of a field of dead grass at eight in the morning, wearing riding gear and struggling to listen to Theo drone on about the parts of a bike and each step to learning to ride one.

"Are you listening, little reaper?" he asks, snapping his fingers in front of my face.

I reach out and grab the fingers, bending them back until he winces. "Don't ever snap your fingers at me if you want to keep them unbroken."

"How violent."

"I'm serious." I wait for him to nod before letting go. "You need to pay attention. Mistakes can be lethal."

"Then how about I just don't learn?"

I expect him to throw our agreement in my face, but instead, he says, "Because you want to learn. I can see it in your eyes every time you get off the bike. You're chasing the high."

My lips press into a thin line, which makes his rise into a wide smile.

"Now, what's this?" he asks, pointing to a little pedal in front of the right foot peg.

"Rear brake."

"Good!" He moves on, quizzing me for ten minutes before announcing that it's time I get on the bike and get used to the mechanics.

"No," I say.

"What do you mean 'no'?"

"I mean, no, I'm not getting on the bike."

"Why not?"

"Because I don't want to." Part of me does want to, but the cautious side of my brain screams now is *not* the time. Not with how unstable the fire in my chest is. And not when it's solely me and Theo here.

"Why are you being so difficult?"

"Why do you insist on telling me what to do?"

"I'm trying to teach you."

"And you have. I think that's enough for now."

"Come on, little reaper," he says, patting the seat, his eyes almost pleading.

I shake my head.

The vein in his neck that always seems on the verge of bursting bulges. His fingers curl into his palm, and he stalks toward me. I realize what he's planning to do a second before he leans down to pick me up. With record speed, I dodge his grab, yank the knife from my boot, and press it under his chin. He freezes, holding his palms out in surrender.

"Try it. I dare you," I all but growl. Theo was going to physically force me onto the bike like I'm a doll he gets to manipulate whenever he wants.

His eyes jump around my face, possibly looking for a hint that I won't slit his throat. Any other day, I might not, but today, right now? All I can hear are the crackling, roaring flames, and all I can feel is the scorching heat. My body begs me to press a little deeper and drag. My skin aches to feel his warm blood cover my hand.

Seemingly deciding that I am, in fact, serious, Theo slowly steps back. "I see it again," he says. I cock my head in question, keeping the knife raised. "That thing in your eyes, like you need something right now or you might lose all sanity," he clarifies. "I get it. I feel the same thing. It's like a tornado in my brain, and every second I don't feed it, the winds grow stronger, and more shit is sucked in until I feel like it'll break every aspect of who I am."

I almost drop my hand in shock. That's exactly what the fire feels like. I've never had someone explain it so perfectly. No teacher, therapist, or client.

But I carefully don't move or speak. I won't admit to Theo that what he sees is a desperate need to take a life.

"What is it? What does your tornado need?" he asks.

"Nothing," I say, though there's no power in the word.

"Little reaper."

"Stop it. Stop calling me that!"

Frustration tugs at the vein in his neck and the muscles in his jaw. A second later, he throws his hands to the side in defeat. "Fine. Don't tell me. But don't say I didn't offer. Let's go. I'll take you to the office."

Reluctantly, I lower my knife. Then I climb on behind Theo and promise myself that I'll do it this weekend, whatever it takes. There's a list of backup victims in the hidden compartment at my office. None of them are fully researched, but all have been verified as men deserving of death. It won't be my cleanest kill, but it'll be enough.

It'll have to be.

THIRTEEN

Theo

June didn't forget last week's agreement that she wouldn't have to come on today's ride. She insists on staying at the house, even though I know she enjoys riding. It's pride keeping her from admitting it. Or maybe whatever version of her tornado I keep seeing is acting as a barrier between herself and the possible joy she could be experiencing.

Thankfully, she's followed through with other aspects of our deal. She pitches in around the clubhouse without fighting, she helped Benny cook before church last night, and she's been making friends with the others, particularly Benny and Luna.

Meanwhile, she's digging her heels in at home, refusing to let her guard down for even a second. It's like our night watching *Die Hard* never happened.

Her bad mood is starting to irritate me. What she really needs is to be tied down, blindfolded, and gagged while I have my way with her. That would put her back in her place.

James thinks the entire situation is hilarious.

"Sorry, T," he says, barely concealing his amusement at my most recent failed attempt to talk to June. We're sitting on the back patio at the clubhouse, and June just stormed inside when I told her she couldn't go home without me. "I've never seen you pine."

"I'm not pining," I say.

"You're always staring at her. You complain about her all the time. You've had me search her house and office four times. I don't know what you think you're doing, but it looks a hell of a lot like pining to me."

"I watch her because she's a threat. I complain about her because she's maddening. And I've had you search her things because we need more information on her and her extracurricular activities. You're the one who always preaches about knowing your enemies and gathering information before a job."

"I also say not to take unnecessary risks, and keeping her around is the definition of an unnecessary risk." He takes a breath and lowers his voice, adding, "But I get it, I really do."

"Whatever," I mumble, pushing up from the chair. Ignoring James's knowing grin, I march inside and scan the crowd of bikers for June. Instead, Kip finds me, demanding my attention before I can locate the little reaper.

"Boss, can I talk to you for a bit?"

"Go ahead."

Kip glances over his shoulder. "Outside?"

I frown, not sure what he would need to talk to me about in private. Our last job went off without a problem, and we don't have another one planned. It could be about June and the supposed debt she has to me, but Kip has so far refrained from mentioning that. Still, I nod and turn around, heading back outside.

"Rejected again?" James asks when he sees me emerge. His eyes widen for a fraction when he sees someone else following me, then relax at the sight of Kip.

"Shut the fuck up."

"Careful," James says. "Both your James-vein and your chick-vein are making an appearance. Two at once is always dangerous."

"Then stop trying to piss me off."

"Boss," Kip interrupts before James can retort. "I just got a call about a possible job. The solo kind."

"Okay?" I say, prompting him for more information.

"It's Lorry. He wants our assistance in furthering an investigation," Kip continues, referring to his detective brother-in-law, who inadvertently helped us start this very lucrative little side business.

I remember his visit to the Iron Cage four years ago, during which he asked around about a local drug dealer. I could tell several Saints wanted to beat him up just for stepping foot in our space, but luckily for him, I knew the drug dealer he was after and wanted him gone. The guy targeted kids in the system who had no one and nothing, got them hooked on the tamer stuff, then tricked them into the hard-core and dangerous narcotics. I told Lorry to get the guy off the streets before I did it myself. Lorry then explained all the bullshit bureaucratic red tape he was restrained by and hinted that he needed a reason to get a search warrant and to find plenty of the drugs to put the guy away for life.

Most of our clients are law-abiding citizens with good intentions, but once Lorry got a taste of how our help makes his job easier—and gives him an impressive closing rate—he became a regular, no matter the case or crime. He has a love-hate relationship with the law. Meaning he loves enforcing it but hates obeying it.

Our business may not exist without him, but I still don't like the guy. These days, I'm rarely sure the suspects he wants us to frame are always guilty.

Still, he pays good money, and it's extremely convenient having a cop in our pocket.

"Who is it this time?" James asks, a sneer pulling at his lips. He despises Lorry more than I do. "Some mom he's convinced is lying about her kid's volunteer work on college resumes?"

Kip chews on his bottom lip, eyes jumping between us. "A murderer."

"When did he get promoted to homicide?" James asks.

"He hasn't," Kip answers. "He's investigating on his own time."

"Why?" I ask. The blood seems to run faster through my veins, and I'm not sure why.

"Because the department doesn't think there's a case, but he thinks it's a serial killer." Kip's words are steadily getting shakier, and his eyes have dropped from mine. "Three years ago, his cousin disappeared, and though everyone, the guy's wife included, is positive he ran because of his insane gambling debts, Lorry is convinced he was murdered."

"Three years ago, and he's just now hiring us?" James asks.

My heart pumps louder than normal. Like the sound of a distant storm crawling closer.

"He just found the killer. At least, he thinks he found them."

"Good for him. Why does he need us?" James asks.

He knows. So do I. But Kip seems to need a nudge to say it out loud.

"There's no physical evidence linking the killer to the disappearances. Honestly, there's hardly any circumstantial evidence. I'm not sure why he's so confident about this theory. It seems thin. He brought it to me yesterday, and he doesn't know… I don't think he realizes… I told him it was ridiculous, but he—"

"Kip!" I interrupt. The tips of my fingers are going

numb, and my pulse has reached an alarming rate. "Get to the point."

He sucks in a shaky breath and finally meets my eyes. The fear roiling in their depths makes my legs weak.

"He thinks the killer is June. He wants us to frame June Graves for murder."

FOURTEEN

June

How any of these people have real jobs is beyond me. If they're not riding, then they're at the Iron Cage or here at the clubhouse, drinking, smoking, doing drugs, fucking, literally anything but actually working or sleeping. It didn't take long to learn who to avoid and who is tolerable.

Like Luna. She'd fit in seamlessly with me and the girls. Theo and I were at the clubhouse for five minutes after his ride before I left his side to find her. She's the only one I trust myself around right now after the disaster of this afternoon. My target, Keith Burrows, was surrounded by people all day, so I couldn't follow through with the kill I started planning Thursday night. He's the closest optional target on my list, meaning I didn't have to travel far to get to his house. I was able to sneak inside and plant a camera, so my phone will alert me when he gets home, hopefully alone. Then I'll have to find a way to ditch Theo for a few hours.

Burrows has been on my radar for a while but never a prime target. He's an old pervert who used to work at a high school before someone discovered he had a secret camera in the girls' locker room. Burrows was fired, and there was a lawsuit that went nowhere, though he's yet to get another job at a high school. One of my old clients was a young man who went to the school and used to buy drugs from Burrows. Since then, I've kept him as an option. He might not have physically touched a girl that I know of, but he took advantage of his position.

"Watch, watch," Luna whispers next to me, momentarily pulling my thoughts away from the soon-to-be-dead man. "He's going to ask if she wants to try on his cut next," she says, a giggle in her voice as we watch Raphael attempt to flirt with Lydia, Benny's cousin, across the room.

Sure enough, barely thirty seconds pass before Raphael starts to take off his jacket, motioning for Lydia to put it on. She shakes her head, pushes his shoulder back, and walks away. Luna and I crack up, which Raphael must hear, because he turns and scowls at us.

"Oh no, busted," Luna says with a grimace. "Come on!" She grabs my arm and pulls me down the hallway, passing Nico and his friends preparing lines of coke. Luna pulls me through a door, and I stumble in, laughing.

"How he ever got a woman to sleep with him is beyond me," she says, locking the door behind us.

"He's attractive," I admit. "It's when he opens his mouth that he loses all chance."

"I pity those of you who are attracted to men. That should be proof enough that sexuality isn't a choice."

I snort and flop onto my back on the queen-sized bed. A brief worry that this bed belongs to a biker and is probably therefore disgusting enters my mind, but I ignore it. "Agreed. But also, it doesn't make sense to me that anyone is fully gay or fully straight."

Luna lies on her side, propping her head up with her hand. "So, you're not?"

"Not what?"

"Fully straight?"

I turn to look at her, glancing briefly at her curved lips. "Who is?"

"Liars."

My mouth feels dry as Luna's eyes travel down my body. She reaches out to brush a strand of hair off my face, letting her touch linger.

"My apartment is above the garage," she says. "No one would know we're there."

"You'd take me to your apartment knowing what I really am?"

"Fuck yes. I don't know how anyone, girl or guy, can be this close to you and not want you."

I shrug as best I can while lying down. "I doubt my friend Sadie does. She's pretty damn straight. And she's a big fan of men. Always has at least three in rotation."

"And you let them all live?"

Luna's tone is teasing, but the question still sends a crack through whatever tension was forming between us. I straighten my neck, looking at the ceiling. "One I didn't." The admission takes me off guard, but Luna seems perfectly at ease.

"What did he do to her?"

"How do you know he did something?"

"Because you don't kill indiscriminately. You only off men who deserve it, right? Abusers, rapists, drug dealers."

My forehead scrunches with a frown. "Am I that obvious?"

"I know a survivor when I see one, and I can tell when someone has a good heart. You're both, so it makes sense that your… urges are directed at predators. It's pretty *Dexter* of you. Very sexy." Her words are like a physical touch, and my cheeks warm.

"He tried to rape Sadie," I say, as if trying to cool my body's reaction. "She managed to fight him off, but he still got far enough. He hurt her."

"So you killed him?"

"He deserved it."

"I agree." A beat of silence, then Luna asks, "What did Theo do to deserve it?"

The question isn't surprising, but I still wasn't prepared. "You don't know?"

"I know he's not a hero, but he'd never hurt a woman. *That* I'm positive of."

"Maybe you don't know your leader as well as you thought." My words are hard, and I expect her to get upset or walk away, but she just scoffs with a grin.

"There's plenty I don't know about Theo, but I would bet my life on this."

Before I can think better of it, I ask, "What about Amber?"

"That's what this is about?" For the first time, she sounds taken aback. "Amber betrayed him. She betrayed all of us. She was an addict and got in deep debt with the South Five. She tried selling Saints secrets to clear her debts."

The information is so unexpected that my lungs take a moment to suck in a breath. I was beginning to suspect that Amber wasn't as innocent as Jennifer made her out to be, but that still doesn't justify hurting and killing her.

Although maybe he didn't. Maybe the other gang did and Theo covered it up. I know I should ask, and I want to know, but before the question forms, my phone buzzes. I pull it free and see a notification that Keith Burrows has arrived home. I sit up, ignoring Luna's question of where I'm going, and open the app.

He's alone. Perfect.

"I have to go," I say, heading for the door.

"Wait, why? We don't have to talk about Theo or any other guy. Actually, I prefer that."

"Another time." I leave the bedroom, planning to sneak out the side door before someone can see me. But, just my luck, Benny notices and makes a beeline for me.

"June! I want to introduce you to my cousin, Lydia. She's—"

"You know, I'd love to, but it'll have to be another time. I need…" I scan the room for some excuse and find Theo by the back door, watching with his brows low and lips pressed in a thin line. "To talk to Theo," I finish, shrugging out of Benny's hold. Theo opens the door, and I follow him onto the back patio.

"What's up?" he asks as soon as we're outside. He crosses his arms with distinct annoyance.

"I'm not feeling great, so I'm going to walk back to the house."

"You're not going back without me."

"You're going to force me to stay?"

"You didn't come on the ride today, so yes, you're staying and spending time with the Saints. We'll leave together in a couple of hours."

"Seriously?"

"Yeah, seriously," he says, raising his voice in a mock tone. "What about the last few days makes you think I'd trust you enough to walk out of here by yourself?"

"Fuck you," I spit, turning and storming back inside.

The interaction fanned the flames, and knowing that Burrows is home, probably perving over his videos of underage girls, does nothing to help. Recklessness roars in my ears, drowning out logic.

If I leave right now and Theo realizes I'm gone and doesn't find me at the house, he may turn me in to the police.

I don't know how much evidence he has against me, but anything is too much. I don't want the cops to even know I exist.

No part of me cares, though. I don't spare a thought for anyone else in the house, just head straight for the front door. Burrows's house is close enough to walk, so I double-check the directions, check the cameras to see he's in his bedroom, then drop my phone in the saddlebag of Theo's motorcycle. A fever fills every inch of my body as I walk, the fire growing larger, wilder, and hotter than it's felt in years.

The forty-minute trip to Burrows's house warps time, somehow taking half a blink and several hours. While I walk, the blazing inferno launches me back into memories that threaten to melt the bones under my skin.

"Honey, it's time to go," my foster mom says.

Tears I failed to hold in slide down my cheeks. "I want to stay here with you and Papa."

"I know, baby. But she's your mom, and she misses you."

I sob, shaking my head until a headache pounds my skull. "Don't make me go!"

There's a knock at the front door, and I know she's here to take me away from my home. My family for the last five years. I barely remember her. She's not my mom.

Soft arms wrap around me, and my foster mom's rosy smell surrounds me. She holds me tight, her shoulders shaking along with mine. "You're going to be okay, baby. Don't cry now. This is a happy day. You're going home."

But I'm not. I'm leaving my home. And I'm not coming back.

After my mom married Calvin, we started feeling more like a family. It wasn't perfect, and Mom still had bad days, but sometimes, when I closed my eyes, I could pretend like life was normal. Then something always ruined it.

Calvin's daughter, Imogen, is crying. I lean over the edge of the top bunk to see my stepsister. She's sitting at the head of her bed with her knees pulled up to her chest, tears streaming down her face.

"What's wrong?" I ask.

"Nothing, leave me alone!" she says, turning to face the wall.

"Talk to me, Emmy," I say, swinging over the edge of the bed and dropping to the floor.

"Don't call me Emmy!"

My eyes burn. I swallow a heavy lump in my throat, forcing the tears to stay at bay. Crying never got me anywhere, and it won't help now.

Michael fought for time with me, but I wasn't an idiot. I'd turned fourteen, and I knew my dad wasn't there for me. He was there for Calvin's money. He thought if he could be a part of my life, he could scam my mom and Calvin out of enough money to disappear forever. I almost wished he would.

I remember those days after my mom went to prison, before I went to the foster home. Dad hated me, especially when he was drunk. I tried to be as small and quiet as I could, but sometimes I was too loud, and he would lock me in a closet for an entire night or throw me across the room. Crying made him angrier. I was weak. A coward. Worthless.

I didn't want to be that anymore.

A year later, that weak, cowardly side of me melted in the fire of anger, pain, grief, and injustice. I became someone who fought back. I would save the girls who couldn't save themselves, like the girl I used to be.

Being a slave to the flames was worth it.

Burrows's house is quiet and small, exactly where you'd expect a sad, lonely man to live. It's easy to sneak through the back door, knife held tightly in my right hand. Each step is silent as I walk on the balls of my feet. He still seems to be in his bedroom, so I gather the camera in the main room first, then retrieve a rag from his kitchen.

Without my drugs, I had to improvise. Thankfully, Theo had bleach and rubbing alcohol under his kitchen sink, so I made a little homemade chloroform and have kept it in my back pocket, ready for this moment when I could douse it on the rag. With that ready, I start toward the bedroom.

Burrows is sitting in front of his computer, his pants discarded and porn playing at full volume. He's so engrossed in tugging at his wrinkly old dick that he doesn't hear me enter. By the time I have the rag pressed over his nose and mouth, it's too late. He struggles for a few seconds before the fight drains away and he's unconscious. His kiddy porn plays on a loop on his computer. Disgusted, I pick it up and slam it to the floor, satisfaction following the shattering of the screen. I then turn back to the old man who personally violated the privacy of dozens of teenage girls and sold drugs to the children in his care, and consider the quickest and most painful way to end his disgusting life.

I smile. The best place to start would be with the limp dick between those thin legs. I'll take it away in pieces, dragging the pain out for several minutes.

He won't wake up for at least ten minutes, if not longer. I use the time to duct tape him to his chair, then slap some over his mouth, an unfortunate necessity since we're not in my sound-proof basement. Then I begin searching for his sick memories I'm sure he keeps so it's the first thing the police find when they come looking for the rancid smell of his rotting corpse. I hate leaving bodies, but I can't avoid it this time. I'm not worried, though. The cops won't find any DNA or evidence of my existence in the house, and there's no reason for them to consider me in the first place.

I've found five pictures by the time he's stirring awake. Excitement flutters in my stomach as I make my way back to his bedroom.

"Welcome back, Mr. Burrows," I say. He groans, eyes still not open. I flip the knife in my hand and kick the front of his chair where his legs are spread.

A wailing siren stops me before I reach him. The alarm grows closer by the second, and though there isn't anything to suggest the cops are coming here, my body doesn't care. I'm frozen in place, listening to the approaching siren as if it's my own breath.

Then there's a sound like a floor creaking under someone's weight. Hair on end and heartbeat doubling in speed, I spin around, half-expecting to see a dozen cops waiting with their guns trained on me.

Instead, I see Theo Zervas, hands in his pockets and eyebrows raised.

"You've got yourself in quite the pickle, little reaper."

FIFTEEN

Theo

In a series of blinks, her expression turns from fear to shock to confusion to rage. Watching the transitions is slightly disorienting, and when she bares her teeth, I want to laugh. But time isn't on our side. Those sirens are attached to cop cars heading straight to this house. If we're here when they arrive, we're both in deep shit. Especially with Lorry already on June's tail.

"What the fuck are you doing here?"

"Saving your sorry ass. Now let's go. They're seconds from surrounding this house."

"You called the cops on me?" she asks, incredulity sharpening the edge of her voice.

"If I did, would I risk my own freedom to save you? We can argue later. Right now, we need to get the fuck out of here."

Icy anxiety creeps through my limbs as I watch June look back at the slowly waking man, as if she's contemplating whether killing him is worth the risk of being arrested. Thankfully, she decides against it and follows me outside. We leave through the back door, and the sirens are so loud they sound like they're coming from inside my head. I run as fast as I can, June impressively keeping pace. Red, blue, and white lights fill my peripheral vision, and I know any second now, someone will see us fleeing the scene. My lungs burn as I push my muscles to the limit, and we turn around a fence corner just as the cops converge on the old man's house.

Reaching my bike at the curb, June wastes no time grabbing her helmet and buckling it under the chin. She throws her leg over the seat, looking like she's spent her life on a bike. The sight momentarily punches me in the chest, and when her sky-blue eyes pierce into me through the open eye shield, my lungs empty of air.

"Theo!" she yells, snapping me out of the trance her beauty lured me into. I get on the bike, push up the kickstand with my heel, and rev the throttle before we take off with a squeal that I'm sure leaves skid marks. She holds onto my waist with all her strength, and though it makes it difficult to breathe, I don't care. The pressure is a reminder that she's here, safe.

I make the drive home in record time.

If I expected gratitude for saving her, then I was sorely mistaken. She climbs off the bike and storms inside without a word, slamming the front door shut behind her. I allow myself five seconds to take a deep breath before following. The door to her bedroom is shut, but I had the lock removed before she moved in, so I stroll over and throw it open.

She's pacing the small room, one hand in her hair, tangling the blonde waves, and the other closed in a fist around the handle of her knife. At my entrance, she whirls around, eyes wild.

"What the fuck was that?" she demands.

"I could ask you the same. Didn't I say to stay at the clubhouse?"

"Fuck you, I'm not a dog for you to order around."

"Clearly. A dog would be easier to train."

She answers by stepping forward and swinging her arm, the tip of the knife aiming for my neck. In a flash, I grab her wrist, halting her mid-swing. Then I yank her forward so her chest is flush against mine. "This is familiar," I say. She struggles against my hold, pushing at my shoulders and attempting to stomp on my foot. "Calm down."

"Let me go!"

"Drop the knife and I will."

Her eyes meet mine, and I swear steam billows from her nose as she lets out a huff. A moment later, she opens her hand, and the knife clatters to the floor. With my foot, I slide it backward out of reach, then let go of June. She instantly launches back, both hands curling into fists.

"Why the fuck were the cops there?" she asks.

"I don't know, but I intend to figure that out," I answer.

"Why were you there?"

"I thought that was rather obvious."

"How did you know I was there? I left my phone in your saddlebag."

"Yes, clever of you. But you had your wallet."

She pauses. Her eyes widen at the realization. "You put a tracker in my wallet?"

I shrug, which seems to exacerbate her anger. I can nearly see sparks fly from her eyes, and I fully understand then. I think I realized what created her tornado days ago, but it's finally real now.

June Graves truly is a reaper. She needs to kill, or the tornado will sweep her away. Or, more accurately with the rage emanating from her like heat, the fire will consume her if she doesn't give it the blood it craves.

She's every bit the ruthless murderer James warned me of and the serial killer Lorry suspects her to be.

And I'm more certain than ever that I'll do anything in my power to keep her safe. Both from her own flames and those who would seek to extinguish them.

"It's a good thing I did, or you'd be in the back of a cop car right now," I say, relieved that my voice doesn't give away my self-realization. "As much as I'd love to see you in handcuffs, that isn't quite the situation I imagined."

"Did you plant trackers on me anywhere else?"

Instead of answering, I say, "You were almost caught. You have to be more careful."

"I don't need you to save me."

"Of course not."

She growls in frustration. "I could have at least killed him before we left."

"Maybe if you hadn't wasted time knocking him out and waiting for him to wake up to start torturing him."

"I wasn't—"

"I was there," I remind her. "I saw enough."

Her face pulls taut, then she lets out what almost sounds like a howl. It's a sound of anger, yes, but also of pain.

I take a tentative step toward her. "How long has it been?"

She glares up at me, not flinching at my approach. "What do you mean?"

"Since you killed someone. How long since you satisfied that hunger?"

"Fuck you," she says, as if struggling to keep her guard up around the dirty secret she's trained herself to keep hidden.

I move closer, making her tilt her chin up to keep her eyes on mine. "If that'll help."

June reaches up to shove me back, but I grab hold of her wrists as soon as her hands hit my chest. They smell faintly of chemicals. "Stop it."

"Tell me," I order.

"No."

"If you need to kill someone, I can arrange that. The Saints have no shortage of enemies."

Her lip lifts in a disgusted sneer. "I'm not going to kill someone simply because you don't like them."

"You can pick the target. But you can't just go killing people without telling me."

"I can do whatever I want. Contrary to what you believe, I'm not your little reaper."

I raise my eyebrows. "Aren't you?"

Fire fills her glare, and I suddenly want nothing more than to feel the heat of her flames on my skin.

"Let me go." Her demand has lost some of its strength, but she continues tugging at my hold on her hands.

"Why? Isn't this what you want? A fight?" I push her backward until she's pressed against the dresser behind her. Her chest rises with a stuttering breath, and I feel her legs press tighter together.

"No."

"Yes, it is." Then, to prove my point, I force my leg between hers. The friction makes her inhale sharply. Her eyelids flutter, and her hips move, attempting to grind against my thigh. I smirk. "That's what I thought." Then I lean down and slam my lips against hers.

I didn't realize how badly I've been wanting to kiss her until it's happening. She matches my ferocity, our teeth clanging together. I push my tongue into her mouth and her answering moan shoots straight to my dick. She rolls her hips against my leg and grips my shirt. I let go of her wrists and plunge my hands into her hair, tugging at the strands and maneuvering her head back, allowing better access to her neck. Then I lower my lips, sucking the skin at the crook of her neck between my teeth. She's as hot as I imagined, and I can't spare a thought for the consequences of this. She could burn every inch of my body, and I wouldn't care.

"Theo," she moans. The sound shatters any memory of self-control I had. I reach down, grab her legs, and lift her up without breaking contact with her neck. She gasps and clings to my shoulders with her arms. Before she can fully wrap her legs around my waist, I turn us and throw her on the bed.

The sight of her lying there, flushed, hair a mess, teeth biting down on her bottom lip, undoes me. I climb on top of her, one hand traveling up her side, pulling her shirt with it, the other propped next to her head to hold my weight. She meets me in a kiss when I surge down. Her hands thread into my hair, and her nails scrape along my scalp, eliciting a groan. Slipping my hand under her shirt, I palm her left breast. She's wearing what feels like a lacy bra, and the thought of what it looks like curdles any logic with lust. I pull it down and pinch her nipple, pleased when she moans.

I abruptly sit up, and before she can look confused or upset, I grab the hem of her shirt and rip it up. She manages to lift her arms so I can pull it all the way off, and *fuck,* she is wearing a black lace bra.

"Holy fuck," I groan. She smiles and wraps her leg around my middle, pulling me back down. I grind my hips into hers, desperate for relief, and she matches the movement. Leaning down, I pull the cup of her bra away for direct access. Her loud gasp transforms into a moan when I suck her tit into my mouth and clamp my teeth around the nipple. Glorious pain radiates from my scalp when she pulls hard on my hair. I bite and suck until I'm sure there will be a bruise, then move to the other side. By the time I'm done, she's writhing beneath me, desperate for more.

And who am I to deny the reaper herself?

I reach down, unbuckle her pants, and push them down enough to plunge my hand inside and slide my fingers beneath her underwear.

"Fuck," I breathe. "My little reaper is so wet for me."

"Shut up," June barely gasps, her hips raising in search of more pressure.

I chuckle and simultaneously bite down harder on her nipple, pushing two fingers inside. Her answering moan is nearly a yell. I return my mouth to her lips and swallow her next gasping breath. My fingers move deeper, and I press my thumb to her clit, making her push harder against me.

"That's it, ride my hand." By the tightening around my fingers, she likes the encouragement. "Come on, little reaper. Show me how much you want me."

She does. She grips my back hard enough to leave bruises. My thumb circles where she wants it most, and I watch her eyes squeeze shut at the sensation. "You're so fucking tight," I say as I scissor my fingers. My aching cock wants nothing more than to replace them and some distant part of my mind knows that I'll never be satisfied until I'm buried deep inside her.

But not tonight. Right now is about cooling those flames enough to get her through a few more days.

So I work her with my fingers, letting her grind against my hand and swallowing every delicious sound she makes. After I add a third finger, it's not long before she arches her back and lets out the most beautiful sound I've ever heard. I feel her flutter and squeeze my fingers as an orgasm flows through her. We're both breathing hard, and she's still holding tight to my shoulders. I work her through the release, then pull my hand free from her pants. I wait for her eyes to open before sliding my fingers into my mouth, her taste shooting south with the rest of my blood.

"Fuck, you taste amazing." She watches me with half-lidded eyes in a satiated relaxation. I sit back on my legs, and her eyes jump down to the evidence of my arousal. "Not tonight, little reaper," I say, despite the overwhelming desire. She no longer looks like she's on the verge of combustion, and that's what matters.

I climb off her bed, leaving her lying there boneless and half-naked. "Sleep now. Tomorrow, we'll talk about finding a more lasting solution to those flames in your eyes." Then I turn and walk away, knowing that I just irrevocably changed everything.

SIXTEEN

June

Miraculously, I fall asleep after Theo leaves. But it doesn't last long, and my eyes fly open at five a.m. I rub my legs together and nearly moan at the warm need pulsing between my thighs.

My first thought is *Shit, did I just have a sex dream about Theo?*

My second thought is *FUCK, did I let Theo finger fuck me last night?*

My third, and loudest, thought is, *I was almost caught last night. How did the cops know I was there?*

I might understand if the police somehow knew I was trailing a target, but Burrows was a backup. It's been three years since he was fired from that high school, and I barely followed him at all before last night. He might've been under surveillance for a different reason, but then the cops would've already been outside his house when I arrived, right?

There's only one thing that makes sense. Theo was involved. How else would he have known where I was *and* that the cops were on their way?

But why would he call the cops then risk himself to save me? Was it some delusional attempt to earn my trust?

It kind of worked, since you let him finger you, I think. Then I banish the thought. My adrenaline was through the roof last night, so I was already aroused and the logical side of my brain was taking a nap. Letting him get me off means nothing. I only woke up wet and wanting him again because it's been a while since I've had decent sex, and Theo happens to be great at getting women off. He should be, with how many people he's fucked.

I tell myself it's a natural reaction, even as my hand travels down my body under the covers. It's normal to still be aroused after excess adrenaline. My eyes flutter shut, and my fingers lift the band of my underwear. I rub my clit and bite my tongue, pushing my hips up. An image of Theo leaning over me, keeping me immobile with a hand on my hip as he has his way with me, fills my mind. Turning my head into the pillow, I bite the corner, muffling a gasp as I pick up the pace. There's a twinge of pain when I move my fingers to push into my opening, which serves as a reminder of Theo roughly shoving three fingers inside a few hours ago.

I finish to the memory of Theo licking his fingers clean.

Then logic returns, and I groan, throwing the blanket off. I head to the bathroom to wash my hands and brush my teeth. My hair is tangled, and the circles under my eyes are prominent. Deciding I need to wash everything from yesterday away, I lock the bathroom door and turn the shower to the hottest possible temperature.

By the time I feel clean enough to turn the water off and get dressed, it's nearly seven, so I'm unsurprised to find an empty coffee pot in the quiet kitchen. I hadn't realized until now that there's always been coffee waiting for me in the morning, and it takes ten minutes before I find the bag of grounds in the freezer.

"Who the fuck keeps coffee in the freezer," I mutter, measuring out enough scoops for at least four cups.

"People who get already-ground coffee as gifts from idiots who don't realize good coffee starts going bad after you grind it."

I whip around, heart jumping at the unexpected response. James is standing a few feet away, scowling. There's a bruise on his cheekbone that wasn't there yesterday and a split in the middle of his top lip.

"Shit!" I whisper. "What are you doing awake so early?"

"Could ask you the same thing, Ms. I-Take-Hour-Long-Showers-At-The-Ass-Crack-Of-Dawn."

Right, his room is on the other side of the bathroom we share. Oops.

He passes close by on his way to the fridge, and the bruising on his cheek is even more evident.

"What the hell happened to your face?"

"Had a late fight last night. I was distracted, so he got in more hits than he should've."

I'd nearly forgotten that James occasionally participates in underground fights. I watched one in November while I was following Theo, and he beat his opponent unconscious in less than five minutes.

"Why were you distracted?" I ask, unease turning my stomach.

James shuts the fridge door and turns back around. He twirls a plum in his hand and presses his lips together. "Family stuff."

Instinctively, I think back to my research on James. All I really know is his dad passed the role as the Saints leader to Theo instead of him. I've wondered why James didn't take over, but I doubt that's what's bothering him now. I don't believe he'll tell me what is.

So, instead, I ask, "Did Theo tell you what happened last night?"

His eyebrows raise. "What happened, *little reaper?*"

My cheeks flush, but James wasn't here when Theo and I got back, and *that's* not what I'm referring to anyway.

"So, no?"

He takes a bite of his plum and shakes his head. "Got back late, T was already asleep."

"Oh, okay."

"But I remember he left the clubhouse abruptly. Didn't tell anyone where he was going. I'd bet anything that has to do with you."

"It doesn't matter."

"It matters as long as it affects my brother," James says, an uncharacteristic edge to his words.

"Then ask your *brother,*" I say, turning back to the coffee maker. It's not finished, but there's enough to fill a mug, so I pull it free and ignore the hiss when a splash hits the exposed hot plate. I walk out the front door, holding the full mug close to my chin. Not wanting to deal with another fight once Theo wakes up, I drop onto one of the porch chairs, even though I'd love to go on a morning walk.

Taking advantage of the peace and quiet, I open my phone, which I'd retrieved from his bike last night, and start replying to messages, making sure to give the girls a long— and false—update. I say I went back home after Taco Tuesday and spent the entire time there before returning to Theo's last night, since I missed a call from Evelyn while I was at the clubhouse. Then I launch Google and scroll through local news. I want to search Burrows's name, but I resist in case I can be placed at his house last night. I don't want to give the police any reason to connect me to him.

I last fifteen minutes before giving in to frustration and searching "Keith Burrows."

The most recent article is about him being found innocent two years ago. Nothing from last night. Nothing about the cops going to his house or him reporting a break-in or assault.

"What the fuck?" There should be *something* about why the cops were sent to his house. Even if it's a false alarm. Burrows has been in the news before, so any report would at least *mention* him. But there's shit all.

Did Theo lie? Maybe the sirens weren't for him after all. Maybe it was a coincidence, and the police were going somewhere unrelated.

If that's the case, then Theo stopped me for no fucking reason.

Then dragged me back to this fucking house to take advantage of my body's natural arousal from the adrenaline.

"FUCK."

Coffee sloshes over the edge of the mug when I slam it onto the table and jump up. I storm inside, through the now-empty kitchen, and to Theo's room. I don't bother knocking, just throw open the door and step inside.

His bedroom is nearly three times the size of mine. His bed is in the center, and I'm pretty sure it's a California King. Despite being the only one who sleeps in it, Theo is firmly on the left side, leaving the right open.

At my loud entrance, he jerks awake and seems to naturally grab a gun from behind his bedside table. He already has the weapon aimed toward the door before he registers who I am with a few blinks. He lowers the gun and drops his arms to the side. "Reaper," he says with an impressively level voice.

"What the fuck did you do?" I demand, stopping inches from the foot of his bed. Dimly, I register that the rug beneath my feet is incredibly soft and the whole room looks meticulously organized.

"You'll have to be more specific."

"Last night!"

Theo smirks and returns the gun to its hidden spot. "If you want me between your legs again, just ask."

"At Burrows's!" I clarify, refusing to let him distract me from the anger. "Those cops weren't headed to his house at all, were they?"

His lips drop into a frown. "Pretty sure they were."

"*Why?*"

"Typically, when police believe—"

"Why do you think they were going there?" I interrupt. "How did you know?"

"That doesn't matter."

"Yes, it fucking does. There's *nothing* in the news about Burrows being arrested or found tied to his chair. Which means the cops were never there."

"Or they just didn't tell the media."

"That kind of shit always ends up in the news. Journalists religiously listen to their police scanners."

"Maybe they didn't talk about it over their radios."

"Then how would you have known about it?" Before he can reply, I add, "Tell me the truth, Theo! Either you had some inside knowledge, or you lied to me and stopped me for no fucking reason."

"I wouldn't do that."

"Because controlling me is so out of character for you?"

"This isn't the same, and you know that!" Theo says, finally climbing out of bed. I carefully don't look below his face, where he's wearing nothing but boxer briefs. "Haven't I made it clear that I want to help you with your… *needs*, not smother them?"

Something curls in my gut at the way he says 'needs' and how he steps close enough for his natural scent of coffee, gas, and an unidentifiable smell that is so noticeably *Theo* to reach my nose.

"Then explain what's going on. How did you know the cops were on their way? Why were they going to Burrows's? Why did you show up?"

"God, June!" he yells. "Do you ever just shut the fuck up and say, 'thank you'?"

Before I can think better of it, I slap him. His neck turns with the force, and there's a breath during which I know I made a mistake, and fury fills his eyes. Then the next second, his hand wraps around my throat and pushes forward until my back is against the wall. He presses so close that his hot breath brushes my face. I claw at his hand on my throat, but he doesn't budge. His fingers tighten enough to keep me in place but not enough to cut off airflow.

"You just *have* to provoke me, don't you?" His voice is low, but he's close enough for every word to be audible. "Just because I haven't hurt you yet doesn't mean I can't or won't."

I clench my thighs together, silently cursing my body for the way his hand on my throat and his words fill me with desire, not anger or fear.

Even worse, Theo is so close to me that he doesn't miss the movement or the way my breath hitches.

"And I'm pretty sure you'd *like* that, wouldn't you, little reaper? I bet if I tied you up and punished you the way you deserve, you'd be begging for my cock in no time."

"Fuck you," I snap.

Theo tightens his hand, fully cutting off my air. "Keep saying that, and one day I will." He leans closer, and I struggle against him, gasping for a breath I won't get with him choking me like this. "You might be the reaper, but I haven't been afraid of death in a long time."

The next second, his hand is gone, and he steps back,

giving me room to double forward, coughing and sucking in air.

"I'm not like every other monster you hunt, little reaper. Don't forget that."

By the time I can stand, no longer lightheaded, Theo is gone.

SEVENTEEN

Theo

I twist the throttle and lean to the right, briefly riding the shoulder to zip around an SUV. The speedometer steadily climbs, and with each number, the wind in my brain clears. But it doesn't matter how loud the exhaust roars or the wind howls, I can still hear her fucking voice. That little breath hitch when my hand went around her throat still plays on repeat at a deafening volume.

James was right. She's gotten too far under my skin. I've only ever felt that blinding rage mixed with drowning desire with one other woman.

And her death nearly ended me.

"FUCK!" My shout is lost to the rushing air as the needle tips into triple digits. I fly down the center of a somewhat empty two-lane highway until the red tinge fades from my vision.

My next breath feels cleaner, and I let up on the throttle. Ten minutes later, I'm slowing to a semi-safe speed several miles outside the city limits. Dirt and pebbles kick up behind the tires as I pull off the road. I stop next to a small cactus and push out the kickstand before climbing off the bike.

I've always had a temper. It kept me from sticking to a

foster home for longer than a few months at a time and got me thrown into juvie twice before I turned sixteen. It was Rocket who taught me there's a way to secure a leash on my temper and only let it out when it was beneficial. He and James are the sole reason I wasn't thrown in prison long ago. Sure, it's still slipped my grip a few times, but never so quickly or without any warning like it did with June.

It wasn't even the slap that did it. It was the accusation. The sanctimonious look in her eyes when she asked me about last night. Like she finally saw who I truly am under the mask.

What really pissed me off is I'm afraid she did. Maybe she realized I'm nothing but a hypocritical lowlife criminal happy to get other people arrested for the exact same crimes I commit on a regular basis. If she knew about last night… I shake my head, guilt forcing me to relive that conversation.

"He wants us to frame June Graves for murder. But it's not her, is it? She can't be a… fuck."

Kip saw the truth in my eyes last night. My story about some bullshit debt June owes went up in smoke in that moment, and though I didn't explain the details, he knows enough.

Not just him. His brother-in-law. A cop is on June's trail. Soon, Lorry will learn that June lives with me and is apparently my girlfriend. If he hasn't figured it out already.

"Maybe it's a test," James had suggested.

"What fucking for? To see if I'll send my girlfriend to prison for him?"

"Will you please explain what's going on? Is Lorry right? Did June kill his cousin? Has she killed others?" Kip asked. He was thinking out loud; he didn't need us to verbally answer. Maybe we would've had time to explain if Luna hadn't come outside asking what happened and where June went. As soon

as I realized she was gone, I knew. I could feel it in my bones.

If I'd been five minutes later in finding her, she'd be behind bars right now.

The thought makes me feel sucked dry.

Something buzzes in my pocket, shocking me from my thoughts. James's name flashes on the screen.

"Wanna tell me why I just found your girl digging through drawers in your bedroom?" he asks in a laughable interpretation of a greeting.

"Of course she's snooping." I rub my thumb and forefinger down the bridge of my nose and blow out a heavy breath. "Is she okay?"

"Besides a suspiciously red neck and a really pissed off attitude? She's fine."

I turn and stalk back to my idling bike. "We got in a fight."

"I figured. Did you tell her about Lorry?"

"Fuck, no! You didn't, did you?"

"Did I tell the already unhinged serial killer that me and her fake boyfriend slash jailor were hired to frame her for murder? Totally."

"Hilarious, James, really."

"Kip texted. He wants to come over and talk about it."

"Not with June around."

"I'm not an idiot, T. But what do you want me to do? And where the fuck are you?"

I give him my estimated location, then ask, "Can you get her out of the house for a few hours? Tell her she can go see her friend Sadie or something."

"You want to send her off while she's this angry at you? Are *you* an idiot?"

"She won't do anything, trust me."

"What makes you so sure?"

Absurdly, the first thing I think of is the way her lips parted and her eyes squeezed shut as she moaned and came all over my fingers.

I clear my throat and say, "Mutually assured destruction."

His pause tells me he's not at all happy with the command, but he still says, "You're the boss. I'll tell her."

"Thanks. Make sure Kip doesn't show up until after she's gone. I'll be back in twenty minutes." After a few more quips from James about how I'm going to get us all murdered, I hang up and push back the kickstand. A ring of dust fills the air as I spin around and head toward the city and my mutually assured destruction.

~

"Is someone going to start explaining any time soon?"

I hear Kip's voice even before I'm inside. Our head road captain is usually quiet, controlled, and meticulous, so hearing this loud, ruffled version of him is more than unsettling. At least I know June somehow listened to James and left. She was probably eager to seize the opportunity to escape for a few hours.

With a heavy breath, I throw open the door and stroll in, hoping to appear more in control of the situation than I am. Kip spins around at my entrance. His location between the kitchen, dining room, and sunken living room suggests he's been pacing. James is sitting at the dining room table, the dark bruise on his cheek and slightly ungroomed beard lending to his overall stressed appearance.

"I'll explain, but you have to calm down," I say.

"Boss," Kip says, every muscle in his body taut. "What is going on?"

I let out a heavy sigh and drape my jacket on the back of a chair. "It appears your brother-in-law is a much better detective than I ever gave him credit for."

Kip crosses his long arms, tattoos climbing out from under his sleeves. "There's no way this is true. Are you fucking with me?"

"You know T doesn't have a sense of humor good enough for a joke like this," James says.

"Thanks," I grumble. Then to Kip, "It's not a joke. I don't know for certain if June did kill Lorry's cousin, but it wouldn't surprise me if she did. June has a bit of a temper… and a very low tolerance for asshole men."

"So, she's a serial killer?"

"Kind of."

Kip's mouth drops open. "How can someone *kind of* be a serial killer?"

"T's giving her more credit than she deserves. She's one hundred percent a serial killer. She has some sort of revenge murder honor code and targets men who abuse women. In fact—"

I whip my head in James's direction, my glare successfully cutting him off before he can reveal that June tried to kill me. That part must stay a secret, because the more Saints who know of June's failed plans, the more likely one of them will try to get revenge on my behalf. And I'd really hate having to kill one of my own for laying a hand on her.

"About a month ago, I found her watching the club," I say, filling the awkward moment with the story I came up with on the ride back. "She was hunting for her next target and thought he'd be a member of the club. I tried to convince her no one here deserves her vigilante justice, but she had no reason to believe me. So, we agreed on this arrangement. She gets to know the Saints and no one dies."

"You mean you willingly let a murderer into our midst *knowing* she was spying with the intention of killing one of us?" Kip asks, disbelief in every word.

That's where I felt my story snag, too. But it's the most believable without being the truth. The best I could come up with in half an hour, at least. Still, I'm not sure how to respond in a way that'll stop Kip from asking more questions.

Thankfully, James comes to the rescue, as he always does.

"She's not a threat if none of our men are abusing women, which they're not. And June already had plenty of evidence of our club's one percent activities stashed away as a contingency, so we couldn't just kill her. Besides, T didn't want to kill her. He really is smitten."

"I'm not fucking smitten."

James snorts. "Sure you're not."

I glare at him. His help always comes with strings.

"Sorry, boss, but you're *something*. That much is obvious," Kip adds.

I fist my hands. These two will make me break our code by fucking strangling them. "Whatever. That's not the point right now. The point is, yes, June has some stabby tendencies. But we will *not* be helping Lorry lock her up. In fact, we need to figure out how to get him off her trail completely."

"That won't be easy. He called me this morning to ask if I'd talked to you guys about it. He's nervous because he's been watching her house for nearly a week and hasn't seen her once. I didn't tell him she's here, of course."

"And he doesn't know?" James asks, sounding just as suspicious as I feel.

"This is all new, June dating Theo and hanging around the club. Lorry was busy with another case and couldn't get back to his June investigation until Tuesday. Since it's unofficial and on his own time, he only has so many resources. He mentioned June arriving at her office with another woman on a bike last week, but he didn't know it was Luna. Must not have seen her jacket."

"You're *sure* he doesn't suspect June's involvement with the Saints?" I ask.

Kip shakes his head. "No, I'm not sure. But I think he would've asked about it if he did. He'll figure it out soon, though."

"Maybe we should let her drive to work on her own for a few days," James suggests.

"No."

"T—"

"I said no," I interrupt before I've really considered the suggestion. It'd be a good idea, and I'm reasonably confident June won't try anything.

But no. Ubering every once in a while is one thing. Letting her drive her car wherever she wants is something else entirely.

"Either way, Lorry will figure it out. Clearly, he's not terrible at his job," I say. "We have to come up with a plan that'll convince Lorry of June's innocence without making him suspicious of us."

"He's been looking into this for years," Kip says. "Anything you say will make him think you're trying to cover up for your girlfriend. There are only so many crimes he'll overlook for us."

"Can you get his research? We need to know what he knows and what he suspects."

"He keeps all his files for active cases in a safe in his home office if they're not at the station."

"Does your sister know the code to the safe?"

Kip shakes his head. "She doesn't even have a key to his office."

"Picking the lock will be easy. We just need to figure out a way into the safe so we can make copies of his file on June."

"We'll need to get him and Bethany out of the house for

a few hours," James adds, referring to Kip's sister. She and Lorry have two children, but they're both away at college.

"I could do that," Kip says.

"Perfect. Then James and I will get in, make copies of the files, and get out."

"We should make sure Luna is here watching June," James says. "If she suspects anything, she'll follow us. And I'm assuming you don't want to tell her about this?"

"Fuck no."

"So, a Luna distraction it is. She'll have a blast."

An image of how exactly Luna might occupy June's time for a few hours fills my mind, along with an intoxicating combination of jealousy and lust. If I think about Luna distracting June for too long, I'll be stuck with a raging hard-on.

I force my mind to move on from the daydream. "Once we have the files, we can figure out next steps. We need to do this quickly, before Lorry learns June is here."

"I can't believe you're letting a serial killer of men live under your roof," Kip says.

"You have no idea," James mutters.

EIGHTEEN

June

On the way to Sadie's apartment, I stop at the store to buy recording equipment. There's something going on with Theo and James, and I want to know what it is. Basically forcing me to leave the house they're keeping me prisoner in and suggesting I go see my friend who isn't a Saint can only mean it's a big deal, whatever *it* is. Maybe a few planted microphones will shed some light on the situation.

I double-check my neck before heading inside, confirming that the makeup I applied earlier covers the marks Theo left. I'm not worried about Sadie seeing them, because she understands how rough sex can leave bruises, but I don't want to deal with the questions from Evelyn and Rose if Sadie tells them.

"The prodigal daughter returns!" Sadie shouts, throwing open the front door before I've reached it.

I roll my eyes. "We Facetimed on Friday."

"But I haven't seen you since Tuesday!" she says, pulling me into a hug. "For all I know, you could've been killed or thrown in prison or something."

Laughing at how close to the truth she is, I follow Sadie inside and greet Soot, her giant dog. "You'd be my first call if I was thrown in prison."

"I'd expect nothing less. So, why the last-minute hang?"

"Can't I just miss my best friend?" I wipe slobber from my face with my sleeve and stand, following her to the kitchen.

"Duh, but that's not what this is."

"How do you know?"

Sadie grabs her teapot, giving me an unamused face. Her square tortoise shell glasses slide down her nose, perching on the end to give her a sexy librarian look. "We've been best friends for five years. I know you."

You know part *of me.* "Fine. It's just…" I use the time it takes to pull in a deep breath to conjure a reason that doesn't involve Theo. Or, at least doesn't *directly* involve him, because what I come up with is, "Evelyn has ignored all my calls and texts since Tuesday."

"Maybe she's busy."

"She's been texting in the group chat."

Sadie frowns, evidently attempting to come up with another reason that'll make me feel better. She fills two loose-leaf tea steepers with a dried mix that doubtless came straight from her greenhouse, hopefully not the one I sometimes break into that has the more dubious plants and flowers. "I doubt she's ignoring you on purpose."

"She is, and we both know why. She's pissed at me for dating a criminal. She thinks I'm disrespecting our professions or something."

"Maybe it's just bringing up her own bad experiences," she suggests.

My hand pauses mid-petting Soot, and the dog looks back at me, whining. How had I not considered that? Evelyn rarely talks about her past, but we all know the highlights.

Emotionally abusive father, mother arrested for prostitution, sister arrested for dealing drugs, which Ev helped make happen by testifying against her, and a narcissistic ex-husband. After the shit show that was her first twenty-four years of life, she now spends every second trying to keep other kids from similar situations.

So, yeah, I should've realized that my being involved with a group of criminals would trigger some stuff.

"Fuck."

Sadie pats my arm sympathetically. "Give her time. She'll realize it's not the same situation."

No, it's not.

It's worse.

~

Shockingly, Theo is at the house when I return. I expected him to be at the clubhouse or Iron Cage, but he's standing in the kitchen facing the stove. I automatically sniff, stomach rumbling at the smell of garlic and baked bread.

"Little reaper," Theo says, looking over his shoulder.

"Tinkerbell," I say, remembering the nickname I haven't used since our amicable night watching *Die Hard*.

"I highly caution you against making that a nickname," he says.

"You get to have one for me."

He doesn't respond. Instead, he lets his brown eyes rake over my body, and our last interaction fills my mind. His hands around my throat, desire pooling low, his promise to tie me up.

The images vanish when he asks, "Do you like pasta?"

"What?"

"Pasta, the food. Do you enjoy it?"

I nod. "Uh, yeah. Who doesn't?"

"I've known people who don't." There's a story behind that, I can tell. But I don't have the chance to ask. "I'm making garlic butter chicken pasta. There's also garlic bread in the oven."

I drop my bag on the dining table and venture into the kitchen. "Making sure I'm not a vampire?"

He chuckles. "You can never have too much garlic."

"Look at that, we agree on something." I stop next to him at the stove, and my mouth waters at the sight of the food.

"Have fun with Sadie?"

"Yeah. Going to tell me why James kicked me out of the house?"

"No."

At least he didn't deny kicking me out. "How about last night?"

"Can we not do this again?" he asks, a genuine plea in his voice.

"We wouldn't have to if you just told me the truth."

He sighs, stirring more cheese into the pasta. "I have a contact in the police force," he says. I'm so shocked that he's giving me an answer that I nearly forget to breathe. "Sometimes he gives me a heads up before the cops are going to raid somewhere in the Saints' territory, especially if he thinks one of my people may be around. He said they were about to raid a known drug dealer's house based on an anonymous tip, and he always warns me if drugs are involved, even though most of the Saints don't deal. Anyways, he told me where it was right after I learned you'd disappeared, and I somehow *knew* where you'd gone. All I had to do was check the tracker in your wallet to verify my suspicions."

"Why didn't you just tell me that?"

"You already think so little of us. I worried knowing I

have a cop actively keeping us off the police radar who, for some reason, assumes a Saint is involved with every little crime in the area, would somehow prove your belief about how terrible we are."

An odd twinge fills my chest at that answer. "Theo, I… I don't think you're all terrible."

His eyebrows raise. "No? Just me then?"

Now would be the time to tell him about Amber. To ask him what happened. Did he kill her after finding out she betrayed the Saints? Or did someone else get rid of her?

But the twinge in my chest won't let me ask. It travels low, twisting at the base of my stomach and morphing into a very different need than the fire.

"You did tell me you were a monster just this morning. Right after choking me."

The memory pulls Theo's eyes to my neck, where the marks are still covered by makeup. He turns away from the stove and takes a step closer to me. "You were being a brat."

My mouth drops open. *Did he just call me a brat?* "Do you typically choke people for being brats?"

"Just the ones who want me to."

Annoyed and more turned on by the second, I reach my hands to his chest, preparing to shove him back. Instead, he grabs my wrists and tugs me closer. My neck strains as I attempt to hold eye contact.

"I think it's time you remember your place here, little reaper." His voice lowers, void of any humor that was present moments ago. His pupils are blown, and he licks his lips.

"And what's that?" I feel him hardening in his jeans and privately hope he'll push me to my knees.

But before he can respond, his phone rings, the shrill sound demanding.

"I'm going to kill him," Theo mutters, reaching blindly down the counter for his phone without letting me go.

"You don't even know who it is."

"I don't care." He finds his phone and presses it to his ear. I shift forward unconsciously, pressing my body against his erection. He answers with a curt, "What?"

The answer makes him freeze. I promptly stop moving, sensing trouble when his muscles tense, and the veins in his arms bulge.

He steps back, and the loss of his weight and body heat lingers like a cold ache. "God, what a fucking idiot," he says, knuckles turning white with how hard he grips the phone. "Yeah, I know." He turns off the stove and oven, then races to his bedroom, saying something else into the phone.

I follow, catching the end of his next sentence. "—if he's even still alive tomorrow." The anger in his voice is different than when he's mad at me. It's the type of disappointed, partly scared anger that parents have when their children disobey and do something dangerous. He heads to the closet in his bathroom and squats in front of a metal safe. "I'll be there in five minutes." He hangs up, keys in the code on the safe, and pulls out a gun.

Instinctively, I tense and reach for my knife. But then Theo is securing the gun into the back of his pants and walking past me, a scowl on his face.

"What's going on?"

"Issue at the Cage," he answers curtly. "I don't know when I'll be back."

I'm close on his heels, desperately trying to catch up with the turn of events. "What? Wait, no."

He pulls on his Saints of Purgatory cut, turning to face me. "Sorry to leave you like this. But I'll make it up to you, little reaper. Promise."

I grab his forearm, nails digging into the leather jacket. "No."

"I have to go."

"Fine, but I'm going with you."

He frowns. "No, you're not."

"Isn't our deal that I take part in Saints activities?"

"Not this stuff. It'll be dangerous."

My eyebrows raise. "I can do danger, Theo."

"I won't be able to focus on you."

"I don't need you to. I can take care of myself."

A muscle jumps in his jaw as he glares at me, warring with himself. Finally, he sighs and says, "Fine, just be careful and don't do anything stupid."

"Always am."

He rolls his eyes then heads outside. I sprint after him, grabbing my helmet on the way. We both climb onto his bike, and I hold him tightly when he speeds away. In less than five minutes, we're at the Iron Cage, where the lot is fuller than I've ever seen it, with more than just the Saints' bikes. The shouting from inside is clear when Theo turns off the engine. We leave our helmets with the bike and run inside to find a dozen strangers facing off against most of the Saints. James is in front of the Saints, fresh blood dripping from his nose and a cut on his arm. In between the two groups is Nico on his knees, face beaten so badly that one eye is swollen shut and the other is halfway there.

Theo wastes no time stepping between the two groups and standing right in front of Nico. He gives the boy a quick glare in warning that promises punishment for whatever he did to cause this standoff, then turns to the strangers. I realize they're all wearing the same jackets and catch the name on the back of one.

The South Five. The same gang that Amber supposedly owed money to and betrayed the Saints for.

"Bowie," Theo says, greeting the man in front of the

other group. "You seem to have forgotten that you're in Saints territory."

Bowie, who is nearly as tall as Theo and has a large burn scar on his neck, sneers. "It wasn't one of my guys who crossed the line first. It was yours." He juts his chin out to Nico, who has scrambled to his feet and backed away, fear filling his disfigured face.

"Simply entering another's territory isn't grounds to attack at my bar," Theo says. He's not growling or yelling, but his voice still sounds deadlier than I've ever heard it.

Bowie gives a fake laugh. "Oh, that's not all the little shit did."

I can tell Theo doesn't know what Nico did, but he doesn't give that away. He says, "Careful what you start in my territory."

Bowie looks over Theo's shoulder at Nico, saying, "Care to share your transgression with your fearless leader?"

Nico whimpers, and I suspect he's only on his feet because of James's hold on his arms. Behind them are several other Saints, Benny, Raphael, and Luna included, all poised for a fight. None of them spare me a look, instead keeping their attention on the intruders.

To Theo, Bowie says, "Your trust fund *pet* has been fucking my baby cousin. Found their messages on her phone earlier today."

Theo doesn't give away his surprise, but I can tell it's there in the way his fingers press into his palms harder. "Your *baby* cousin is twenty; perfectly capable of giving consent."

"She's been defiled by your dirty mutt!"

"And that's no reason to attack him outside of my fucking bar."

"You clearly need to keep your men on a tighter leash."

Theo rumbles, "I don't need you telling me how to lead my club."

"And what a club you lead. Letting a little pussy nearly tear it apart not once, not twice, but three times."

At the word 'three' Bowie points at Nico. I briefly wonder what all three instances he's referring to are. Amber must be one, but who was the other?

His words do their job, though. All the veins in Theo's body are on display, and his face turns red. "Watch it."

Bowie steps closer. "Why? Can't handle a little reminder of your failures? Don't want to remember the snake you welcomed into your bed?" He's offensively close to Theo now, and I know before he says them that his next words will push Theo over the edge. "Or are you too weak to hear someone remind you that it was your fuck ups that killed your beloved Scottie?"

In a blink, the entire bar is lost in a bloody battle between the Saints and the South Five. Theo punches Bowie so hard that I almost think his neck snaps. But he stays on his feet, blood streaming liberally from his nose, and wastes no time returning the attack. Theo blocks his punch and catches him in the middle, slamming him to the floor.

The rest of the Saints are fighting too. James has two opponents who appear to be twins. Luna is punching a skinny boy over and over. Raphael is pinned by a giant muscle of a man.

I run forward and tackle the man on Raphael. He huffs while we roll. When we come to a stop, his eyes widen when he sees a girl straddling him. Before he can push me off, I slam the palm of my hand into his nose, feeling a satisfying break.

I nod at Raphael, who mutters, "Thanks," and takes over the fight. I look around, but most Saints are faring well in their personal fights, so I head to aid James. He's exhausted and bleeding, probably having already been in a fight before Theo and I arrived.

I jump and catch one of the twins around the waist with my legs. My momentum takes us both to the ground, and I carefully spin so the guy takes the impact. I attempt to pin him, but he's faster than the other guy and throws me off. I hit the floor with a huff and don't get in a breath before the guy is on me, throwing punch after punch. He catches me twice in the face before I manage to get my arms up to block him.

"June!" James yells. He has the other twin cornered at the bar. He doesn't pause in his fighting, just tosses me a glass from off the bar. I catch it and bring it down on the back of the guy's head with as much strength as I can. He gives a sharp cry and falls off me.

Leaping to my feet, I kick him a few times, then am grabbed roughly from behind. A large, sweaty arm is around my throat, and a fist lands in my side, knocking the breath from my lungs. The arm tightens, so I can't replace the air. Stars spark in my vision. I try stomping on his feet or elbowing him in the groin, but the guy dodges every move.

Just as I'm about to lose consciousness, he lets go. I lean forward, sucking in a quick breath before spinning around. There's Luna, smiling wide at me. "Hey, killer!" she says, sounding gleeful at the bloodbath.

"Thanks," I rasp.

"No problem."

Movement behind her snags my attention. My already-spiked adrenaline goes through the roof.

A man is raising a gun. I follow the direction he's aiming and see Theo still pummeling Bowie.

"THEO!" I scream. Nearly everyone in the room freezes. Theo launches away from Bowie, whipping around. Panic fills his eyes as he searches for me.

But I'm already moving, running for the shooter with

my knife pulled free. The rest of the room doesn't exist in this moment. There are no eyes on me. There's no other danger in the vicinity but the man and his deadly weapon pointed straight at Theo. Logic is dormant in my mind, fully taken over by years of instinct.

I reach the man and manage to shove his arm up half a second before he pulls the trigger. The bullet soars over everyone's heads. There's not a moment's pause or hesitation before I impale the knife in his throat. He screams, arms wildly flying up to attempt stopping me. But my body is moving faster than even my mind can keep up with. I drag the knife with me, pulling it through his throat. I feel it catch on bone and adjust my hold accordingly so the knife has no obstruction from one side to the other.

One second. That's how long it takes for me to turn from an innocent girl Theo introduced to his confused club into a vicious killer grinning at the intoxicating feeling of hot blood spurting all over my face. The liquid *finally* smothers the fire in my chest, and I feel alive again.

The man hits the floor. I stop moving, chest heaving with a deep, cleansing breath. There's gurgling as blood spills from his mouth. Then he goes still and silent.

And reality sets in.

I haven't killed in front of anyone in twelve years.

I don't do witnesses.

And now I have over two dozen.

I look to the rest of the room, unable to focus on the many shocked faces, wide eyes, and slack jaws facing me. All I see is Theo.

He looks pissed. His lips are pressed together, and he stares me down with hard eyes.

Then he turns to Bowie and orders, "Get the fuck out of my bar if you don't want to be next."

The man scrambles to his feet, spitting blood on the floor. "This isn't over, Zervas."

"Out."

The Five leave, each one bruised and bloody in some way. Then it's only me and the Saints, all of whom are still looking at me with shock.

"You too. All of you." He finds Nico in the crowd and says, "I'll deal with you later." The boy drops his eyes, then Theo addresses the rest of the Saints. "Whoever isn't out of this bar in the next five seconds will have a bullet in their forehead."

I feel nailed to the floor, unable to look away from a very on edge Theo as everyone moves, racing for the door. Luna brushes past me, whispering, "Happy humping, killer."

The door shuts behind her, and I straighten, preparing for a verbal lashing.

Instead, Theo says in a reverent tone, "You are the most stunning reaper I have ever seen." He closes the space between us and slams his mouth to mine. I gasp into his mouth, arms circling his neck. The bloody knife clatters to the floor.

Theo kisses me hard. He pauses to suck in a breath and say, "I'm going to fuck you so hard that you'll see the hell you send your victims to."

NINETEEN

Theo

I'm in a free fall into oblivion. Aches scatter my body from the few hits Bowie managed to land. My heart pumps on overdrive. Roaring lingers in my ears from the moment of blinding fear when I heard her scream.

None of it registers compared to the all-consuming desire burning in my veins.

She moves like an angel. She kills like a demon. I can't decide if she's of God or the devil, but either way, I'm ready to worship at her bloody altar.

Her back arches into my kiss, and her fingers snake into my hair, leaving a sticky trail of blood in their wake. When I pick her up, her legs naturally go around my waist so she's hanging on me like a monkey. Her mouth is hot against mine, and I can already imagine how amazing her cunt will feel around my cock.

I moan into her mouth, moving us toward the closest booth to set her on the edge of the table. The body of the South Five member is still close behind us, but that does nothing to slow me down. If anything, the memory of how easily she killed him, how ruthless she was when saving my life, only makes me more desperate to be inside her.

We come up for air, and she takes the opportunity to pant out a question. "You're not mad?"

I blink. "Why would I be mad at you for saving my life?"

"I killed someone in your bar."

"He's not the first person to die here, and he won't be the last."

"Your entire club knows I'm a killer now."

I'd really love for the questions to stop so I can put my mouth to better use.

"The Saints know you'll murder to keep their president safe. They probably like you more now."

Her frown is filled with uncertainty and a hint of fear. The sight is a clamp around my heart. I wonder what she's been through to make her so distrustful and afraid of allowing anyone to truly see her in all her reaper glory.

I gently brush my hand over her forehead, pushing hair away from her eyes. The cuts and bruises littering her skin make me want to rip out every South Fiver's throat. But her eyes are bright blue again, free of the flames that have been growing more noticeable every day.

"Little reaper, you are powerful, deadly, and beautiful. There is nothing wrong with you. In fact," I reach back and pull her hands away from my neck, positioning them between us. There's still blood staining the skin, though they're not as wet as they were before she started running them through my hair. "The more I see of you, the more unworthy I feel to be at the end of your blade, much less between your legs." I lean forward and stop an inch from her mouth while pressing a hand over her pants against her heat. She pushes into my touch, and I bite her bottom lip. "But nothing short of the reaper herself will keep me from fucking you now."

Our lips meet again in a greedy kiss. I quickly unbuckle and unzip her pants, pulling them off with her help. Her panties go next, and when she reaches for my own pants, I stop her with a hand around her wrist. She lets out a whine of disappointment. I smirk, lift a brow, then lower to my knees in front of her.

The sight of her has the potential to turn me into a drooling mess. She spreads her legs further, and I groan, palming my painfully hard cock.

Unable to wait another second, I dive forward, dragging my tongue up her center. Her blood-covered hands return to my hair, nails digging into my scalp. She tastes better than anything I've had in my mouth before, and I would happily spend eternity on my knees before her. Closing my eyes, I devour her. She starts rocking into my face, and I smile, pulling her clit between my teeth. Her moans and pants grow more desperate when I add fingers, pushing two in at once, then twisting them to press against her inner walls. It doesn't take long before she comes undone. She rides her climax out on my face, and when she starts to come down, I pull away and stand up.

She's going boneless, so I make quick work of unbuttoning my own pants and pushing down my boxers. I pull out my rock hard cock and drag her forward to the very edge of the table with a hand on her lower back. Her eyes open and look down. She whispers "Oh," and sucks her bottom lip between her teeth when she gets her first look at me and the Prince Albert piercing. I almost come right there just at the sight of her bloody, sweaty, satisfied face.

I barely have the presence of mind to ask, "Are you on the pill?" She nods. "Clean?" Another nod. "Good." Then I drag the pierced tip up her soaking center and don't wait for any other confirmation before slowly pushing inside.

If I thought tasting her was heavenly, then this deserves a completely new word. I've never felt anything as good, including riding my bike at top speed. It's slow at first as we both get used to each other, her to my size and me to her sheer tightness. But once I'm fully inside her, it's all over. I pull out then slam back in, earning a delighted shriek from her swollen lips.

Her nails dig into my back as she holds on while I start pounding into her. When her head falls back, I descend, teeth sinking into the skin between her neck and shoulder. We move together faster and harder, panting and moaning, sweat and spit and blood passing between us.

"Yes, Theo!"

"That's my good reaper," I growl. I pull back her shirt and bite down on the top of her breast hard enough to leave a bruise. Then I press a kiss to the red mark from my teeth. "Let me hear you."

"FUCK!"

She lifts her head to meet me in another open mouth kiss. Our thrusting becomes more frantic and erratic, and I know she's close. I grip her ass, pulling her hips forward for better leverage. The slight change has me hitting that spot that makes her nails dig so hard that I feel skin break. I manage to get one of my hands between us and rub my thumb over the top of her pussy. At the same time, I move my mouth to her other tit, biting lower this time. The combination of sensations pushes her to climax. She screams my name as she comes, clamping down on me and dragging me over the edge with her. The orgasm rips through my body harder than it has in years.

Spent, she falls back onto the grimy table. I follow, lying half on top of her and barely managing to stay on my feet. For several long moments, the only sounds are our heavy breathing. Her hands fall to her side, leaving a cold loss behind.

Each second we lay there, pieces of reality return like an image slowly coming into focus. Pain pulses around my rib cage and flares from my jaw, eyes, knuckles, and back. I'm not even sure what injuries I've sustained in the last half hour.

Then I think of Bowie and the South Five. The Saints aren't a gang, but we have our territory, and stepping out of line strains the tenuous peace we have with actual gangs like Bowie's crew. After today's events, we've likely started a war with them. However I look at it, the Saints will be at fault for starting it. The Five will claim that Nico sleeping with Leticia, Bowie's cousin, was the initial offense, and their following pummeling of Nico was justified.

Or, if not, it'll be when I punched Bowie for mentioning Scottie.

The final nail in the coffin was June killing that grunt. Not that I'll ever regret that moment. I'd happily watch it happen again and again. Still, the Five won't forgive and forget. We drew first blood.

So, now I have that to worry about on top of dealing with Lorry's investigation into June.

Plus, there's the looming reality that my deal with June is nearly halfway through. We have two and a half more weeks before she'll decide what to do next. Risk it all by killing me or letting me go and moving on with her life.

Either way, I'll lose her. My chest seems to tighten at the thought.

"My feet are falling asleep," June mutters.

"Right." I push back to a standing position, the movement causing my dick, which is still buried inside her, to shift. With a moan, I look down at where we're joined, the sight sending fresh blood south. But I want the next time I fuck her to be in a bed. Or at least somewhere slightly more comfortable.

I pull out, watching with fresh hunger as both my cum and hers drip out. Once free, I retrieve her underwear and pants from the floor, handing them to her without getting a rag for her to clean herself with. Let her feel my cum leaking out of her on the ride home.

"Give me ten minutes, then we can go." Before walking away, I place both hands on her knees, push them up her legs and inside her thighs. With a thumb on either side of her cunt, I say, "Don't think I'm done with you yet. By the end of the night, you won't remember anything but the way your body weeps for me."

I turn to face the corpse in the center of the room. Blood is no longer flowing, but the puddle spans several feet. The cut is so clean and deep that it takes my breath away. I knew she was a reaper, but seeing how deadly she truly is up close is a different thing entirely.

Fishing out my phone, I call Ace, who owns a specialized cleaning company. They're my regular custodians who help clean up similar messes from Saints. After they approve a dispatch team, who should arrive within three hours, I call Axel and Bella to come back and wait for the custodians while clearing the other carnage in the bar.

With that settled, I turn back to June. "Ready?"

She nods, lips curled into a grin. I'm not sure if it's because of the sex or the kill, but I'm willing to give her as much of both if I get to see that smile more often.

I match it with a more devious one of my own. "Then let's get out of here, little reaper."

TWENTY

June

The combination of a fresh kill and mind-blowing sex creates a euphoric high I'd give anything to ride forever. Leaning against Theo's back on the ride to his house, I replay the last hour, skipping over fear and uncertainty to focus on the parts that make me momentarily forget who I am. The kill was faster than normal, but it did the job, and now I'll have at least a few weeks with smoldering coals in my gut rather than molten-hot flames.

And Theo. It's apparent now why someone would stay with him even if he's an asshole. I'm already aching for that second round he promised.

Once back at the house, I look down at myself and the blood that's soaked my shirt and stained my hands. I've never left a kill site with so much evidence on me before. Much less left the body behind in a building with cameras.

"The security cameras," I say, turning to Theo.

"I'll deal with them."

"I want to destroy them."

He levels his gaze on me. "I said I'll take care of it."

"Or you'll save them for more blackmail on me. I'll destroy them."

An eyebrow cocks and he saunters closer. My mind says to back up because his closeness seems to fuck with my logic, but my feet stay planted. "I have plenty of blackmail. I don't need this. Besides, we were in *my* bar surrounded by *my* people and the tape will show everything that happened after you went all reaper on that jackass. Trust me, I will take care of the tapes."

I frown. "Why would I trust you?"

He grabs the back of my neck, applying enough pressure to force me to look up at him. "Because I'd have to gouge the eyeballs out of anyone who dared to watch me fucking you on that table."

My lips part, and my pussy clenches. "Not a fan of voyeurism?"

"Watching, sure. But no one else will see you like that."

"What if I want them to?" I ask, not bothering to hide the challenge in my tone.

He squeezes harder and pulls me up to my toes. "I don't really give a shit what you want." His mouth crashes to mine then, tongue instantly exploring my mouth. I bite down on his bottom lip hard enough for him to hiss. The kiss breaks, and he growls. "Didn't I warn you what would happen if you kept provoking me?"

"Didn't I tell you to stop ordering me around?"

"I have seventeen more days, little reaper. I'll do whatever the fuck I want with you in that time." Then he effortlessly scoops me up and throws me over his shoulder, carrying me to his room.

"Theo! Put me down!"

Of course, he ignores me. It's not until he's gotten something out of his bedside table that he throws me on the bed. I start to scramble away, but he's on me quickly, legs pinning me down. My attempts at bucking him off do nothing to deter him from his mission. He pulls my hands over my head, holding them together. I strain my neck back and watch upside down as he ties my wrists together with something soft. He adjusts his legs so his feet help keep me still while he reaches for a restraint tied to his bedpost. It doesn't take him long to connect the silk ropes around my hands to the restraint, then he climbs off me and repeats the process with both legs so they're spread wide.

"Untie me right now or I swear to God I'll slit your throat in your sleep," I threaten.

In response, he cranks the ratchets, adjusting the tightness of the ropes so there's no slack. I yank at them, trying to bend my knees or pull down the headboard, but all that accomplishes is causing the ropes to dig into my skin.

Theo stands next to the bed and surveys his work with a sinful smile. "Threatening me with violence isn't the deterrent you think it is, reaper." He turns to walk out of his room.

I'm momentarily stunned. Is he planning to leave me like this?

I almost scream for him to get back here and let me go but decide to use the time to try and undo the restraints. Craning my neck, I study the knots he used around my wrist, hoping to find a weak spot. But Theo knows his knots, and there's no way I'm getting that undone from this position.

"You don't move until I decide to let you."

Theo is back, leaning in his bedroom doorway and twirling a pair of scissors on his fingers.

"And James isn't home, so screaming won't do you any good either."

Vexed, my joints stiffen. "Theo. Let me go."

He shakes his head. "Not until you've learned the consequences of provoking me."

"What? You going to spank me?"

"I don't think that would be much of a lesson for you, would it?" He walks forward, spinning the scissors once more. He snips the air once, as if to scare me, and I hate how a thrill crawls up my legs. "Lay still." He rests a knee on the bed for balance, then grabs the hem of my shirt, placing it between the blades.

"Don't you fucking dare."

He snips, cutting a long slit into the shirt, and sets them down on my stomach. The cool metal causes goosebumps to form, which spread to my toes when he grips either side of the slit and yanks, ripping the shirt down the center.

"Theo!"

He spreads his warm hands along my shoulders, pushing the shirt back. "Gotta burn it, little reaper. It's covered in evidence of your extracurricular activities."

I press my lips together because he's not wrong. There's no fully getting blood out of clothing. Still, that doesn't mean I'm okay with him literally ripping my clothes off my body.

Which he continues to do with my pants, underwear, bra, and socks until I'm lying, tied to his bed, completely naked. With my legs forcibly spread like this, I feel more vulnerable and on display than ever. Theo is standing at the foot of his bed, fully clothed and looking me over like a slab of meat he's considering taking home to roast.

"Stunning," he whispers, almost to himself. A traitorous blush rises to my cheeks. "But I'm the only one who gets to watch."

My lips turn down in confusion because there's no one else here. Then he pulls a black silk eye mask from his back pocket and moves to the head of the bed.

"Don't." I attempt to dodge his hands, but I'm helpless in this position, and he tightens the mask around my eyes.

"Open your mouth," he orders.

I clamp it shut.

"Such a bratty little thing." Fingers squeeze my jaw, forcing it apart. As soon as my mouth is open enough, Theo stuffs fabric inside. "Use this as a reminder that you want me just as much as I want you." He wraps another silk tie around my mouth so I can't spit out whatever fabric gag this is.

As I process his words, a taste registers on my tongue, and I realize exactly what I have lodged between my lips.

My underwear. The same pair he just cut off my body that's soaked in both of our cum. I gag at the same time that I feel more desire pool between my legs.

"How do we taste, little reaper?" He adds, almost as an afterthought, "Three quick tugs on the restraints if you want this to stop."

Right, I can't speak to call out a safeword if needed. The thought ramps up my anticipation.

Suddenly, cold metal presses against my shin. He drags what I assume are the scissors up my leg, lingers on the inside of my thighs, then up my waist. He circles my nipples with the blade, moving it so the sharp tip digs into the flesh of my tits. But he never breaks skin.

Once he has the scissors against my throat, he leaves it there, and his next words are hot against my ear like he's inches away.

"This is my new favorite knife. Watching you drag it through that throat like it was butter was the sexiest thing I've ever seen."

Knife. Not scissors. Theo is dragging the knife I just killed someone with across my body.

I pull against the restraints, though only once. He laughs and kisses my cheek. His heat suddenly disappears, as does the knife against my throat. Then, just as quickly, teeth land on my inner thigh, and sharp pain explodes when Theo bites hard. He sucks the skin of my thigh into his mouth, working it between his teeth until I'm pulling so hard on the restraints that the circulation is starting to cut off to my feet. Then he pulls back and pushes a finger into my waiting pussy.

"I knew you'd like this," he says upon finding how wet I am. He removes his finger, and I whine at the loss. When I'm penetrated next, it's by something bigger and harder than his finger. I don't think too hard about what it is, focusing only on the building need in my core. I push down on the object as best I can, and Theo flattens a hand on my hip to keep me still. "Your cunt swallows the handle so perfectly."

Handle?

He pulls the object out, then thrusts it back in, faster this time. He continues, speeding up with each thrust. "Come on, little reaper. Let me see you come all over your knife."

I moan and press my head into the mattress as I fight the restraints to try and ride the handle of my favorite knife. He moves the hand on my hip down so he can rub my clit. Then his teeth fasten to my other leg. He lets go and moves his lips further in, kissing the space between my thigh and groin. At the same time, he pinches my clit and thrusts the knife as deep as possible.

I scream. The panties muffle the sound as I climax, squirting all over my knife and Theo's hand. He pulls the handle free, and I go limp on the bed, muscles depleted from my third orgasm of the evening.

"Don't get too comfortable, little reaper," he says, the gloating audible in his voice. "We're just getting started."

~

If you can die by having too many orgasms, then Theo is trying to murder me. After the knife, he gets me off with his tongue without even touching me with his hands. Then he fucks me, making me come twice before he shoots his load. While it's dripping out of me, he walks away, leaving me lying there, tied up, blindfolded, gagged, and exhausted, for almost half an hour while he gets a snack and talks to James.

He returns whistling, announces he's refueled, and wastes no time returning to his task of coaxing out as many orgasms as he can. I pass out after the eighth.

I wake up on my side, a heavy sort of satisfaction draped over my muscles. I blink, and it's a few seconds before I realize the blindfold has been removed, along with the underwear gag. I groan, rubbing my eyes as I roll onto my back.

"There you are, little reaper." The bed moves as if someone next to me has climbed off. I take a few long, aching breaths, then the bed dips again. I sigh when Theo's oil and coffee smell reaches me. "I need you to open your eyes for me. Take these." His hand brushes over my face with the gentlest touch, then lingers on the back of my neck, supporting me as I gather the energy to follow his command.

My eyes finally open to find him sitting on the edge of the bed in front of me. He's holding out two little pills, which he drops into my hands when I open a palm. He gives me a glass of water next, and I swallow the pills before chugging all the water.

Theo smiles. "Good girl."

Something curls in my chest at the two words. "What time is it?" I ask. My voice is hoarse from the moans, cries, and screams he coaxed out of me.

"Three in the morning." He tucks a stray piece of hair behind my ear. "I iced your wrists and ankles for a bit after you passed out. I'd offer a massage and heating pad now, but you really need more sleep. So we can do that later."

I frown. A grogginess in my mind contorts his words, making it much harder to interpret them and come up with a response. He must realize this because he moves to my side and pulls me into him, strong, tattooed arms holding me close. "Go back to sleep, little reaper."

So I do.

I'm still wrapped in his embrace when I wake up next.

"Good morning."

His voice is so tender that my cheeks warm.

"How are you feeling?" he asks.

"Mmm," I roll out of his hold and stretch, muscles burning in the best way. "What time is it?"

"Seven. Do you have an appointment this morning?"

I groan. "At nine. I should leave for the office soon." I don't want to. I'd rather lie in this bed that has no right being as comfortable as it is. But I can't cancel on clients who need me just because I'm tired from a night of countless orgasms after I finally soothed the fire under my skin by slitting a man's throat.

"I'll take you." Theo leans forward and presses our lips together, his fingers moving to the back of my neck and threading through my hair. My body twists closer to him, and my mouth opens, inviting him into a deeper kiss. He obliges, and soon my pussy is aching for him again. Instead of giving me what my body craves, Theo pulls back. "You need to shower. You're covered in blood, sweat, and cum."

Fuck, I forgot that I never showered after the events of last night. I also didn't use the restroom after sex. I better not get a fucking UTI.

Grudgingly, I sit up and climb off his bed. My muscles are tight and sore, particularly between my legs. I look around for my clothes, then remember he cut them off.

"Use my shower. James is still here."

"I need my stuff."

He stands, stretching his arms over his head. My eyes fall to his bare chest. I was blindfolded for most of the night and never got a good look at him. A bruise covers his right side, and his arms and chest are nearly covered in tattoos.

"I'll get it," he says, snapping my eyes back to his face. He smirks, having caught me checking him out. "Go get in the shower. I'll bring everything to you."

I nod and head to the bathroom. It's bigger than I expected, with two sinks and a separate shower and bathtub. It's also clean, only half the counter filled with toiletries organized by size. I turn on the shower and look in the mirror, gasping at the sight. A bruise covers my cheekbone, and it won't be long before it's a black eye. There's a cut in the middle of my right brow and my bottom lip, which is red and inflamed from kissing. More injuries decorate my body, both from Theo and the fights. My wrists and ankles are red, though not as bad as I would've expected, thanks to Theo's soft, silky restraints. There are, however, marks from his teeth on my tits and my inner thighs and a hickey on my neck. Plus the bruises from him choking me still circle my throat.

I'll have to apply liberal amounts of makeup so my clients don't think I got attacked by a super horny mugger.

The shower is filled with steam when I step inside. Hot water pelts my back, and I sigh in relief. Soon, the bathroom door opens, and Theo walks in, his arms filled with bottles. My first instinct as he walks to the shower is to tell him to leave everything on the counter and get out, but there's no reason. He's seen every inch of my body now and been inside me more times than I remember.

"I wasn't sure what all you needed, so I just got everything."

"Thanks." I push open the shower door, plucking the bottles from his arm and setting them on the shower bench next to Theo's soaps. While my back is turned, I hear the shower door shut. A second later, thick arms wrap around me and pull me back against his chest.

"I have to shower," I say.

"I'm not stopping you."

"You have to let me go."

Theo nuzzles his head into my neck, softly kissing my skin. Unease furls in my gut. I could justify last night as a heated night of passion driven by high adrenaline and a murder-fueled haze. It was frantic and dirty and primitive. I wasn't thinking.

But now, in the light of morning with a clearer mind, guilt and logic can no longer be ignored. Showering with him, allowing him to gently kiss me, is a whole different level of intimacy.

"Theo, I'm serious, I don't have time for this. I need to get ready."

He lets me go but doesn't leave. Instead, he examines the bottles and picks up the shampoo. I turn, watching as he uncaps it and says, "Let me help you."

I stop him, taking the shampoo. "I can clean myself."

"I know, but it'll be so much more fun if I do it."

I dodge his attempt to grab me. "I don't want you to. Now get out so I can clean all this shit off."

He frowns, noticing my scowl. Finally, he turns and exits the shower without another word. A moment later, the bathroom door shuts.

Despite the hot water raining down, I suddenly feel cold.

TWENTY-ONE

Theo

"Kip guarantees three hours, but we should try to be out in two just in case," James says from the Jeep's driver's seat. I left June on the couch, where she fell asleep soon after we got back from her office. Luna will likely get there before she wakes up. Before we left, I stared at her, considering once again waiting until tomorrow to break into Lorry's house while June is at her Taco Tuesday. But the plans for Kip to get Lorry and his wife out of the house tonight were already set, so I reluctantly left June and haven't stopped thinking about it since.

"Sounds good." I open the camera app on my phone to see that June hasn't woken up yet.

"You did a number on her, didn't you?"

I realize James has clocked me spying and lock my phone. My neck tenses in response, and I think of what I did to her. And, more specifically, what she did to me.

"Daryus asked a lot of questions about her last night," James says. "So did some of the other guys. Seemed to think not just any girl could kill someone like that, even with their fight or flight on full blast."

"I don't really care what they think."

"You should. They're your club. You really want them asking questions about your girl's past?"

"She's a badass fighter, that's all they need to know."

"They don't know her. Right now, they see a random girl who showed up two weeks ago and managed to gain their president's trust enough to go to church and live in your house even after everything. Then she brings down a turf war on us by murdering a South Fiver in front of everyone."

"To save my life," I bite, forearms tightening as I curl my hands into fists.

"I get that, and most of the boys do too. Raph was going on and on about how amazing she is. Bonnie and Clyde are ready to adopt her. Nico was singing her praises. And you know Luna is her biggest fan. But still, you can't ignore the fact that this changes things."

"So, things will change."

"T…"

"I get it, James," I interrupt. "I do. But I don't care. I can't… I won't…" *lose her.* The words refuse to form.

James reaches over and squeezes my arm. "I know." He moves his hand back to the steering wheel and faces forward, letting the conversation end there.

For the rest of the drive, I think about what to tell the club, how to deal with the South Five, and what to do about Lorry. I check the cameras in my house one more time before we get to Lorry's and see June has woken up and is now eating pizza in the kitchen with Luna.

"Ready for this?" James asks, parking a block away.

I nod. Lorry and Bethany are already with Kip, so the house is empty. I pass James the jamming device from the glove compartment and keep the LED laser for myself. He turns on the device when Lorry's house is in view, hopefully drowning out the security system's Wi-Fi signals to disconnect it from the network. In case that's not enough, I shoot the lasers into the lens of each camera we pass to blind it and keep it from filming us. Lorry shouldn't have any reason to check his security tapes, but if he does, I want it to look more like a mistake with the system than someone intentionally tampering with the cameras.

I pick the front door lock, and we carefully follow Kip's directions to the office in the back of the house on the first floor. That lock is slightly more difficult to pick, but once we're in, I find the camera and blind it while James drapes a black rag over it. We'll be in this room too long to risk the cameras coming back on and catching us.

"Alright, where's the safe?"

I head to the closet, push open the door, and reveal a shining black safe about five feet tall. "Have at it," I say, waving James in. I'm better at picking locks, but James has a way with safes. He'll be much faster than me, and we only have two hours.

So, I spend the next hour and a half standing in the office, keeping watch while James works on the safe. I check my house cameras a handful of times and find June in the living room with Luna. Finally, James shouts in celebration. I turn to see him pulling the safe door open.

"I deserve an award!"

"I'll plan a ceremony," I say, crossing the room to help him dig through the safe. The second file I flip open has a picture of June at the front. It's thinner than I expected and takes less than five minutes to make copies of everything.

"Dude, he has files on all the Saints, too," James says.

"Really?"

"Yeah, here." He walks over to the copier holding a stack of other files, many of which are much thicker than June's. "We have time, let's copy these too."

So we do. We've already returned everything to the safe and made it out when Kip texts us that Lorry is headed back. I flip through June's file on the drive home and pause on her personal history, which Lorry has dated back to her childhood. My research on her was much less extensive.

According to Lorry's investigation, June's mom, Heidi, went to prison when she was five, and she lived with her dad for a few years until CPS removed her after one too many ER trips. I'd bet anything several of the old scars I saw in hidden places on her body were from that time in her life.

She was in foster care from age seven to thirteen. Her foster parents tried to adopt her, but Heidi was released from prison, got a job and an apartment, and ended up getting June back. Heidi remarried a respectable man, Calvin, who legally adopted June after the wedding. He already had a daughter, Imogen, from his first marriage. June's dad showed up less than a year after Calvin and Heidi got married, probably wanting some of Calvin's money, and when June was fifteen, the man mysteriously died in what the cops assumed was a drug deal gone wrong. Lorry thinks he was June's first kill. I, unfortunately, agree with the assumption. I almost wish she hadn't killed him so I could do it for her, but I'm also glad she had the satisfaction of ending the miserable man's life.

Imogen had a baby when she was seventeen and moved to San Antonio after high school. June, meanwhile, went to college at The University of Texas, graduated at twenty-one, turned twenty-two in July, and moved here the same month. That August, she started school at the University of Arizona and graduated with her master's in counseling in two years.

Lorry had compiled a list of every possible disappearance or death he thinks could be linked to June. From a quick glance, I could eliminate over half of them. June wouldn't kill a guy for having gambling debts or abandoning his family.

Which means if she did kill Lorry's cousin, the man deserved it.

"Anything good?"

"He's zeroed in on June, that's for sure," I say. "I'll study it more later." We're almost home, and I haven't checked the cameras in a while, but the last time I did, they were drinking and playing some sort of board game.

I don't expect to walk inside my house and find Luna completely nude and June wearing only a small pair of underwear, showing off all the marks I left on her skin. She shrieks at our entrance and struggles to cover herself, even though I've seen it all before, including Luna. She may be gay, but we have very similar tastes in women and have noticed that women who like one of us often like the other too, so Luna and I have shared more than once.

Which is why when she drunkenly suggests we share June, I'm not completely surprised.

Watching June get off with Luna between her legs, drinking like her arousal is nectar from heaven, makes my cock twitch in interest. It hardens at the thought of June exploring another woman's body with her tongue. Imagining all the other ways Luna and I could use June and make her see stars has my entire body burning with need.

But all those images also twist the veins in my chest and compress my throat. It's almost painful to think about anyone other than me being inside her, making her come. Hearing anyone else's name on June's lips, even Luna's, might shatter me.

The fucked up, masochistic part of my brain wants to try it, to see how much I can handle or when I'll start daydreaming of ripping Luna apart.

Tonight is not the night to figure that out, though. June is in no shape to be consenting to anything, much less a threesome. She's barely keeping her eyes open.

So, I tell Luna later. That we can do it once. Because more than that would be dangerous for everyone involved.

"You've never been so stingy and jealous before," Luna whines. Next to her, June falls against the edge of the couch, her eyes shut.

"You've never seen him falling in love before," James says.

For the first time since entering the house, I pull my eyes from the naked serial killer in my living room to glare at my best friend. "I'm not in love."

"Maybe not, but you're on your way. I mean, look how possessive you are with her."

"He may be right, boss. You've got the evil twinkle eyes," Luna says.

"You're drunk," I say. "Go to sleep."

"I'm not drunk, I'm just happy and very good at Battleship."

"Either way, you're sleeping here tonight. You can take June's bed," I say, crossing the room to scoop a passed-out June into my arms.

"Ooh, yay!" Luna says, jumping to her feet. She instantly sways and falls onto the couch.

"By yourself. June will be in my room."

"Booo!" Luna calls after me.

I ignore her and take my little reaper to bed, where I tuck her into the freshly cleaned sheets. I set a glass of water and a few painkillers on the bedside table and a trash can on the floor, just in case. After brushing my teeth, I pull off my clothes and crawl in next to her. As soon as I'm settled, June mumbles something unintelligible under her breath, then turns over, curling into my side.

James's words come back to my mind as I run my fingers through her hair and kiss her forehead.

Fuck.

TWENTY-TWO

June

Work is excruciatingly long. Several times, I have to drag my mind from memories of last night or thoughts about Theo and force it to focus on my client. By the end of the day, I'm so exhausted that I pass out on Theo's couch as soon as we're back.

The smell of pizza drags me from a blissful dream of riding Theo in the middle of a puddle of warm blood. I crack my eyes open and see the TV is on, the volume low enough not to disrupt my nap.

I sit up, rubbing sleep from the corners of my eyes. Luna is in the kitchen, facing away from me, her hips swaying as she hums something under her breath. She's wearing jean shorts that barely hang lower than her underwear and a loose-fitted mesh top over a blue bra. A spiderweb tattoo on the back of her neck disappears into dark hair cut close to the scalp.

My bare feet are nearly silent as I walk to her. "Whatcha doin'?"

Luna squeals, jumps, and spins around. "Damn, killer!" She presses her hand to her chest. "Don't sneak up on people like that."

"I wasn't sneaking."

"Then you just naturally move like a fucking shark."

I grin at her exaggerated reaction. "A shark?"

"They're really quiet predators," she says, shrugging. Without warning, she pulls me into a hug, squeezing hard.

"What's going on?" I ask with a laugh.

"What? I can't hug my friend?"

I didn't know we were friends, I think. "We saw each other yesterday."

She lets go. "Yeah, during a brutal bar fight in which you were almost strangled to death before you nearly decapitated a man to save Theo's life."

"I didn't nearly decapitate him."

Luna moves a pizza box from the counter behind her to the island next to me, flipping it open to show a pepperoni and olive pizza. "Close enough. It was hot too, the way you just slit his neck without pause. Everyone was talking about it all evening."

I wince. I haven't had much time to consider what the Saints are saying about my display. "Talking about how insane their leader's new girl is?"

"More like how badass you are. I think Raph would propose if you weren't dating the boss. They're all expecting him to officially name you his *Ol' Lady* soon." She picks up a piece of pizza, using her finger to break long strings of melty cheese.

"No one is… I don't know, disgusted? Or thinks I'm a deranged psychopath?"

Luna shakes her head, keeping the end of the pizza steady with her other hand to blow on it. "I think a few might be scared of you now, but that's not a bad thing in this world."

I shift my weight back and chew on the inside of my

cheek. Another girl's voice from over a decade ago echoes in my ears.

"What did you do? Oh, my god, Juniper. You're a psychopath!"

All I can think to say is, "Oh."

"Grab a piece. You like olives, don't you?"

"How do you know that?"

"T told me."

With a frown, I grab a slice of the pizza. I've never eaten olives with Theo or told him I liked them, so how does he know?

"What are you doing here?" I ask.

"Thought we could have a movie night."

"Why?"

"Because I'm bored," she says, dropping her eyes to the pizza. I can tell there's more.

"And?"

She meets my eyes and tries to shake her head, but I raise my eyebrows, and she groans. "I've decided I don't like serial killers. You're too perceptive."

That makes me laugh. "So? Why are you here?"

"Theo asked me to come. He had to go out for the night with James and wanted me to keep an eye on you."

"Seriously? He still thinks I'm going to… run away or set up a bomb in his bedroom or something? Even after—" I snap my mouth shut, cutting off the sentence.

"After what?" Luna asks, wagging her eyebrows suggestively. "After whatever followed Theo threatening to murder us if we didn't leave? After he left those marks on your neck and wrists?"

I look down at my hands, forgetting that I pulled off the sweater I wore during work as soon as we got back. A blush heats my cheeks, and I take a bite of the pizza.

"By how deep you were sleeping when I got here, I'd say you had a good time."

"Why is he making you babysit me?"

"I'm not babysitting you, I'm hanging out with you. T has club business, so he had to leave, but he didn't want you to be alone after everything. My guess is he's worried that the last twenty-four hours will catch up with you."

"I'm a grown-ass woman. I don't need you to hold my hand because I killed someone and had rough sex. Neither of those things is new to me."

"I know that. He knows that. But there's nothing wrong with a girls' night. And I really am bored." Luna finishes her pizza, then wipes her hands together, sending crumbs falling to the floor. "So, are you going to keep interrogating me about the motivations behind my friendship, or are we going to watch a movie and get drunk?" She presents a bottle of wine that must've been behind her.

I hesitate, wanting to push her more on where Theo is and why *exactly* he wants me babysat, because I don't believe it's out of some concern for my mental health.

"Come on, killer."

I roll my eyes. "Fine. But I get the last pizza slice."

She smiles wide. "All yours."

We end up watching old Jenna Marbles YouTube videos and playing Tipsy Battleship, which Luna digs out of a very messy closet. After my third loss, I hit the table and yell, "You are so cheating!"

She laughs, face rosy from the wine. "I am not!"

"You are!"

"How would I be cheating?"

"I don't know!" I realize my voice is much louder than normal, but the pleasant buzz prevents me from caring. I turn my empty cup upside down over my mouth, pouting when nothing miraculously falls out.

"I'll get more drinks." Luna jumps up, clearly not tipsy at all, and heads to the kitchen.

"But we're out of wine!" I call, twisting her Battleship board around to study it for signs of cheating.

"Have a little faith, killer!" She comes back with an expensive bottle of brandy. "I've known these men for three years. I know where they stash the good stuff."

"Nice!" I reach for the bottle, but she holds it out of reach.

"Let's make the game a little more interesting."

A frown of suspicion pulls on my lips. "Interesting how?"

"I'm thinking we raise the stakes. Each ship sunk, we drink. Or, even better, Strip Battleship!"

"Strip Battleship?"

"Yeah! An article of clothing for every ship."

I study her clothes, then my own. "We'll be naked after one game."

She winks. "Sounds like a good game to me."

I'm not about to fuck my way through the Saints, even if I do find Luna very attractive, so I counter with, "How about a mix of the two? We sink a ship, and the other gets to choose which we do: drink, strip, or answer a question."

"Answer a question?"

I nod, a plan piecing together in my sluggish brain. "We get to ask anything we want, and the other has to answer honestly."

Luna readily agrees.

"No doing the same thing twice in a row. If we strip once, the next round has to be a drink or a question," I add.

"Sounds good to me. Game on."

She pours brandy in both our cups, then settles on the couch across from me. "We're starting over. I know you looked at my board while I was gone."

I spend twice as long preparing my board as before. Once we're both ready, I cast my first shot. "B6."

"Miss. F5."

"Miss. J2." It takes four guesses before I get a hit and five more before I sink her ship. I impulsively want to ask a question, but her filter needs to be thinner. "Drink."

"Boring!" She obeys, downing half her glass. When she sinks my submarine, she predictably says, "Strip."

I'm still wearing both socks, but I pull off my shirt, watching Luna's eyes drop to the lace bra holding my hickey-covered chest. "D10."

Luna's eyes tear away and flick to her board. "Fuck, hit."

She sinks the next one and makes me drink. Then I sink her battleship and ask, "Why did you join the Saints, other than to rebel against daddy dearest?"

"Hmm." She taps her lips in thought. "I was always different from my family. Gay, not as well mannered, hated going to church, into tattoos and horror, I'm even smaller than most of them. I started riding motorcycles in high school to try and get the attention of this smoking hot chick on the soccer team. I fell in love with riding, but I never even considered joining a club until I met James. I was in town for my twin brothers' high school graduation, and I left the celebration early because the Mcintyres in a group setting are suffocating. I ran into James at a bar. He was… drowning his sorrows, so he was pretty drunk. But when a guy hit on me and called me a dyke when I turned him down, James still punched him in the face. In that one second, a stranger defended me more than my entire family had in over two decades. So, yeah, I guess I joined the Saints because I wanted a family I belonged to."

It's a much longer answer than I expected, which bodes

well for future questions. "I'm sorry you didn't have that with the Mcintyres," I say. "I get it, though. The desire for a real family that stands by your side."

"Yours wasn't like that?"

I wag my finger in the air. "Sink a ship to get an answer."

Luna rolls her eyes and takes her next shot. She drinks when I sink another of hers, then the following round, she throws the final shot to sink my carrier. "What was your family like?"

I huff at her look of satisfaction. "My mom is… a lot. She was in prison for a DWI until I was eleven. It was her third strike, and I was in the car, so she got eight years but got out in a little over six. She remarried when I was thirteen. My stepdad is a quiet, patient, wealthy man. He has a daughter a year older than me who lives in Texas with her son now. None of them are bad people, but I never belonged."

"And you're dad?"

"Dead."

"How?"

I cock an eyebrow and look pointedly at the boards, and she groans. She sinks the next ship and makes me strip again. This time, I pull off a single sock. To even things, I tell her to strip when I sink her fourth boat, leaving only one left for both of us. Several guesses later, she wins the game.

"I think that means I get one of all three. Strip, drink, and question."

"We did not decide that!" I argue.

"Then just two. Drink and answer."

"Ugh, fine." I finish my drink, building the courage to answer her question. Staring into my empty glass, I say, "He was murdered."

"By who?" The way she asks it tells me she knows the

answer. I start pulling the pins out of my boards to set up again while she says, "I know, I know. Gotta sink a ship. But I don't need to win to know your answer."

"You seem pretty confident."

She shrugs. "If I were a serial killer, I would've killed my dad too." And with that, we start our next game. We drink until we're both far past tipsy, strip until we're both in our underwear, and ask questions until I feel safe enough to get to the real answer I want.

"What happened to Amber Wallace?"

Luna squints at me, confused. "Seriously? Why do you care so much about that bitch?"

"That's not an answer."

"Amber was a threat to herself and the entire club. Theo took care of it. The rest of the story is his to tell."

That's still not an answer, but Luna won't give me anything else. And I know I shouldn't care, but I don't like the way my question made her face fall and annoyance fill her voice. I like Luna, and I want her to like me, too. "Okay. It's your turn."

She studies me for a moment before throwing the next guess. Three ships later, I'm answering her question, that no, I've never had a threesome, when the front door opens and Theo and James walk inside. They freeze upon seeing the two of us, me topless and Luna fully naked, in the middle of their living room.

"Hey, boys! Down for a game of Strip, Drink, or Truth Battleship?" Luna asks cheerfully. I lunge for the couch, which we moved off of an hour ago, and grab a blanket to cover myself with. Theo's heated gaze follows my movements.

"A game of what now?" James asks.

"Strip, Drink, or Truth Battleship!" Luna repeats. "So far, I've learned that June here likely killed her dad, refuses to answer who the craziest client she's ever had was, despite the rules of the game—"

"Because of HIPAA," I interrupt.

"—had the best sex of her life last night, and has never had a threesome. Also, she has absolutely magnificent tits."

"Luna!" I shout.

She giggles. "Sorry."

I drop my face in my hands. Tomorrow, I'll be mortified at everything Luna just revealed, but right now, I'm too drunk to really care.

"Well, okay, then," James says.

"They are pretty magnificent, aren't they?"

That comes from Theo, and his voice is husky, filled with desire. I expect him to get angry that I let Luna see me naked, but he doesn't.

"I think we should change those last two truths, don't you agree, T?" Luna asks.

I don't understand her question, but Theo seems to. "Careful, Lu. She's not a random hookup."

I look up, glancing between the two of them. Luna is grinning wickedly, facing Theo, whose dark eyes are still pinned on me. "I know. She deserves both of us to worship her, don't you think?"

"How much have you had to drink?"

I realize he's asking me that question, and I furrow my brows in thought. "Five... six glasses?"

Theo turns to Luna. "Not tonight." I follow his gaze in time to see Luna pout, still not bothering to cover herself up despite being completely naked. "But later, when she's sober and will feel everything, yes. Just once though, Lu. Then you don't get to look at her again."

Just once what? I think. That last glass seems to have doubled the effects of all the previous ones. My eyes shut. I bet I could fall asleep sitting up.

"Why once?" Luna asks. Her words are slurred. Or my ears are slurred. Can ears be slurred? "You've never been so stingy and jealous before."

I'm not sure who responds, because whatever is said next disappears as I drift off, falling asleep against the couch.

TWENTY-THREE

June

Bits of the night before stick to my memory, mostly playing Battleship with Luna, but I don't remember much after Theo got home. I think I was already nearly naked at that point, which means James probably saw me, too. I definitely don't remember coming to Theo's bed. Or what we did.

I sit up as Theo walks into his bedroom holding two mugs of steaming coffee. He kicks the door shut behind him and smiles when he sees me. He's wearing sweatpants and no shirt, so I get a good look at those lean muscles and colorful tattoos. There's a vibrant red and blue devil woman on his side that's cracked in half with a skeleton crawling out of the hole. On his forearm is a large scorpion curled around a bleeding moon. Over his heart is a bird soaring above a willow tree in a scene that seems to radiate an odd mix of tranquility and sadness.

He sets a mug down on the bedside table next to me. "How're you feeling?"

The pounding in my head is less intense than I expected. Still, I swallow the pills he left with half the water. "What…

Did we?" I look down at my still bare chest. Part of me hopes Theo says *yes, we did fuck*. But I don't know if I want him to say that because I want a justifiable reason to hate him, or because I genuinely like the idea of him using me while I'm unconscious.

As though he can read my mind, Theo smirks. "No, we didn't. Next time I come home to find you naked and drunk, though, don't expect me to be such a gentleman."

The idea has heat filling my core.

At the sight of me squirming, his smirk grows, and he cups my chin with a hand, running his thumb over my lips, and says, "You gave Luna some ideas last night."

I swallow. "What ideas?"

"In your time stalking me, do you remember seeing the kinds of guests I'd have?"

"Lots of women." Even when he was still dating Amber, he'd have other girls over. Once or twice, Luna would follow.

Theo sets his coffee next to mine and sinks his hand into my hair. "Luna's guests are similar. Now that she's gotten a look at all you have to offer…" His eyes fall to my tits and my nipples harden at his intense gaze. "She wants a taste."

"Would you cut her tongue out along with her eyes?"

"Do you want me to?"

"Of course not."

He strengthens his grip on my hair, and I hiss. "Really?" He leans closer, and I wonder if he can hear how loudly my traitorous heart is beating. "Because I think a little violence turns you on just as much as it does me."

"I don't want you to hurt Luna," I manage to say, though my voice is quiet and hoarse. "She's my friend."

"Do you want your *friend* to consume you? Do you get wet at the thought of Lu between your legs, fucking you with her tongue? What if I tied you down again and let her have her way with you?"

My mouth is dry, and my underwear is anything but. "What if I said yes?"

"Then I'd throw Luna at your feet and watch as she feasts on your delicious pussy until you can't stand anymore."

"And?" I prompt, licking my lips and spreading my legs slightly under the sheet.

Theo climbs over me, close enough that I can feel his body heat. He leaves one hand in my hair and drags the other down my neck to my chest. "Then I'd put you on your hands and knees and make you suck my cock while Luna fucks you from behind. Or maybe we'll pin you on your back so I can fuck this tight cunt and Luna can ride your face." He rolls my nipples between his fingers, and my hips jerk.

"Would my little reaper like that? What if I chained you up in the clubhouse and let every Saint have their way with you?"

"You wouldn't," I manage.

His soft laugh is a dark sound that promises corruption. "You're right. But Lu? I'd give her a taste."

"I'm not yours to give."

"Yes, you are, little reaper." Before I can respond, he presses his lips to mine. In seconds, he has the sheet removed and literally rips my underwear off. I shout, but the protest is lost in a moan that he swallows while sliding two fingers into me. "Always so wet for me."

My hands go to his back, nails digging into his hot skin. He growls, bites my bottom lip, then pulls away enough to push his sweatpants down. He's not wearing any underwear, so his hard cock is immediately free. Then he's on me again, tongue eagerly exploring my mouth. There's no warning or warm-up before he thrusts into me. I gasp, head falling back. Theo kisses my neck and slides a hand under my back to lift my hips, straightening so he can look down at where I'm lying naked, legs spread, hair a mess, and back arched. He maneuvers my legs, bending them so they can help keep my hips up. In his position on his knees, he has the perfect angle to hit that spot deep inside that fills me with resounding pleasure. My fingers clutch his sheets, and my mouth falls open with gasps and moans as he slams into me over and over.

"Open your eyes," Theo commands.

I obey and meet his gaze. Blown pupils make his brown eyes look black. He reaches forward and wraps a hand around my throat. My pussy clenches, and he groans, grip tightening. I grab his wrist, as if to hold onto something. The harder I squeeze his wrist, the tighter his chokehold becomes. Soon, he's cut off my air completely. I strain my neck, pushing my head back and gasping, instinctively looking for air.

"You're mine, little reaper." His hips slam forward. "Fuck, you take my cock so well." Stars dot my vision, and just as I begin fading, his grip loosens, allowing me to gulp in a breath. He doesn't let up for long, though. He removes his other hand from my back and rubs two fingers over my clit. I claw at his wrist with both hands now, nails sinking into flesh.

"Come on, baby," he coaxes. "If you want to breathe, you'll come for me."

Seconds later, my body arches off the bed, and I'm coming apart under his hold. The orgasm tears through me, stealing the remaining bit of air and strength I have. My arms fall to my side, and darkness envelops me as I lose consciousness. I'm only out for a moment before my eyes snap open, and I suck in a lungful of air. Theo is still pounding into me, both of his hands gripping my hips. He's holding me so hard that I'm sure his fingers will leave bruises. He's still staring at me, like he'll never be able to look long enough.

I push into my heels, lifting my hips even further, and clamp down on him. It pushes him over the edge, and his thrusts stutter.

Once finished, he pulls out and leaves to get a wet rag. I lay with my legs spread, body fully melted into his mattress, and let him clean me up. While wiping the inside of my thigh, he licks his lips and drags a finger up my center. I jerk at the sensation, and his eyes shine with delight. But instead of forcing another orgasm, he tosses the dirty rag away and lies down next to me. Resting his head on his arm, Theo reaches over and grabs my tit, the entire thing disappearing into his hand.

"Little reaper?"

"Hmm?"

He pinches my nipple so hard that I gasp in pain. "Don't ever take off your clothes in my living room without me again."

I scowl at him. He really gets off on ordering me around. *So do I.*

I banish the thought and pull his hand away. "Tink?" He scowls at the nickname. "Keep trying to control me, and I'll walk naked into the Saints' clubhouse." With that, I climb out of his bed and walk into his bathroom, locking the door behind me.

~

Taco Tuesday is canceled because Sadie is sick and Evelyn has to work. I'm suspicious that Ev's reasoning has more to do with my relationship with Theo than her relationship with her job, but I don't say anything. Instead, Theo takes me out for another riding lesson, which lasts for maybe an hour before we end up making out on his bike.

Back at the house, I use the evening to catch up on work and sleep, which I manage to do in my bed instead of Theo's.

I still wake up with an aching need for him I have to satisfy with my vibrator. But it proves to not nearly be enough, so I suffer through work inappropriately turned on by a man who isn't even there. By the time he arrives to pick me up, I'm too lost in desire to do anything but drag him into my office and ride him on the same couch where dozens of people tell me their problems every day.

"Feeling up to facing the club?" Theo asks once we're finished.

I pause buttoning my shirt, the haze of lust clearing and making room for self-consciousness. "What?"

"I was thinking we'd go to the clubhouse. You haven't seen anyone but James and Luna since…"

"Since I killed someone in front of them." The last three days have been so consumed by horniness mixed with confusion and guilt that I haven't had much brain power to spare for the Saints. I haven't even seen Luna since Monday night, and James has been too busy to say much beyond hello and goodbye.

"I talked to them. They shouldn't give you any trouble," he says, shrugging on his jacket.

"What did you tell them?"

"That you take a lot of self-defense classes and were just trying to save my life."

"What about the South Five?"

"Haven't heard a peep. I have Bonnie and Clyde looking into it. Their daughter lives in the Five's territory, so they can easily check it out without looking suspicious. They won't be in their colors, of course."

"Nico?"

He scowls. "Laying low. They did a number on him, broke a few ribs." He sighs and sets his hands on my shoulders. "It'll be fine, I promise. None of my people are snitches, and they'd never say anything about their president's girl. Most of them really are amazed by you and thankful that you protected me."

"Most?"

"Nobody can please everyone at once."

I bite my cheek, only now realizing how anxious I've been to see them after Sunday. Theo settles his palm on my face, thumb swiping lightly over my bruised cheekbone. "Don't be ashamed of who you are or afraid of letting them see you. You're not broken. You're *everything*."

My eyes burn, and I avoid looking directly into Theo's.

"These people live in purgatory; they're not going to turn their backs on the reaper."

A soft smile lifts the corner of my lips. "Fine, let's go."

Like our first visit to the clubhouse, over a dozen bikes are out front. I'm just as hesitant to head inside now as I was then, but for completely different reasons. And like two weeks ago, our entrance earns the attention of everyone.

It's silent at first, as everyone turns to us. Then there's an eruption. People cheer and holler. Raph shouts something about me being the new savior of purgatory, and Luna winks from where she's standing by the fireplace, beer in hand.

My cheeks burn, and my hand sweats in Theo's grasp. He squeezes it once and says, "You idiots suck at not making a big deal."

"Sorry, boss," Benny says, though he doesn't sound or look sorry with a smile that stretches ear to ear.

"We missed you, Graves," Valor says.

"Alright, that's enough," Theo says. When people don't look away, he repeats, "That's enough," in a more commanding tone that makes everyone shift their attention away from us.

Luna skips over. Today, she's wearing a short, red

leather dress that's so tight I'm not sure how she rode her bike over here. Though I have seen her ride in a pair of pants, then take them off when she's done riding. "Killer, long time no see." Her smile shows off the tips of her teeth, giving the illusion that she's a vampire studying her next meal. Pieces of Monday night and Theo's words yesterday morning return, and my core pulses with interest.

"It's been two days," I say, accepting her hug with one arm since my other hand is still clasped firmly in Theo's.

"Around here, that's like an eternity." She looks at Theo, who towers over her short stature. "Hey, boss." She doesn't say anything else, but there's a clear suggestion in her expression.

He frowns and says in a low, almost threatening voice, "Later."

She still presses a brave kiss to my cheek before rushing off. His hold on my hand turns painful, and he mutters something about murder under his breath.

I chuckle and whisper, "Which one of us is the reaper again?"

He shakes his head. We continue through the room I intimately know now after spending hours here, often exploring on my own. Today, Theo stays glued to my side, like leaving me was never an option.

For the most part, the Saints act normal and don't bring up Sunday. Some of the braver and dumber ones, like Raphael, do make comments.

"You never mentioned how badass you are," he says.

I raise my brows. "Didn't realize I had to."

"Guess you didn't. Just, with the boss's history…" He catches Theo's warning glare and quickly changes lanes. "Anyway, I'm glad he found you. He deserves someone who has his back."

That hits me harder than I expected.

Do I have Theo's back? I did save his life, but it was the heat of the moment. I was in fight mode. I hadn't killed in too long. I saw a threat and acted. It wasn't only about Theo. And these people don't know what I planned to do to their leader.

My breath catches when I process that I *planned* to kill Theo. Not that I *plan* to.

Because I don't. Not anymore. There's no way I could kill him now. What does that make me? A hypocritical coward? I know I'm not some transformed person who no longer has the psychotic need to kill. The fire still burns. I'll still have to douse it with blood.

It'll just be someone else's. Not Theo's.

The rest of the night is fun, and I'm actually disappointed when Theo says we're leaving.

The disappointment vanishes when he whispers in my ear, "We both have early mornings, and I plan to spend at least an hour making you scream my name before I let you sleep."

The next day, he says he'll be busy all evening, once again with the mysterious "club business" he refuses to give me any information about. I decide to use the night to see the girls and text them about hanging out. While Sadie and Rose argue about what we're going to do in the group chat— Evelyn is suspiciously silent—I text Luna to ask if she's free to drive me somewhere. She asks where, then wastes no time suggesting I invite the girls to Theo's house so all five of us can hang out. Or more likely all four of us, because I doubt Evelyn will join.

Sadie and Rose enthusiastically agree, and soon I'm standing in the middle of the living room, looking around for anything to clean or hide before my best friends show up at the house of the criminal motorcycle club leader whom I tried to kill and am now fucking at every possible chance.

I'm straightening the couch where I found a pair of my underwear stuffed behind a pillow when the front door swings open. "Killer!" Luna shouts, stopping in the kitchen to set the two bags she's holding on the island counter.

"Lu!" I say. "There's nothing overtly illegal in sight, is there?"

"You mean serial killer trophies or drugs? Nope!" She pops the 'p' on the end of the word and smiles wide.

"Cool, thanks."

"Nervous for your goody-two-shoes friends to see your boyfriend's house?"

"He's not my boyfriend." The answer comes automatically but with barely any weight.

"Sure." She winks and helps me unload the groceries for a taco bar and margaritas. "And your Skittles," she finishes. I take the extended candy bag and set it with the margarita ingredients.

"These are for the drinks."

"How are Skittles for drinks?"

"You'll see."

The island is fully stocked with every taco topping by the time there's a knock at the front door. My heart skips a beat, and I nervously straighten my top, pausing at the look on Luna's face.

"What?"

She shakes her head. "Nothing."

I frown at her, then head to the front door.

"Hey!" they both shout, throwing themselves at me. I laugh, catching them and returning the fierce hugs. Rose's dark brown hair is in its natural curls now, a big difference from the box braids she had last week.

"So, this is the home of the sex god?" Sadie says, turning in a slow circle. She meets Luna's eyes and says, "You're Luna!"

Luna nods, eyebrows raised. Looking from Sadie to Rose, she says, "You're Sadie? And Rose! I'm so excited to finally meet you."

"*You're* excited? Bitch, I've never heard June talk about anyone like she talks about you guys."

"Oh?" Luna smirks at me, and a blush colors my cheeks.

"Okay! Introductions over!" I shout, preparing to drag the girls to the makeshift taco bar.

I don't get the chance before Rose saunters over and adds, "Introductions just began! So, Luna, I hear you're gay?"

I drop my face in my hands. Luna laughs. "Very. I hear you're queer and, you, Sadie, are 'pretty damn straight,'" she says, making air quotes with her fingers.

"Oh, I must know this conversation," Sadie says.

Luna happily obliges. It's like we've all been friends for years. After filling our tacos and making margaritas, I grab a handful of Skittles and say, "I'm about to change your life," then drop them into Luna's glass.

"Skittles, fuck yes!" Sadie says, doing the same to her drink.

Luna takes a hesitant sip, then smiles.

"Ha! Told you!" I shout.

"I never doubted you."

"Did I tell you guys that Vanessa wants to give up sugar?" Rose says, adding a rim of it, instead of salt, to her glass. "I think we have to break up."

I scoff. "You'd never break up with Vanessa."

"Ooh, Vanessa," Luna says in a singsong voice. "Do tell!"

Rose tells. With enough detail to fill the twenty minutes

it takes for us to eat several tacos sitting in the living room. Sadie and Luna are next, sharing their stories about various partners. Then all three look at me. I wipe a line of salt off my lip and swallow a mouthful of margarita.

"Oh no. No, no, no. You all know plenty. You," I point to Luna, "know too much."

"Not enough yet," she mutters into her glass. Since she's sitting next to me, I'm the only one who hears.

"I need more!" Rose says. "Like, does he have any siblings? Where did he grow up? Why did he become a biker? How many tattoos does he have? Does he like your tattoos? How big is his dick?"

"Rose!" I shout.

"I can help!" Luna.

"Don't encourage them, Lu!"

"Please, encourage us, Lu!" Sadie says.

I groan. "You get *one* question."

"Six," Sadie says.

"Two."

"Five."

"Three."

"Four."

I shake my head. "Three."

"Fine, three. Deal." Sadie extends her hand. We shake on the agreement. Luna watches the entire interaction with bemused intrigue.

"You want the first one?" Sadie asks Rose.

She nods. "What's his family like?"

I frown. "The Saints are his family. And they're… a lot. Some of them," I gesture to Luna, "are amazing. James, his roommate, is basically his brother. He's tall, ginger, and tattooed. He's nice but protective. I get the feeling he doesn't let people in easily."

"She's not wrong," Luna adds. "But killer here is getting past those hardened walls."

"Killer?" Rose asks.

"She thinks she's being clever," I say. "I've gotten a lot of nicknames based on Graves."

"Nah, it's because you're a lady killer. Or man killer, I guess. Really, an everyone killer with that face," Luna says. I hear the double meaning in her words, but she's thankfully nonchalant with how she says it. Still, Sadie's eyes twinkle as she turns her inquisitive gaze from Luna to me.

After a moment, she says, "Okay, my turn. How big is his dick?"

"I haven't measured it, Sadie!" I say, cheeks reddening despite expecting the question.

"Just ballpark! Small? Average? Big? Huge? Painful?"

Knowing I won't get past the question, I make a guess and hold my hands nearly seven inches apart. Luna reaches over and pushes my hand further. "You're right," I say without thinking. Both Rose and Sadie look between us, brows pulled together. "What?"

"I thought you were…" Rose says.

Luna shrugs. "Doesn't mean I don't know how big things are."

"And he has a Prince Albert," I say.

Rose's face contorts in a painful expression. Sadie grins and says, "Oh, hell yeah. Love a pierced man."

Deciding I don't want to explain Theo's dick further, I ask, "Next question?"

Sadie and Rose discuss before asking, "Does he love you?"

Luna and I answer at the same time.

I say, "No."

She says, "Yes."

"Lu, he doesn't love me."

"Is she always so blind?" Luna asks.

"No, she's normally pretty perceptive," Sadie answers. "But when it comes to believing people love her? Yeah. She can be obtuse."

"I'm not obtuse."

"No, you just don't believe you're worthy of love."

"That's not fair. Trust me, Theo doesn't love me." He loves fucking me, sure. But after what I've done, of course he doesn't love me.

Sadie's look is almost pitying. "Babe."

"Nope, not doing it. No therapy."

She holds her palms out in surrender. "No therapy, promise. But forgive me for believing Luna on this."

"I like her," Luna says.

"That doesn't surprise me."

Thankfully, their focus doesn't stay on Theo long. Three hours later, I start to worry they'll still be here when he gets home, and I don't want to deal with that tonight. But then my phone rings while Rose is working to convince Luna to come to hot yoga. I stand and head to my room before answering.

"Hey."

"Hey, little reaper," Theo says, his voice soft. "You doing okay?"

"Is this you checking up on me? Why don't you just check the cameras?"

His silence suggests he didn't expect me to know about his hidden cameras. "How long have you known?"

"How long have I been here?"

He chuckles, but there isn't much life in it. He sounds exhausted. "That's on me for thinking you wouldn't notice, isn't it?"

I grin. "Yes, yes, it is."

"I did see we have guests. How are Sadie and Rose getting on with Luna?"

"Like long-lost triplets. I worry you'll never be rid of them."

"That's fine with me." He lets out a heavy sigh, then says, "I don't think I'll be home for a while, so don't wait up for me tonight. I'm sorry."

Leaning against the dresser, I'm surprised at how disappointed the news makes me. "Is everything okay?"

"It will be. But I'd much rather be there. I'll make it up to you tomorrow."

I cross my feet, anticipation already curling low. "Oh yeah? How?"

"I'm thinking on my knees, feasting on you until you can't see straight."

"Hmm, that might make it up to me."

"It definitely will. Hey, I got to go, but have fun tonight. I'll see you tomorrow when I pick you up from work. Luna will take you in the morning."

"You won't be back by then?"

"I'm sure I will, but I'll be too tired to safely take you to work. Don't worry, I'll be more than ready to make this up to you later."

"Okay."

"Oh, and little reaper?"

"Yeah?"

"If you need help relaxing before going to sleep, check the drawer in my bedside table. But be sure to smile for the camera if you do, so I can see exactly what I'm missing."

My thighs push tightly together at the idea of what he has in his bedside table. And of him watching me get myself off over a security camera.

"Get back soon and watch it in person," I purr.

There's a moment's pause, then a low, "Fuck. I'll do my best. Now go back to your friends. They're starting to roam, and I don't want them exploring my room."

"Bye, Tink. Stay safe."

"Only for you, little reaper."

Then he hangs up, and with a controlled breath, I return to the living room to corral my best friends and try desperately not to think too much about the aching yearning in my chest for Theo's return.

TWENTY-FOUR

June

The first thing I do when the girls leave is go to Theo's room, lock the door, and open his bedside drawer. A small soft bag sits in the center. I open it to find a LELO wave dual stimulation vibrator. I pull the silky toy out of the bag and study it. It's like a rabbit vibrator but more of a U shape so the internal G-spot part and the clit suction nearly touch.

Grinning, I set up my phone against his headboard with the front-facing camera on. Then I walk to the corner of the room where Theo's camera is, drag a chair underneath, and stand so I'm inches from the lens. "Watching me is a privilege, Theo. Maybe I'll let you see my recording." I blow a kiss, pull off my shirt, and grab the tape from my back pocket. Stretching up, I tape the shirt to the ceiling so it's hanging in front of the camera.

I hop off the chair and take off all my clothes before climbing onto the bed. I sit on my heels once I'm in the phone's camera frame, then start the recording. Even though Theo isn't watching me right now, my pussy throbs with anticipation that he'll eventually see this.

My need to get off has steadily grown every minute since his phone call two hours ago. I'm so wet and ready that when I position the thicker end of the toy at my entrance, it easily slides in. Even without turning it on, the pressure has my lips parting. Once the toy is all the way in, I move the external stimulator until it's positioned over my clit. Then I look straight into the camera and press the button to turn it on.

The vibration shoots up my spine, and my head drops back. I let out a moan and rock into my hand, imagining Theo beneath me.

My legs shake from the vibration abusing my G-spot while the suction pulls on my clit. I lean forward, pressing my palm into the mattress a foot from the phone and dropping my head between my shoulders.

The vibration grows more intense until my breaths come out short and staggered. I sit back and reach up to squeeze my tit, rolling the nipple between my fingers. A second later, an orgasm hits me with virtually no warning. Instead of pulling the toy out, I turn it off long enough to move onto my back, feet on either side of the phone so the camera is facing the toy buried in my cunt. With a breath, I turn it back on, and my hips instantly leave the bed. It takes less than a minute to come again. I don't even turn it off, just let my body rock and chase another climax.

"Fuck, Theo!" I call, my legs shaking as the orgasms ripple through me. The vibrations are painful now, so I turn off the toy and let my arms fall to the side, not bothering to even take it out. Fully out of energy, it's several moments before I'm able to turn enough to reach my phone. I hold it above my face and give an exhausted smile to the camera.

"Just a reminder of what you missed." I wink, then turn off the recording. My chest rises with heavy breaths, and I know I should get up now, but I'm far too relaxed and comfortable. I fall asleep with the toy still inside me, but wake up only fifteen minutes later, climb off the bed, and walk to the corner of the room. After pulling my shirt down, I take the toy out and hold it and the phone up, screen paused on the first frame of the video.

"If you want the video, you'll have to prove it when you get back." Without cleaning it, I set the toy on top of Theo's pillow, gather my clothes, and walk out. Still relaxed from the several orgasms and earlier margaritas, it doesn't take long to fall asleep.

I wake up wet, needy, and moaning. The sound of a muffled happy hum comes from the foot of the bed, and I instinctively rock my hips up into the face between my legs. Two large, tattooed hands grip my hips, right near the lingering bruises from Theo's fingers.

Sleep fades, and I focus fully on the tongue thrusting into my cunt and up my middle to slide over the bundle of nerves. My hands find their way to Theo's head, and I grip his hair like it's a handle. His thumbs rub in a circle, kneading under my hip bones.

"Fuck." I press into his face, searching for more. "Harder."

He groans, the sound a vibration at my core, and speeds up his licking, then sucks my clit between his teeth, working it lightly. My hips shake with an oncoming orgasm.

"Yes, Theo. More," I moan. Keeping one hand gripping my hip, he moves the other down to shove two fingers inside, all the way to his knuckles. He twists and crooks them, rubbing the spot the toy was pressed against earlier. Black patches fill my vision when he flicks his tongue, and I pull on his hair so hard that strands come free. I gasp as he coaxes me over the edge then works me through the orgasm. When I relax into the mattress, he removes his fingers and presses a kiss on the inside of my thigh.

"Missed you, little reaper," he whispers, sliding up my body until we're face to face. He licks the seam of my lips, and when they part, he hooks his tongue on my teeth. I sigh into his mouth when he presses his lips to mine. Already, sleep is pulling me back under, and I don't bother fighting it.

I'm alone when my alarm wakes me up what feels like five minutes later. I have four missed texts, three in the group chat from Rose and Sadie raving about Luna and telling Evelyn she missed a great night. The fourth text is from Luna, saying she'll be here to pick me up by seven thirty.

Nothing from Theo. I'm not sure if I imagined his visit last night, but I know he's back because his jacket and helmet are hanging up, and his bedroom door is shut. Unfortunately, work keeps me from barging into his room to wake him up and ask where he was last night.

The first half of my day is simple, though one of my clients tells me about recently learning her little brother was molested by their childhood pastor. I make a note to investigate him, thinking he may be my next target. Pastors who prey on children are my favorite kind to slice up.

During my lunch break, while I'm looking over my next client's files, I realize Jennifer is coming in. She missed her last appointment, so I've only seen her once since meeting Theo. That was when I was still planning his murder.

Now I'll have to look her in the face knowing I've been happily fucking the man who may be responsible for her niece's death for almost a week.

"Jennifer, hey," I greet, opening the door. She comes in with a soft smile and settles on the couch. "How have you been?"

She shrugs. "Since the cops refused to look into Amber's disappearance, I've been asking her old friends, the people she hung out with before getting mixed up with that awful gang."

An icy feeling fills my chest. What if she decided to confront Theo or the Saints? What if she showed up at the Iron Cage and saw me there, dancing with the people who ruined her niece's life?

"And?"

"Most of them say they hadn't seen her for a while. One said she was selling drugs. But I know she isn't selling drugs. My baby would *never* do that. It must've been that gang banger."

Theo doesn't sell drugs, I think. Axel and Bella run all the drugs that go through the Saints' territory, selling from the Iron Cage. They're very particular about what drugs they'll sell and who they'll sell to.

"I can admit that she may have tried weed at parties," Jennifer continues. "But she doesn't do drugs, much less sell them."

"*Amber betrayed him. She betrayed all of us,*" Luna had said. "*She was an addict and got in deep debt with the South Five.*"

"Have you heard from Amber since that text?"

Jennifer shakes her head. "Maybe he took her phone. My baby wouldn't cut me out like this." With that, her carefully controlled demeanor shatters, and Jennifer starts sobbing. I help work her through the breakdown and manage to get through the rest of the appointment without falling too far into my own mind. But when she leaves, the guilt slams into me with the force of a dam breaking.

I'm betraying my client. Her life has been torn apart because her niece got involved with Theo and the Saints. And I have the audacity to sit here and tell her she's going to be okay knowing full well that Theo will pick me up in a few hours just to take me back to his house and fuck me senseless.

It's not just Theo. The club's weekly church meeting is tonight, and I'm looking forward to going. I want to see Luna, James, Benny, Valor, Bonnie, and the others. Then tomorrow is the long ride with the entire crew, and I get excited bubbles in my stomach when I think about it.

This started because I had no other choice. Theo stopped me from killing him. It was either agree with his insane plan or put my fate in his hands, which meant death or prison.

But I can't lie. That's not what this is anymore. If it was, I never would've let Sadie and Rose into that house. I wouldn't have been sad when Theo told me he wouldn't be home last night. I wouldn't be wet and needy at the thought of him.

I wouldn't be avoiding thinking about the fact that our agreement is halfway over, and I have less than two weeks left with the Saints.

~

Theo is leaning against his bike outside the office, ankles crossed and hands propped on the seat under him. He's wearing his jacket and sunglasses, his long hair in a bun. He smiles at my approach.

"Little reaper."

The guilt grows when my heart jumps at the sight of him. "Tink."

He stands and holds out his hand for my bag. I hand it to him to store in the compartment. Then he wraps an arm around my waist and drags me closer to him until our chests press together. My breath hitches, and he captures it with his mouth.

I pull back, laying a hand on his chest. "What are you doing?"

His brows pull together. "Kissing you."

"In public?"

He lets go. "I didn't realize I was only allowed to kiss you when you're tied to my bed or asleep in yours."

Last night was real, not a dream.

"Well, you can't kiss me outside my work."

He nods once, the motion stiff. "Alright. Then let's get away from your important job and get back to the hole where us dirty criminals hang out."

"Theo—"

"Come on," he interrupts. "We've got church."

The emotions in my chest feel like they're caught on a spiderweb, unable to break free. There's pain for Jennifer's loss. A fiery need to take justice into my own hands. Guilt for abandoning Amber. Longing for Theo. Fondness for the Saints. Regret for putting that pained look on Theo's face.

Too many to say anything now. So, I pull on the helmet and climb onto the bike, leaning into Theo's back.

My third church with the Saints is leaps and bounds better than the first two. I can still tell some of them are angry at me for being there, but the rest welcome me in, and Luna makes me sit next to her and Raph rather than waiting toward the back of the room. The meeting stretches on, though there are moments that are interesting, like when Kip explains the club's next chop hit or when Theo goes over interested prospects.

Toward the end, he brings up the South Five and how the club will prepare for retaliation. I want to shrink into myself at the feeling of gazes on me like shards of ice. It's not that I'm embarrassed or ashamed. I don't regret killing that guy. But that's a part of myself that has never risen to the surface for someone to notice. Before Theo, only one person knew I'm a murderer. Now, in the middle of an entire room of people who literally watched me kill another human, I feel flayed open, naked down to my soul. My body begs to hide for my own survival or fight back to eliminate the threat, neither of which I can do.

I have no choice but to sit here, Theo's voice an unintelligible roar, and endure the sharp edges of dozens of sets of eyes cutting into my skin.

"Alright, that's all for tonight. Ride starts at ten tomorrow. Don't be late," Theo says. He walks up to me while the Saints disperse. "You good to hang out for another half hour or so? I need to talk to Axel."

He still sounds upset, and it makes no sense that he'd care so much about kissing me in public. It's not like we're dating.

"That's fine," I say. "Everything okay?"

"Yeah."

I open my mouth to ask more, but Theo doesn't give me the chance. He turns and walks away, the muscles in his back tense.

"Trouble in paradise?" Luna asks.

"I don't get him."

She chuckles and stands, nodding toward the kitchen. "I'm scheduled to help Benny clean up. Join us, and I'll try to explain the paradox that is Theo Zervas."

I follow, picking up empty cups on the way.

"Sweet, I have the killer helping me out, too," Benny says. His gloved hands are submerged in the sink filled with soapy water.

"Oh great, I'm so glad that nickname is catching on," I say, voice monotone and full of sarcasm.

Luna shrugs. "What can I say? I'm a natural leader. I can't help but influence others."

"How about you influence everyone to call me by my real name?"

"That'd be boring," Benny says.

"Killer here needs our help understanding the boss," Luna says.

"Aren't you the therapist?" Benny asks. "You should be helping us understand that asshole."

Luna starts loading the dishwasher with the dishes Benny isn't hand-washing. "We've both known him several years longer." She turns to me and asks, "So, what's going on?"

A few Saints mingle near the kitchen, and I suck my lips between my teeth, uncomfortable with anyone else hearing me talk about my "relationship" issues with their leader. Luna knows the truth, but Benny only sees what we want him to see. What if this conversation ruins everything?

Then I think about Theo's face falling earlier and how much he pushed to learn about the fire he saw in my eyes so he could help. I think about his anger in my office for reducing him to his looks and claiming that we're both villains. I remember how he called me beautiful and powerful. His words after I killed that man in the Iron Cage ring in my ears. *"The more I see of you, the more unworthy I feel to be at the end of your blade, much less between your legs."*

I think about Amber and the mysterious "Scottie" Theo punched Bowie for mentioning, and his childhood in foster care.

There are too many questions I need answers to, and if Benny and Luna can help scratch the surface, then it's better than nothing.

"Why does he care so much about public perception?"

"What do you mean?" Benny asks.

"Like… it bothers him that I don't like PDA around my office."

"Is it the PDA around your office bothering you or Theo's presence in general?" Luna asks.

My cheeks burn. "A lot of my clients are already nervous around men, and Theo doesn't necessarily emanate trustworthiness."

Luna and Benny share a loaded look. I wish I could grab it to unwrap and study. With a sigh, Benny passes me a pot to dry and says, "Theo has had troubles in the past because of his looks and lifestyle. The cops have targeted him because he fits a certain profile. I mean, they do it to most of us, it comes with the territory—"

"Especially when you are a bunch of criminals," Luna interrupts.

Benny rolls his eyes. "Right, well, we're all used to it. But Theo has had it worse. I think it brings old stuff up for him."

"What kind of stuff?"

"You'll have to ask him that," Luna says.

I grind my teeth together and decide to move on to my next question. "Why was it such a big deal that he brought me to church that first time?"

Luna laughs and Benny says, "That's an easy answer. Theo has only ever brought two women to church before. Both relationships ended badly, and the entire club was affected."

"Amber and Scottie?" I guess.

Benny looks shocked. "You've talked about Scottie?"

"Not with Theo," I say. "But that guy, Bowie, mentioned her, and I've heard some stuff."

"Yeah, well," he coughs, "I never met her. I wasn't in the club when they dated, but she's still talked about now. Apparently, Theo was so broken after she died that he was volatile for a while. Beating people up, pulling jobs by himself, drinking more. The way some of the older guys talk about him back then makes him seem like a different person."

"How did she die?" I ask.

"Suicide," Luna answers. "But if you want to know anything else, you need to talk to him."

My heart feels like it's cracking, and I want to know, but I also can't imagine asking him to relive what was probably one of the worst times of his life just to satiate my curiosity. "So, the club is worried I'll either betray them or die?"

Luna shrugs. "The club has trust issues, and we're all protective of Theo. No one wants to see him hurt again, and everyone can see how much he cares about you."

Thankfully, I remember Benny before I argue. I decide to make a joke instead. "You sure they're not just scared he'll stab them for looking at me too long? His jealous streak is pretty violent."

"That's actually new," Benny says.

"What?"

"He's right," Luna says. "I've never seen Theo so territorial. Granted, I've only seen him with one real girlfriend, and they were hardly exclusive. Most girls, other than Amber, were around for a few days or weeks, if they were lucky. He had no problem sharing them."

I frown. "You're kidding."

"Nope."

"He wasn't even that possessive over Amber," Benny says. "Anytime he caught her making out with someone else, like Raph, he just told them to wear a condom because he didn't need two Raphs when one was already too many."

If Theo caught me making out with one of his men, I genuinely think he might kill them then lock me in the bedroom, chained to his bed, for the next month.

"You see why people were hesitant at first?" Luna asks. "Theo's not supposed to have many weaknesses, and here you are, a stranger who could have him on his knees with nothing but a smile."

"I'm not... I don't..." I stutter, unsure how to respond.

Benny grins and unplugs the sink, letting the dirty water drain. He pulls the gloves off, revealing the tattoos covering the back of his hands and all of his knuckles. "Theo isn't as complicated as he seems. He might be a badass, deadly biker with few qualms about breaking the law and almost no fears, but at the end of the day, he only wants one thing."

"Which is what?"

Something sad falls over Luna's face. "Family."

Family.

The word feels too small for all it represents. The pain, hope, love, heartbreak, and disappointment cannot fit in six small letters. So much comes back down to that one simple yet endlessly complicated word. Every person who has stepped foot in my office has had a suitcase of baggage because of family. Hell, my own life is drenched in the stains of family.

So why did I expect Theo to be above it all?

TWENTY-FIVE

Theo

After a week of trying to lead Lorry's investigation in the wrong direction, all I want is to pin the little reaper to my bed and fuck her until she begs to show me the video she recorded. I hadn't planned on visiting her this morning when I finally got home, but she left the unwashed toy on my bed, still smelling like her, and I couldn't help myself. I had to taste her.

It was exactly what I needed to fall asleep after the shit show that was last night. Lorry finally saw me with June when I picked her up from work on Wednesday. Unfortunately, that's the day we fucked on her couch, so he watched me arrive, park, go inside, and take twenty minutes to leave.

He didn't confront me until yesterday.

"What the hell were you doing with Graves?"

I look up from my desk to see Lorry standing in the doorway of my office. "What do you mean?"

He barges inside and kicks the door shut behind him. "I asked you to help me put a serial killer away, and you, what… start fucking her?"

I lean back in my chair, carefully not revealing any reaction. "Lorry, I'm going to need more information."

"Don't play stupid." His face is red, filled with anger. "I saw you at her office yesterday. You went inside, then she left with you. On your bike."

I'm surprised it took him so long to figure this out, but it works for me. I interlock my fingers on my desk and pull in a measured breath. "Of course she did."

He pauses mid-pace, surely not having expected me to admit it so quickly. "What?"

"Lorry, this isn't like other cases. You want me to frame someone for murder. Actually, you want me to help you put away a serial killer who, according to the rest of the police department, doesn't exist."

"Since when do you ask questions? I'm not asking you to investigate! I'm asking you to help stop a killer." His volume is rising, and though the Iron Cage isn't full right now, I still would rather not be overheard.

"Sit down." I gesture to the chair across from me. He doesn't sit, but he does cross his arms and wait for me to continue. "I'm not investigating. But this isn't a case of planting some drugs on someone or breaking a taillight. I don't have a body I can drop in Graves's house. And I'm sorry, but I'm not going to frame a random woman, who appears to be a perfectly respectable member of society, for murder without a little more information."

"I don't pay you to investigate."

"No, you pay me to break the law so your job is easier."

"She killed my cousin."

"I believe you have reasons to think that, but you haven't shared them with me, and you haven't listened to any of my other findings or theories. You're confident this Graves woman is the killer, and I don't know why." He opens his mouth, but I barrel forward before he can interrupt. "I'm not saying you have to share your investigation with me. But this isn't a simple job, and

there isn't a simple answer. I have to get into her life, see how she lives. The more I know about her, the better I can help you. You may not believe me, but I don't kill without reason, and I won't kill someone just to frame her. I'm guessing you don't want me to wait for her to kill someone. So, yeah, I was at her office, because the best way to get into someone's life is if they invite you."

"So, what? You're dating her now?"

I shake my head. "I tried that, but she's not going to date me. I'm clearly not her type." The lie is sweet in my mouth. "But she does have a bit of a hero complex, and she's been writing a book on the psychological reasons people find belonging among broken or 'sinful' people. Or something like that. The way she said it sounds much smarter." In reality, June briefly mentioned that she'd love to study why people like Luna feel happier and safer with a found family that, to the rest of the world, is more dangerous than their blood family. But it gave me this cover story idea for Lorry.

"And?"

"And, what better case study than the Saints? So, I'm letting her believe she's saving me while getting the chance to observe the Saints and interview some of our members."

Lorry finally sits, lowering slowly into the chair. "You're bringing her to the Cage?"

I nod. "And while she's with me, we know her house is empty. James has looked around a few times. Found nothing yet, but we set up a few cameras. I told you, this isn't like the other jobs. It'll take time."

He chews on his cheek, looking for something to fight me on. "When will you be done?"

"I don't know, Lorry. But you'll need a lot of hard evidence to convince a jury that someone like June Graves is capable of cold-blooded murder."

"Just be careful. Don't let her fool you. Trust me, this woman is a killer."

I know, *I think.* *"If she is, then you'll put her away. But not tomorrow."*

"Next time, tell me what you're planning to do before I catch you picking the killer up from work," Lorry mumbles.

"Sure thing. Now, I've got work to do."

I followed Lorry after that and was unsurprised to see him go to June's house. I had to sneak in and turn on the lights and TV to keep him from breaking in or learning that she hadn't slept there in two weeks. I already removed everything incriminating from the house but didn't want Lorry digging through her drawers.

I spent the rest of the evening looking into the disappearances he's attributed to my little reaper. Four of them I'm reasonably confident were June's work, and I can for sure link two of them to her. The rest aren't her. Two of them aren't bad guys at all, which leads me to believe that Lorry has no idea what type of victims June prefers.

After searching the house of one of her assumed victims, whose wife used to see June, I decided to check my cameras at the house. There was my reaper, drinking with Sadie, Rose, and Luna. Seeing her happy in my living room, comfortable enough to invite her friends over, filled my entire body with warmth.

Unfortunately, I was distracted when the dead man's widow arrived. Thankfully, I managed to hide and spent an hour watching her with her new boyfriend before I snuck out. Enough time to hear the man verbally abuse her. Her taste in men hasn't gotten better.

Which means I have two plausible suspects I can pin the guy's disappearance on. Cops are much more inclined to think a widow or new boyfriend is guilty of murder than a random serial killer.

Before I could go home, Axel called about seeing some drugs pass through the Cage that neither he nor Bella sold. With the South Five on our backs, I couldn't put that off.

The thought of taking June home and fucking her senseless was the only thing that got me through the exhaustion of last night and today. When I knew Lorry wasn't watching me at her office, I couldn't help but kiss her. My body ached for her touch. My mind begged for the respite of losing myself in her.

Sometimes I forget that I'm temporary to her.

After church, Axel says he has an update on where the drugs are coming from. June seems fine to hang out longer, and I try not to feel jealous that she's getting so close with the other Saints.

But whatever conversation she had with Benny and Luna didn't go well. She looks lost in her head when we leave, and her hold on me is more desperate as we ride home.

"Can we talk?" she asks as soon as we're inside.

I toe off my shoes and sigh, thinking about church and how everyone looked at her when I brought up the Five. "Look, it's not your fault. This war with the South Five has been building for months."

She shakes her head. "Not about that." Her chest rises with a deep breath, and her next sentence comes out like one word. "It was Amber Wallace."

My movements slow as I process her words, brows pulling together. *Amber?* I thought we were past that. "What?"

"That's why I was going to kill you. Amber's aunt is a client of mine, and she said you'd been abusing Amber. I watched you for a while, and there was clearly something wrong with Amber. You'd get in fights, and the next day she'd have bruises all over her arms. Then, when Amber disappeared, Jennifer was sure you killed her."

"Fucking bitch," I swear under my breath. I knew Amber's aunt hated me, but is that really what she thought? She doesn't know her niece at all. What must she have told June? Of course, June hated me if all her information was coming from Jennifer.

I sigh, rub my face, and nod to the bedroom. There's no point hiding this from her, and maybe the truth will help break down some of her defenses. "Alright, come on, let's do this."

I shut the bedroom door behind us and carefully don't think about June on my bed or how she tasted this morning. "I wasn't abusing Amber. She was—"

"I know," she interrupts. "A junkie trading secrets to the South Five. But you were still rough with her."

"I'm not going to lie and say I was the perfect boyfriend. Hell, she was way too young for me. But at first, she was just so…" I make a wild gesture, lost on how to explain Amber or why, after seven years of not dating anyone for more than a few weeks, I chose to bring home a twenty-one-year-old. "She was fun, and she fit in," I manage. "She reminded me of an easier time in my life, and I liked how little I thought around her. Then her using got out of hand and, yeah, I was angry. But I didn't kill her."

She sits on the foot of my bed, pulling her feet up. "What did happen?"

I lean against my dresser, arms crossed at the memory of those last few days with Amber. Sometimes, I'm surprised I didn't kill her. "Rehab."

June's mouth drops open. "What?"

"I'd already broken up with her, but she still hung around the Iron Cage for a while. Then I found out what she'd been doing with the South Five, and I told her to fuck off and never step foot near me or the Saints again. The next night, she showed up at my house on a ton of shit. She locked herself in my bathroom, and I had to break the door down. I found her on the floor, seizing. She'd overdosed. I took her to the hospital, then forced her into rehab. I called last week to check on her. She's doing good, apparently, but she still refuses to talk to her aunt or anyone else in her life."

"Jennifer thinks she's dead."

I shrug. If she wants to put her aunt through that kind of hell, that's on her. "Amber isn't my problem anymore."

June frowns but doesn't argue. She lets a long moment pass, then says, "I'm sorry."

"What for?"

"All of it. I'm sorry you had to deal with that. I'm sorry I judged you too harshly too quickly. I'm sorry I rejected you outside my office today."

I drop my arms. I didn't expect that. The apology should make me feel elated, but I'm just tired. With a sigh, I sit next to her on the bed. "I expected you to be okay with whatever I wanted without considering where you were coming from or giving you all the information."

"I don't know what I'm doing," she admits, her voice no more than a whisper.

"Me either."

We sit silently side by side for several minutes. The peace between us feels delicate. I can feel her mind still working, and I don't want to interrupt her thoughts.

"Can I ask you another question?" After I nod, she asks, "What's up with going to the playground on the second Tuesday of every month?"

My chest tightens, the weight enough to split my rib cage and send splinters through my heart. I swallow hard, forcing down the memories.

I can't tell her that. Not now. But I can give her part of the truth.

"That's where and when Rocket asked me to lead the Saints almost five years ago. I go to remind myself what this responsibility means."

"Rocket is a Hartley, right? James's dad."

"Yeah. He would've given the reins to James if he wanted it, but we all knew I'd be better for it."

"James still seems to take the lead pretty often."

"He's vice president. It's his job."

"Why did Rocket step down?"

I lick my lips, stalling for time. The heaviness of reminiscence settles on my shoulders when I think of Rocket and everything that happened before he left. "He was tired. He'd had enough. And after what happened, I don't think he had it in him."

"What happened?"

"You don't know?" My tone betrays my disbelief. There's not much information about the Hartleys out there, but I figured she at least knew this. "What about your impressive research?"

"There's shockingly little about most of you online."

A smile threatens to pull up my lips, but they barely twitch. "That's how we like it."

"So? What happened to Rocket?"

I stand again and walk away from the bed. The memories are weapons in my mind. Thinking about this is like swallowing burning water. "His daughter killed herself."

"James's sister?" she asks in a whisper, as if saying it quietly will make it not real.

I nod. "Seven years ago. Rocket stayed as long as he could, but he was done. And he had the right to be. Rocket gave so much of his life to this club and the members for two decades."

"And James?"

"What about James?"

"Is that why he's not the leader? Because he lost his sister?"

I face her, hoping she doesn't see the threat of tears in my eyes. Time makes it possible to talk, but it doesn't remove the pain. "Partly. James doesn't have the edge of anger and lack of morals that the Saints' president needs. I also don't think he wanted to lead. He wasn't ready. Or maybe he let Rocket pass the reins to me because he knew I needed something to hold onto, a responsibility I couldn't and wouldn't abandon. That's something he'd do."

She nods. "What was her name?"

She asks it like she already knows the answer. I remember Bowie mentioning Scottie at the Cage and wouldn't be surprised if June has heard things from the other Saints in the last couple of weeks.

Still, I want to answer her. I *have* to. Refusing to would feel like a betrayal.

"Scottie."

"When did you start dating?"

"I was eighteen. She was seventeen." My next breath struggles over the knot in my throat. "Rocket had all but taken me in by then, and I'd just become an official member of the Saints. Rocket never let anyone younger than eighteen join."

"And y'all were together until she died?"

I nod. "For the most part. Seven years is a long time to be with one person, especially when you're a wild kid. But at the end of the day, it was always me and Scottie."

Hesitancy seems to sap her next question of strength, so her words are little more than a whisper. "What was she like?"

A year ago, answering would've brought me to tears.

Now, I smile at a mental image of Scottie, gorgeous and laughing. Her red hair, wide brown eyes full of false innocence, ears covered in chains and earrings, and pierced tongue. "She was her own person and didn't care what anyone thought. She loved to meet new people and always sucked the air from every room she walked into. She hated pasta and ate a bag of sour gummy worms every day. Rocket had her on a bike before she could walk, so she was an amazing rider, though she was never a member of the Saints. I think she would've hated it, but she was still mad at Rocket and James for not letting her join."

"James didn't want her in the club?"

I shake my head. "Definitely not. Partly because he was protective of his little sister and didn't want her near the danger. But mostly because she would've been a terrible member."

"How so?"

"She was Daddy's Little Girl, and Rocket let her get away with everything. It would've been worse in the club. Even when she was just hanging around the Iron Cage or coming to club meetings as my Ol' Lady, she'd cause trouble. She had a habit of inciting fights by pushing people's buttons and somehow blaming someone else for it. She was pretty wild until…" I pause, running my tongue over my bottom lip. Talking about *that* will always come with tears, I think. "She eventually calmed down. She never stopped being herself, but she mellowed out, became more responsible, started putting family first."

June is quiet, watching me, probably wondering what caused my smile to fall. "She sounds great."

"You would've loved her. In some ways, you remind me of her. In others, you couldn't be more different."

"Do you know why she…" She trails off, but I don't need her to finish the question.

Do you know why she killed herself?

I nod but don't answer.

Thankfully, she doesn't push. "I'm sorry you lost her. I can tell you really loved her."

I shrug. "We were kids."

"You were in love. How old you were doesn't change that."

"Yeah…" A rope made of memories and lost futures tightens around my throat.

There's a slight sheen in June's eyes, as if she, too, is fighting tears. "I'm not sure if Luna told you, but I killed my dad when I was fifteen," she says.

I almost grin. I knew that already, but I appreciate what she's trying to do. She's offering a secret, something painful from her past, so I don't feel as vulnerable.

I return to the bed, sitting at the head now so she turns to face me. "She mentioned her guess. You were obviously too drunk to remember."

She winces. "My dad was a real asshole. He lost his punching bag when my mom went to prison, so I became his new one. In the two years it took before CPS intervened, he managed to break my arm, crack a rib, and give me a concussion."

I knew he was abusive, but hearing specifics fills my veins with rage and coils my muscles. I fist my hands, fighting the desire to murder someone who's been dead for over a decade. I'd love to resurrect the bastard just to kill him again, slowly and painfully.

"I didn't see him again until I was fourteen," June continues. "My mom had recently married Calvin, who's well-off. My dad showed up with the pretense of wanting to patch up our relationship, but he just wanted Calvin's money."

She pauses to suck in a long breath. "Anyway, he couldn't hurt me anymore, but I wasn't the only one around. Calvin has a daughter of his own, Imogen. She's a year older than me, and she wasn't the prettiest girl at school, so she was kind of desperate for love and naive to how the world really works. I tried to protect her, to be her friend, but she never liked me."

Her words shake slightly, and she drops her eyes to the bed between us, like she's too afraid to look straight at me while telling the story. As if I'd ever judge her for killing the man who hurt her. If I knew her then, I would've been by her side to hold the knife.

"One night, I couldn't find Imogen anywhere. Calvin and my mom thought she was at a party, but she didn't go to parties. So, I checked her phone's location on her laptop and realized she was at my dad's house. I took my mom's car to his house and found them in his bedroom. He was on top of her, choking her while he... while he..." She closes her eyes and gulps in a breath. I reach forward to grab her knee and squeeze. She doesn't need my words, but she does need an anchor, something to remind her that she's safe here with me, not back in that room with her father.

"I stabbed him in the neck with my pocketknife. Imogen screamed, of course. Afterward, I managed to convince her not to tell anyone by saying she'd be culpable for the murder just as much as me and that the cops may even think it was her. I had left my phone back home, so only she could be placed at the scene, and only she had his DNA inside her. And his blood on her. It was fucked up. *I* was fucked up. But she was freaking out. I had to convince her not to go to the cops." Tears are falling in earnest. She shoves them away, sucking in another broken breath.

"Imogen hated me after that, of course. She was in love

with my dad and convinced he loved her too. When she found out she was pregnant, she told our parents the father was a guy from a different school and she didn't want anything to do with him. She moved to her aunt's house in South Texas before having the baby. I've still never met him."

The shards of my ribs shred my heart to ribbons. I wish I could swallow June's pain for her. I want to yell some sense into Imogen. She shouldn't be alienating or judging June. She should be worshiping her for saving her life.

I know I do.

"Imogen hasn't spoken to me in nearly twelve years." A hiccup follows her words.

I lean forward, grab her waist, and tug her across the bed to tuck her into my side. She wraps her arms around me, and I use one hand to wipe tears off her cheek and the other to rub her back. I'm not sure how much time passes with us lying there in the quiet aftermath of so much vulnerability. Our breaths sync, and my eyes grow heavy. June's tears eventually stop falling, but neither of us speaks. There are no hollow sentiments to make us feel better.

That night, I sleep better than I have in years.

TWENTY-SIX

Theo

A soft breath fills my ear. I blink open tired eyes and focus on the small body pressed against me. June's leg is between mine and her arm is on my chest, fingers gripping my shirt. Looking down, I see she's still asleep.

"Dirty, dirty little reaper," I whisper. Both of our pants came off at some point in the middle of the night, so the only barrier between my bare leg and her pussy is a thin piece of cotton. She's hot and wet from whatever dream she's having.

Her next word is barely noticeable, but with her mouth close enough to my ear, I make out both syllables. "Theo."

"*Fuck.*" My morning wood grows impossibly harder. June starts rocking into me, and I don't care what time it is or that she's still asleep, I roll on top of her, pull my cock out, and rip her underwear to the side. I slide the tip up her center, rubbing my piercing over her clit, before pushing inside. There's a small amount of resistance at first, and the pressure finally wakes June up. Her eyes fly open, and she holds onto my neck as I push fully into her.

"Theo!" is her first cognizant word of the day.

Her chin lifts as she presses the back of her head into the

pillow. I lick up the length of her throat and pull her earlobe between my teeth. "What were you dreaming about, little reaper?"

"I don't…"

"I woke up to you riding my thigh. Feel how wet you already are?"

Her nails dig into the back of my neck. I slam forward, filling her completely. She gasps with every thrust, and far too soon, I feel an orgasm rising.

"If you want to come, tell me what you were dreaming about," I demand, snaking a hand under her to raise her hips more. I feel my piercing drag against her pulsing inner walls and moan.

"You," she breathes. "You were taking me in your office at the Iron Cage."

"Ooh, my little reaper wants to play in public?" I smile, the idea sending more blood traveling south. My next thrust is harder, and a shrill gasp rips from her throat. I press my hand over her mouth. "Shh, James is still asleep." She bites my palm, the flash of pain adding to my pleasure.

"If you're good today on the ride, maybe we can make that dream a reality." I remove my hand and reach between us, slipping my fingers between her folds. I feel myself thrust in and out, soaked from my little reaper, and use her natural lubrication to rub her clit, savoring the jump in her breathing that precedes her moan. "Now, come for me, baby."

It takes one more thrust to push her over the edge, and she's squeezing around me. She buries her face into the crook of my neck to muffle her scream. I follow close behind, spilling into her.

"Good girl," I whisper, dragging my wet fingers up her body and over her lips. She's spent, and her eyes are still shut, but they open at that and find mine in the dark. "Good morning." I pull her bottom lip down with my thumb, studying her perfect face with the minimal light coming through the window.

"Morning," she whispers.

Our mouths are an inch apart, and her eyes flick down to my lips. Thinking about her rejection outside her office yesterday, I pull back, refusing to kiss her. Her face falls, but if she wants that again, she'll have to initiate it.

I head to the bathroom to get ready and am disappointed that she doesn't join. But when I head out to the kitchen, I smell the coffee and find her making pancakes at the stove.

"I didn't know we had pancake mix," I say, caging her in from behind.

"I made it from scratch."

"You like to cook?"

She shrugs. "Baking is more fun."

"You adding chocolate chips to these?"

"Of course."

I hum in delight and reach up her torso to her tits while she pours more batter. "We leave in half an hour."

She nods just as James comes out of his room, dressed and ready to leave for the ride. I step away from June and fill a mug with coffee while he sidles up next to me to do the same. Upon seeing the pancakes, he says, "I could get used to this every morning."

Me too.

After eating delicious pancakes, the three of us head out and meet the rest of the Saints outside the clubhouse. June relaxes almost instantaneously, with none of the stress or uncertainty she had on the first ride. She holds me tight, her helmet between my shoulder blades. We're at the tip of the formation, with James's front wheel parallel to the middle of my bike.

Her gloved hands start moving an hour into the ride. They travel down my torso, fingers softly tugging on my jacket. She presses her palms into my thighs, then slides them down the inside, framing my dick with her hands, and squeezes. I shift slightly, my cock twitching in interest. I don't know if she senses it or if this is just her game, but June inches one hand further in. She palms my cock, groping me while I ride, squeezing and pulling up, practically giving me a hand-job through my pants. From her hand and the adrenaline of the ride, I'm hard within seconds.

"Fuck," I mutter under my breath.

"What's that, boss?" Daryus asks, his voice in my ear from the microphones we wear during rides.

"Nothing," I growl. I swear I can hear June laugh. She keeps playing with me over my pants, and my grip on the handlebars tightens so much that the tips of my thumbs go numb. She wiggles her hips behind me, and I imagine her attempting to subtly hump the seat to relieve her own growing desire.

I need to bring her on more rides alone, just the two of us. Or take her skydiving. Or do anything that'll get her adrenaline pumping. My little reaper is turned on by danger and excitement, the same way she's turned on after a fresh kill.

The last thing I want to do is stop her, but I refuse to come in my pants in the middle of a ride. So, I finally reach down and grab her hand, pulling it away from my crotch. She thunks her helmet into my shoulder, clearly disappointed that I've stopped her fun, but keeps her hand at my waist.

For the first time ever, I want this ride to be over sooner rather than later.

~

"That's a new record for how long a cop has followed us!" Raphael shouts after most of the bikes have been parked and turned off outside the Iron Cage.

One of the boys responds with something that earns a loud laugh, but I'm too focused on watching June's leg swing off my bike. I miss whatever James says behind me because she takes off her helmet next, pulling her wavy blonde hair with it. A few strands are stuck to her sweaty forehead even as she shakes her head.

"Boss?" someone asks.

"Ask James," I say in their general direction. Not waiting for a response, I grab June's hand and haul her with me inside the bar.

"Hey!" she shouts.

Once inside, I lean down, scoop her up, and throw her over my shoulder.

"Theo! Put me down!"

Ignoring her, I march to my office, lock the door behind us, push several papers off the desk, and drop her on it. I grip the edge on either side of her and hover a few inches from her face. Her eyes pinned to mine, she hooks her heels around my thighs, pulling me closer.

"I could've wrecked," I whisper, knowing she can feel my breath on her lips.

"You're too good to wreck."

"Sure, but I've never had you against my back, your hand on my cock, while I'm riding."

Her smile is full of depravity as she drags her leg up my thighs and lifts her hips. Her hands go to the buttons of my pants. "Why don't I finish what I started?"

The growl starts in the back of my throat. I reach up and grip her hair, pulling hard so her head is forced back. I lean down enough so my lips are barely an inch from hers. Her breath hitches, and her hands pause halfway through unzipping. "What are you waiting for?"

With half-lidded eyes, she finishes unzipping, reaches back to my ass, and shoves my pants and boxers down. She yanks the front down next, freeing my already half-hard cock, and grips the base. She pulls her hand up, drags her finger to the tip, and tugs slightly on the piercing.

"Fuck, little reaper," I grunt through gritted teeth.

She lets go, lifts her hand, and spits into her palm. This time, her hand moves easier. She twists at the top and licks her lip. My fist in her hair squeezes.

This just won't do.

"Stop."

Her hand pauses, but she doesn't let go. Confusion and a hint of hurt fill her eyes. I step back, forcing her to let go.

"On your knees."

Instantly, the look in her eyes transforms into eager lust. She hops off the desk and drops to her knees.

"Remember recording a certain video on my bed?" I ask. She whimpers. "And then turning my balls about as blue as they could be while I'm leading a club ride?" Holding my cock, I set it against her chin, the ring resting on her bottom lip. "I think it's time you're punished for both of those."

"Theo…"

While her mouth is open, I slide past her lips. She doesn't fight. Her cheeks hollow as she sucks, a hint of her teeth grazing the underside. "You can take it." I grip her hair again and push until I hit the back of her throat.

She raises her hand, attempting to grab the base that isn't in her mouth.

I pull back. "Nuh, uh," I tsk. "Hands on your thighs." She obeys, and I pause once I've pulled nearly all the way out. "Ready?"

While she's nodding, I slam forward, forcing her to take everything until my cock is deep in her throat. She gags, and tears fill her eyes.

"Good girl," I say, pulling back and repeating the motion. I scratch her scalp, and she swallows me down until there's a vacuum sensation around my cock.

"Fuck," I moan. My muscles tighten as I pull her head and thrust forward, fucking harder and faster. I desperately want to spill into her and force her to swallow every drop, but I muster my last ounce of willpower to pull out. Drool drops down her chin, and tears gather under her eyes. She's stunning like this, on her knees in my office, wrecked and gasping, probably dripping between her legs.

"Up."

She slowly stands. Once she's on her feet, I spin her around, reach between her legs, and roughly palm her over her pants. She gasps, hips jerking forward. "My eager little reaper," I coo in her ear as I undo the buttons and zipper, then shove my fingers into her underwear, finding her soaking. Wasting no more time, I tug down her pants until they're at her ankles. Then I plant my hand on her back and shove her forward until her chest is flat against my desk. I slap her ass hard enough to leave a red welt, and she yelps.

Reaching past her, I grab the back of my chair and pull it closer, positioning it so the wheels are hooked on the leg of the desk. I hit the inside of her thighs and nudge her feet. "Wider," I say. She spreads her legs, and I prop my foot up on the chair. With this position, it's easy to slide inside.

"Fuck!" she moans. Her nails dig into the wood of my desk, and as much as I like having her spread before me like this, I wish those nails were on my skin.

Another day. Right now, it's time to make her dream come true.

It's hot and fast and brutal. The desk rocks with our movement, and she slides further onto it, so much that I have to drag her back twice. She moans and cusses and shouts my name, all of which is thankfully drowned out by the music now blaring in the bar beyond my locked office door. Sweat drips down my back and forehead from the effort, and the muscles in my thighs burn. I relish every feeling. If I could, I'd spend an eternity buried in her.

Her inner walls squeeze in warning that she's close.

"Come on, little reaper," I coax. "Come on my cock." Neither of us has touched her clit, and she's started rocking forward with my thrusts, searching for some sort of friction, but she's not getting it. Not right now. She'll come solely from a brutal fucking.

"Now, June." My demand is followed by a particularly rough slam into her pussy, and I lean forward to latch my teeth onto her exposed neck. She screams, and I manage to slap a hand over her mouth quick enough to muffle the sound. Waiting long enough for the orgasm to ripple through her, I stand back up, grip her hips tighter, and yank her back onto me. With three more thrusts, I'm following her over the edge.

She winces when I pull out. I lean down to grab my pants and press a kiss to the red mark on her ass from my hand. She turns around while I'm tucking myself back into my boxer briefs, her chest rising with a deep breath, and her hair sticking to her forehead.

"As good as your dream?"

She smiles. "Better."

God, I want to kiss her.

Instead, I nod to her feet where her pants are discarded, noticing the trickle of my cum on the inside of her thighs, and say, "Get dressed. The others are waiting for us."

I don't miss the hint of sadness on her face.

But she doesn't say anything, and I try not to let myself feel too disappointed. After all, we have less than two weeks left. Then she'll be free of me.

The sharp pain in my chest at the thought is too overwhelming to ignore.

TWENTY-SEVEN

June

Groping Theo while riding was almost as much of a high as the actual ride. Or maybe more of a high by the way he let himself loose on me in the office. The power I felt on the bike, combined with the near-degradation in his office, was invigorating.

After several hours of dancing and drinking at the Iron Cage, Theo and I return to his house and fuck again in the kitchen. Each time is more addictive than the last, like a drug that gets better every use. Or maybe our disagreement Friday and the following conversation after church has added a layer of intimacy that I didn't expect. I know telling me about Scottie was significant for Theo, an invitation to not only see his pain but lay among it. The presence of another so close to the bruises of your past is both uncomfortable and comforting.

At least, that's how I felt telling Theo about my family. The abuse, foster care, fear, death… I haven't thought about how the satisfaction of finally ending my dad's miserable life was tainted by Imogen's rejection in a long time. Saying it out loud was like throwing up. Excruciating in the moment, but worth it when the nausea alleviated.

I think about Imogen's little boy all the time. My mom and Calvin have sent me pictures of Grayson, and I wonder if my mom suspects who his real father is. He looks so much like Michael that I can't imagine she's never considered it.

No one has mentioned anything to me, though.

It's not lost on me that Theo is the only person in the world I've told that story to. Sadie, Rose, and Evelyn have gotten versions, but not everything. I can't tell them how I stabbed my dad in the neck and smiled at the shock and fear in his eyes when he realized he was about to die.

Something shifted in my chest on Friday. Lying next to a sleeping Theo tonight, still feeling the aching pleasure from having him between my legs, sends my brain on a rollercoaster. Not a smooth one, either. One at a state fair that's too fast to be held together with rusted bolts and flimsy wheels.

I want this to be simple. I want to examine the feeling in my chest without being obstructed by preconceived assumptions, others' opinions, or fears. I want to be able to use normal words for whatever this is. I want to scrub the beginning of my association with Theo, those months of following him and the first few weeks being here, from existence.

If we weren't weighed down by our beginning, then maybe we'd be strong enough to have a future.

All I'm certain of is here and now, and even that isn't pure. I still have questions. He still has secrets. There are hurdles I'm not sure I can clear because I have no idea how tall they are.

But maybe I can eliminate just one unknown.

While Theo sleeps, I unlock his phone with no problem since I've known his code for weeks. Going through his messages somehow feels like too much of an invasion of privacy, so instead, I open his call history. Most of the calls are with other Saints, a few are to someone named Lorry, and a ton are spam or random numbers. But there's one from over a week ago to Cottonwood Tucson, and a quick Google search reveals it's an addiction treatment center.

Just like that, I've found the rehab facility where Amber is. According to their website, visitation hours are on Sunday. Unfortunately, I'm not Amber's family. Fortunately, I'm a licensed professional counselor and a very good liar.

I could ask Luna to take me, but I don't particularly want Theo to know where I'm going. So, I text Sadie, who's more than happy to "go on an adventure" tomorrow morning. She's even happier to come back to Theo's house, especially while he's home.

With that settled, I return Theo's phone to his bedside table and settle into his side, letting my eyes shut and my brain take a break from the jolting roller coaster.

He's awake before me the next morning. I find him sitting on the couch, phone in hand.

"Hey, Tink," I say, dragging my finger along the arm of the couch. He looks up at me, frowning at the nickname. The frown quickly disappears when I swing a leg around to straddle him. "Sadie had a bad date last night." I rub my hands down his chest, and his expression turns suspicious. "She needs a girls' day. So, we're going shopping for a few hours. She's coming to pick me up."

"Are you asking permission to go out with your friend?"

"No, I'm telling you I'm going out with my friend. I think we're past the whole jailor routine, don't you?" My hands travel under his shirt, meeting hot skin. He hisses at the contact, and I feel him harden beneath me.

He grips my hips, pulling me closer. "When is she getting here?"

I purse my lips in thought. "Ten minutes."

"That's enough." He surges forward, lips latching onto the base of my throat, and sneaks a hand between us, cupping me over my pants. "Take these off," he says, pushing me off his lap. I look toward James's room, and Theo says, "He's asleep."

"It's almost ten in the morning."

"On a Sunday, he's asleep. Now hurry. We're down to nine minutes."

I obey, shoving my pants and underwear off. Theo simultaneously pushes his sweatpants down enough to free himself. Already slick and ready, I straddle him again, positioning over his cock. He holds the base, guiding me down, and the cool metal of his piercing sends a shiver up my spine. We both moan, our foreheads pressing together until I'm fully seated. With my hands around his neck, I start rising until only the tip is still inside. Before I get the chance to lower again, he simultaneously thrusts up and pulls my hips down, setting a rhythm.

The fact that James could walk out of his room and see us, or Sadie could arrive at any second, only makes this hotter. I rock forward, grinding down on him to alleviate the throbbing. We both pick up the pace, chasing release. His head falls back to rest on the couch cushion, blowing out a heavy breath.

Briefly, I think about the fact that this is the fourth time we've had sex in two days, and he hasn't kissed me once. I didn't expect to miss that part of fucking, but as I stare at him biting his bottom lip to keep from yelling, I long to replace his teeth with mine.

Instead, I dig my nails into his skin through his shirt and continue bouncing until I feel myself reaching the crest.

"Theo!" I shout without thinking. He abruptly covers my mouth, muffling my next moan.

He lifts his head, eyes boring into mine. "Now, little reaper."

Fuck, I should be worried about how turned on I get when he orders me around. But hearing the demand in his voice mixed with a croak of desire sends me over the edge. I gasp into his palm. The sensation of my orgasm drags Theo with me. We slow down, both breathing heavy.

My body begs to stay put, but Sadie will be here soon, and I don't want to still have Theo inside me when she arrives. So, I carefully lift off him, then reach down and cup myself, catching his cum before it can leak down my thighs.

Theo lifts an eyebrow. "What are you doing?"

"I don't want to have to change my pants," I say, scooping up my underwear and pants, then running to the bathroom. Clean and redressed, I'm in the process of washing my hands when the doorbell rings.

"I'll get it!" I yell through the shut door. I stumble from the bathroom in my rush, but Theo beats me there.

"Miss Oliver, so good to finally meet you," he says.

"Sexy biker!" Sadie replies. She leaps forward, wrapping her arms around Theo in a tight hug. She's taller than me, so she barely has to lift onto her toes to hug him.

Theo looks back at me, a bemused expression plastered on his face. His arms are out to the side awkwardly, like he's not sure what to do. I'm tempted to let him figure out how to deal with my best friend, but I want to get her out of here more than I want to see Theo struggle.

"Sadie, seriously?"

She lets go, turns in my direction, and beams. "What? I'm finally meeting the man who managed to not only capture your attention but also have you essentially living in his house in less than three weeks."

"I don't live here," I lie.

"No, you're just having girls' nights here and sleeping here most of the week and having me pick you up from here when your car is in the shop."

He tilts his head forward. I try to communicate with my eyes that I had to come up with a lie about why I don't have my car that's not the fucked-up truth. The slight rise of his lips tells me he understands.

"Can we go now?" I ask.

"Uhm, no?" Sadie says. Then she grabs Theo's hand and tugs him to the kitchen table, pulling out a chair and dropping across from him. I grudgingly sit between them, accepting that she won't give up any time soon.

"So, tell me, Mr. Criminal Biker Man—"

"Sadie!"

"Are you a wizard?" she asks, smoothly ignoring me.

Theo frowns. "What?"

"Do you have a magic ding dong? Are you blackmailing her?"

If I had coffee, I would've choked on it.

"Or, I know!" She claps her hands together. "You're a US Marshal, and Juney here is in Witness Protection?"

"If I were in Witness Protection, I'd have a new name and be moved to a different state."

She waves her hands in the air, brushing me off and keeping her attention locked on Theo. "So?"

He still looks confused, which makes me laugh. "I don't…"

"She's trying to figure out how you got me so… captivated."

"Oh," he smiles and nods. Turning to Sadie, he winks and says, "I knocked her on her ass."

"Theo!"

"Wait, what?" Sadie gasps. Her grin widens further as

she looks between us. When she asked how we met, I gave her some vague answer about running into each other after Taco Tuesday.

"Yeah. It was late one Tuesday, and she was walking through a park. I was the only other person there, and I guess I was walking too close, because she tried to hit me, and I tackled her to the ground."

I'm shocked at how much of the truth he's giving her. "I did not *try,*" I correct. "I did hit you." I think. I can't truthfully remember the details of our first meeting.

"I still pinned you."

"I cut you first."

"Barely."

"I almost had you!"

"You had as much as I wanted you to have, little reaper."

I bite my cheek, catching myself before I can keep arguing and possibly give away too much in front of Sadie, who's watching the exchange with enraptured eyes and a splitting smile.

"Little reaper?" she asks.

"He thinks he's clever."

"I am clever," he says. "Her last name is Graves, and she has a cemetery tattooed on her arm."

Sadie spreads her hands over the kitchen table. "Let me get this straight. You decided to go for a walk, alone, at night, in the woods, and when a strange man who has a good ten inches and a hundred pounds on you started following you, you decided to fight him instead of calling 911 or, I don't know, running?"

"It was a park, not the woods."

"You're lucky he turned out to be a biker with a soft heart and not a fucking serial killer." She gives me a look I can't quite interpret and don't have the time to because Theo laughs, and I turn my glare on him.

"In her defense, she's a good fighter," he says when he's done laughing.

"I'm a *great* fighter."

"You two are adorable," Sadie says.

He smirks, satisfaction leaking from his pores. I hear steps behind me, and Sadie looks down the hallway, her lips parting. Her eyes move up and down, filling with the recognizable glint of attraction.

"Hey, James," I say, before turning to see him walking over. His eyes are also trained on Sadie, with thinly veiled suspicion. He's wearing tattered jeans and an old AC/DC t-shirt that leaves most of his tattoos on display. His normally slicked-back red hair is hanging loose, strands falling over his forehead.

"Morning, June, T," he says, nodding to us both. Then he looks at Sadie, his lip twitching. "Sadie, right?"

Oh, right. I forgot they stalked me almost as much as I stalked them.

"Yeah. And you're the Weasleys' badass uncle who left to become an American biker."

James frowns, his brows lowering in confusion.

"She's making a joke, dumbass," Theo explains. "You know, the Weasleys from *Harry Potter*? Family of redheads?"

"Right." He nods. "Nice to… meet you."

"You too. So, you're Theo's roommate and basically his brother?" Sadie's voice sounds like it's dancing, and I know she's loving every second of this.

I avert my eyes but still feel James's sharp look in my direction. He's probably wondering how much I've told my friends.

"Yes."

"James is the vice president of the Saints," Theo offers.

"What's that like?" Sadie asks.

"A headache," James says.

"He's pretty much the parent of fifteen psychos," I say.

"Sixteen," he corrects.

"I wasn't including Theo."

His eyes narrow on me. "Neither was I."

My cheeks burn. I clear my throat and push against the table, the chair scraping against the floor. "Alright, that's enough." I motion for Sadie to follow. "Let's go."

"But—"

"Sadie."

She pushes her bottom lip out in an exaggerated pout. "Fine." She and Theo both stand and follow me to the front door. James stays by the table, hands in his pockets. "It was good to finally meet you, Theo," she says, standing on her tiptoes to kiss his cheek. Then she looks past him to James and winks. "And you, Weasley."

James dips his chin in her direction.

Theo says, "You too, Miss Oliver," then calls to me, "Be safe, little reaper."

I hold up my middle finger, ignoring his laugh and the answering warmth that blooms in my stomach.

Miraculously, she waits until we're locked in her car before saying, "Holy shit, you live with two Adonises."

"I don't live there."

She waves her hand in the air. "Semantics. So, where are we going again?"

I plug the address into her phone, and directions show up on the dashboard screen.

"And we're not telling your boyfriend because?"

"Because I'm going to talk to his ex-girlfriend," I admit.

She briefly glances at me with wide eyes. "Becoming an obsessed new girlfriend, are we? I support it."

I chuckle. "I love you, you know that?"

"'Course you do."

We listen to Olivia Rodrigo, starting with "Obsessed," much to Sadie's delight. When we arrive, I take a deep breath to calm my racing heart. "You can wait either inside, out here, or go get coffee then come back and pick me up."

"I'll wait here. How long do you need?"

"No more than an hour."

She nods, then looks back at the building. "You think dating Theo is what landed her in rehab?"

Yes. "No, I just have some questions."

"Text me if you need me."

"Thank you." I open the door and jump out, then take a deep breath before heading inside.

"Good morning. Welcome to Cottonwood," the older woman behind the welcome desk says upon my entrance. "How can I help you?"

"I'm here to see Amber Wallace," I say, setting my credentials and ID on the counter.

"Are you family?" she asks, examining my driver's license first.

"Family therapist."

It takes a few minutes of careful conversation before the woman leads me back to a meeting room with three sections of chairs and couches, one section already occupied. A thin, pale, Scandinavian-looking man sits in an armchair. Next to him on the corner of the couch is a woman about the same age, with dark brown skin and long black hair. They're holding hands, both wearing wedding rings. By the man's torn cuticles and bouncing leg, I'd guess he's the resident here. Next to the woman is a man a few years older, who looks like he could be her brother. A little girl sits cross-legged across from them, wearing headphones and holding an iPad in her lap. She looks up as I walk past, her glistening eyes meeting mine.

"You can wait here," the employee tells me, gesturing to the couch furthest from the family. "Amber will be out in a few minutes."

"Thank you."

She nods, gives me one more look as if I'll announce my less-than-honorable intentions, then walks off. Five minutes later, I'm leaning my forearms against my knees when a young woman arrives, dark eyes full of suspicion landing on me. I recognize her immediately, though she's gained a bit of much-needed weight and her hair is longer, still choppy, the remnants of a pixie cut that has grown out unevenly. None of her tattoos are visible.

I stay seated as Amber approaches and drops into the chair across from me.

"You're not my therapist." She has one of those sexy raspy voices.

"No." I almost tell her I'm Jennifer's, but that would be yet another HIPAA violation, and I can only stomach betraying my clients so many times. What I decide to say is still a grey area, though. "I know your aunt, though. She's really worried about you."

Amber scoffs. "She doesn't give a shit about me."

"You're all she talks about."

"Don't mistake that for family love. Jennifer only cares about herself and what people think about her."

"She cares about you."

"When I was a kid, she cared about proving to my parents that she was a successful person with an enviable life, despite being alone and childless. She only spent time with me to pretend she cared about my mom. They had some fucked up sister passive-aggressive rivalry thing going on."

"And now?"

"Now, she just cares about controlling me. She got stuck

with me, and her perfect single life was over. She resented me until she realized I could be an extension of her. People pitied and respected her. 'Poor Jennifer, losing her sister and brother-in-law like that. How wonderful of her to take their troubled daughter in,'" she mocks. "She wanted me to be the perfect woman, a beautiful and successful model that reflected her brilliant parenting. She let me know every day how much I disappointed her."

I open my mouth to respond, then clamp it shut again. I'm not here to have a therapy session with Amber. She gets one of those every day in this place. She's saying this to try to prove she doesn't care who I am and has no intention of talking to her aunt.

"I don't want to talk to you about Jennifer."

She crosses her arms and leans back in the chair. "Then why the fuck are you here?"

I glance over her shoulder, noticing that one of the employees is standing in the doorway. He's not looking at any of us, and thankfully, he's too far away to hear us.

"Who gave you that scar?" I ask, referring to the raised white scar on her neck.

Her brows fall into a scowl. "The car wreck."

"You weren't in the car with your parents," I say. Jennifer has gone over the day her sister died in detail. "And that scar is newer."

"Why do you care?"

"I've heard you got caught up with a bad crowd."

"Did Jennifer tell you that?" Amber interrupts. "Last time I saw her, she yelled at me for 'whoring myself out to a bunch of lowlife gang bangers.'" She makes air quotes with her fingers, then crosses her arms again.

I try not to look surprised that Jennifer would say something like that. It's possible those aren't her exact words, and Amber just interpreted them poorly. There's no way to know for sure. *And it doesn't matter*, I remind myself.

"Did they do that to you?"

"What is this? Are you some undercover cop trying to get me to rat on the Saints? Or…" her eyes widen, realization filling them. She uncrosses her arms and leans away from me, her face going slack with fear. "You're with *them*. Look, I already told Bowie—"

"I'm not with the South Five," I interrupt.

"But you know about them?"

"And your debts to them." Amber moves to stand up, but I hold out my hand. "I want to ask you about Theo."

"Are you kidding me?" she says, voice rising.

The man in the doorway turns his head in our direction, and I focus on Amber, making my voice as level and calming as I can. "I'm not here to judge you."

"Judge me all you want, I don't give a shit."

Deciding that jumping around the topic will do more harm than good, I ask, "Did Theo give you that scar?"

"He might as well have."

"What does that mean?" I recognize my 'therapist voice' that I usually save for the office. Amber must hear it too, because she rolls her eyes.

"It means when you get involved with a group of people who use violence to solve every problem, you're bound to walk away scarred. If you walk away at all."

"Is that the reason you're in here? To get away from Theo?"

"Theo is an asshole, okay?" she bites. False anger fills her voice in an attempt to mask what she's truly feeling. Like dumping a tablespoon of pepper on a double chocolate brownie to try and eliminate the sugar. "Is that what you want to hear? He's a thug who fucks anything that moves and lost interest in me as soon as I wasn't the perky, innocent, young little girl he first met. When I started standing up for myself, I became a nuisance, and he shoved me in this hellhole."

"Why didn't he just break up with you?"

"He wanted to get rid of me completely."

"What does that mean?"

She catches the look in my eyes and says, "He wasn't going to kill me if that's what you're thinking." She shrugs bony shoulders and adds, "But not because of some moral code. I mean, dude is a predator. I was twenty-one when we met. He was thirty."

She's desperately trying to villainize him. Or maybe he *is* a villain, and I'm the dumbass making excuses for a bad guy because he's decent in bed and has a pierced dick.

"I'm sorry you went through that," I say. "I don't mean to minimize your trauma. I'm just asking if you were ever afraid of him. Did you notice anything off or more dangerous than normal?" I think about the last week and how often Theo has been disappearing for "club business." James is almost always with him, and Luna seems to know what's going on even if she's not directly involved. But the rest of the club only cares about riding, partying, pulling off chop jobs, and fucking up the South Five. "Was he keeping stuff from the rest of the Saints of Purgatory?"

She frowns, premature wrinkles forming on her forehead. "He leads an outlaw motorcycle club. Of course, he's dangerous."

I roll my lips between my teeth. It's an effort not to get visibly annoyed. "But did you notice—"

"You're fucking him," Amber interrupts.

"What?"

Her mouth split into a wide smile. "Oh, my god. You're

fucking him. What is this? Stalk the ex-girlfriend time? God, shouldn't a therapist be less pathetic?"

"No, I'm not."

"Yes, you are. Wow. This is unbelievable."

"Theo could be a danger to—"

"Shut up. Seriously."

"I'm sorry?"

She shakes her head, still grinning. "Look, I know he's good at fucking, but that's all he's good for. The moment you're no longer new and exciting, he'll screw you over. So, enjoy it while it lasts, and I'll see you in a few weeks when he decides your pussy isn't tight enough and he shoves you in here with me." Before I can respond, she stands, turns around, and walks away.

Sadie is still waiting for me outside, and, being the best friend in the world, she doesn't ask about my conversation with Amber.

After a few hours of shopping and a quick lunch, we stop at a cafe to drink tea, surrounded by bags of newly purchased clothes, books, and jewelry. My phone rings, Theo's name and a picture of him scowling at the camera flashing on the screen.

"Oh, the marshal is calling," Sadie says.

I roll my eyes, pick up the phone, and stare at his picture, considering whether to answer. Then I see it's nearly four p.m., which means he's let me enjoy over six hours with my best friend without interruption. So, I accept the call.

"Hey."

"Little reaper. How's your girls' day?"

"Sadie's smile says great. My credit card disagrees."

He laughs, a little puff of air through the speakers. "Did you go anywhere interesting?" He says 'interesting' with a barely noticeable lilt, and I worry he knows about my

Cottonwood visit. But no, there's no reason for him to know. I turned off my phone's location services and got rid of the tracker in my wallet. I even checked for any others he could've planted on me.

"We went to a new boutique downtown."

"And what did you buy at this boutique?" he asks suggestively.

"You'll have to wait and see."

"When do you think you'll be back?"

"I'm not sure."

Sadie must hear Theo's side of the conversation because she whispers, "I need to get back to Soot anyway."

We could easily go back to her house and hang out there, but I know what she's doing. A week ago, I would've taken the opportunity to spend more time with her, away from Theo. Now, I can't wait to run my fingers through his hair and feel the rumble of his voice with my head on his chest.

"We're headed back soon," I say.

"Want anything specific for dinner?"

"Surprise me, Tink. Just no pickles."

"Tink?" she mouths.

"Careful, little reaper. I may have to fuck that name out of your vocabulary."

My cheeks burn, growing hotter when Sadie's jaw goes slack.

"I'll text you when we're on the way," I say, words half filled with air.

"Be safe."

"Bye," I hang up before he can say anything else, then hold my hand up, stopping her just as she opens her mouth. "Not a word."

She grins, and I know I'm going to regret answering that call in front of her for the rest of my life.

TWENTY-EIGHT

Theo

"Chick vein alert," James says as I watch June's location on my phone. She's half an hour away. Thirty minutes has never felt so long.

"Weren't you going to the gym?" I ask.

"'Bout to leave." He sits across from me, shaking the bottle full of his pre-workout. "Want to talk about it?"

"No."

He pops the top off his drink and raises an eyebrow. "Is it the friend? Because I'm going to have to veto that one moving in too."

"Fuck off, James."

"And here I thought things were going well. I mean, I just heard you call a girl to ask her when she'd be back. Every day you fall more."

"I'm not falling."

"T."

"J."

"You've been off all day. It's giving me whiplash."

I don't cognitively think about saying it, but the words come anyway. "She went to see Amber."

James pauses mid-drink and slowly lowers his bottle. "What?"

"She figured out Amber is in Cottonwood, and she went there this morning." She turned off her location on her phone, but I had James put a tracker in Sadie's car over two weeks ago, assuming June would try to escape with her friend after a Taco Tuesday. She was sitting in the parking lot for an hour before driving away.

"Why do you care? You already told her about Amber, didn't you?"

"That doesn't mean I want the two... hanging out."

"Worried Amber is going to scare June away?"

I shake my head, clicking my phone back on to watch June's dot head in my direction. "I guess I just... thought we were past this."

"She's an obsessive serial killer. Of course she had to verify the story. Loathe as I am to admit it, she's a decent person. She's driven by a need for justice. That drive wasn't going to shut off because someone told her justice was already done. She had to see it for herself."

"I know." I've gone over this a hundred times in my head the last few hours. I've opened her contact on my phone a dozen times to call her. I considered calling Cottonwood. I convinced myself it was fine, that talking to Amber didn't push her to disappear. Or try to kill me again. I watched her location as she went from store to store and pictured her telling Sadie the truth, begging for help escaping me. I've gone back and forth about confronting her about it when she gets back.

When I couldn't take it anymore, I called her. By her voice and words, everything is okay between us. But I won't fully relax until she's here, writhing beneath me.

"She's also not an idiot. She probably saw right through

Amber's bullshit," James says. I nod, and he stands, slapping my shoulder. "Stop brooding. If you two can get past attempted murder, you can survive meeting the exes."

"Sure," I mutter. A moment later, I hear the door open and shut, then the rumbling of his bike.

When June is ten minutes away, I pull myself off the couch and head to the kitchen to start the marinade to soak the pork in, pop the cork off a bottle of wine, and am pouring the glasses when the front door opens. June strolls in alone. She sets a handful of shopping bags on the dining room table, finds me in the kitchen, and smiles.

That's a good sign.

"Wine?" she asks, raising her eyebrows and toeing off her shoes. "Are we celebrating something?"

I shrug. "You've been here for eighteen days. That seems like enough to celebrate."

"Only eighteen?" She lets out an exaggerated sigh. "Feels like a lot longer than that."

She crosses the room and accepts the offered glass of wine. Watching her bring the rim to her lips and swallow a sip of the red liquid has my mouth going dry. Then her tongue darts out to capture a drop from her bottom lip and my cock twitches in interest.

"We've come a long way."

"Does that mean I'm off the hook?" I ask, sipping my own wine.

She tsks and shakes her head. "I still have twelve days to make that decision."

I set down my glass and step forward, my feet positioned on either side of hers. My hands land on the counter so I'm caging her in. Her breath hitches, and she holds the wine closer to her chest as she looks up at me.

"And I have twelve days to make the reaper beg for

mercy." I kick her feet apart and grip the back of her neck, keeping her head in place. She gasps, and I pluck the glass from her hand. "Open your mouth." I wait for her lips to part, then pour half the glass of wine past her lips. A bit dribbles from the corners. "Swallow." Her throat moves as she obeys, and I lean down, licking the trail of wine up her throat to the corner of her lips. Lingering an inch over her lips, I set her glass on the counter behind her. With my now empty hand, I pop open her pants and push under her underwear. "Come on, you can get wetter than that," I whisper, my breath brushing her lips. She shudders and pushes her hips into my hand. I dip my fingers into her pussy, coating them before returning them to her clit.

Her eyes shut, and she grips my shirt, holding on tight as I rub and pinch and fuck her with my fingers. She lets out a breathy moan and presses her forehead to my chin. When she's nearing her orgasm, I pull my fingers free. Her eyes pop open, and before she can complain, I shove my fingers into her mouth.

"Clean them, little reaper."

She scowls, even as her tongue slips between the digits. She licks every inch, then tries to yank her head back, but doesn't get far since I'm still holding the back of her neck. I press her tongue down and slide my fingers deeper in until she gags. Only then do I pull them free and let her go. She sags against the counter and glares at me.

"What was that?" she asks.

I retrieve my wine and say after a drink, "I don't know what you're talking about."

She crosses her arms, pouting. It's so cute that I look forward to causing it several more times tonight. I lean against the counter across from her and peer at her over my glass.

"Are you going to tell me about your day?"

"I did on the phone. It was fun. We went to a few stores. I bought a couple of books I've been wanting to read."

"Is that what you got at the new boutique?"

"If you want to see what I got at the new boutique, you can't leave me with lady blue balls."

I chuckle and almost decide to give her what she wants. But she hasn't earned that yet. "How is Sadie?"

Her face is blank for a moment before she remembers the story she fed me about Sadie's bad date. "She's okay. The day was good for her."

Fuck, I can't do this anymore. "Even the hour of waiting while you talked to my ex-girlfriend?"

"Shit," she mutters, running her hands through her hair and scratching her scalp. "I knew it. Fuck." She crosses her arms again. "How on earth did you find out?"

"We've established that you're not the only one who's good at stalking. But that's not the point. Are we going to talk about it?"

"There's nothing to talk about."

"You snuck into a rehab facility to interrogate my ex, who you used to think I abused then murdered, and you think that's not something we should talk about?"

"Clearly, you didn't kill her, so that's settled, and we can move on." She starts to move, and I extend a leg to block her.

"If I need to tie you down to force you to talk to me, I will."

"It's not a big deal. She's angry and hurt and scared. I get it. She blames you for everything that went wrong in her life, but I know you didn't hurt her. Not like that, anyway."

"And?"

"And she's a traumatized kid getting the help she needs. That's it."

I raise my eyebrows. "That's it?"

She lets out a frustrated huff, then deflates and meets my eyes again. She nods and says, seriously, "Yes. I just had to check on her, okay? But that's all."

I believe her. I don't know what that says about me or means for us, but I believe her. I know looking Amber in the eyes was something she needed to do.

"You could've told me. I would've taken you."

She shakes her head. "I had to go myself."

"Next time, just tell me where you're going."

"Maybe I don't want you to always know where I am. That's a sign of a controlling relationship, you know."

I smirk. "Are you saying this is a relationship?"

She frowns and rolls her eyes, then walks away.

"Where are you going?"

"To shower!" she calls over her shoulder. "Alone!"

Feeling lighter, I return to the couch, slowly sipping the wine. I'm checking Valor's records from the Saints of Purgatory's meetings and correspondences with outside organizations, reports on our latest jobs, suggestions for future jobs, and updates on the South Five, when I get a message. I click the name on the top of my screen and smile, typing out a response.

Then I drop my phone and head to the bathroom to bring my little reaper to the edge again.

~

We watch *Die Hard 2* while our dinner cooks, finishing half the bottle of wine. After dinner, I get on my knees between June's legs and feast on her for dessert, letting her reach the crest over and over but never quite falling. The third *Die Hard* has just started when she climbs off the couch to go to the bathroom and comes back wearing a thin pair of black panties and a lacy black corset with attached garters.

My cock is instantly hard.

"The new boutique had the cutest selection," she says, voice low and seductive. "I thought you'd like this one."

"Goddamn, little reaper." I glance at the clock, see it's nearly eight-thirty, and thank whatever freaky god likes to watch people fucking.

She circles the couch, stops in front of me, and leans down, giving me a perfect view of her ass. "Well?"

Quickly, I stand, pick her up, and carry her to her bedroom, where I drop her on the bed.

"Why are we in here?" she asks.

I pull the furry leather handcuffs I put in my back pocket earlier and make quick work of securing her arms behind her back. "Because only I'm allowed to fuck you in *my* bed."

"What does that mean?"

Right on time, the front door opens. June's eyes go wide when I yell, "We're in here!"

I keep my attention firmly on my little reaper so I can watch her expression turn from horrified to shocked to nervous but interested when Luna walks into the bedroom.

"Hey, killer," she says, voice dripping with mischief. "Ready to have some fun?"

TWENTY-NINE

Theo

June uses her feet to push back on the bed, her wide eyes going from Luna to me. Something white-hot vibrates in my chest as my body wars with the simultaneous desire to throw Luna from the room and shove her forward so she can take June apart with that troublesome mouth of hers.

"What is this?" June asks, looking down at the sexy outfit she put on to try and persuade me to finally give her an orgasm.

Luna walks past me and stops by the head of the bed. "Don't you remember?" She leans down and strokes the side of June's face. "I was promised one time to have some fun with you."

Realization fills her eyes as she remembers my promise to give Lu a taste.

"Fucking Battleship," June mutters under her breath, even as her legs rub together. I practically see her thoughts filtering through her mind like a jukebox unable to land on a specific song. Rather than leaving her on shuffle, I want to see her lost in a song of desire.

"Go ahead, Lu," I say.

She needs no more encouragement. Luna flattens her

palm against June's stomach over the corset and trails up, between her tits and to her neck. Her hand goes around June's throat, and I worry for a second that she's going to kiss my little reaper. That was my one rule when I agreed to this little game. No kissing. If I can't taste that delicious mouth, no one can.

But Lu knows to obey, and she applies pressure, guiding June to her back. June lets out a huff of pain when her arms land uncomfortably behind her, thanks to the handcuffs.

"Goddamn, what is this outfit?" Luna moans, eyes traveling down June's body and snagging on her thighs where the garters cut into skin.

"She bought it today," I say.

June's hips twist as if she can physically feel our eyes on her. Luna crawls onto the bed and straddles June, moving both hands to cup her tits and rub down her side.

"Luna…" June pleads.

"Easy, killer." Lu skims her fingers under the corset and rolls her hips down. "How do you want to do this, boss?" she asks, not tearing her eyes from my reaper's face.

"Make her beg," I order.

"Gladly." Luna moves down, hovering over June's pussy. She pulls in a long breath through her nose, then looks back at me and smiles. "Delicious."

"Wait until you taste her."

June sits up, arms bent behind her and abs clenching to look down at Luna with unchecked need in her eyes. "Please," she says.

I close the distance between us and shove her down with a large hand on her chest. She hits the bed with a gasp, and I palm her tit over the lingerie, then imitate Luna and place my hand on June's throat. I squeeze, much harder than Lu did, and nod at her to continue. She obeys, ripping off June's underwear and burying her face in the reaper's sweet pussy. June's mouth opens with a gasp that has no noise since I'm cutting off her air.

"That's it," I say, feeling her pulse quicken under my fingertips. "You like having Lu's mouth on you?" I keep the pressure until her lids start sliding shut, then I let go of her throat. She sucks in a breath, her eyes glassy, and moans when Luna's hands join her mouth.

"Please..."

"What do you want, baby?" I ask.

"I want to come."

Luna's eyes flick up, looking at me over June's pelvis. I nod once. She hums, diving back in. June writhes, and the sounds of her breathy moans make my cock strain against my pants. My fingers go around her neck again, this time closer to her chin, forcing her to look up at me.

"Come, little reaper. Now."

Like the good girl she is, she obeys, back arching, secured arms straining behind her, hips following Luna's mouth. She lets out a shout that's been held in since the first orgasm I denied her over three hours ago.

"Holy fuck, killer. You taste incredible," Luna says, fingers digging into June's thighs as she peers up at us, lips and chin glistening.

June sucks in a heavy breath, sweat coating her skin. I waste no time pulling off my clothes, telling Luna to take off June's handcuffs as I do. Once she's free, I say, "On your back, Lu." Smiling wide with anticipation, she climbs up the bed and drops onto her back. She's already reaching for June when I say, "Sit on her face, facing me."

June's legs are shaky as she obeys, hovering over Lu's face as if she's afraid to drop all her weight. But, unsurprisingly, Luna grasps June's thighs and pulls her roughly down, mouth open and ready. June moans, head falling back. I give her a second to enjoy it, stroking myself as I watch. *Fuck*, I didn't realize how much I'd love watching her get used like this. But only by someone I trust, like Lu. And only once, because as turned on as I am, I also feel a burning jealousy that feels like actual fire licking my bones.

June rocks forward, riding Lu's face and chasing another orgasm. Her nipples are hard beads under the corset, which is latched and tied at the front. I quickly undo it, ripping the garment away from her body. Her full tits bounce with her movement, and I gather them up in my hands, nails digging into flesh. Goosebumps bloom over her chest. She gasps out, "Theo, please."

Who am I to deny her? I lean over, suck a nipple into my mouth, and bite down. Satisfaction runs through my veins when she yelps a response. I circle her puckered nipple with my tongue, then move to the other breast.

Straightening, I move my hands to her hair and fist the strands. With a hungry whimper, June reaches for my dick, wrapping a hand around the shaft and stroking. She uses her thumb to swipe over the tip, gathering the glistening pre-cum, then rolls the piercing between thumb and forefinger.

"Fuck," I groan, abs tightening. "Hold on tight, Lu," I warn, before yanking June down by her hair and shoving my cock in her mouth. The tip hits the back of her throat, and she gags and jolts. "That's it, baby. Choke on me." I pull back, then slam forward again, all the way to the hilt. Tears fill her eyes as she chokes, but she doesn't pull away. She holds onto my thighs, and we set a rhythm of me fucking her mouth and her rocking on Lu's face.

Several minutes pass, and when I feel an orgasm cresting, I pull out completely, not yet ready to be done. I keep my fingers tangled in her hair and watch her face as I say, "Another one, little reaper. Drown Lu." She rocks forward once more, then her entire body goes rigid, and she bites her bottom lip. I pull her lip down with my thumb. "I want to hear you."

"Fuck!" she shouts, her nails digging into my waist so hard that she breaks skin.

I don't give her a moment to breathe before I pick her up off of Luna and spin her around, dropping her back on the bed on her hands and knees. "Back up, Lu, and take off your shorts," I say.

She scoots back on the bed, then wiggles out of her bottoms so her bare pussy is level with June's head. I hold onto June's hips with one hand and grab the base of my cock, angling myself at her entrance.

Before pushing in, I tell June, "Show how much you appreciate her, little reaper." I wait until her mouth is an inch from Lu, then thrust inside. She lets out a sound that's half gasp, half curse, momentarily overwhelmed by taking all of me at once. Her empty lungs attempt to refill, and I press my hand to the back of her head, pushing her down to Lu's pussy. She starts licking and sucking, and either she's done this before or she's just a natural because Luna is writhing immediately, eyes squeezed shut.

"Shit, you're so tight." I pound into her again, rocking her entire body.

"Holy goddamn," Luna mumbles, lost in the sensation of June's mouth.

The combination of seeing her eat another woman and the feeling of being buried in her cunt is almost too much. I set a bruising rhythm, and soon the headboard is banging against the wall. Obscene sounds of skin slapping skin, my cock sliding in and out of her wet pussy, and Luna's moaning and praising June fill the room.

"You're so good," I say, rubbing my hand down her spine. "Fuck, little reaper. You were made for this. Made for my cock." *Made for me.*

She groans happily, and Luna arches off the bed, her knees bending and hand twisting into the sheets as she climaxes. June lifts her head, and I imagine her giving Lu a look full of satisfaction. I reach around her waist, fingers finding her clit, and start rubbing. They slide easily because of how wet she is, and her cunt tightens around my dick. I move my other hand to her stomach and pull her up so her back is flush against my chest. The new position makes her feel like a vise around my cock.

I'm close, but I have no intention of going alone. With my mouth next to her ear, I whisper, "Come with me, little reaper. You can do it. One more." I pull out to the tip then pinch her clit and ram into her, throwing her over the edge. She comes with a shout and clamps down on me. I follow, cock pulsing. She goes limp, and I steady her with arms around her middle. My lips find their way to her neck, kissing softly. I lick at her salty, sweaty skin and wonder if you can become addicted to someone's taste.

"Holy shit, boss," Luna says. She's still sitting against the headboard, eyes wide from watching me fuck June. "Your killer is the sexiest woman I've ever seen."

"I know." My hand travels to cup June's chin, and I turn her face enough to lick up the side of her neck and kiss her jaw. "Now go wait in the living room. You've had your fill."

Lu sticks out her bottom lip in a pout.

"Now, Lu." The warning growl in my voice compels her off the bed.

She grabs her clothes and heads for the bedroom door but pauses, looks back with a smirk, and says, "Thanks for the taste, killer."

Once she's gone, I flip June around so we're face to face. Her eyes are heavy, pupils blown, and her cheeks are rosy. She's so fucking beautiful. It's like a collar around my heart, and I worry at how easily I'd hand her a leash.

"Did I accidentally agree to any other threesomes?" she asks with a tired voice.

I shake my head, grinning. "I hope you enjoyed that, because it's the last time anyone but me will ever be between these milky thighs." I grip her muscular thighs and slide my hands up to where they meet her hips. "Or inside your sweet cunt." My thumbs dip inside, inches from said location.

She shifts on my lap, knees squeezing my sides. Blood once again travels south, but there will be time for another round later when Luna isn't here. I take a moment to let my hands travel up her body, grope her tits, circle her throat, and sink into her tangled hair. Her lips part, and I desperately want to bite the bottom one until I taste her bleeding for me.

I settle for pressing my lips to her forehead, lingering there for several seconds before I pull away and replace my lips with my forehead so our eyes are level with each other.

"What does this say about me?" she whispers. "That the only thing that makes me feel sane is killing monsters and the only thing that makes me feel alive is the touch of the one monster I couldn't kill?"

I smile, tucking hair behind her ears and cradling her jaw. "Maybe you just need someone to see all of you and not be afraid." I pull back to study her and gently brush my thumb over her cheek. "I'm not afraid, June Graves. I'm mesmerized."

THIRTY

June

Blood sprays from James's mouth, splattering the floor. He staggers but stays on his feet, the bikers surrounding me all shouting, and I follow suit, cupping my hands around my mouth to amplify my voice.

"Knock him out!" I yell.

James swipes the back of his hand across his forehead, then swings his fist, catching his opponent under the chin. I wince at the snapping sound, but my blood hums at the sight of him flying backward, body hitting the floor with a loud *THUNK.*

"Nice, James!" Theo shouts. We're in the front row watching James's fight with most of the Saints, having come straight here after a later Saturday ride. Energy sparks in the air like every spectator is an individual generator. James is transformed in the ring. He has gasoline in his veins, and he starts each round by lighting a match.

He kicks when the other fighter tries to stand, sending him flat on his stomach, eyes shut and blood spilling from his nose. The referee counts down, hits the floor, then declares James the winner, still undefeated. He raises his fists in the air, and the crowd is on their feet, screaming and clapping. Smiling wide, I turn to Theo, who's glowing with pride at his brother. With another cheer, I jump, and Theo catches me with ease, raising me up.

After the fight, I'm so wound up and turned on that Theo drags me to a closet, pulls my underwear to the side, and impales himself inside me. We fuck hard and fast, my back against the shelf and Theo gripping my ass with bruising strength.

James gives us a knowing look when we finally make it back to personally congratulate him on the win.

Back at the Iron Cage, I find myself joining in on the celebration, dancing for several hours, sweaty and drunk.

I spent the week settling into a routine that became normal so quickly that I almost don't remember when life was different. Theo took me to work every day, I met the girls for Taco Tuesday, he gave me another riding lesson that I excelled at, we hung out at the clubhouse a couple of times, and we spent every free second becoming experts on each other's bodies.

Despite all that, I still feel the fire sparking in my core. They're flames now, and I know I'll have to appease them soon. The spontaneous kill to save Theo wasn't enough. It was a handful of nuts when what I'm craving is a Thanksgiving feast.

I shake my head, trying to banish any thought that isn't about dancing to the reverberating beat of the song. I want to cling to the happiness born from the fight and celebrations. Someone comes up behind me and I look back, expecting Theo. But I don't recognize the man. Sparks dancing in my stomach, I pull away from the stranger and head to the bar, eyes scanning for Theo. When I find him, a cold sludge of apprehension seems to fill my mind. He's in the back corner with Kip, their heads bent together and Kip occasionally looking around, as if worried about being overheard.

It's probably nothing. Still, the phone call I overheard yesterday morning replays in my mind, Theo's low voice biting back in response to something I couldn't hear.

"Will you just calm down and be patient? I know what the fuck I'm doing. Look, she trusts me now. I'll get something we can use against her."

He wasn't talking about me. He couldn't be. It was Saints business. Had to be.

But as I watch him talk to Kip, his entire face frowning, an intrinsic part of me knows the truth. Swallowing down the unease, I turn to the bartender and order a fifth shot of vodka.

My memory of the night ends there. I'm not surprised when I wake up naked in Theo's bed, head pounding and pelvis sore. I groan, roll over, snatch the painkillers on the bedside table, and throw them back with the entire glass of water Theo left for me. I've slept in his room every night this week, and he, without fail, brings me a fresh glass of water before bed and in the morning. There's also a bottle of painkillers, ointment, and lotion that seem to have a permanent place on my side of the bed, just in case one of our sessions of bringing each other blinding pleasure becomes too rough.

"Coffee?"

The voice is a gong in my ears. Theo chuckles at my protests, and the bed dips when he sits. "You okay, little reaper?"

"Mm, too loud," I mumble. I turn, curl closer to Theo, and ask, "Did we fuck last night?"

"Do you want us to have fucked last night?"

My eyes inch open halfway. My cheeks flush, and heat curls between my legs at the idea of Theo using me for his own needs. He knows it, too. His eyes darken, and an eyebrow raises.

"You were so good for me last night," he says. "Very eager and obedient."

I press my thighs together, wishing I could remember what we did.

I'm about to ask what the day's plans are when he stands, leaving a mug of coffee next to the empty water glass.

"I have an errand to run with Kip. We're scouting out a possible hit for the boys. They're getting antsy."

I know how they feel, I think. I start to push the covers off to get ready. "Give me thirty mi—"

He interrupts with, "Stay here. Rest. It's not going to be fun or interesting. I won't be gone long. James should be home in an hour or two."

I frown. "Where did he sleep last night?"

"No idea, but if you find out, please share." Curiosity wakes among the fire in my chest. In the three weeks I've been here, I've never seen James with anyone, and no one has talked about a current partner or an ex.

Theo presses a kiss to my forehead before leaving, which reminds me of another mystery. He hasn't kissed me on the lips in over a week. I should ask him about it, but every time I think to, I'm distracted by his mouth landing somewhere else on my body.

It takes an hour to finally get out of bed and get dressed. The painkillers have kicked in, subduing the headache, and a smoothie staves off any nausea. Bored, I venture back into Theo's room, surveying it with fresh eyes. I dug through most of his drawers and under his bed after our fight that first week, but James interrupted me before I found anything. And I haven't thought to keep snooping since then. Deciding Theo is innocent—well, innocent *enough*—drove off ideas of invading his privacy further.

But now, that phone call fills my ears.

"She trusts me now. I'll get something we can use against her."

Uncertainty is a predator in my gut, sniffing for a hint of its prey. It propels me to his bathroom, where I know there aren't any cameras. I search and find nothing interesting in the cupboards or drawers except for a vibrator that should've found its way to his bed before now.

I check his closet next, getting on my hands and knees to look behind hanging clothes and a shoe rack. I open the gun safe, finding nothing new, and am about to give up when I notice a large binder hidden behind it.

Why would Theo hide something behind the fireproof, locked safe? Maybe he knows I have the safe's combination and thought *behind* would be safer than *inside*.

I drop to the floor, cross my legs, and stare down at the binder that looks more like a photo album now that it's in front of me.

Guilt is a rare feeling for me. I've killed fifteen people and didn't feel bad about a single one. I've never once felt guilty about invading people's privacy. But the sensation crawling up my spine feels suspiciously like guilt.

Something about this binder feels more important than an unregistered gun or a dossier of drug dealings. Tingling fingers trace the edge of the book as curiosity wars with the potential guilt of crossing this line.

I've just decided not to look when there's a voice from the closet doorway. I'd been so lost in my own thoughts that I didn't hear James arrive.

"What are you doing?" he asks.

I jump and push away from the binder. "I didn't... I wasn't..." Shame swallows the last half of those sentences.

James frowns, eyes falling on the binder. Color leeches from his cheeks. When he speaks, his voice is shaky. From fear or anger, I'm not sure. "June, tell me you didn't look at that."

I shake my head. "No. And I wasn't going to. I was about to put it back, I swear."

He takes a slow step forward. From the look on his face, I was right not to open the book. "Why do you have it?"

"I overheard Theo on the phone mentioning some girl he got to trust him, and I..." I swallow, though the embarrassment stays lodged in my throat. "I thought he was talking about me, and I don't know what I was looking for, but I had to know what he meant. If all this was real or if he's just been using me."

"You thought it'd be easier to find the answer in his personal belongings than by asking him?"

The blush deepens in my cheeks. I forgot how much I hate feeling ashamed. "You're right. I'm sorry."

"Don't apologize to me. It's not my privacy you're invading."

I nod, looking back at the binder. James's reaction to it simultaneously makes me want to look even more than before and incredibly glad that I didn't. "Was he talking about me?" I ask, keeping my eyes on the book. "On the phone call?"

"Again, I'm not the person you should ask."

My eyes burn. I'm not even sure why.

"Put the binder back, June."

His words are stern, and I prickle at being ordered to do something by anyone other than Theo. Still, I know he's right, so I grab the binder, return it to its hiding spot behind the safe, and push past James to walk out of the closet. I feel him on my heels and attempt to shake off the last few minutes before we're in the living room.

I didn't do anything wrong, and I still don't know what Theo's call was about. He could've been manipulating me this whole time, just like Amber said. So, until I have answers, I refuse to feel guilty for trying to protect myself.

While James showers, I put on old episodes of NCIS but barely pay attention. He joins me twenty minutes later, red hair still damp and water dripping from his beard onto his bare chest—I learned early on that shirtless is his typical state. He takes his normal spot in the large armchair to the right side of the couch.

"Have a good night last night?" I ask.

"Yup."

"What did you do after the Cage?"

His brows lower. "Why do you ask?"

"Because you're my friend and I'm interested," I answer honestly.

"Did Theo put you up to this?"

"I'm offended at the implication that my interest in your life hinges solely on Theo."

That *almost* earns me a smile. When all this started, I thought Theo would be the grumpiest of the two and that James would warm quickly to me. The exact opposite has proven true. I know James likes me, but he only recently started letting his guard down, and now I'm worried finding me in Theo's closet brought it right back up.

"Going to start stalking me next?"

"Ha ha. Seriously, though. Do you have a secret girlfriend stashed away on the other side of town? Or maybe a secret boyfriend?"

"If I told you, they wouldn't be secret, would they?"

I cross my arms, leaning back on the couch. James must play poker, because there isn't a single clue to what he's thinking on his face. Sensing that he won't be giving me any juicy details about his evening, I return my attention to the show. We watch in silence for nearly two episodes, then a roaring engine approaches. My stomach clenches, and my palms suddenly feel damp.

"Just ask him," James says with a surprisingly gentle voice. I look at him with wide eyes, and he offers me a soft smile that somehow bolsters my confidence. "Trust me. But… if he's not ready to tell you, don't push him."

I nod, unable to verbally respond. Logically, I've done nothing worse than what I've done in the past. But logic does nothing to ease the anxiety drying out my mouth.

Theo walks inside, sets down his helmet, and kicks off his shoes, catching sight of us in the living room. He pauses in the middle of shrugging off his jacket and raises his eyebrows in a silent question.

James pushes out of the chair, says, "Hey, T," then heads for his bedroom. He pauses at the mouth of the hallway, looks back at me, and silently mouths, "Trust me."

After watching James disappear into his room without a word, Theo cautiously heads toward me. "What was that about?"

Deep breath. "I uh… I need to talk to you about something. Well. Two things, actually."

He frowns, lowering to the couch. "Okay?"

"I overheard you on the phone on Friday. You said, 'She trusts me now. I'll get something we can use against her.'" I resolutely keep my eyes trained on Theo, watching him breathe in through his nose while his lips stay pressed shut. "Were you talking about me?" I'm expecting to analyze his expression for a hint of a lie, so his response takes a second to process.

"Yes."

My heart starts falling. "What?"

"But I was lying. I…" He pauses, huffs in frustration, and runs a hand down his face. "James, Kip, Luna, and I sometimes do smaller jobs with individual clients outside of the Saints. Basically, we help make problems and people go away."

"How does this—"

"Please, just let me explain," he interrupts. I nod for him to continue. "Okay. Sometimes, the problem is getting rid of a car involved in a crime. Sometimes it's hacking into a computer or breaking into a house to delete or steal incriminating photos or videos. Then there are people. We get rid of them in creative ways. One of our first clients was a young woman being stalked by her ex. The police couldn't, or wouldn't, do anything about it. Luna drove him out of the state by getting him fired, alienating him from his friends, and calling his mom."

"How did she do that?"

"She seduced him, got him drunk, and stole his phone to send herself his mom's contact info and sent a company-wide email of a video of him doing body shots. Then she took some pictures of him making out with a guy he thought was Luna and sent the photos to all the most recent guys in his messages with the text, 'I wish this was you.' She topped it all off by calling his mom on her phone, pretending to be pregnant."

I can't help but laugh. God, I love her.

"Other times, we've gotten people put in psychiatric hospitals or drained their bank accounts. Most people we end up framing for a crime, and the majority were guilty of *something*.

"Our most frequent client is a detective, Lorry McCoy.

He hires us to help put away criminals who'd otherwise get off on a lack of evidence or a technicality. Recently, he…" Theo pauses, closes his eyes, and takes a heavy breath. When his eyes open again, he looks desperate. "Three years ago, his cousin was murdered, but there's no body, and everyone else thinks the guy just ran off. Lorry hired us to frame the killer for murder."

My body suddenly feels full of helium. It's a shock to look down and see I'm still sitting on the couch. I almost miss Theo's next words, but I don't need to hear them to know what they are.

"His cousin was Solomon McCoy."

Solomon howled as more blood fell, adding to the pool of bodily fluids beneath him. I held the freshly severed finger in front of his eyes, grinning. "This little piggy touched its sixteen-year-old babysitter." I set the finger on the center of his chest, and he jerked away, causing the digit to fall to the floor. I frowned when it landed in the center of a puddle of urine. "Gross. Guess I need a new one."

I got four of his fingers before he passed out, which felt poetic seeing as I knew of at least four babysitters between the ages of fifteen and nineteen he fucked while his child slept in the neighboring room.

It wasn't even one of the babysitters who was my client. It was his wife, Charity. She told me about finding him with the most recent sitter, who was eighteen but had been working for them for two years. Charity blamed the girl. She cared more about Solomon's gambling than his serial raping of teenagers. Part of me wanted to do a two-for-one special and kill her as well as Solomon, but I wasn't going to orphan three children. And she didn't deserve it like Solomon did. Charity needed therapy and a reality check, not a butcher's knife.

Remembering that especially satisfying kill momentarily took me out of my current reality. But Theo lays his hand on top of mine, and the touch sucks my attention back into the room with dizzying speed.

"I'm not doing it, of course. I'm trying to get him off your trail. He thinks I'm tricking you into trusting me so I can find a way to frame you. But I promise, June," he squeezes my hand, emphasizing the use of my real name, "I will not let him or anyone else take you away. I'll kill him before that happens."

Fuck, I believe him. That doesn't make this okay, though. "Why didn't you tell me?"

"I didn't want you to get scared and do something reckless."

"What? Like kill a detective? I'm not a fucking idiot, Theo! Or were you more worried that I would leave you?" I pull my hand from his, anger weighing my bones back down. "You should've told me! There's a fucking detective investigating me!"

"I know, I know. I should have. I'm sorry."

"Oh, that makes it better," I say sarcastically.

"Look, you didn't know about our side business, and I was nervous about what you'd think. It's stupid, I know. I thought I could handle Lorry before you needed to know. I thought I'd be able to derail his investigation and he'd forget about you."

"And?"

His shoulders slump slightly. "He's pretty determined. But he doesn't have anything substantial. He barely has circumstantial evidence."

"He's still a cop! If they're looking at me—"

"*They're* not," he quickly adds. "Only he is. He hasn't shared his investigation with the others because no one thinks there's a case. He's the only person who doesn't think Solomon just ran away. You did the job well." He smiles like a little compliment is going to fix everything. But the idea that Theo's been actively involved with an investigation into me, whether official or not, has the fire in my chest fanning to alarming heights.

"How long have you known about this?"

"I—what?"

"How long have you fucking known that a detective is watching me? When were you *hired* to frame me for murder?"

He hesitates for a moment. Then, "Two weeks."

Two weeks.

Two fucking weeks.

I'm going to kill him.

I clasp my hands together, nails digging into skin until the sharp pain helps focus my mind. With an immense effort, I say, "Were you ever going to tell me?"

"I was going to wait until the month was over."

"You were going to let me go another week without knowing about this? Why? Didn't want to lose easy access to pussy before our deal was over?"

"No, June. I didn't want you to have to deal with it yet. I told myself, and Kip and James, that if I couldn't fix this by February fourteenth, I was telling you."

"So, Kip knows the truth?"

Theo nods.

"Anyone else?"

"No."

The oxygen that enters my nose feels searing hot, like I opened an oven and breathed in the air trapped inside. "What evidence does he have?"

"Not much. He knows Charity was your client. He has

a record of you hiring one of their old babysitters to clean your house a few times. He has paystubs from your visit to a shooting range and a picture Solomon and Charity took at a fair. You're in the background of the photo. The worst thing he has is an image from a security camera of you getting in an Uber outside of the train station two days after Solomon disappeared. Solomon's car was found abandoned at the station a week later. It's all circumstantial."

"If it's so circumstantial, then why is Lorry sure it's me?"

"He's looked into you and thinks more people have disappeared or showed up dead around you than should be normal."

"Wait, he doesn't just suspect me for Solomon, he suspects I'm a serial killer?" I nearly scream because this is *so much worse*. Putting away a serial killer is a career-making, life-changing thing. Cops latch onto these cases like they're the only donut in a house of vegetables.

"I stole his files. Most of it is bullshit. A few I think were you. But I've been working through them. I found three of the guys who disappeared and managed to anonymously point the cops in their direction. One of the murdered guys was a gang kill, which the cops have officially labeled as. One was already labeled a suicide, but Lorry wasn't sure at first. He is now, after an anonymous donation was made in honor of the guy to the American Foundation for Suicide Prevention. The cops are only investigating two of the guys I suspect you killed. One, I haven't gotten a chance to look into much. The other is labeled as a missing person, but there's quite a lot of new evidence pointing to his wife's new boyfriend, so they're looking into him. Lorry also decided you weren't responsible for that one."

"You framed someone for a murder I committed?"

"Not enough for the guy to be put away. Just enough to

keep Lorry or any other cop from looking too hard anywhere else."

"That's what you've been doing every time you disappear for 'Saints business,' isn't it?" I knew he was hiding something. I just didn't realize he was spending hours cleaning up messes I wasn't even aware of. Giving money to charities so Lorry thinks someone, maybe a family member, was confident about the manner of their loved one's death. Tracking down missing people. Planting evidence on strangers for my crimes.

"Yeah," Theo says. "You're good at what you do, though. There hasn't been much to cover up. But the fewer names on Lorry's list of your possible victims, the better. Most are easy to fix. Unfortunately, Lorry knows my work, so I can't just frame a bunch of people. I can't make it obvious what I'm doing."

Though the anger doesn't disappear, it does soften, dulled by the effort Theo has put into keeping me out of prison. "You should have told me, Theo. This is my mess. I should be helping clean it up."

"I know," he admits. "I'm sorry. I'll tell you everything you want to know. I have a copy of Lorry's files in my office I can show you."

I nod. "Thank you."

Theo's answering exhale is drenched with relief. Then his next words are like a bucket of ice over my lingering anger when I remember that I, too, have something to confess.

"You said you needed to talk to me about two things. What's the other?"

"Right." I straighten my back. "When I didn't know what your little call was about, I got nervous and decided to finish snooping through your shit."

"Naturally," he says with a hint of amusement that I expect will disappear any second.

"I found something. I didn't look at it, but James saw me with it before I could put it back, and he… well, I could tell it would've been bad if I had looked."

"What was it?"

"A binder behind your safe."

The words stretch all the oxygen to a breaking point, making the room feel smaller. Color seems to drain from Theo's cheeks and eyes. It's not anger, fear, or betrayal shaking the foundation. It's something much, much worse.

It's sadness.

The visceral kind that has a heartbeat of its own. The kind that latches onto your lungs so every breath you take has to struggle against the added weight. The kind that demands attention, even from those who don't own it.

I want to take my words, and all this terrible sadness, back. I want to rescue Theo from whatever thoughts are now holding him captive.

I want to go back in time and stop myself from ever seeing that binder.

But the only way to survive a moment suffocated in this sadness is by acknowledging it. So, I gingerly touch his forearm and whisper, "Theo? What's in the binder?"

His voice is nearly unrecognizable. "My daughter."

THIRTY-ONE

Theo

Thinking about her is like lying in a coffin full of broken glass and willingly being buried alive. But it's also like climbing free of that coffin and feeling the sun on my face after months of darkness. Memories of her are weapons and warm blankets.

Unable to look at June, I stare down at her hand on my arm as I say, "Her name was Shiloh. Scottie had her when we were twenty. She was adorable. Not the smartest kid in the world," I grin thinking about her trying repeatedly to draw with a marker that still had the cap on, "but so happy all the time. She loved being around the Saints and would always shriek and clap when someone rode up on a bike." I pause, heat singeing my eyes and a rock lodging in my throat. Shiloh's perfectly round face fills my mind, dark red hair bouncing in pigtails and giant brown eyes always shining, excited to explore the world.

I swallow, but the next words are still choked and heavy with unshed tears. "When Shiloh was three, I took her to the playground. She was spinning on one of those little merry-go-rounds. I could hear her laughing. I was sitting on the bench, watching her, when this woman came over to talk to me. I looked at her baby in a stroller for maybe thirty seconds. When I looked up, Shiloh was gone."

June gasps and tightens her hold on my arm. I chance a glance at her and see tears silently streaming down her face. The sight breaks the dam holding my own back, and I feel fat drops fall from both eyes.

"I looked everywhere. Called the cops. Called Scottie and James and Rocket. I was screaming my head off, and all the other parents and nannies were helping me look. But she wasn't anywhere. She'd disappeared."

A hiccup interrupts my words, and I drag my hand down my face, sniffing. "The cops arrested me, convinced I did something. They saw the tattoos and the bike and jumped to conclusions. They held me for forty-eight hours before they let me go because they didn't have anything. But the whole time they were interrogating me, someone was out there with my baby." A sob escapes my throat, and the tears and snot are falling in earnest now. "They found her body a week later. Scottie lasted a year before she couldn't survive the grief anymore."

June throws her arms around my neck, tugging me into a hard, long hug. I shake as I cry, ears full of the sound of Shiloh's laughing mixed with how I imagine she screamed and cried before she died. June doesn't offer any platitudes or ask any questions, just gives me time. She rubs my back and runs her fingers through my hair. By the time the tears slow and I'm able to breathe normally, I pull back, wiping my cheeks with the back of my hands.

"Second Tuesday?" she asks.

I nod. "Rocket took me to the playground to ask me to take over the Saints. I think he wanted to create a happy memory there for me. And he said it was a reminder of my strength and resiliency. He said, 'Any man who can lose a daughter and still have space for someone else's grief is a man worthy of leading. I know, because I'm not that man.' Rocket tried. He tried hard. But he lost a daughter and a granddaughter. He couldn't handle talking to James, much less leading the Saints. In his grief, he forgot that James lost a sister and niece, that the rest of the Saints lost two girls they loved. He even often forgot that I lost my girlfriend and daughter. When he came to his senses, he knew he couldn't stay."

"I'm so sorry, Theo," June whispers. "I can't… There are no words." Her hands reach up to my face, cup my jaw. A thumb swipes under my eyes, catching gathered tears. "Rocket was right. I don't think I've ever met someone more worthy. You are endlessly strong, and I'm sorry you've had reason to prove that strength."

I circle her small wrist with my fingers and lean into the palm of her hand. Then I pull her hands off and stand.

"Where are you going?"

"Wait there." My legs are weak as I walk to my closet, retrieve the photo album, and return to the living room. I perch on the edge of the couch and lay the album on the table. June inches forward, her thigh pressed against mine.

"You don't have to," she says, laying her hand on mine to stop me from opening the album.

"I want to. Shiloh deserves to be seen." With a steady hand, I open the photo album to the first page, the day Shiloh was born.

A decade younger version of me is sitting next to an exhausted Scottie lying in a hospital bed. Her hair is in a messy bun that has several loose strands, and in her arms is a little bundle, the baby's face barely noticeable. I'm smiling wider than I have in years, my eyes locked on the baby in Scottie's arms.

The second picture on the page is of only Shiloh, sleeping wrapped like a burrito. The next few pages are variations of the same: infant Shiloh in her crib, infant Shiloh in my arms, infant Shiloh lying on James's legs. Then she's on her stomach in one of her playpens, staring at the camera with eyes a lighter brown than they'd become. There's a picture of her reaching up to play with a spiked choker around Scottie's throat, one sitting naked in the bath floaty, one holding her little feet up by her head. By the twelfth page, Shiloh is sitting up, wearing diapers, smiling. There's even a tuft of fuzzy strawberry blonde hair. There are countless pictures of her with bikers or being held on the seat of a bike, usually by me, James, or Rocket. Photos show her in dresses, in little biker baby outfits, and naked.

"She has your eyes," June says, not even realizing she used the present tense.

"She had my temper, too. Thankfully, she had Scottie's hair and infectious joy." I flip the page and prove my point. We're halfway through the photo album, and every single picture shows Shiloh with a full head of red hair and a constant smile.

"This is one of my favorites," I say, touching the corner of a large picture. Shiloh is wearing a helmet that's far too big, and she's sitting on my shoulders, her little hands holding my hair like handles. I flip to the next page and laugh. "And this one. She walked around all day saying, 'I Daddy.'" Shiloh is standing with her arms held out to her side, skin covered in little temporary tattoos. There are ponies, princesses, dinosaurs, dogs, and even a few skulls. I remember the day better than I remember this morning. "Shiloh showed the tattoos to anyone who looked in her direction. Every member of the club got a full, though mostly unintelligible, explanation of each individual tattoo. She'd point at someone's tattoo, like the scorpion on my forearm or the snarling wolf on James's shoulder, then at the most similar one on her body and clap, like the matching art was the most wonderful thing."

"She's adorable," June says, leaning closer to study the picture. Hesitantly, she reaches for the bottom corner of the page and looks at me with a question in her eyes.

"Go ahead."

June turns the page to see a picture of Shiloh covered head to toe in mud. She takes over flipping through the album, laughing and sniffling. She asks occasional questions and lingers on some photos, most of which are also my favorite or include me or Scottie as well as Shiloh. There are seven pages in a row of photos from Shiloh's third birthday party, which was themed after her favorite movie.

"*Tinkerbell*," June whispers. She looks at me with glistening eyes.

I nod. "Her favorite movie."

"And yours."

"Yeah."

"I'm so sorry. I shouldn't have laughed. Or… fuck, called you Tink. You must have—"

"Don't," I interrupt, cupping the back of her neck so she looks at me. "You didn't know. And, yes, I hate the stupid nickname, but not because of Shiloh. If anything, the reminder of her is nice."

"Theo…"

"Don't grow a conscience on me now. I can handle talking about Shiloh and Scottie. I can't handle you looking at me like I'm broken because of it."

"I've always looked at you like you're broken."

I smile. "Sure, but a sexy broken. Not a pitiful broken."

Her forehead wrinkles as she raises her brows. "A sexy broken, really?"

"Little reaper, I got rock hard watching you slit a man's throat, and you got off when I fucked you next to his body. What else would you call it?"

"Fair." Rosiness colors her cheeks at the memory. She turns back to the photo album and continues flipping through. The birthday party photos show Shiloh with huge, tattooed bikers and little kids, half of whom were there with their straight-laced parents. There are six more months of life documented in the photos. The last picture, of Scottie holding Shiloh over her head, was taken four days before I took Shiloh to the playground and lost everything that mattered to me.

June sits in silence, staring at the picture of the two girls whom I loved more than anything or anyone. Sitting next to my little reaper, a different man in a different world, makes this picture look like a snapshot of a dream. It's surreal and intangible, yet just as real as the feeling of June's hand sliding into mine, lacing our fingers together.

"Thank you," she whispers after a long stretch of silence.

"For what?"

"For sharing her with me. I don't take that lightly."

I smile at her, and something slots in place in my chest. Maybe it's because I finally told her about Lorry or maybe it's remembering Shiloh, but it's like my lungs have been punctured until now and they're finally inflating for a real, full breath. I know the truth lodged in my ribs, curled right next to my heart.

I love June Graves, and that might kill me.

THIRTY-TWO

Theo

"That's it!" I shout. "Don't forget the clutch." I watch from the edge of the parking lot as June brings the motorcycle to a jittering stop. She balances herself by putting her left foot to the ground first, then switches the gear to neutral and drops her right foot before letting go of the handlebars. I rush to her side, clapping. "Fantastic!"

June takes off her helmet, blonde hair plastered to her forehead. She's beaming, cenote-blue eyes free of any smoke from the fire inside her. "Told you I could ride!" she yells over the thundering exhaust. The heat from the bike coats the surrounding air, and sweat beads down June's temple as evidence. I get the sudden urge to lean forward and lick the sweat off her skin.

I laugh, standing next to the front wheel so my leg brushes hers. "You still have quite a bit to learn, little reaper."

"Like what?" she asks with a smirk.

The suggestion in her voice dares me to bend her over right here, but Lorry called this morning demanding an update on the case, and he slipped in a threat about me getting too close. Which means he's probably watching her more than I expected. She was in my bed, freshly fucked, when he called, so I had to tell her everything.

Having a detective looking into her is bothering her more than she's letting on. But she won't mention it, not after learning about Shiloh. After I put the photo album away, neither of us brought her up again. There was a slight shift in the air that always comes from sharing secrets, but nothing drastic. June didn't lie down bubble wrap or look at me with pity. She even called me *'Tink'* again.

Her last client of the day left at three, and when I arrived to pick her up, I found her on the edge of her desk chair, flipping through a file, biting her nails, sparks flying in her eyes.

"Found a new victim?" I asked.

She shrugged. *"I can't decide between the guy I was planning before you or a new one."*

The irony of a therapist discussing who to murder with the president of a criminal motorcycle club wasn't lost on me. I plucked the file from her hands and pulled her out of the office, ignoring her protest, certain that a riding lesson would help clear her mind.

Standing beside the bike now, baking in the sun, her grin proves the decision was the right one. "For one thing, you still shift too early when changing gears," I say with a wink. "Now, how do you feel?"

"What do you mean?" She turns the bike off, and silence flows over the rumbling exhaust pipe like a wave swallowing the shore.

I tap the space between her eyes. "The fire, little reaper."

"It's weird that you can read me so well."

"It's easy to recognize something I've experienced too."

"You've experienced the all-consuming need to feel a heart stop beating under your hands?"

"Well, not *that* exactly," I say. "But I have been overwhelmed with my own violent impulses. So, tell me, how long do we have?"

She sucks her lips between her teeth, thinking it over as she studies me. "I'm not sure. Recently, I could safely go about seven months between kills. But the South Fiver was quick, spontaneous. And the two before that were interrupted."

I give her an apologetic look that neither of us believes. "So, you're experiencing serial killer blue balls?"

She frowns. "That's one way to put it."

"Riding helps?"

"Some. It's like any other adrenaline rush. Like sucking a little oxygen away from the fire. It doesn't put it out, but it does temporarily shrink it."

"What did you use before biking? Skydiving? Roller Coasters? Horror movies?"

"Some of them. The biggest is tattoos."

"You have, like, three," I say, thinking about the doves on her rib cage, the lion on her thigh, and the cemetery on her arm.

"You think I got the whole sleeve in one sitting?" She smiles and leans forward on the bike, bringing her face closer to mine. "Never thought to ask what the gravestones were for?"

I move so my forearms are resting on the handlebars, and my hands are dangling closer to June's thighs. "I have a guess."

"A stone for each kill. I add the fire later, when it's burning in me again."

"When the flames consume you, they consume the grave that suffocated them last time," I say. I counted the stones on her arm while she was sleeping once. Fourteen. I'd guessed they were for each of her victims.

"Exactly."

"Did you have a spot saved for me?" I rub my hand up her arm, squeezing where I know the sleeve is hiding under her jacket. Her body is a magnet, and I'm powerless to resist its pull.

"I had an idea."

"You haven't gotten one for the Fiver you killed in the Cage."

"It's not like I've had much free time, Tink." She winks, and the words settle low in my gut. Clearly, it doesn't matter how long I spend inside her or how many times we fuck in twenty-four hours, I'll always want more.

"We could go get it now," I suggest.

"My artist doesn't work on Mondays. I need to make an appointment with them."

"Then make the appointment. I'll come with you."

Her eyes widen with excitement, the anticipation of something to look forward to coming alive in her expression. "I'll text them."

Spontaneously, I say, "See if they can squeeze a small one in for me, too."

"What are you going to get?" Her eyes rove down my body. "Better question, *where* are you going to get it?"

"It's a surprise."

She shifts on the bike while typing out a message, and I wonder if she's throbbing for attention between her legs.

"Alright." I step back into the cold air absent of heat from both my bike and my reaper. "Again."

June looks disappointed for a second before she pulls the helmet back over her head, turns on the bike, and hits the kickstand with her heel.

~

Her tattoo artist, Dom, can squeeze us in on Wednesday afternoon. June looks excited, but all I can think is that's two days before the end of our deal. What will June do after the thirty days are over?

"Sadie wants you to come to tacos night," June says when we get back to the house from her office on Tuesday.

"Of course she does."

"You should come." She says it with forced casualness, like she doesn't care if I do or not. But the tension in her shoulders tells me she does.

"Your friend Evelyn wouldn't appreciate that." I don't remind her that it's the second Tuesday, so I'll be busy tonight. For the first time in years, I consider not going to the park. But the thought fills my throat with bile. I won't betray Shiloh like that.

"She'll get over it. Rose has brought Vanessa before. And Sadie has brought two of her past boyfriends." She freezes mid-kicking off her shoes and slowly turns, a blush climbing up her neck. "I didn't mean… I'm not—"

"Relax, little reaper," I say, grinning. As much as I love watching her get flustered, especially since it doesn't happen often, I don't think now is the time to have the complicated labels talk. "I can't tonight anyway. Lorry is demanding to meet to go over our progress."

She instantly forgets about her boyfriend slip. "Why don't you share that progress with me first?"

"Honestly, I'm surprised you haven't demanded to see everything sooner." I retrieve the files on June from my safe, both Lorry's and the one I put together, and bring them to the dining room. "This is a copy of Lorry's from a few weeks ago," I pass her the first file, "and this one is mine."

She accepts the second file, shooting me a glare.

"My guess is only four of the guys Lorry has as your possible victims are correct." I sit next to her, watching as she flips through the file. "Like I told you the other day, I've eliminated one of them, Adam Brewer, by pointing the cops' attention to his wife's new boyfriend, who also seems like someone you'd want to add to your list."

"Seriously?" She stops at the page of a fairly messy kill a few years ago. It's unsolved, but the cops are pretty sure it was the guy's ex-girlfriend. "This is insulting. I would never leave such a mess behind. Think of the forensics!"

I chuckle. "How rude of him."

She flips the page more aggressively this time, lingering on one of the missing men I think June is responsible for. I couldn't find a link to her, but learning if people go to therapy is nearly impossible. Still, the man seems like an actual dirtbag. Two women have filed restraining orders against him, and there've been assault allegations from three others.

"That one of yours?"

She shakes her head. "I wish it was. But no. Did you find him?"

"No, that's why I thought you killed him. He dropped off the face of the earth."

"The cops looked into these other women?"

"Two don't live in the state anymore, one was in prison, one was thirty weeks pregnant, so the police didn't think she had the energy or strength to do anything. The last woman didn't have an alibi or anything, but she's living a pretty good life down near Linden, so no one thought she had the motive."

"Police assume he just left town?"

I nod. "I've learned they tend to always assume that."

"Yes, they do. It makes my life so much easier." She throws me a wicked smile and continues flipping through the file, making comments every so often.

"He thinks I'd shoot someone in the head? Where's the fun in that?"

"A girl? Does he know serial killers at all? She doesn't fit the victim type."

"This guy disappeared nearly six years ago. I'd lived here for like a week. I made it eight months here before I killed someone."

"Wow, eight whole months?" I tease.

She shoves my shoulder. "Eight months *after* moving here. A year total since the last kill."

Her smile vanishes when she turns back to reading Lorry's file. By the time she's finished, her lips are dropped into a permanent scowl.

"He's got three right," she says.

"Including Brewer?"

She nods, returning to one of the last pages on a guy named Dakota Peterson. He was the first guy I knew June must be responsible for, because there was an obvious connection to her. The cops ruled it an accidental overdose, which fit his reputation, but Lorry disagrees.

"Sadie's ex," I supply.

"He was an asshole." The words are like grinding gravel as she holds in her rage. "If she had one more drink that night, or if she didn't go to those self-defense classes with me, or if…" The sentence breaks, and she pulls in a long breath through her nose. "Just because he failed at raping her that time doesn't mean he would've failed next time. Or that he failed with other women in the past."

"You're right," I agree, imagining my little reaper finding her best friend hurt and terrified, having just barely escaped an attack from her boyfriend, then turning around to seek vengeance. The idea of her, pissed and bloodthirsty, turning that guy into another nameless asshole defeated by his own vices makes my cock harden. "You left a body."

She rolls her neck back, eyes flicking to the ceiling with

annoyance. "It was an impulse kill. I've only done that three times. Well, four now, I guess. But it wasn't hard. We were at this club, and I just kept supplying him with alcohol laced with drugs and drugs laced with more drugs. Then I told him to meet me in the supply closet and locked him inside. I figured if the alcohol and drugs didn't kill him that night, I'd plan something better in the future."

"What about cameras?" James tried to access the video recordings but didn't have any luck. The cops got them, though, because there are notes about it in Lorry's file.

"They were just in the main area of the club, not the back rooms or hallways. I made sure it saw me dancing in the middle of the room, then I snatched a hat from this guy, tucked all my hair inside, lured Dakota to the closet, and was back dancing in less than five minutes. Not enough to make the police suspicious and definitely not enough to convict me."

Fuck, I shouldn't be rock hard from listening to how good she is at murdering people. I shift, trying to reposition myself without drawing June's attention. Fortunately, or unfortunately, her attention is back on the file, where she's flipped to an earlier page.

"Tim Bidwell," she says, tapping her finger on the guy's picture. He's an average-looking man, cheeks a little full and brows too thin, but he was young and popular, which earned his disappearance more attention. "Pastor. You know, out of the fifteen people I've killed, four of them have worked in a church of some kind. That might not seem like a lot, but it's kind of a crazy percentage when you think about it."

I scoff. "I'm not surprised."

"Tim is my most recent pastor. His high school girlfriend, Alexandria, was in the same MSW program as me. We weren't super close, but the nature of the program meant we shared a lot of our pasts with each other. I could tell he hurt her, but didn't realize to what extent. Then one day, she told me that a girl she used to babysit reached out. Turns out, Tim's tastes didn't grow out of high school with him. Alexandria was gone, but as the youth pastor, he had a steady stream of girls for the picking."

My hands curl into fists, anger stretching the tendons. "He suffered?"

Her lips curl into a full smile, though one without any real joy. It's all malice, the smile of someone who knows they're going to hell but plans to be ruling it before the night is over. "One of my longer kills. Five days."

I whistle, leaning back in my chair. "Damn, reaper. Impressive."

She gives a fake little bow in my direction, which brings her face closer to my dick. It's softened since she started talking about this Tim guy, but with her proximity, it stirs again. Then she's lifting too soon, her eyes meeting mine. "He took a while to break, I'll give him that. But once he did, he cried and begged more than most."

"The cops looked into his disappearance, didn't they?"

"For a few days," she says. "Then his family got some messages about him finally deciding to follow God's calling to Cambodia. He continued messaging and posting updates for a few weeks. Enough to make the police lose interest. That was over two years ago. I haven't revisited him much, so I bet his family started worrying again when he stopped replying. But you know how dangerous those Godless places can be. Anything can happen." She sounds so innocent when she says it, I'd almost believe her. But I know her face and the intricacies of her cadence and voice. I see the truth behind the facade. The pride at ridding the world of one more scumbag without an ounce of suspicion pointed her way.

Well, until Lorry, that is.

"Lorry is operating under the, I presume correct, assumption that you sent those messages from his phone," I say.

"Did he check the IP addresses? They'll say Cambodia."

Shit, she's brilliant. "I don't know."

"What makes him think I did it?"

"Lorry's cousin's wife was in a sorority with Tim's sister. That's what originally got his attention. I think he was looking for other disappearances within a year of Solomon's. The fact that Tim wasn't the type to disappear and that all his family and friends had were a few messages and social media posts kept his suspicion fueled. He was looking for more connections to you, but I'm assuming you used a fake name and disguise when you went to the church."

"Who says I went to the church?"

I raise an eyebrow, and she dips her head forward, conceding. "Black wig, platform shoes, bigger, padded clothes, no one looked my way."

"Lorry doesn't have much on Tim's disappearance," I lie. "So, I doubt it's one of his main cases against you. I also don't know if he's tried linking anyone else to you since I stole these files a few weeks ago. You've killed fifteen people total, right?" She nods. "How many since moving to Tucson?"

There's a moment's hesitation as she studies me, fighting a decades-long instinct to keep that part of her life hidden. When she gives in, I can't help the warmth of pride that fills my chest at realizing I've gained her trust. "Eight," she says. Then shakes her head and corrects, "Nine. Including the guy two weeks ago."

Nine people in five and a half years. And only four of them have caught the attention of anyone in law enforcement.

"And you're positive none of them, other than these guys, can be linked to you?"

"You doubting my skills, Tink?"

"Not at all. But no evidence for a crime no one knows exists is a lot different than no evidence for a crime someone is actively trying to link to you." I slide Lorry's file to the center of the table and open mine, moving past the basic stuff, like where she's from, when she graduated, who her friends are, and land on her crimes. Most of it is stuff I picked up when she was following me. Information from the cameras in her house, times she spent with her friends, and how often I caught her following me. Past that is what I've been able to pick up in the weeks since Lorry called.

"How did you know about Jared?" she asks.

"I watched who went into your office a few times. Then I looked into Clarissa's past after we… met."

Color drains from her cheeks. "My clients… You…"

"I wanted to know why you were following me. Then why you wanted to kill me. But I didn't document anything about any of them," I say, knowing that clients' privacy is a big deal to therapists.

"Do you think Lorry knows who my clients are? I'll have to email them if my client list was compromised."

I hate how scared she sounds now. Reaching over, I lay my hands over hers. "He's watched you arriving and leaving your office a few times. But he's never had time to sit outside your office and watch people come and go."

She sniffs, though no tears have welled in her eyes, and looks down at our hands. "Okay."

"Lorry doesn't have anything."

"Nothing substantial. But how am I supposed to…" She gestures into the air, "with a cop watching my every move?"

"We'll figure it out."

Her lips press together, and she bounces her knee, staring dully at the table. I don't think she has a specific picture in her vision, just smoke from the fire clouding everything she looks at. I hook my foot on the leg of her chair, turning it so she's facing me. Keeping one hand over hers, I move my other to her jaw, fingers touching her hair. The smoke clears enough to let her hold my gaze.

"I won't let you burn, little reaper. Even if I have to drag a victim into my living room and strap him down for you. I promise."

Her eyes jump between mine, then down to my lips. Her body softens in my direction, and she relaxes her head into my hand.

"Why?" she whispers.

My brows cinch together. "Why what?"

"Why do you care to help me this much?"

The answer is growing in my chest, aching to climb up my throat and pass my lips. But I won't say that. Not now.

"I've lived most of my life either running from death or chasing it. You've shown me how to respect it. That's no small thing, June Graves."

A little breath passes her lips. Then, before I can blink, she swallows the distance between us and crushes her lips to mine. After over a week without this, the kiss feels suffocating. I smile and tug her closer, ready to empty my lungs if she asks.

THIRTY-THREE

June

"Hey, Dom!" I say, heading to the chair in the back of the tattoo parlor. Theo still hasn't told me what he's getting, but he says it's small and shouldn't take long.

Dom is young and has big curly hair that's mostly black with an outer grey layer. One arm is covered in colored tattoos, and the other is mostly bare. "Hey, Graves," they say, spinning around on their chair. "And Graves's tall guest."

"Theo," I say.

"Oh, right. I got your message on Instagram," Dom says. They smile, showing off the shining gem on their outer incisor.

"Nice to meet you," Theo says.

"Alright, another grave, Graves? Or flames?"

"Just the headstone for now. I'll be back later for the flames," I say. The first time I came to them, not long after I moved here, I asked if they would add to an existing tattoo, because the first artist I visited refused. Dom took one look at the cemetery, said, *"Damn, and I thought I took the name 'Dom' too seriously,"* then enthusiastically agreed. I worried that they'd get suspicious with me coming in every few months to get a fucking gravestone tattooed, because how would the actual symbol of death not raise red flags, but I lucked out with the most ironic last name since Remus Lupin. And I'm pretty sure if Dom found out I was killing asshole men, they'd give me that literal sparkling smile and comp my next tattoo.

"Still no dates or names?" they ask.

I shake my head. I considered getting the date of each kill, but decided that was far too conspicuous.

"Where are we putting this one?"

I pull off my jacket to show I'm wearing only a strapless bandeau underneath. Twisting my arm, I point out the spot on my tricep that's still free. My entire forearm and most of my upper arm is already full. Two or three more graves, and I'll have to move onto my shoulder and back.

Dom nods, snaps on their gloves, and starts shaving. They grab the pre-printed headstone stencil and prepare my arm to apply it.

"How's that?" they ask.

I head to the nearby mirror to look. The stone fits perfectly among the others, right next to the one for Jared. Theo walks up behind me, touching two fingers to my elbow to lift my arm for a better look. Despite being a gentle, innocent touch, it still causes goosebumps to prickle up my neck.

"So?" I ask, meeting his eyes in the mirror.

He bends over, kisses the skin under my ear, and whispers, "My badass little reaper."

The words instantly make me wet, and I know the tattoo will only add to that.

"I'm assuming that's a yes?" Dom asks.

I spin around. "It's perfect!" I lay down on my stomach,

holding my arm at an awkward angle so they can start the tattoo. Theo sits on my other side, and I turn my head so I can see him while Dom works. The needle touches my skin, sending the addictive slice of pain down my arm. It bites away at the smoldering logs in my gut, forcing the fire to decrease.

Theo's eyes turn murky with desire when he sees me smile. "Of course you'd like being repeatedly stabbed by a tiny needle."

"What can I say? I'm a masochist."

"She is one of my only clients to literally fall asleep during a tattoo," Dom says.

"That doesn't surprise me at all," Theo says. "So, Dom, how long have you been tattooing?"

"About eight years," they answer, launching into the story I've already heard about how they were a third-grade teacher before and were fired when they wore a dress one day that left a few tattoos on display. "Private schools. They're a whole different world."

Not much later, they roll away and announce, "Finished!"

I return to the mirror and give them a wide smile when I see yet another flawless headstone tattoo. Seeing evidence of a recent kill fills me with a similar feeling of euphoria that the actual kill provides. Not nearly as intense of an emotion, but enough to satisfy the craving for a few more weeks.

"Your turn, Theo," Dom says while they wipe down the chair, switch out their gun and needles, and prepare the new ink. Fifteen minutes later, they're transferring the stencil to the outside of Theo's right knee. I try to lean over to see it, but he holds out his arm, stopping me.

"Not yet," he says.

I rock back on my heels and cross my arms, pouting.

Theo winks, approves the location, then moves the extra chair to the head of the tattoo table. He nods for me to take a seat, knowing I won't be able to see Dom working from the location. I hesitate, and he grips my shoulders, forcing me down. I squeeze my thighs together, trying to ease the burn that grew from the pain of the tattoo and flares now as Theo manhandles me.

He lies on his back to give Dom the best access to his leg. Unable to see Theo's face, I reach forward and run my fingers through his hair. He relaxes into the feeling, nearly purring when I scratch his scalp.

His tattoo takes longer than mine, about half an hour. After telling Dom he loves it, he says, "Alright, little reaper, come look."

I eagerly jump up and circle the chair, taking Dom's recently vacated spot to look down at Theo's brand-new art. As soon as my eyes land on it, my lungs deflate, like Theo's tattoo became a physical object and punctured them.

It's a scythe. The weapon carried by reapers. Etched into the blade of the scythe, less visible in white ink, is a small outline of two familiar-looking wings. A second later, realization slices down, this time through my heart.

Tinkerbell's wings. At first glance, they're not noticeable, but their location almost makes them look like a reflection in the blade.

Tink and the reaper.

Suddenly, the scorching fire and the burn from the tattoo are nothing compared to the heat filling my eyes. A bubble of tears gathers on my lower lids and breaks when I flick my eyes up to Theo, causing two fat tears to roll down my cheeks.

His eyes shine, reflecting my feelings back. Something undefinable, an emotion that feels too big, yet I never want to lose. A giant bubble of pure air living among the smoke and flames and dust I've been choking on for over a decade.

"Good?"

I nod. "Perfect."

We thank Dom, pay, and leave in a hurry, the ache to be on him, in him, have him in me growing until it feels uncontrollable. He goes well over the speed limit on the ride back, and I tempt fate further by groping him, effortlessly causing a pronounced bulge as his cock grows harder with each passing second.

The front door isn't fully shut before Theo slams me against the wall, mouth on mine and hands pushing up my shirt. His fingertips drag over my hips, stomach, and rib cage, carving a trail into my skin. Our teeth and tongues tangle with a savage demand for *more*.

Holding onto his neck, I tighten my core and lift my legs to wrap around his waist. His hands drop to my ass, helping keep me steady, and I bite his bottom lip, then say into his mouth, "I need you to fuck me, Theo. Please."

He groans. I stay clinging to him, and our kiss doesn't break when he turns and heads for his bedroom. We bump into something, and I hear what I think is a chair clattering to the floor, but neither of us cares. He kicks his door shut and lowers me to the bed, stopping the kiss long enough for him to pull off his shirt and me my bandeau. Then he's on me again, exploring my mouth with his tongue.

He moves down my body and closes his mouth around a nipple. Head dropping back, I suck in a breath and focus on the sensation of his teeth biting down. The next second, his hand is on my neck, fingers settling into invisible grooves molded perfectly to his hand. He squeezes, and exhilaration follows the loss of oxygen. He moves to my other nipple, probably leaving marks behind, not letting up on my throat. My hips buck up, rubbing against his thigh. Just as glowing black spots begin filling my vision, he lets go of my throat and sits up. I open my eyes and see him looking down at me, pupils blown. He slaps the side of my breast, and my breath hitches. Then he grabs them, one in each hand, and massages, pinching the sensitive nipples.

"You're so beautiful," he says, almost to himself.

I run my hand down his chest, studying the tattoos and marred skin with a brand new appreciation. It's like whatever bubble of emotion that formed in the tattoo parlor is providing me enough oxygen to see him clearly for the first time.

"Please," I beg, not caring how desperate I sound.

He grabs my hands, stopping their exploration of his pecs, crosses my wrists, and lifts my arms, elbows bent so my hands are about an inch above my head. Leaning forward, he gently kisses the new tattoo, lips touching the Saniderm rather than my skin. With one hand wrapped around my wrists, keeping them still, he reaches down with the other to unbutton my pants. He slides his hand beneath my underwear and pushes his fingers down my center.

"Holy fuck, little reaper," he growls. "You're so fucking wet."

As if to prove my readiness to be fucked, I lift my hips, forcing his fingers deeper. He chuckles, hovering his head above mine. "Such a good little slut."

My pussy flutters at that, and I reach up to catch his lips in another kiss. His fingers curl, hooking into me. Before I can appreciate the new pressure, it's gone. I don't get a chance to whine at the loss because he interrupts our kiss by shoving his fingers into my mouth. I taste my own arousal and moan at the evidence of how much I want him.

Instinctively, I close my lips and run my tongue up his fingers, licking them clean. Theo lets go of my hands and pulls his fingers free, then stands to easily kick his pants and boxers off. I follow his lead, wiggling out of mine so we're both fully naked. My eyes find the Saniderm-covered skin outside of his knee, and the unnamed emotion, that bubble of fresh air, expands further.

His cock is fully erect, Prince Albert piercing glinting. He grips the base and gives it one pull before climbing back on the bed. I widen my legs and lift my hips in preparation, painfully throbbing for him.

Theo props himself up with one hand on the bed next to my head while he uses the other to guide his cock to my entrance. Once he's lined up, he thrusts forward, entering me all at once. I gasp, neck straining and eyes squeezing shut. Each time is better than the last, and I wonder if I'll ever get used to the size of him or the feeling of his piercing dragging inside me.

He moans. "You were fucking made for me," he says before pulling out and pushing in again. His hand finds its way to my throat again, choking as he pounds into me, stealing my breath as he fucks me hard and fast, occasionally loosening his grip on my throat long enough for me to suck in air. Then he moves his other hand down to rub my clit with brutal efficiency. It's not long before I'm coming, back arching with the intensity of the orgasm.

I don't get to relax or fall back to the bed. He pulls out, then flips me around onto my stomach, grabbing my hips and yanking me back so I'm forced on my hands and knees, then pushes inside again. He continues slamming into me, his grip on my hips tight enough to leave bruises. I gasp and moan his name, which drives him over the edge, his dick pulsing as he fills me. We both collapse, me turning so I land on my back and Theo lying with his head on my chest.

We lay like that on the bed, breathing heavily, without speaking. I realize my fingers are in his hair, running through the strands without even thinking. His own fingers are softly drawing circles on my side, like we're both mindlessly searching for active ways to continue touching each other.

I feel his cum leaking out of me but don't even consider getting up to clean off. My eyes are heavy, and I could fall asleep if my mind wasn't on overdrive. Despite the deep satisfaction, I want to scream at my brain to quiet. It should feel nothing but content after the past few hours.

But the silence gives it time to think.

It's Wednesday.

In two days, the month will be over. There's no question that I no longer want to kill Theo, but other than that, I have no idea what's next. I'm not going to continue living here. I have a life, a house and a car and friends that I want to return to.

But I don't want to leave him behind. I don't want to forget about Theo or the Saints of Purgatory. Plus, that detective is still looking into me, and I have no idea if the South Five will retaliate against me personally for killing one of their members.

It's too much. There's no simple answer. I know we should talk about it, but I don't want to ruin the evening. I want to shut my brain up and continue indulging in Theo. So, after a few more minutes of lying together, I tug on his hair, coaxing him to look up at me. His eyes are soft, and I drift my hand down his face.

"Round two?"

His smile turns evil. He answers by meeting me in another kiss. This time, I roll him onto his back and sink onto his cock, riding him from the top. We moan and pant and move together, attempting in vain to drown the uncertainty of tomorrow with the pleasure of today.

THIRTY-FOUR

Theo

"Holy fuck," I groan, hips thrusting forward faster. My cock bumps the back of June's throat, and she chokes, saliva falling down her face. Her hair is a mess from sleep and my hands, and she looks up at me through watery lashes before sucking further, throat working to accommodate me. She lets her teeth gently scrape the underside of my dick. Soon, my hips stutter, and I come down her throat. She swallows, then pulls back, wiping the corners of her mouth.

"You're fucking fantastic," I mutter, tugging her up the bed to meet me in a messy kiss. She woke me with my cock in her mouth, and I want to return the favor, but she catches sight of the clock and jumps off the bed in a hurry.

"Fuck, I'm going to be late," she says. The rest of the morning is a blur as she rushes to get us out the door in as little time as possible.

Once at her office, I stay on the bike but pull off my helmet, prepared to bring up evening plans since it's our last night, but she doesn't give me the chance. She stands on her toes and steals a quick kiss before turning and heading inside without a word.

Clearly, she has no problem kissing me in public anymore. But that doesn't necessarily mean much. And it doesn't provide answers about tomorrow.

I kick the bike back into gear and peel out of the lot.

June pored over the files I gave her on Tuesday, and though we talked through some of Lorry's investigation, there's still stuff she doesn't know. I removed a few pages from the files before giving them to her.

From my file, I hid the list of her clients, their addresses, diagnoses, families, and any other information I thought was prudent. I didn't want her to know how much I violated her clients' privacy, especially because only a few of them were helpful. I found who I think were her three victims before Jared, besides Dakota, Sadie's ex-boyfriend.

There was Adam Brewer, whose wife spent a lot of time in the E.R. before she started seeing June in early 2022. By September, Brewer disappeared. Eight months later, Curtis Mills, the father of one of June's older clients, disappeared from his home in a senior living community. He's considered a missing person, but Lorry didn't think twice about him because he's in his seventies. I guess he thinks seniors are beneath June. I know better. She doesn't care about age. She's an equal opportunist murderer. If the man is an asshole, she's going to slice him up. Simple as that.

Then there was Mario Narvaez. He was the foster brother of one of June's clients, and he abruptly quit his job via email and moved away last February. No one has heard from him since. He's not in Lorry's file because he lived in Utah, which means June traveled several hours for that kill.

I also took a single page out of Lorry's file. A new one that Kip retrieved for me on Monday. It's the most damning piece of evidence he has against her, and he found it over the weekend. I knew she'd freak out if she saw it.

There's a witness.

A twenty-year-old guy saw June, not in disguise, with Tim the day he disappeared. He didn't tell the cops because he didn't think anything of it. But Lorry tracked him down, showed him a picture of June, and the guy, Miles, confirmed that June was with Tim. According to Lorry's files, Miles said June picked Tim up from the church, kissed his cheek, and drove off with him. That was the last time he was seen. I think Lorry talked to him again yesterday, but I have no idea how that went.

I intend to find out.

It takes twenty minutes to get to Miles's townhouse. I park and head to the front door, knocking first. A minute passes, then I ring the doorbell. It takes two more rings before the door swings open, revealing a disheveled man with a chubby baby face, circles under big eyes, and a large shirt hanging over a thin frame.

"What the hell do you want?" he demands.

"Miles Harrison?"

"Depends…"

That's a yes. I push his arm off the door and force my way into his house.

"Hey! What are you doing?" Miles yells. He's oddly brave, considering he's nearly a decade younger than me and a hundred pounds lighter.

Once inside, I throw the door shut and cross my arms. "You talked to a cop, Lorry McCoy, last week."

Miles frowns, eyes dropping down my body. For the first time, he shows some fear as he assesses his now precarious situation. "So?"

"I want to know exactly what you told him."

"Why do you care?"

I take a step closer. "Tell me."

His eyes glance behind me, then to the side, probably looking for an escape or a weapon. To disabuse him of the notion, I grab his throat and slam him against the door. He screams, and I press into his windpipe, shutting him up.

"I'm going to let go, and you're going to tell me what you told him if you want to keep all your appendages. Blink once if you understand."

He blinks. I release his neck, but don't step back.

"He came asking about my old pastor. I told him he up and left, went to Cambodia. Pissed me off, too. I was his assistant at the church. His replacement said he didn't need one. Lost me my job."

"And?"

"He showed me a picture of this girl. I remembered her because she was gorgeous. Sexy as hell. I saw her a couple of times with him. Nothing against Tim, but she was way out of his league."

My blood boils. I want to rip out his tongue and gouge out his eyes, but he has more to tell me.

"Did the cop seem interested in her?"

"Yeah, duh. I thought he might be a new boyfriend, but then he said she was dangerous and asked me to think more about it, call him if I remembered anything else."

"Did you?"

His eyes jump away, and he licks his lip, fidgeting. "No."

Liar.

"Think carefully, Miles. Did you call the cop again?"

"No, man! I swear!"

I pull a rag out of my pocket and jam it into his mouth. He looks confused for a moment, then he's screaming into the rag, veins in his neck sticking out and face going red when I reach down and break two of his fingers at once.

I wait for him to stop screaming. His chest heaves, and

tears run down his cheeks.

"Scream and it'll be your arm next. Now, what did you tell McCoy when you called him again?" I pull the rag from his mouth, and he sucks in a shaky breath that's broken by sobs.

"I remembered that I saw that girl again the night Tim disappeared. Or maybe the next day, I don't know. But I went to the church in the middle of the night 'cause my girlfriend and I got in a fight, and sometimes I'd sleep on the couch in his office. She was there when I showed up. She was on the computer, so she didn't see me. I left. Figured she was his girlfriend or something and didn't want to intrude. But the next day, people were talking about how Tim cleared out his office. Took his computer and some books and such. But it was all there that night when she was there. I know it."

"Why didn't you tell anyone sooner?"

"I don't know, okay? I didn't think anything of it when it happened. I didn't even remember until that guy came around with the photo and got me thinking about it again. Please, that's all, I swear!"

"You didn't remember the first time McCoy talked to you?"

"No!"

"Why not?"

"I don't know, I swear!"

I start to shove the rag in his mouth, but he shakes his head wildly, snot flying as he cries. "I was drunk! I didn't tell anyone or remember 'cause I was drunk! My parents would've killed me!"

"How did you get to the church if you were drunk?"

"I drove! Okay? I was an idiot! I drove! But I remember her being there. I didn't make that up. Please, that's everything. Please let me go."

"Are you expecting another call or visit from McCoy?"

"No!"

"Did McCoy record your story?"

"What? No!"

"Have you told anyone else?"

"No, I swear! And I won't. I won't tell anyone you were here."

"Were there cameras in the church offices?" I know the answer but want to make sure there aren't any other surprises.

"They were broken. Broke a few weeks earlier and hadn't gotten fixed yet."

"Did anyone else know that girl was there? Or see her with Tim?"

He's shaking and crying and soon, he's going to piss himself. "No. No. I don't know. Tim was single, that's all anyone knows."

Good. So, it's just this guy's testimony, which is shaky at best.

But it's still too much. I don't want Lorry knowing anything about June. Any hint of evidence she may be involved needs to be eliminated.

"Thanks, Miles," I say, grinning. He starts to relax, which makes snapping his neck slightly easier.

I step back, and his body crumples to the floor.

"Fuck." That was dumb.

There's no reason for this kill to be traced to me, but Lorry will suspect June. He probably will anyway, but I can't leave the body here. I also can't carry him away on my bike.

Grinding my teeth, I grab my phone and call Ace.

THIRTY-FIVE

June

Theo and I don't talk about tomorrow. He picks me up, we visit the clubhouse for barely an hour, then we go back home, where we fuck and watch movies and drink wine.

I should mention tomorrow. I know I should. I need to know what the plan is. Unasked questions and anxiety about the future play on a loop in my head. Theo's eyes are a television screen that I stay glued to, ignoring the outside world.

We fall asleep in each other's arms again. When we wake up, we go through the motions of the morning like it's any other day. Until we're pulling on our jackets and shoes, about to walk outside.

"I can have James drop me off at your place later, then I'll bring your car to your office. I'm sure it'll be nice to have that again."

He could easily pick me up from work and take me back to my house. But this way, I'll have to drive him back to his house, which I'm sure is the plan. Get me back, then maybe I won't want to leave.

"Wow, I almost forgot I have a car," I say with a soft huff of laughter. I haven't missed the freedom of having my own vehicle in a while. I like the bikes.

"Maybe you should get a bike." It's supposed to be a joke, but I hear the seriousness behind his words.

"I'm not sure I'm ready for that."

"A few more lessons and you will be."

Lessons. Those were supposed to end with the month, too. I know he doesn't want them to. And while I don't either, I also want to reconnect with my old life. I need to remember who I am without Theo and the Saints. How can I do that when keeping one foot in their world?

"We'll see," I say with a pitiful excuse of a smile.

Once on his bike, he takes the familiar route to my office. I wish I wasn't wearing a helmet, so my face could press flat to his back. The wind whipping past me feels like a threat of time. The rumble of the engine is a song I've grown to love, and I dread the moment it'll go silent.

He turns off the bike long enough to kiss me and quietly say, "I'll see you later today."

I nod as best I can with his hands holding my face. Without another word, I step away from him, and he turns the motorcycle back on, peeling out of the parking lot. Allowing myself ten seconds to breathe, I tilt my head back and look up at the sky before going inside to start the long day of work.

~

"Amber called me from rehab," Jennifer says. "We could only talk for a few minutes, but she sounds okay."

"I'm so glad to hear that," I say. I called Cottonwood Tucson earlier this week and made sure they had the correct contact info for her aunt. I had a hunch that either Amber or

Theo gave a fake number, which would've been why Jennifer hasn't heard from her. Turns out, I was right.

"She can't need rehab, can she? I mean, when did she… how did she…" She stops to pull in a shaking breath. "It had to have been that boyfriend of hers. I knew he was bad news."

I let Jennifer talk and wonder if I should be worried that I no longer feel any guilt about my time with Theo. I know he's not the bad guy Jennifer makes him out to be, but he did leave Amber unprotected and vulnerable among drug dealers, criminals, and men who didn't care about her.

That doesn't seem to matter. Not anymore.

It's a struggle to stay focused during each session and give my clients the attention they deserve. Most of them talk about their plans for the evening, which continually reminds me that it's Valentine's Day. Somehow, I had forgotten.

Did Theo forget too? The Saints are still having church tonight. Maybe celebrating Valentine's Day isn't a priority for them. Though, I can imagine some of the guys, like Raph and maybe even Luna, will troll bars for easy lays. And I'm sure Bonnie and Clyde will want to go out. Would Theo? Did he and Scottie celebrate Valentine's?

My eyes flick to the clock every few minutes like I'm a junkie waiting for my next fix. By the time I'm heading outside to wait for Theo, my entire body is on edge, and I don't know whether it's from the desire to see him or the fear of his reaction when I tell him what I've decided to do.

I'm rocking from heel to toe and back, watching the mouth of the parking lot, when a door slams behind me. I turn to see a man, middle-aged and well-built, walking toward the office door. He's wearing light-washed jeans and a short-sleeved button-up. He gives me a disarming smile. I nod once, then turn back around, pulling my phone out to call Theo.

The next thing I know, blinding pain explodes at the back of my head, there's the sensation of falling, then blackness.

THIRTY-SIX

Theo

I'm sitting at my desk at the Cage, failing to do any work at all as I think about seeing June in two hours, when Raphael walks in.

"Hey, boss," he says, dropping into the chair across from me. "I was wondering how late church is going to be tonight? A few of us wanted to go out later."

I give him an unimpressed, blank look. He's not the first one to ask a version of that. None of my guys would consider missing church, not for something as trivial as Valentine's Day, but they'll happily try to get out early if there's a chance of getting laid.

"It won't be long." If I'm honest with myself, I may cancel church so I can spend the entire evening picking June apart with my teeth, depending on how it goes when I pick her up.

"Sweet." He doesn't move to stand, and a flicker of hesitation crosses his face.

"What is it, Raph?"

"I just… You know that cop? The one who hires you occasionally?"

My brows pull together. "Lorry?"

"Yeah. Well…" He licks his lips as if his mouth has gone dry, then shifts in the chair, breaking eye contact. "He was here earlier. Asking about June."

There's a stutter in my chest. "What about June?"

"Just, you know. Who she is. How long you two have been together, that sort of thing."

"What did you tell him?"

"Nothing!" he quickly says. "Just that she's your girl and y'all have been together a little over a month."

Fuck. That could ruin my story about getting close to her for Lorry. He only came to me three weeks ago, if that. But Raph is an idiot, so it won't be hard to explain this away as him not knowing what he's talking about.

"And that's all?"

Raph hesitates. I sit forward, eyes boring into him. Finally, he says, "I didn't think anything of it! I know he's been a client for a long time. I swear, I didn't tell him anything bad. He just asked what she was like. I said we all really like her. He asked how often she's here. I started getting unsure then, so I just said a bit, ya know, like she's here some, but I didn't say it was all the time. Then he asked if she partakes in club activities, and I know we're not supposed to talk to outsiders about that shit, so I just shook my head."

"Okay…" I dangle the word like a noose, waiting for Raph to wrap it around his neck.

"He asked if she ever got violent. Of course, I didn't tell him about that day she saved your life. I'd never do that, boss."

I'd think not. "Did he ask anything else?"

Raph shakes his head. "No, no, I swear. He talked briefly to Bella, but I think she told him to fuck off, because he left in a hurry after that. I thought maybe he was just interested in the boss's new girl. I mean, who wouldn't be? But I dunno. It was a bit weird."

"When was this exactly?"

"Like fifteen minutes ago, I swear."

I lean further across the desk, letting some of the lethal darkness rise to my eyes. "If I find out you've said *anything* more about June to *anyone* outside of the Saints, especially a fucking cop, I will rip the skin off your arms and hang you with it from the ceiling of the Cage so everyone can watch you die, do you understand me?"

His Adam's apple bobs with a swallow. He nods, pushing back as if adding a few inches of distance between us will save his life.

"Make sure everyone knows not to even *breathe* in Lorry's direction."

He nods again and scrambles up from the chair. "Yes, sir, of course."

"Good." I settle back, forcing myself to appear calmer than I am. "Send Bella in here."

Raph runs out quickly. Bella saunters in minutes later and tells me that Lorry asked her about 'the boss's new girl,' and she told him to fuck off if he wasn't going to order a drink. I believe her, and a quick look at the cameras will confirm her story. Dismissing her, I turn back to the computer and rub my temples, wondering what the *hell* Lorry was thinking.

This is bad, but it's not the end of the world. I can explain away anything Raph says.

But now it's even more imperative that we put an end to Lorry's investigation as soon as possible. If he's gotten to the point that he's asking my guys about her, then his tentative trust in me must be growing thin.

I text June to remind her I'll be by later with her car, and she likes my message but doesn't text back.

The next hour and a half are sheer torture. The clock moves slower than it ever has.

Finally, blissfully, I'm parking her car in front of the office. I text her first, and after waiting ten minutes, in case she still has a client, I decide to get her myself. The front door is unlocked, but the space is quiet. Her office is locked, and there's no response when I knock.

"June?" Stepping back, I notice there's no light coming from under the door. With a frown, I turn to check the other doors in the office building. All but one are shut. The open one has a black and gold nameplate. Inside is an older man with small rectangular glasses and blonde hair. He looks up from his desktop when I knock.

"Can I help you?" he asks.

"Have you seen June Graves today?"

His forehead wrinkles as he takes in my appearance. I try not to bristle under his scrutiny. Ever since the police wasted precious time assuming I did something to Shiloh rather than looking for the actual sick fuck who took her, it pisses me off when anyone makes assumptions.

"And you are?"

"Theo, her friend. I'm supposed to pick her up today."

"Ms. Graves left about twenty minutes ago." He drops his attention back to his computer, silently dismissing me.

An instinctual seed that something was wrong planted in my gut when she didn't respond to my text. Now it feels like a quickly growing poisonous tree.

Twenty minutes? She didn't text me. I pull out my phone and click her name, but the call goes straight to voicemail. Hurrying back to her door, I grab the doorknob and use all my strength to break the flimsy lock and force it open. The office is dark and empty, everything put away and organized. Not a single book, pillow, or tissue is out of place. Her desk computer is turned off, and there are no phones in the drawers.

Starting to panic, I call her again. Then I try James, but his phone goes to voicemail too, which would worry me if I didn't know he's in practice. He always turns off his phone during practice. Luna is next, and she answers after two rings.

"Sup, boss?"

"Have you heard from June today?"

"I texted her earlier to ask if she was coming to church tonight, but she never replied. I figured she was busy at work. James reminded me it's the end of the thirty days. That doesn't mean she's going to stop hanging around, though, does it? Because if you brought this badass little killer into my life just to—"

I hang up, trying June again. Voicemail. Her trackers are all off, which isn't surprising because since the one in her wallet, she's found anything I've tried planting within hours and destroyed them. The cameras I still have in her house show no movement. Neither do the ones in my house.

But Sadie... the tracker in her car flashes at her house. Maybe June decided to go there so she wouldn't have to see me at all now that the month is over.

Almost hoping that's the case, I find Sadie's contact in my phone and click dial. There's not even a full ring before she answers.

"If you're calling for the best friend's advice on what to get June for Valentine's Day, then I'm sorry to inform you that you're too late."

"Is June there?"

"No? Why?"

"Has she called you today?"

"No..."

"So you haven't heard from her at all?" The tree of

poisonous panic has reached my lungs, vines squeezing them tight.

"Not today. Why? What's going on?"

I turn in a circle in the office without answering. June's not at her house or mine. Her trackers are off. Her phone is off. She hasn't talked to Luna or Sadie. She supposedly left twenty minutes ago.

No matter what she planned to do now that our month-long deal is over, she wouldn't just disappear like this. Not when she knows about my past.

My breaths have turned short and sharp, loud enough for Sadie to hear. It takes a moment for my ears to register that she's nearly yelling into the phone.

"Theo Zervas! Tell me what the hell is happening! Where is June?"

I shake my head even though she can't see me. "I don't know. I don't... I was supposed to pick her up from work. She's not here."

"Maybe she went—"

"Her car is here." No need to tell her that I drove it here.

"Hold on, I'll text her."

"No point. Her phone is off."

"*Fuck*," she hisses. "Okay, you stay there. I'll call the girls. Maybe I should call the cops."

"No!" I shout. "No cops."

"Why? If she's missing..."

"Sadie, no." Fuck, June can't have more cops looking into her life. Even to find her. I don't think she'd be labeled a missing person; after all, it's not a crime to run away or stop talking to your friends, and there's no obvious threat to her life, but still. She can't be on their radar *at all*. Not when she's already on...

"Lorry." I don't realize I've said it out loud until Sadie

asks who that is. "It doesn't matter," I answer. I should hang up. June would kill me if I told her best friend about her bloody hobby.

"Bullshit it doesn't matter! You tell me my best friend is missing and I can't call the cops, and then you say some random lady's name?"

"Lorry is a guy," I correct automatically.

"That's worse!"

"Look, don't worry. I'll figure it out. I'll find her."

"Fuck that. You've known her a couple of weeks. She's been my best friend for years."

"Fine! Ask Rose and Evelyn if they've seen her. Check with her other friends," I say, hoping to keep Sadie busy long enough for me to figure out what the fuck is happening. "I'll talk to the Saints and let you know what I find out."

"I'm not an idiot, Zervas. You know exactly what's happening, and it's scaring you. Tell me or I'm calling the cops."

"Sadie—"

"NOW!" she screams. "Or so help me god, I'm hanging up and calling 911. They'll be raiding your little bar within minutes."

I grip the phone so hard I'm surprised it doesn't crack. I don't give a shit if the cops go to the Cage, but they can't know that June exists. So, reluctantly, I say, "Fine. Fine. The only thing I can think of is Lorry McCoy. He's a detective."

"A detective? But you said…"

"I don't have time to explain right now. But I need you to call Luna and tell her that June is missing and to talk to the Saints. Tell her I'm going to talk to Lorry, she'll know what I mean."

"I—"

"Please." My desperation must show in how I beg, because she doesn't bother arguing.

"Okay, yeah. I'll call her now. Just, please, call me later. I need to know she's okay."

"I will," I promise. June is so going to kill me for getting Sadie involved. But I don't care. All that matters is that she's okay. If I find her alive, I'll sharpen the knife for her to slit my throat.

After hanging up, I immediately call Lorry. Unsurprisingly, he doesn't answer. It goes straight to voicemail without ringing. I try four more times, feet dragging me out to June's car. By my sixth attempt at contacting the detective, my heart feels like a hammer slamming against my sternum. The car's tires squeal as I speed out of the parking lot. I call the police station next. They inform me that Detective McCoy isn't in the office and ask for my name. Before I can respond, my phone flashes with an incoming call from Luna. I gladly hang up on the station to answer.

"He took her," I say in lieu of a greeting.

"I know," Luna says without a hint of the carefree humor from mere minutes ago. "Kip is on his way to Lorry's house to check there."

"He won't keep her there."

"He's close enough to check just in case and to look for any clues about where he would take her. Maybe he can ask Bethany, too."

I don't point out that Bethany, Kip's sister and Lorry's wife, is likely to be in her office at the university today, which is where I'm headed now. Kip will politely ask his sister about Lorry and June.

I'm so far beyond polite that by the time I find June, I might truly be the type of monster she hunts.

"Have you gotten a hold of James?" I ask.

"Yeah. His trainer answered the phone, thank god. He's on his way back from the gym."

"Ask everyone if they've talked to Lorry recently or if anyone has come by asking about June. Lorry was at the Cage earlier today talking to Raph."

Luna swears under her breath, and I hear movement on the other end. Lorry had to have talked to someone or heard something to make him act now. Why else would he *personally* kidnap June? He never gets his hands dirty like this. He prefers to pay me to bend the law for him. And he'll throw a criminal in prison before enacting personal justice every time.

Something changed. And I have to figure out what.

I push down on the gas pedal to fly through a yellow light, and a thought occurs to me.

Miles. The possible witness I killed yesterday.

"Call me if you learn anything," I order Luna, then hang up without waiting for a response. The next call connects soon after, and a low, somewhat raspy voice answers.

"Actaeon's Custodians."

"Ace," I greet. "Were there any issues with my cleanup order yesterday?"

There's a moment of silence as Ace checks over his records. "No. I took care of it personally an hour after you called. No one was inconvenienced by the mess, and we were able to clean it completely with no problem." Meaning no one saw the dead body before they got there, and no one saw them getting rid of it.

"And the resident?"

"He's unfortunately come down with a bad flu. A classmate is taking notes for him, and he ordered some pain meds."

So, I should have a few days before Miles's disappearance is noticed. Unless Lorry decides to check in on him sooner. Miles had said he didn't expect a visit or call from the detective, but he was under duress at the time.

Fuck. I shouldn't have killed him like that. Of course, Lorry is going to blame June.

"Has anyone complained about the mess?" I ask Ace.

"No."

"What about any other mess recently? Like the one a few weeks ago?"

"Of course not," Ace says, sounding slightly annoyed. He's the best in the business, and any suggestion that he may have made a mistake would be a personal insult. "Your account is safe, Theo. No one on my crew has reported anything out of the ordinary."

"Thanks, Ace."

"I might remind you that should you meet any problems on your end, your contract prohibits any mention of Actaeon's Custodians."

"I'd never jeopardize you or your work," I say honestly. "Thank you again."

"Yup." There's a break, and I'm about to hang up. Then he adds, "Call my personal phone if you need anything, T."

"I will." Then I hang up.

Ace has been the Saints' custodian ever since I took over the club. But before that, he was my friend and foster brother. It's been a while since we talked outside of business deals, but I don't doubt that he'd be there in an instant if I needed him.

Ignoring signs that I need a faculty pass, I pull into a parking spot closest to Bethany's office. People look my way as I walk through the building, but I keep my eyes locked forward. Bethany's door is at the back of the building in the HR department. I open the door and walk in without knocking.

"Hey, you can't... Theo?"

I lock the door and turn to face the woman. She's

attractive in the blandest sense of the word, wearing large glasses and a tweed dress, which she smooths down after standing from her desk. "What are you doing here?"

"Sit down, Bethany."

She frowns at me. "What—"

"Now."

Her eyes go wide, and the pulse in her neck jumps from fear. She glances at the door, then her phone. I take a threatening step forward. She sits.

"Where is Lorry?"

"I don't know…" she says, her voice shaking now. "The station, probably."

"He's not."

"Maybe he's out on an investigation. He didn't say. Is everything okay?"

I brace myself against the edge of her desk and angle myself closer to her so she can see every inch of my face and the anger simmering in my eyes. Bethany has no idea about my business dealings with her husband, of course, but she knows we've come in contact. Her brother is my third in command, so of course her cop husband has checked into the Saints.

"Do you have his location on your phone?" She shakes her head. I lower my voice and add, "I can have you unconscious before you can even open your mouth."

She swallows. "I really don't have it. But I can call him."

I raise my eyebrow in a silent command to do that. She picks up her phone, and I watch her navigate to the favorites list in her contacts. After she clicks his name, I snatch her phone and click speaker, holding it between us. It rings, which means he has me blocked, but he still doesn't answer. This time, when it goes to voicemail, I leave a message.

"One hair on her head and I'll make your wife wish she

never met you, Kip be damned. If anything happens to June, I swear to every god you can imagine that I won't sleep until your name is wiped from this earth, even if that means I have to kill everyone who has ever met you. Think very carefully about what you do next, Lorry. I'm exceptionally good at making people disappear." Then I hang up and pocket the phone. Bethany is watching me with eyes so wide and red that I won't be surprised if she's crying by the time I leave. She's frozen in her seat, her fight or flight instinct forcing her to remain still as if the predator won't see her. "I suggest you think twice before telling anyone about my visit. I have no qualms about following through on every single one of those threats. Do you understand?"

She nods.

"If you hear from your husband at all today, you call me or Kip. Use someone else's phone, because I'll be taking this one," I pat my pocket, "in case he decides to call you. Understand?"

Another nod.

"Good."

I turn around, unlock her door, and return to June's car. The hammering of my heart has started splintering my sternum. It won't be long before every bone in my chest has shattered and the splinters have shredded my heart and lungs.

THIRTY-SEVEN

June

There's a rock in the base of my skull that keeps dropping over and over, creating ripples through my head. It flows over my brain, down my throat, into my eyes, on my tongue. Everything pulses. Throbs. The signal to tell my eyes to open gets lost halfway, and my eyelids shudder with the abandoned action.

What happened?

The question expands with a fresh breath, taking up space in my mind until it's all I can think about. A skipped track twirls in my ears, repeating the question over and over.

"What happened?"

"What happened?"

"What happened?"

I think about the rock in my mind and how it's not a rock at all but a pounding headache. And the headache originates from the pain at the base of my skull. Did I fall?

No, I was hit. I'd been standing outside of my office waiting for Theo, and something—some*one*—hit me in the back of the head.

The realization expands the next ripple of pain, and I groan.

"I didn't hit you that hard, you should be awake by now."

The voice is warped in my ears, but I'm pretty sure it's coming from in front of me. I try to orient myself and realize I'm sitting, hands behind my back. I shift, barely moving an inch, and my shoulders protest with a shout of pain.

"Getting tangled with the Saints of Purgatory was a bad idea," the voice says. "Were you even aware that your boyfriend has been killing and framing people behind your back?"

The Saints.

Theo.

Where's Theo?

He was supposed to pick me up. He probably already arrived at the office, so he must know I'm missing. Unless he dropped off my car and left.

If he realizes I'm gone, maybe he'll know where I am.

Where am I?

I try to open my mouth to ask, but my tongue is still too heavy. Instead, I focus on opening my eyes. It's like trying to pry superglue off my skin, but eventually they peel apart, and a soft light pierces my vision. Dizziness rocks me, and my eyes promptly spring shut again.

"I'll give you this, you're good at covering your tracks. Not perfect, but pretty damn good."

"Wha…" My voice cracks. I grimace and manage to open my eyes again. This time, I glance around, cataloging my surroundings. The walls are discolored, like freshly installed drywall that hasn't been painted yet. There's a dark hallway to my right and a shut door to my left. All the windows are covered with cardboard. Sheets of plastic lay on top of whatever furniture is in the room, fluttering at the slightest breeze. It's like a house in the middle of a renovation.

I gently move my limbs, finding my ankles tied against chair legs and my hands cuffed behind my back.

Directly across from me, standing in front of what looks like a covered fireplace, is a blonde man with dark circles under small eyes. He's the same guy from outside the office earlier. Why is he...

Then it hits me.

Detective Lorry McCoy. I should've recognized him earlier. I looked him up after Theo told me about his investigation. There were photos of a recent ceremony where he was recognized for his work as a narcotics detective. How many of those cases did he close because Theo did his dirty work?

It seems he's ready to get his own hands bloody.

"You've been out nearly two hours. I started worrying that I hit you too hard."

He walks toward me, spinning like he's on a merry-go-round. I bite the inside of my cheek, trying to force clarity through my brain.

"Why am I here?" The question comes out as a croak.

He sneers. "Because there's no way you'll go away for what you've done. Not with those fucking *criminals* covering for you."

"What are you talking about?"

"Fun fact." McCoy scoffs and stops a foot away from me. "A buddy of mine has a C.I. in the South Five. The other day, he comes up with this crazy story about why we've noticed some increased gang activity. Apparently, one of their own was killed in a bar on someone else's territory. He didn't know names, but it didn't take much pushing to learn the killer wasn't a member of the Saints of Purgatory. She was a small blonde girl with a sleeve tattoo."

I wince, glancing down at the cemetery inked on my skin.

"Imagine my surprise when none of my questions about this mysterious murderer yielded any answers. The Saints in particular were adamant that nothing of the sort ever happened in their bar."

Theo has an impressive amount of control over his club. Either that, or they're all just so loyal that selling out an outsider wasn't even an option because their leader liked her.

"That made me start questioning the work Zervas, Kip, and the others do for me. I've never had any reason to doubt them before, but all I've gotten these last three weeks has been evidence of your innocence and empty promises that he'd get the job done."

His words are starting to string together, and I squeeze my eyes shut for a second. I swallow down a wave of nausea, cursing my fucking body. I clearly have a concussion.

"So, I followed Zervas yesterday. Watched him take you to work. Kiss you." He sounds so disgusted that I wouldn't be surprised if my nausea transferred into him. "Want to know where he went after dropping you off?"

I don't nod or reply. McCoy isn't discouraged, though.

"To a townhouse near the university. Last week, my case finally started going somewhere. I struck gold, without the useless help of the Saints. I found a witness to your involvement with Pastor Tim Bidwell."

My eyes snap open and snag on McCoy's smug grin.

A witness? There's no way. They would've come forward.

"I didn't realize Zervas was going to the house until he was there. He wasn't inside for long, but he left in a hurry.

Imagine my surprise when I decided to check on my witness, only to find him dead on his floor. Your little boyfriend snapped an innocent man's neck all because he could place you with Bidwell before he disappeared."

I gape at the detective, unsure whether to believe him. Did Theo really kill someone yesterday? To protect me?

"I would've assumed you did it, had I not seen Zervas with my own two eyes," McCoy continues.

"You didn't see Theo kill anyone," I say. My brain may be bruised from the blow earlier, but I heard McCoy's words. He watched Theo go into the house, then walk out. He didn't see him kill anyone. That's probably why he didn't call it in. And he would've had to explain that he was following a citizen without orders and entered a private residence without probable cause. "Maybe he was dead already." It's a thin argument, but enough for me to hold onto. I don't care that Theo killed someone, but I don't want him to go to prison because of me.

"You sound like a defense attorney."

"What do you want from me?"

"I want you to pay for killing my cousin!"

I recoil from the shout, another bout of sickness washing through me. This time, I don't tamp it down. I lean forward, projecting the vomit forward so it lands on McCoy's shoes. He exclaims in disgust and jumps back.

"Sorry," I mutter. "Concussion."

He gives me a look worthy of a rotting carcass on the side of the road. After a beat, he says, "There are two ways you're getting out of this. You can either walk out of here to confess to your crimes, or you can leave in a body bag."

"Thought you were too good to be a murderer."

"You're not human enough for it to be murder."

"That's not very nice," I say, even as the irony registers.

My victims are bad men. Monsters. I tell myself that killing them is different than killing innocent women, like other serial killers. But that doesn't mean it's not murder.

Cops have a term for people like me. An organized, mission-oriented killer. Or a vigilante killer, though I don't belong with the vigilantes. My consistent ritual and lack of remorse puts me squarely in the serial murderer category.

"You murdered my cousin," McCoy says, pausing after each word for dramatic emphasis.

"Who?" I ask innocently.

"Solomon."

"Don't know him."

"You're *lying*!" he screams. His face turns red, filling with rage.

Unpredictable. That could either be good for me or very, *very* bad.

"You're right, I'm sorry." Sarcasm drips from my lips. "Solomon. King of Israel, right? I went to Sunday School."

In a blink, McCoy's fist comes flying at me, then an explosion of pain sparks behind my nose and in my skull as my head snaps to the side. The chair doesn't budge, which suggests that it's bolted to the floor. Smart. I sniff, wince at the burning, then spit. Unsurprisingly, the saliva is red. Pressing my tongue against my cheek, I feel the cut where it slammed against my teeth.

McCoy paces away from me, hands in his hair as he attempts to breathe through the anger. Using his brief distraction to my advantage, I do a quick inventory of my person.

McCoy took away my pocket knife *and* my small bracelet, which has a tiny hidden knife inside I might've been able to use to shim out of the cuffs or cut the ropes around my ankles. My shoes are gone, so I don't have shoelaces, but

I think he left my earrings in. Twisting my hands, I blindly study the handcuffs to confirm that he used an average police-issued pair. He activated the second latch to lock the cuffs in place, which means they won't tighten any further, but it'll also be impossible to shim out of them.

I could probably dislocate my thumb then tug my hands free, but I'd prefer not to. Thankfully, I've been on alert ever since Theo told me a detective was looking into me. Clipped on the tag inside the waistband of my pants is a micro-clip handcuff key, which I usually wear or tie into my shirts before a kill. I made sure to always have one on me the first two weeks with Theo, but then I got complacent and went several days without one. Since learning about McCoy, I started wearing them again.

Unfortunately, the awkward angle I'm at and the chair makes reaching the key difficult. I won't be able to while McCoy is in the room. It'll be too obvious.

"I really am sorry," I mutter. "But I don't know who Solomon is. I've never killed anyone."

He spins around. "Don't do that."

"Do what?"

"Play innocent. It's pointless. I know you killed him. And I know Zervas knows. Otherwise, he wouldn't be going to such lengths to protect you."

"Why would he protect me? He wouldn't do anything to put the Saints in jeopardy."

"I think he would for you."

I actually laugh at that. "Theo would never pick me over the Saints."

"He broke a boy's neck for you just yesterday."

My expression stays frozen, giving nothing away. "I'm a therapist. I volunteer at the children's hospital." Though I haven't done that in a while. "Why would I kill anyone?"

"I don't care about your motives. I care about justice. And you've avoided it far too long."

"Our justice system generally frowns upon kidnapping people and tying them to chairs."

"There are holes in our system that let people like you get away with murder without consequences."

Yeah, it does. It also has safe pockets where abusers and rapists and narcissistic assholes can comfortably sit, knowing they'll never be locked away.

"I didn't kill anyone," I insist through gritted teeth. I know his mind is never going to change. He's decided I'm a killer and that's that. The fact that he's correct doesn't matter, because I won't be admitting anything. Not to a cop. Especially not when I'm likely being recorded. Arizona is a one-party consent state, so while any recording he gets may not be admissible in court, it would be legal for him to do so.

"You did. And the families of the people you killed deserve closure."

His watch flashes, and he pauses to look at the little screen. His jaw ticks as he looks back at me. "Think about your situation for a bit. You can either do the right thing or you can meet the same fate as your victims." Then he disappears down the dark hallway.

As soon as he's gone, I work on maneuvering my hands up and over the slits in the chair. Pushing with my heels, I angle my hips up, bringing the back of my pants closer. The metal edges of the handcuffs slice into my skin, and I hold in a hiss as blood drips down my fingers. Finally, a finger hooks over the waistband of my pants. Sliding my back up the chair and pulling down with my finger, I manage to nudge the tiny key just as the sound of a bang makes me flinch.

"FUCK!" McCoy's returning footsteps are loud, an

ominous threat following him. He slams to a stop in front of me, eyes wild with fury and fear from whatever phone call he just received. Spit flies from his lips as he yells, "If Zervas touches my wife, it's more blood on *your* hands, understand?"

"What?" I gasp, leaning away from the detective.

"Zervas wouldn't pick you over the Saints? Then why the fuck did he threaten Kip's sister to get to me?"

Kip's sister. Lorry's wife.

Theo's looking for me.

I smile. "Want to keep your wife safe?" I ask as sweetly as I can. "Maybe you should let me go, *detective.*"

Another punch, this one with more force than before. I feel my nose break, and the blinding pain that follows makes me momentarily forget where I am. Then he lands a punch in my stomach, and I huff, falling forward as much as I can while cuffed. I cough and gasp, curling in against the pain. Red saliva falls from my mouth and lands on my knees. Blood trickles from my nose, and I fight the urge to sniff.

"You have an hour to decide how this ends."

His threat is clear.

Confess or die.

And by the sound of it, if I die, Theo will break. Last time, he almost destroyed himself.

This time, he may take all the Saints down with him.

THIRTY-EIGHT

Theo

"Boss?"

I whip around. The last three hours have been an endless tunnel headed straight to Hades. The fall fills my ears with a roaring that gets louder every time I close my eyes. Everything and everyone I look at is blurred on the edges, like they're on the other side of a camera that won't focus.

Every member of the Saints has been looking for June or Lorry since I left Bethany's office. She hasn't contacted me, and none of them have found anything useful. Kip talked to Lorry's partner and his best friend, neither of whom have heard from the detective all day. Even Sadie has been helping. She talked to Evelyn, who's checking everywhere June might go, and Rose, who roped her sister into the search. Apparently, Rose's sister is a whiz with computers, and she's been attempting to hack into the police database for a hint at where Lorry might go. Sadie called half an hour ago to inform me that she was on her way to the Iron Cage to help look and get answers. I didn't have the presence of mind to tell her no.

"What?" I bite.

Axel falters from his spot at my door, and hesitation flicks in his eyes. He swallows, throat working as he tries to repress the trepidation he feels at talking to me while I'm so volatile. "I heard from a buddy of mine down near Fairgrounds."

He pauses, setting my teeth on edge. "Spit it out, Axel."

"He said some cops have been asking about an alleged murder at the Cage. They seem to think it was a drug-related incident involving a young blonde woman."

All the muscles in my body inflate to a breaking point, pushing against my bones.

"How the fuck do they know?"

One cop looking in our direction—*June's* direction—is plenty. We don't need the narcotics team snooping around, too.

"Someone must've talked. One of them, I'd guess."

"Well, it wasn't a Saint."

"Of course not."

"Did anyone mention her name?" Axel shakes his head. "Is it an active investigation?"

"It seems like they were asking preliminary questions. Trying to decide if there's any merit to the rumor. But if no one talks, they'll stop looking. Without a body or a witness willing to come forward, they don't have a case. They're not going to waste time and resources on an unconfirmed murder of a drug-dealing gangster."

"Do you know which cop was asking around?"

"There were two. Detective McCoy." *Unsurprising.* "And a Detective Cruz."

"Cruz?" I ask. That's not Lorry's partner.

"Yeah."

"Anything else?"

"That girl just arrived. Sadie something, I think."

I toss my phone onto the desk, agitation rubbing against my veins like sandpaper. "Shit. Okay. Send her back." I circle my desk and drop into the chair.

"Yes, sir." He rushes out, trying to conceal his hurried steps like he isn't terrified to be alone in the room with me.

I know I'm spinning out, and if I don't get a hold of myself, I could make this all so much worse. But the panic is overriding every other emotion. I can't stop picturing June stuck somewhere with Lorry, unconscious, hurt, or tied up. Lorry might be a cop, but he's already shown he has no problem breaking the law. He wants revenge for his cousin, and he probably knows I was never going to help him frame June. He's unpredictable. He might decide he has no choice but to kill June himself or torture her into confessing. The fact that I have no idea what he's capable of or what his end goal is sets me more on edge.

The door swings open, and Sadie storms inside. She stops at the edge of my desk, her body angled toward me like I'm a magnet attracting her anger.

"Tell me what the fuck is going on with my best friend."

I rub the bridge of my nose between my thumb and forefinger, wishing I could get away with slapping duct tape over her mouth, then locking her in my office so I don't have to deal with her until I have June back.

How am I supposed to explain what's going on when she has no idea about June's homicidal hobbies?

"I don't know yet." I let out a heavy breath and push the chair back, muscles tense and prepared for a fight that's nowhere near occurring.

"Bullshit. You called me terrified because she disappeared. You have a bar full of bikers freaking out, looking all over town for her. And you refuse to talk to the cops because some detective with a chick's name is involved?"

"Look, I'll explain more later," I lie.

"You'll explain now."

"Careful giving me orders, Miss Oliver." Any of my guys, Luna included, would hesitate after hearing that tone, the way anger fills every corner of each word.

Sadie, however, doesn't balk. "If you think for a second that I'm going let you walk out of this room without telling me what's going on, then you're delusional."

I stand, forcing her to tilt her head back to hold eye contact. "*Let* me?"

"June isn't the only one who can fight. She's also not the only one who carries weapons with her." She pulls up her shirt, showing a large knife clipped to her pants.

I raise my brows, momentarily surprised.

Sadie drops her shirt. "Don't underestimate my ability to hear the truth and not turn my back on my best friend. I am just as comfortable pushing lines of legality as anyone else in this god-forsaken, beer-soaked den of inequities."

"Den of inequities?" If I wasn't so preoccupied with the safety of the woman I love, then I might've laughed. It's so obvious why she's June's best friend.

Her chest rises with a heavy breath, and she flattens her hands on the desk. "All I care about is finding my best friend, alive and unhurt. If this has anything to do with what you guys do around here, I don't care."

Why didn't I think of that? I mentally chide myself for being so short-sighted while putting on a look of reluctant shame. "Fine. Yes. June is in danger because of me, okay? Is that what you wanted to hear?" The indignation isn't hard to fake. "She got mixed up with me and a dirty cop who helps us run drugs, and now she's paying the price for *my* mistakes."

Sadie's brows furrow. She leans forward, eyes peeling

back every layer of my mask. Then she shakes her head. "No. She wouldn't do that."

"Maybe you don't know her as well as you think you do." I immediately regret the words when she flinches. But the hurt doesn't last long on her face.

"I know that her shithole father was murdered when she was fifteen, and the cops never found out who did it. I know that not twenty-four hours after I told her my boyfriend tried to rape me, he happened to overdose at a club June visited without telling me. I know she's wickedly good at kickboxing and shooting and self-defense. I know that I have a locked room at my nursery with some more... questionable plants and flowers that will sometimes be slightly emptier after she visits. I know that every few months, she gets on edge to the point that if anyone looks at her the wrong way, they're in danger of getting their head ripped off.

"I know my best friend. More than she thinks I do. And I've loved her a lot longer than you. I will continue to love her long after you're a memory we laugh about. So, tell me what the fuck is going on, or I swear to God, I will stab you in the throat and claim self-defense."

My lips part, but no words form. My brain slows and stutters, like a car running out of gas. Sadie doesn't lift her eyes from mine, and the set of her mouth tells me she's not making an empty threat.

She knows.

Maybe not all of it, but enough to *suspect.*

And she still loves June.

Of course, she does. How could she not?

But if I'm wrong and she doesn't know and I say something stupid... "I don't know what—"

"She has a cemetery sleeve tattoo," she interrupts. "No one likes their last name that much. You call her 'little reaper,' and Luna calls her 'killer.' Even the story of how you two met is dodgy at best. I can put two and two together."

"You've never told June your suspicions?" I ask, the volume of my voice several decibels lower.

The question seems to pierce the inflated anger in Sadie's body, because her shoulders fall, and she drops into the chair. "I didn't want to force her out of the murder closet."

I snort.

"Most people wouldn't jump to the conclusion that their best friend is a killer just because she's a decent fighter with a clever tattoo and a few assholes met their predictable ends."

"Most people are idiots and cowards who don't pay attention and think morality is an inflexible bone we're all born with."

"And you don't?"

"I think that if June wasn't exactly who she is, I would've been raped and so would a dozen girls after me."

My lips roll together. I take in every bit of honesty and love in her eyes. "I'm not telling you her story."

"I'm not asking you to. I'm asking you to give me enough information to help. I'm going crazy here. This detective guy. Sherry—"

"Lorry."

"Whatever." She waves her hand in the air. "Did he arrest her?"

"He can't. There's no evidence."

"So, he kidnapped her?"

My fists curl together, and I nod.

She sits back, sucking in a breath. "Why?"

"His cousin disappeared three years ago. He was… not a great guy."

"She killed a detective's cousin? How could she be so stupid?"

"In her defense, he wasn't a detective yet. And I don't think he was super close with his cousin."

"Still," she grumbles. "So, this is his fucked up version of revenge? How does he even know it was June?"

"That's not important," I say, not wanting to go over all that bullshit yet again. "What is important is that Lorry was tired of trying to find justice within the system. I think he realized it was never going to happen. Then there were rumors of someone being killed here at the Iron Cage, and Lorry thinks it was June."

"Was it?"

I shrug. "If said alleged murder did happen here, then the killer was probably just trying to save my life."

"So, it's your fault?" she says with a grin. I know it's meant to be a joke, but the words feel like a fist to my gut anyway.

Fuck. It *is* my fault. Everything. If anything happens to her because of me…

Red. My life would be saturated in it. In anger and blood and fire.

"I'm going to find her."

She nods. "I'm helping."

"I can't let you get involved. If you got hurt, June would succeed in killing me this time."

"This time?"

"Why don't you find Luna? She could use your help looking for anywhere Lorry may have taken her."

"I'm assuming you've checked his house?"

I nod.

"Any friends with vacation homes?"

I shake my head. "I've looked into all his friends, family, any acquaintances I can think of. No one has property in Tucson that is currently unoccupied."

"Could he have taken her out of Tucson?"

"No. He wouldn't risk going too far."

"What about places he's come across on the job? Like drug hideouts?"

"My guys are checking everything we can think of, but most of those places are currently crime scenes."

"Maybe he drove her out of the city and is holding her in his car somewhere."

"His car is at his house."

She groans and leans back in the chair. I'm just about to again suggest she go find Luna when Sadie sits up, eyes wide and shining with an idea. I can't help the hope cracking in my chest.

"Police auctions."

"What?"

"Police auctions! They're held twice a month to auction off retired police equipment or anything that can't be returned to the original owner or has no owner to return to. Abandoned cars, stolen goods, boats, bikes, building equipment, you name it. Half the shit is crap, but it's all cheap. They even sell foreclosed houses or raided crack houses."

"And?"

"*And* this detective would know what's going to be auctioned off next. Which means he knows which houses are currently empty. The houses won't be on real estate sites and are no longer crime scenes."

Shit, she's right. When I considered places connected to Lorry's job, I was only thinking about places his investigations may have taken him. I sent Benny and Raphael to check it all out, but they didn't find anything.

"How would we know what'll be auctioned next?"

"There'll be a list in their database."

"Rose's sister."

She nods. "I'll call her now." Then she's up and out of her chair, phone already in her hand as she taps away, deepening that crack of hope with each touch of her finger.

This is it.

It has to be.

I'm going to find you, little reaper.

THIRTY-NINE

June

The house doesn't have nearby neighbors. That's what I learn while attempting to quietly unlock the cuffs. I've heard a handful of cars drive by but no honking. There was a dog barking at one point, but it was far away. Based on the cracked, discolored, and shitty door and window frames, the house is old and hasn't been taken care of. It's under construction now, either because a new owner is flipping it or because the current owner decided to give it a lift.

McCoy must've bolted the chair to the ground. Or maybe this house is used by all the dirty cops to get confessions out of the criminals they can't muster enough evidence against.

I used to be better at unlocking cuffs, but I haven't practiced in a while, and with my arms at such an odd angle, it takes a while to even get the micro-clip key positioned the right way. Finally, the key slides in, and I twist and jiggle until it *clicks.* Next, I carefully shim the cuffs and loosen them enough to slide my hands free without accidentally tightening them.

When they fall open, I let out a puff of air in relief and pull my arms away from behind my back, leaving the cuffs hooked on a finger so they don't clatter to the floor. I drop them into my lap and inspect my wrists, noticing where the skin has been rubbed raw and blood seeps from small cuts. The rage turns cold and murderous, forming ice around my muscles.

Quickly, I lean forward and start working the knots around my feet free. Unfortunately, they're well done, and I don't have any of my knives. Plus, the change of gravity to my broken nose threatens to restart the bleeding that only recently stopped. I reach up, unclip an earring, and try using the sharpened point to help cut away at the thick ropes.

It's slow work. Too slow. Abandoning the attempt at cutting them, I focus on the knot itself, following the loops to try and learn which knot he used. But my brain is still thundering from the concussion, and McCoy clearly knows what he's doing.

My fingers are aching, and one of the nails has broken off by the time I get one leg free. I'm so focused on the other one that I don't hear footsteps until it's too late.

"Clever one, aren't you?"

"Shit," I whisper, allowing one longing glance at the half-untied knot before I sit up and turn to McCoy. Before I can face him fully, his hands are on my shoulders, roughly dragging me back. I fight against him, even trying to kick with the single freed foot, but he has more strength right now and a much better position. I'm pressed against the chair, and he's moving his hold down my arms to my wrists.

"No!" I shout, throwing my head back. There's a satisfying thud followed by a shout of pain. The impact magnifies my already throbbing headache, but I ignore that in favor of standing up and turning to place the chair between me and the groaning detective. The movement forces my foot to twist at an odd angle, but the ropes are at least loose enough to allow an inch of space.

Fresh tears blur my vision, but I see McCoy wiping blood from his mouth where my headbutt forced a tooth through his lips. With no time to revel in the small victory, I drop to my knee and attack the knot once more.

"You're not going anywhere!" the detective shouts, lunging for me. I slam a palm up, aiming for his throat, but he dodges just in time so the hit lands on his shoulder. He stumbles but manages to throw his arms around me and tackle me to the floor.

Before I got my leg free.

The strength and speed at which he pulls me down yanks my ankle away from the chair.

Agony. Blistering pain slams into me, erupting from my foot. For a moment, all I see is white and black stars obscuring my vision. I scream, lungs emptying and stomach twisting from the pain.

Then McCoy is on top of me, hands going around my throat.

I buck, throw my fists at him, attempting to twist out of his hold.

He doesn't budge. His hands tighten, and any second now, my windpipe is going to collapse under the pressure. I drop my arms, searching for anything to grab hold of.

My fingers brush against something coarse. I don't think. I just grab the object, lift it, and see the rope that had tied my foot to the chair. I wrap it around McCoy's neck and throw all my remaining strength into yanking the noose.

He instantly lets go of my throat to claw at the rope. I suck in a breath, use the moment of his distraction to twist out from under him, and land on my back perpendicular to the chair. My foot is still tied, but the knot is so much looser now that moving is easier. Yanking harder on the rope, I grit my teeth and pull my shoulders in, making myself a smaller target.

McCoy decides trying to fight me off is pointless, and he instead attempts to pull free one of the weapons I'm sure he has stashed on his person. For an extra hold, I lift my free leg and wrap it around his waist, securing him against me so he has even less room to fight.

He manages to get a knife free and blindly stabs at my leg. I don't move it fast enough to avoid the slice on my thigh. I hiss against the pain but don't relent my hold on the rope.

McCoy goes to stab again, this time aiming behind him for my side, and I manage to twist away from it just barely, a new wave of nausea flushing through me at the pain from my probably broken ankle.

He's losing strength, so his next attempt is pathetic. A few more moments and he'll pass out. Then I could either keep strangling until he's dead, or I could stop long enough to tie him to the chair and have a little fun of my own.

I don't get the chance to decide because the next moment, there's a loud crash from somewhere in the house. It startles me enough that I slacken my hold the barest amount. It's enough for McCoy to suck in a tiny bit of air though, and his renewed consciousness goes fully into a desperate attempt to free himself.

He presses back on me, crushing his weight against my body, and lifts the knife, aiming for my arms this time.

The sound of footsteps makes him pause, then several bodies spill into the room. I blink, recognizing everyone but unable to process who they are.

Until Theo.

Theo.

Gun extended, eyes wide and wild, dark hair a mess.

He finds me on the floor with a detective on top of me, a flickering fire of rage so like mine reflected in his expression.

We have a quick, silent conversation, and he nods.

I let go of the rope, flatten against the floor, and push against McCoy's back. He instinctively sits up in an effort to free himself from the danger.

As soon as he's no longer against me, an ear-splitting BANG fills the room as Theo pulls the trigger.

Red mist replaces the air above me where McCoy's head had been a second earlier. The explosion sends blood, bits of skull, brain, and grey matter flying in every direction. It lands on the chair, the floor, the walls, and me.

I shove the detective's lifeless body away. Then someone, James, I think, pulls him off. I attempt to sit up, but gag and sway.

Theo is at my side before I hit the floor. He cradles me against his chest as someone else starts cutting the rope away from my ankle.

"You're okay," Theo says. Words leave his lips in a stream, more a mantra to himself than to me. "I got you. Fuck. You're okay, little reaper. You're going to be okay. I promise."

I don't even realize I'm crying until he gently pulls my head away from his chest and wipes the tears from my cheeks. Even more shocking are the tears in Theo's eyes. His face is pale, and there's a sheen of sweat beading on his brow.

"I'm so fucking sorry."

I shake my head. "You found me." The words are cracked and broken and make more tears fall free.

He tugs me back against him for a tighter hug. "Always. I will always find you."

My chest aches as I cling to him. For a moment, I don't feel all the pain throughout my body. I only feel him, holding me, comforting me.

The sole thing that could tear my attention away from him is the voice of someone I never would've expected at a scene like this.

"June!"

My head whips up and I look around, wondering if I'm imagining things.

I'm not. That's Sadie shoving past Kip. She drops to her knees next to me, and her hands hover in the air for a moment while she tries to decide where to put them.

"Sadie?" I croak.

She decides to wrap her arms around my shoulders despite the blood coating my body. She's sobbing too, and only the shock of seeing her here makes me hesitate before I return the hug.

I meet Theo's eyes over her shoulders. He grimaces slightly and mouths, *"Explain later."*

That's totally fine with me. Because right now, all I want is to hold the people I love most in this world and get out of this shithole house. Then maybe take a bath and get some strong painkillers.

"We need to go," someone says. "I've already called Ace."

"Where are you hurt?" the gentle question comes from Theo.

I let go of Sadie and turn back to him, blinking as I consider the question. "Nose, ankle, and thigh," I say. Then, "And I think I have a concussion."

Theo takes me in, from the top of my head down to my feet. "I'm going to pick you up."

I nod, and he reaches out, sliding an arm under my

knees and another behind my back. I hiss as he lifts me, an ache dropping to my throbbing ankle.

"I've got you," he whispers.

I manage a nod before dropping my head to his chest. The sound of his heartbeat and the heat of his body is hypnotic. As he moves, the last few hours seem to descend on me all at once, and my eyes are too heavy to keep open.

I lose consciousness to the sound of Theo promising me everything is going to be okay.

FORTY

June

"I still think we should take her to the hospital."

"No. No hospitals. They'd ask too many questions."

"Her ankle could be broken!"

"Valor said it's only sprained. Maybe fractured."

"She needs an X-ray. And medicine!"

"Sadie, think about it for two seconds. If I take her to the hospital, they're going to want to know what happened. They may even call the police. And we don't want the police around June, remember?"

There's a frustrated female groan that I belatedly realize is from Sadie. I'm lying on a comfortable bed, surrounded by a familiar smell of coffee, exhaust fumes, and a comforting musk I associate with freedom, ironically.

I'm still in pain, but it's muffled under a blanket of rest and medicine, more of an annoyance than an all-consuming agony.

"He's right," I mumble. A gasp and rustling follow, then the bed dips, and a soft hand touches my forehead.

"How are you feeling?" Sadie asks.

"Better." My eyes blink open to see my best friend, black hair a tangled mess. Her eyes are red behind tortoiseshell glasses.

Guilt at how worried she must have been stabs my chest. Until I realize that she shouldn't even be here because how would she know about Lorry or any of the shit I've gotten myself into? She shouldn't be worried, because I've very intentionally not gotten her involved with this side of my life.

As if hearing my thoughts, Theo says, "She refuses to leave."

I turn my attention to the biker standing at the foot of the bed—*his* bed in *his* bedroom. His large arms are crossed over his chest, and an expression of pure worry carves wrinkles into his forehead.

"Of course I'm not leaving," she says, turning her head to glare at Theo. "She's my best friend."

I reach for her hand, giving it a gentle squeeze even as my mind races to figure out what explanation Theo has given to explain this away.

"How long have I been out?"

"Way too long," Sadie says.

"Four hours," Theo corrects, rolling his eyes. "She's so dramatic."

I chuckle, vibrating my nose in a painful rhythm. "Yeah."

"They won't let me take you to the hospital even though I've told them that we could easily explain away a broken nose, ankle, and concussion."

"What about the cut on her thigh we had to stitch up?" Theo asks. "Or the wounds on her wrists that are undeniably from restraints?"

I glance down at my wrists to see bandages wrapped

around both. I reach up to touch my face, feeling pressure behind my eyes. My fingers barely graze the tape on my nose, and I hiss from the pain.

"That did break, I think," Theo says. "But it'll heal mostly straight."

I register then that someone must have cleaned and changed me. I'm wearing one of Theo's large T-shirts, and there's no visible blood.

"You gave me stitches?"

"Valor did," he says. "He used to be a doctor. He also looked at your ankle and said it wasn't broken."

"Even though it's purple and swollen," Sadie mutters.

"Valor was a doctor?"

Theo nods. "Few years ago. It's convenient as hell. Axel also got his hands on some morphine. Not much, but enough to get you through the night."

"And who… bathed me?"

"I did," he says, words low and threatening.

She laughs. "He wouldn't let anyone near you while he changed and cleaned you. Not even me or Luna. I told him I've seen you naked a dozen times, but he went all territorial alphahole on us."

I roll my eyes, grinning at the thought of Theo refusing to let anyone see me undressed while I was unconscious and covered in blood. "Where is Luna?"

"At the clubhouse," Theo answers. "James is out in the living room keeping guard, and Kip is with Bethany, so I left Luna in charge of handling the Saints. They're all worried and want to come see you. She's fielding questions about what happened. But don't worry about that right now."

I want to ask about Kip and Bethany, but other questions take precedence. "How did you find me?"

"That was all me," Sadie says smugly.

From the way Theo tightens his jaw, I know she's telling the truth.

"What happened?" I direct the question to Theo.

A different sort of worry flashes in his eyes then. A worry not for my well-being, but about whatever he's going to tell me. I let go of her hand to push myself up, grimacing. Sadie helps me, murmuring for me not to move too much.

Before he can start talking, I look at him, then back at her. He can't talk freely with her here. "Wait. First, Sadie, do you mind get—"

"Don't even try," she interrupts. "I'm not leaving. You don't have to worry about me hearing something I shouldn't. I know enough."

Eyes widening, I turn an accusatory glare at Theo. If he told my best friend about my compulsions, I'm changing my decision not to kill him.

He holds his hands out in surrender. "I didn't tell her anything. She already knew. Kind of."

"Kind of?" My stomach gurgles uncomfortably, every nerve ending screaming to change the topic or get Sadie out of this house.

"It's fine, June," she says. "I've suspected for a while now."

Ice fills my body, and my heart beats like a funeral drum in my ears. "What?"

"You know you can tell me anything, right?" she asks. "And I mean *anything*. This isn't *Jennifer's Body*. I'm here for you, and I trust you."

My eyes thaw from hot tears that don't fall. I want to believe her, but she can't possibly mean that. Or she won't mean it if I told her the truth.

Seeing my disbelief, she adds, "Dakota was an idiot and an asshole. Do you think I'm the least bit sad that he's dead?

I hoped you'd eventually tell me yourself. That's why any time we're watching *Criminal Minds* and the unsub ends up being a woman who kills asshole men, I always say that I support her. That's not a joke."

I gape at her. Even though my body is still on edge, ready to flee, my mind is spinning with the desire to believe her. I desperately want this to be real. If she knew and wasn't horrified and disgusted? It would change everything.

"I love you," she says, stressing each word. "No amount of *Dexter* tendencies is going to change that."

Tears fall from both eyes. "Really?"

She nods. "Really."

A fraction of uncertainty remains in my mind. Maybe she'd be okay with a few random murders. But if she knew I've killed *fifteen* people, one of whom was my own father, would she still love me? And what about her safety? If I'm ever caught and the police find out Sadie knew, she'd be sent to prison for aiding and abetting.

So, don't get caught, a tiny voice whispers in the back of my head.

A month ago, I would've confidently boasted that I'd never be caught. But lying here still in pain after being kidnapped by a cop who did catch me shatters that confidence.

"I believe her," Theo says. "Trust me, I've tried everything to get rid of her." He shakes his head, then moves to sit in the empty chair next to the bed across from her. "Do you think if I thought for a second she was a threat to you, emotionally or literally, that I'd allow her to be here?"

The authenticity in his tone obliterates the remaining uncertainty. I nod, turn to Sadie, and whisper, "Thank you."

"You don't need to thank me. What are best friends for if not to support each other's interests? Even of the stabby variety."

I laugh, eyes still blurry with tears. A moment later, I repeat my request for information, and Theo starts talking. He tells me about finding me missing, then calling anyone he could think of, Sadie included. He tells me about killing Miles and figuring out that Lorry must have taken me because of that. He explains threatening Lorry's wife and having the Saints join in on the search. He skims over his fear, but it's evident in how his voice shakes.

"Then Sadie thought about police auctions and..." he trails off, letting her pick up the story.

"Maple hacked their database for us," she says, referring to Rose's sister. "She said it was simple because the auction information wasn't as protected or something like that. We checked all the homes on the list, and three were remote enough for Lorry to have taken you. One was condemned, and one they'd already checked because Lorry was involved with the case. So, we left to check the last one. Your brute of a boyfriend tried to tell me not to come, even threatened to tie me up, but you're not the only badass in this friendship." She winks, and I laugh.

"She threatened to castrate me," Theo says, glaring at my best friend. I laugh harder, then wince at the pain flaring in the base of my skull.

"Yeah, well, you'd deserve it," she fires back. "That's pretty much it. We came to rescue you. Though it looked like you were doing a fine job at rescuing yourself. Were you really about to strangle a detective with the same ropes he used to tie you up?" She whistles when I nod.

Looking at Theo, I say, "If you were two minutes later, I could've added a new stone to my tattoo. Now this kill belongs to you."

"Sorry, little reaper," he says, not sounding sorry in the least. "I would've kept him alive for you to have your fun with, but seeing you two on the floor like that..."

"I know. It's okay."

"Anyway," Sadie says, reclaiming my attention. "After that, we brought you back. Valor fixed you up, Theo has been obsessively watching you sleep like a creep, and I texted the girls that you were fine. Told them your car broke down and you didn't have service to call us. I never told Rose about calling Maple, and she was all too happy to keep everything a secret."

That doesn't surprise me. Maple is a year younger than Rose, but the two are polar opposites. Where Rose is all smiles and pastel colors, Maple barely shows emotions and lives in the shadows. She's helped me with a few things over the years without asking questions, like erasing security footage or making sure messages are sent from a specific IP address. She's always seemed like someone with her fair share of secrets. I would, too, if I'd grown up in a cult. It's a miracle Rose came out of their childhood with all of her infectious joy still intact.

"Thank you."

"Any time," Sadie says. "Now, your turn to tell us what happened." Theo clears his throat, and she must hear an unspoken request because she stands from the bed. "Actually, why don't we talk tomorrow after you've slept? I'll make some valerian tea. I'm sleeping here, so I'll be around when you wake up."

"Of course."

She leans over me, presses a kiss to my forehead, and says quietly, "Reapers deserve love too. Don't forget that." She straightens and heads for the door, winking once before shutting it behind her.

Alone with Theo now, the room feels heavier. Though I'm not sure if the weight is suffocating or comforting. Whatever happens next will determine that.

It takes incredible courage to look at him. I'm too tired to put words to why my lungs tighten when our gazes lock.

He breaks the silence first. "Never do that to me again."

I would laugh if he didn't sound so serious. Or if his eyes weren't glassy and cupped by tired bags.

"It's been nearly eight years since I felt that kind of fear."

The reminder of what happened eight years ago, who he lost, is acid in my lungs, eating up my ability to fully inhale. "I'm sorry."

"Oh, baby." It's more of a broken sound falling from his mouth than actual words. He moves from the chair to the bed, hands going to my jaw. His proximity is like an invading salve in my body, healing my lungs and melting away the nerves and insecurity I hadn't realized were clenching my heart. "*I'm* sorry. This is all my fault. And if something had happened to you, I…"

"Don't." I hook my hands over his wrists and saturate my stare with love. "This isn't your fault. And I'm okay."

He drops his head, shoulders quivering like they're about to start shaking. I pull one of his hands away and move it to my chest so he can feel my heartbeat.

"See? I'm okay. I'm here. I'm not going anywhere."

He makes a strangled sound that I'm not sure was meant to be a word.

"Look at me, Theo."

He obeys, revealing tears falling down his cheeks.

"I'm alive. You found me. I—" My throat spasms, and I close my eyes to take a long breath before looking at him again. "I love you, Theo."

His eyes widen. Then he's on me, lips claiming mine in a way they never have before. I grip the back of his neck, fingers crawling into his hair like they belong there. Falling into this kiss is the easiest thing I've ever done. I barely register the pain from my nose, focusing solely on the heat of his mouth and the fortifying brush of his tongue against mine.

It ends too soon, but Theo doesn't go far. He presses our foreheads together, breathing me in like I'm the first flower after years of a brutal winter.

"I never thought I'd love anyone enough to feel so afraid of losing them like that again. After Scottie. After Shiloh." A tear drops from his nose. He pulls away just an inch so he can look at me properly. "I knew I loved you, but I didn't realize how much until you were gone. I didn't think I was capable of loving anyone like that anymore."

My breath is almost a hiccup, and I realize I'm crying too. "Theo…"

"No matter what you decide to do next, just promise me you'll be okay. I can't lose you. Not like that."

I almost smile. "I told you, I'm not going anywhere."

"It's technically Saturday now. February fifteenth." He doesn't have to elaborate. I know what he's asking.

"I love you. We both know this stopped being about some stupid deal a long time ago. I want more than thirty days with you."

His entire body relaxes, and he mutters, "Thank fuck," before kissing me again.

There's still so much to discuss. What happened with Lorry, living situations, what exactly Sadie knows, what to tell the rest of the Saints, the lingering threat of the South Five. But right now, none of that matters.

All that matters is the two of us, in this second. No longer enemies agreeing to a temporary truce before killing each other, but lovers who have killed *for* the other and will happily do so again.

Deciding to murder Theo Zervas was the best decision I ever made.

Because only he could make a reaper feel so alive.

EPILOGUE

Theo

ONE MONTH LATER

"I don't think this will work. It's way too big between my thighs."

I smirk, barely managing to contain a laugh. June, of course, sees it anyway.

"You're a child. An actual child." She sits back, away from the tank she'd been leaning against. She's straddling a yellow motorcycle, probably the twentieth one she's tried today, and glaring at me even as the corner of her lip betrays a twitch of her own grin. "The *tank* is too big," she corrects. "What engine size is this one?"

I grab the tag hanging from the bike's handles and flip it over. "Thousand. Definitely too much for you right now."

She nods, not arguing for once. When we started looking for a bike for her, I expected way more push back about the parameters I *helpfully* suggested. She argued at first because, *"You're not my warden anymore, and I'll do what I want, Tink."* But she finally agreed with me after a few of the Saints let her ride their bikes to get a feel for what she likes.

James outright refused to let her ride his Harley, and my

Indian Springfield was too big. She hated Raph's chopper because "the handles are too high," and though she had fun riding way too fast on Nico's sport bike, she ended up agreeing that a "crotch rocket" was not comfortable for longer group rides. We've already told him he has a year to trade it for something American-made, anyway.

In the end, her favorite was Bella's Harley Iron 883, which we used for her lessons. The bike is, of course, almost exactly what I told her to get: a power cruiser with no more than a 650cc engine to start with.

Despite knowing what she likes, we've still been in the shop for over an hour while she sits on bike after bike. I swear, I've seen this woman decide to kill someone faster than it's taking her to pick a damn motorcycle.

"Remember, you're not committing for life. A lot of new riders trade in after a year."

"So you keep telling me." She swings her leg off the bike, a sight that never fails to make my pants too tight, and saunters back to one of the first bikes she sat on when we got here, which feels like several years ago.

I follow her, planting my feet on either side of the front wheel. Once she's seated with her feet on the footrests, I pick the bike up, holding it steady upright. She spreads her fingers along the black tank, her mouth pulling into a smile. The stillness in her expression is easily recognizable. It's the look she gets when something temporarily calms the flames in her chest. I see it after a long ride or a round at James's gym, which she joined despite Sadie's protests. It's a softer version of the blissful relief in her eyes when she's coming apart under my touch or slitting a man's throat.

Which is how I know what she's about to say.

"This one." She nods once, smiles wider, then looks up at me. "Definitely this one."

I can't help it. I lean forward and capture her mouth with mine, savoring the immediate submission in her lips as she falls into the kiss. Suddenly needing so much more, particularly of June's body without clothes in the way or the eyes of strangers pointed in our direction, I break the kiss and carefully set the bike back down.

"Then let's get the paperwork started so I can take you home and show you what it really means to have something too big between your thighs."

"You're an idiot." But she laughs and threads her fingers into mine, so I'm more than happy to be an idiot.

~

I already miss having June's body pressed against mine while we're riding. Still, I can't deny that riding side by side to my house, then watching her climb off her bike and shake her blonde hair out after taking off her helmet, is one of the most erotic things I've ever witnessed, even with several strands plastered to her sweaty forehead. I'm on her in an instant, and she has her legs and arms wrapped around me as I carry her inside. All my attention is zeroed in on her teeth pulling at my bottom lip, so I don't immediately register that there are too many voices coming from my living room.

"The marshal returns! Care to cease defiling my best friend for a few minutes so she can back me up?"

June pulls away, and I mutter, "I swear to God, I will kill her."

June just pats my cheek. "Then I'll kill you, and James will kill me, and it'll just be a long chain of murder. And not the fun kind." She jumps down, turning to greet Sadie, who's making showing up here too much of a habit. What's the point of June still having her own house if her friends come *here* all the fucking time?

"I'm needed?" she asks, practically skipping to the

sunken living room, where Sadie is on her feet, facing James sitting in his chair, arms crossed. Luna is lounging in the center of the couch, arms spread out behind her as she watches whatever scene is unfolding.

"This time, she'll agree with me," James says.

"Ha. Am I or am I not beloved by the Saints?" Sadie asks.

I smile, remembering the hour-long phone call June and Sadie had last week, debriefing the night she met all the Saints. She's been coming here with June and Luna more often, but recently, she bumped it up a notch by wanting to go to the Iron Cage and the clubhouse. After James muttered something about her becoming a hang-around, she needed a full explanation of each member and how to be the best hang-around possible. June happily obliged.

"Sorry, Jamesy, but Sadie is pretty popular. Raph and Benny love her," June says.

"They don't count."

"I like her!" Luna adds.

"You definitely don't count."

"Rude."

"Ha. They like me. So, I think they'd trust me," Sadie adds.

"Woah, wait. That's a different question," June says.

James nods. "Told you."

Sadie frowns at June. "Et tu?"

"I'm not saying they *don't* trust you. But the Saints have trust issues. They've been through a lot," June says. Which is an understatement.

After we brought her home from her kidnapping and had Valor stitch her up, there were *a lot* of questions. Particularly since we had to deal with a dead detective and Kip's very upset sister. Unfortunately, the Saints aren't stupid, and they know that no detective is going to kidnap a random therapist without a damn good reason.

Especially not a therapist who easily slit a man's throat, then continued on with life as if everything was normal. Too many members were putting things together. After a long conversation with June, in which I yelled more than I'm proud of, and several more with James, Luna, and Kip, we came up with a compromise. We told the Saints that June and I met on one of my private jobs. To explain Lorry, we offered *some* truth about his cousin, Solomon. Not that June killed him but that she was hired by the father of one of Solomon's babysitters who found out he'd raped her. June was to 'take care of the problem,' which she did, and later Lorry wanted revenge for it.

It was enough. For most of the Saints. I could see suspicion in some of their eyes, though, and they were watching June a little too closely for my liking. But after officially claiming her as my Ol' Lady, no one dared to voice their suspicions, even knowing we lied about who exactly June is and how we met. Still, losing Scottie and having Amber betray us made our lies hit harder.

"Okay, well, they don't really need to trust me for the plan to work."

I frown. "What plan?"

"This is where you'll lose allies," James says.

"You shut up, Weasley," Sadie says. Luna laughs. She's been watching the whole exchange with hesitation, causing a divot between her brows.

"What plan?" I repeat.

The look on James's face makes the back of my neck prickle. I'm not going to like this.

"This amateur sleuth here wants to emulate Amber and infiltrate the South Five to be our spy."

Yup. I hate it. From the look on June's face, she hates it even more. This might be the first time we've agreed on any plan for dealing with the gang.

"Absolutely not," June says.

"You're not a Saint—" I start.

"Which is exactly why it should be me! They don't know me, so they won't suspect me."

"Gangs don't just let anyone in," James says.

"That's why I'll target Bowie. I'm hot. Men like me." She winks at James.

"Women do too," Luna mutters. Everyone ignores her.

"Sadie, no," June says. "This isn't your fight. I don't want you involved."

"It's your fight, which means it's mine," Sadie argues.

"Those guys are dangerous," I say.

"I can hold my own in a fight!"

"Listen, I love a crazy plan as much as the next girl," Luna says. "But I'm afraid they're right. This isn't a good idea."

"Well, I don't need any of your permission. And it's too late anyway." Sadie crosses her arms. "I already have a date with Bowie next week."

James shouts something about being stupid, and Luna shakes her head, but my attention is locked on June. Her entire body has gone taut. A cloud fills her eyes, but not like the smoke warning of her need for blood. It's more like a fog of fear. The sight makes me want to slaughter the cause of her fear.

Since killing Sadie would be counterintuitive, the only other option is to get rid of the threat against my little reaper's best friend.

Dealing with the South Five just became my number one priority.

ACKNOWLEDGMENTS

First and foremost, Mazikeen. Thank you for letting me call you by that dumbass name that has nothing to do with your actual name or personality or anything. This book literally wouldn't exist without you. You were in the Google doc on day one while we brainstormed dark romance book ideas and the hottest guy names we could think of. You helped me research what gang names existed already so we didn't accidentally use one and biker/MC terminology so I didn't sound like an absolute ass. Thank you for sticking with me through the end of this and for loving these weirdos as much as me. I couldn't ask for a better book bestie and can't wait for all the books with insanely long trigger warnings that we'll both read together and write in the future.

Thank you also to my fantastic friends, LJ and Mollee, who agreed to hop into this manuscript and get to editing, having never read dark romance before. You both provided new perspectives and much-needed fresh pairs of eyes.

LJ, I cherish our writing dates more than you know and am so grateful for all you've done for me, from teaching me to ride a motorcycle to bringing me soup when I feel sick.

Mollee, as much as I hate that dumpster toad man, I'm so grateful that Twitter brought us together. Living with you, writing with you, laughing with you, crying with you, I see it all as my own personal treasure.

Thank you also to Marni, who has joyfully read all of my books, both those that have made it to publishing and those that are still biding their time. You make me a better writer.

Thank you to my fantastic assistant, Gabi. I feel like a total knob saying I have an assistant but as long as it gets to be you, I'm happy. Your endless patience, creativity, and hard work are astounding, and you're going to do amazing things.

Lo, I genuinely don't think anyone deserves you. Thank you for being a constant in my Google Docs and my life.

Cate, you're a storm of love and joy, and I'm happy to stand in the rain. (God, that sounds so dumb, but now that I wrote it, it's staying.)

Thor, be it books, video games, TV shows, or just life, I know I'll always have someone to talk to and something to talk about with you in my life, and that's not a small thing.

Alex, this world sucks but you're in it so that's proof that it can still create beautiful things.

Zoe, I could write a whole book about you and what you mean to me, but it all comes down to one thing. You're my person.

This feels like a weird book in which to include my family in the acknowledgments. But I am thankful for them. Without my fantastic parents and siblings, I'd never be here, writing a book about murderers falling in love and fucking each other's brains out.

To all of the life-changing people I've had the honor of calling mine in some way, I'm so proud and glad to know you, and I hope you feel nothing but happiness. And reality-bending orgasms, if that's your thing.

ABOUT THE AUTHOR

Madison Lawson is an award-winning short story author who writes novels full of suspense, social commentary, diverse characters, and complex relationships. And lots of murder. And now sex. The dog NEVER dies, though. Her debut sci-fi thriller, *The Registration*, and its sequel, *The Registration Rewritten,* were picked up for a film adaptation by Sony Pictures.

Madison is represented by Julie Gwinn at the Seymour Agency. She received her B.A. in English with a focus on Creative Writing from Texas A&M University and her M.A. in Literature from North Carolina State University.

Growing up in a small Texas town, Madison began exploring the world through the page so much that she often lost sleep to finish a book, got detention for writing a story in class, and convinced herself it was okay to read *Harry Potter* one more time. As her curiosity expanded, she began writing, reading, and traveling to discover the world, make new ones, and understand her own a bit better.

Madison currently resides in Texas with her dog, Teddy Lupin.

To learn more and stay updated, visit Madison's website, **madisonlawson.com**, and follow her on Instagram@madisonlawson

Stick around for more of the Saints of Purgatory!

We haven't seen the last of our favorite motorcycle club. With more danger on the horizon, the Saints of Purgatory are forced to face the deadly enemies at their doorstep.

As the vice president of a club on the brink of war with a president newly in love with the killer who got them in this mess in the first place, James Hartley takes on too many responsibilities to handle alone. Which is how he finds himself teaming up with the most relentlessly cheery anomaly he's ever met.

Sadie Oliver has only ever wanted to be whoever her people need her to be. If that's a spy to keep her best friend alive, then just call her Jason Bourne. But it quickly becomes clear she's out of her depth, so who better to have as a partner than the surly man who can't seem to keep his eyes off her?

Everything they love is hanging in the balance, but neither James nor Sadie can be prepared for what they'll face next. Or how facing it together could be the undoing they're desperate to avoid.

Other Books By Madison Lawson:

The Registration
The Registration Rewritten